BADGE HEAVY

a Charlie-316 novel

Colin Conway | Frank Zafiro

Badge Heavy: A Charlie-316 Novel

Cover design by Zach McCain

ISBN: 978-1-7368543-9-6

Original Ink Press, an imprint of High Speed Creative, LLC
1521 N. Argonne Road, #C-205
Spokane Valley, WA 99212

For those who shine a light on dark truths.
- Colin Conway

and

For those who have betrayed.
I wish I could forgive you, but I can't.
- Frank Zafiro

BADGE

HEAVY

Whoever fights monsters should see to it that in the process he does not become a monster.
—Friedrich Nietzsche, philosopher

MONDAY

*You are thought here to be the most senseless and fit man
for the constable of the watch, therefore bear you the lantern.*
—William Shakespeare
From the play *Much Ado About Nothing*, Act III, Scene 3

Chapter 1

"Stop! Police!" Officer Gary Stone hollered.

Did I really just yell that?

Not breaking his stride, Tyler Garrett glanced back over his shoulder. Even from this distance, Stone could see the man's disapproving smirk. Garrett looked ahead, leaned forward, and pulled further away.

"Damn," Stone muttered and continued to chase after him.

They raced along the east side of a four-story apartment building in Spokane's West Central, an area of town known disparagingly as Felony Flats. In the yellowed grass, a small group of children sat in a circle. They played with their toys while their mothers, standing flatfooted and wide-eyed, watched the men run along the brick building.

"Tango-fourteen, what's your location?" an irritated male voice barked from the handheld radio swinging from Stone's hip.

The officer didn't have time to pull it from his belt and provide the requested update. That action would slow him down and he was already falling behind Garrett. Besides, what would he tell them? The last location he could easily identify was where the foot pursuit started and that was two blocks ago. He had no idea where he was now. Confessing that humiliation on the radio was far worse than remaining silent.

The late morning sun reflected off the exterior apartment windows and into Stone's eyes, causing him to squint, almost closing his left eye. He wanted to slow and catch his breath, but Garrett wasn't doing that.

Instead, the man disappeared around the corner of the apartment building like a ball player stealing an extra base.

Stone needed to keep Garrett in sight. Losing him would be bad, even worse than admitting he was lost.

Stone lengthened his stride, pumped his arms, and sucked deeper breaths through his mouth until he reached the end of the building. Despite the blind spot, he didn't bother slowing for the corner. Officer safety be damned. Luckily, when he rounded it, no one was there.

The apartment building's rear door was open but slowly closing. Stone raced toward the door and grasped it before it clicked shut. He yanked it open which caused the door to hit the patrol radio on his belt. It popped free and clattered to the sidewalk.

Stone had a millisecond to decide—turn around to collect the radio and hope that it still worked or follow Garrett. There was no choice.

He burst into the building and scrambled up the stairs that met him upon entry. When he hopped onto the second floor, he paused and listened, his senses straining for any sounds over the blood pulsating in his ears.

It took less than a second to register Garrett's boots pounding up the stairs toward the next floor.

Stone grabbed the worn oak banister, pulled himself toward the next set of stairs, and climbed them two at a time. His breath was ragged now, and his heart felt like it would pop, but he wasn't going to let Garrett get away from him. Not today.

He jumped onto the third floor, didn't see the man, and spun upward toward the next flight of stairs.

Stone didn't worry about the noise his heavy footsteps made, nor the loudness of his wheezing. This was not about stealth. This was about speed and he needed to pick it up or be left behind.

When he stepped onto the fourth floor, he witnessed the brutal collision. A woman stepped out of her apartment just as Tyler Garrett was passing. She yelped when Garrett ran into her. The two of them collapsed heavily to the ground in a tangle of arms and legs.

Stone sprinted toward them.

The woman howled in pain as Garrett struggled to free himself from her.

Once near the tangled pair, Stone leapt over them and continued his sprint toward the end of the hallway. He saw the open window now which led to the rusty fire escape.

That's where Bronson Mulvaney, career criminal and the man they were hunting that day, must have escaped. Garrett had been right behind him before colliding with the woman. Now it was up to Stone to catch Mulvaney.

He didn't hesitate and pushed himself harder than before even though his legs felt like wet sandbags. He could no longer rely on Garrett. Catching Mulvaney was now his sole responsibility. The rest of the team, wherever they were, would be counting on him, too. Without his radio, they had no way to know that he was now on his own.

Stone cleared the window and stood on the rusty fire escape. He heard the clanging of footsteps on the lower level of the metal stairs and felt the entire system vibrating. He didn't bother checking who was making the noise and shaking the escape. He instinctively knew its source, and immediately began his descent.

At each platform, he grabbed the escape's support beam and swung himself down several stairs, hoping to catch solid footing, surprised when he did, and hurried over the remaining stairs only to perform the same acrobatic feat again from the next platform.

Mulvaney, a two-time loser with everything at stake if he was caught once more, jumped from the fire escape into the alley and sprinted toward the next apartment building.

Stone was gaining on him, but only slightly, when he bounded from the metal stairs. For a fleeting moment, he thought about his radio and the warm embrace that calling for assistance would bring. He shoved that fantasy away and ran.

How is Mulvaney not tiring yet?

The criminal was five foot ten and a hundred fifty pounds with a lifetime of poor choices, most of which were in direct conflict with physical fitness. Mulvaney wore baggy jeans tightly cinched with a thick black belt around his waist and dirty, white tennis shoes that were tied like his mother had scolded him to do so before school. He wore no shirt, which revealed his heavily tattooed and sweaty pale skin.

It angered Stone that the greasy criminal hadn't quit running yet.

How is this possible?

The rear door of a nearby apartment building was open, but its wooden screen door closed. Mulvaney sprinted toward it, his long black hair flowing behind him. At the building, he frantically pulled and kicked at the screen door, but was unable to open it. He glanced back at Stone before jumping through the dark screen. It collapsed around him as he fell into the hallway. The man quickly stood and ripped the black fabric and thin wood beams away from him.

With Stone rapidly approaching, Mulvaney screamed, "No!" The thick cords in his neck strained and his wild eyes bugged out.

Mulvaney spun and dashed down the darkened hallway, bouncing from one wall to the next as he struggled to regain his momentum. From a nearby apartment, screeching heavy metal music cranked loudly.

When he caught up to him, Stone tackled Mulvaney and dragged him to the ground. The officer couldn't hold him down, though, as the man's upper torso was slick with sweat.

Mulvaney broke Stone's grip and struggled to his feet. He touched the wall for support as he briefly considered his options. When Stone righted himself, he blocked Mulvaney's exit down the hallway. The only way for Mulvaney to escape was back the way he'd come.

Even without his radio, Stone had confidence that sooner or later, the rest of his team would find him and the suspect they pursued. Garrett, especially, couldn't be far behind. His opponent must have sensed the same thing as he suddenly threw two quick punches. The officer lifted an arm to protect his face and the first strike bounced off his upper shoulder. The second swung wildly over his head.

Stone immediately struck back by punching Mulvaney in the face, but it was a glancing blow across his lips and failed to register as more than an irritant. The thin man grinned as blood thinly coated his teeth.

Preparing for a longer fight, the officer lifted his hands defensively. Mulvaney did the same. The two men warily studied each other. Stone saw desperation in Mulvaney's eyes, and a heavy dose of meanness there as well. He wished again that he hadn't lost his radio.

Stone was fatigued and realized he needed to end this fight quick. For a moment, he thought about drawing his Glock to direct Mulvaney to the ground, but they were in the middle of a hallway, no wider than six feet. Introducing a gun into this situation was a bad decision, no matter how he sliced it. Mulvaney would be on him before he got it out of its holster. And if he succeeded? Well, it meant he was more than likely going to have to kill the man, because Mulvaney didn't look like he would give up without a fight. Could he justify deadly force?

No, he decided in a flash. Bringing a gun into this fight was too big of a gamble.

In the millisecond that followed, Stone decided on a course of action.

He lashed out with a leg, kicking Mulvaney directly in the side of the knee. He hadn't intended to hit him there, instead hoping to strike him in the upper thigh. However, when the toe of Stone's boot hit Mulvaney's knee, the man yelped and straightened his remaining good leg.

The kick to the knee was a strike that would not be found anywhere on the department's officially sanctioned Use of Force scale. Yet, it produced a result Stone desperately needed, so he attempted a similar action.

He pivoted and kicked Mulvaney in the ankle of the leg that was still planted on the ground. Mulvaney collapsed into a heap, squealing while he grabbed at his injured limbs.

Stone jumped onto him then, his weight pinning the lighter man to the ground. It took only a moment to position himself onto Mulvaney's sweaty back, slip his right arm under the man's chin, and squeeze with all his might. Mulvaney clawed at Stone's arms, bucked to get free, and kicked his feet against the hallway wall. When that didn't work, he flailed a hand toward Stone's face. Stone tucked his chin to his chest, closed his eyes, and kept compressing the sides of the man's neck.

When the pressure began to work, Mulvaney's resistance faded. The man lightly tapped Stone's arm—the generally accepted signal for submission. Stone ignored the action, though, and the man's hand slowly fell to the floor. Soon, Mulvaney was snoring in Stone's arms.

"Stoney!" Tyler Garrett yelled from the end of the darkened hallway.

Officer Gary Stone didn't move but continued to maintain pressure around the man's neck. It was then he realized how badly Mulvaney stunk.

Garrett pulled a set of handcuffs from his back pocket. "Relax, buddy, I've got him."

The two men worked together then to secure Bronson Mulvaney's hands behind his back. When they were finished, they left him snoring on the floor.

Garrett clapped Stone on the shoulder and smiled. "That was—"

A new, more annoyingly loud song blasted from the nearby apartment.

Thumbing toward the music, Garrett asked with a grimace, "What the hell is that?"

Stone shrugged. "Heavy metal?"

Garrett turned to the apartment and pounded on the door. "Turn that crap down or go to jail!"

A moment later the hallway was silent.

Garrett continued as if nothing had happened. "Impressive takedown," he said, pointing at Mulvaney who was now regaining consciousness.

"You saw that?"

"Oh, yeah."

Getting a pat on the back from former SWAT Officer Tyler Garrett was a big deal for Stone, but he still felt slightly embarrassed for kicking the man in the knee and ankle. "Not exactly department policy," he said.

Garrett put his arm around Stone and playfully shook him. "In a moment like that, buddy, you cheat to win. Ain't no policy manual here in a fight. Your survival is more important than some academy classroom rules or that turd's ability to walk comfortably."

Stone reached down and hooked one of Mulvaney's arms. Garrett did the same and the two men lifted the now semiconscious man.

Garrett sniffed. His nose crinkled and he chuckled. "You made him crap himself, Stoney."

"What?" Stone asked.

"Dude crapped himself," Garrett repeated.

It was then that Stone smelled it over Mulvaney's body odor. He shook his head once, doing his best to ignore it.

The two officers dragged the handcuffed man out of the hallway into the sunlight, dropping him with a heavy thud into the yellowed grass. Mulvaney moaned, but neither of them paid attention to him.

"Will you notify dispatch we've got one in custody?" Stone asked.

"What happened to your radio?"

"I dropped it during the chase."

Garrett smiled. "Nice." He pulled his radio from his belt and said. "Tango-thirteen."

"Tango-thirteen," the female dispatcher said, "go ahead."

"One in custody. Notify a supervisor. Also?"

"Thirteen, go ahead."

"Start medics for an LVNR."

Stone nodded at the request. The application of a lateral vascular neck restraint required a medical response to ensure that the suspect was cleared to be booked into jail. The senior officer would make sure he acted within that policy, at least.

Garrett grabbed Stone's shoulder and shook him from his thoughts. "Hell of a catch, man. You were a straight up meat-eater today. You're coming into your own out here."

Stone exhaled slowly as the adrenaline ebbed from his system. This was the new version of himself. The guy who was no longer going to be pushed around. The guy who was going to make a name for himself on the street. The guy he liked being. A guy Garrett respected.

He heard it before he saw it—a large block engine whining in protest as it rounded a corner. A 1977 Ford Maverick slid to a stop in the small cul-de-sac near where they waited.

"Yin and Yang," Garrett muttered. "Always late to the party."

"Looks like Ray's mad," Stone whispered.

Officer Ray Zielinski had already jumped from the driver's side while Officer Jun Yang climbed out from the passenger seat. Zielinski, a white male in his early forties, wore blue jeans, a black T-shirt, and a ballistic vest. Yang was in her late twenties but wore almost the same outfit. It was the unofficial uniform of the Anti-Crime Team.

While Yang's face remained impassive, Zielinski's was twisted in anger.

"What the hell was that?" Zielinski yelled toward the two men as he stalked closer.

"What?" Garrett asked.

"You two were in foot pursuit of Mulvaney then all radio communication stopped. We've been driving all around the neighborhood looking for you guys."

"I dropped my radio," Stone said, flatly. Garrett was his partner, not Zielinski. If Garrett didn't have a problem with him dropping his portable, then Ray should back off.

"Isn't that convenient?" Zielinski snapped.

"How do you figure?" Stone replied.

Garrett chuckled. "Yeah, how is that convenient, Yin?"

Zielinski's brow furrowed and he stepped toward Garrett. "What did you say?"

"I said, how is that convenient?" Garrett replied.

"You called me Yin."

"I think you're hearing things, old man."

Zielinski ignored the jab. He checked out Stone's hip, confirming that the radio was indeed missing. Facing Garrett, he said, "What about you, Ty? What happened to your radio?"

"Mine works fine or did you not hear my broadcast a minute ago?"

The older cop shook his head in disgust. He looked back to Yang. "You got something to add here?"

She shrugged, not saying anything.

Zielinski muttered something Stone couldn't make out as he turned and stomped back to his car.

"He'll be fine," Yang said to Stone. Then she added to both men, "Nice arrest, by the way."

"Tell that to Stoney," Garrett said. "Today, the man delivered the goods."

Stone smiled then because he realized that he had, in fact, done just that.

Chapter 2

"How is the team taking the news?" Chief Robert Baumgartner asked.

"They haven't missed a beat," Captain Tom Farrell answered. "They're out hunting hippos as we speak."

"Hippos?

"High profile offenders," Farrell told him. "HPOs…hippos."

Baumgartner frowned. "Sounds more like a movie channel than a criminal."

"It's the designation Crime Analysis uses, so it was just easier to adopt it than come up with something else. Besides, you got your flash with the team name."

"The Anti-Crime Team," Baumgartner mused, then shrugged. "If it gives the mayor a way to work the word 'act' into his community speeches, it's a win."

"Well, they have been kicking ass and taking names," Farrell said, his voice lacking enthusiasm.

"Don't sound so overjoyed about it, Tom."

The team was supposed to be a trap for Garrett, to catch him dirty. Not another chance for him to look like super cop.

But he couldn't tell the chief that. Not after keeping his suspicions about Tyler Garrett secret for almost two years. Not until he had incontrovertible evidence to show who Garrett really was.

Instead, he brought up another reason for concern. "This team needs a short leash with a firm hand guiding it," he said. "Sergeant McGinn was our answer to that."

Baumgartner sighed. "It's terrible what happened. I talked with McGinn for a few minutes when I signed his family leave paperwork. The man looked completely shattered."

Farrell didn't reply. Sergeant Christian McGinn's wife had died in childbirth, along with the couple's second child. In addition to dealing with his own grief at losing both his wife and his newborn child, McGinn had a three-year-old daughter at home who didn't understand where her mother had gone.

"Have we done everything we can do for him?" Baumgartner asked.

"For now, yes."

"What about the chaplain and his team?"

"He's been in contact," Farrell said. "The entire chaplaincy will be there to support him."

"And McGinn's got family to help him through this?"

Farrell nodded. "As I understand it, both sets of parents live here in Spokane."

"Good. If there's anything he needs, let's make sure he gets it. If you need me to make it happen, let me know." Baumgartner gave Farrell a meaningful look. "*Any*thing. We take care of our people."

"I'll stay on top of it," Farrell said. "But McGinn's absence leaves a huge hole on the Anti-Crime Team."

"I know. We can't have them running around out there unsupervised for long. Things might be fine for a while, but then…" He trailed off.

"Then something will go wrong, and it'll be bad," Farrell finished. They'd discussed this potential problem at length when forming the team several months ago. The danger of officers in a setting like ACT eventually bending the rules to make an arrest stick was too high. Officers believe they're serving the greater good by making small changes to their ethical core, but behaviors like that, if unchecked, led to greater transgressions. There were plenty of examples out there, and neither Farrell nor Baumgartner wanted Spokane to join that ignominious club.

"What are our options?" the chief asked.

"Simple. Find another sergeant."

Baumgartner frowned. "That's easier said than done."

"It's the only option I see."

"Aren't you being a little myopic? There are other ways to handle this."

"Like what, sir?"

"We could shut down the team until McGinn returns."

Farrell realized his mistake and had to hurry to put the conversation back on the right path. "That's an option. But is that really what you want to do?"

Baumgartner shook his head. "No. They're making good arrests and getting us excellent press. The mayor is thrilled, which means he's poking his nose into other city departments and not ours. I don't want to lose that freedom."

"Even a temporary shutdown gives the naysayers their opportunity to keep the team on the shelf. In this case, it's better to beg for forgiveness than ask for permission."

"That's a dangerous attitude to take at a leadership level."

Farrell considered his words carefully. "I understand. But we don't need more input from outside forces. You've got councilmembers who have already been vocal against it. Neighborhood groups who think—"

"I know who's against the concept, Tom."

"What I'm saying is it could be a while before McGinn comes back."

"And that's the problem," the chief said, more to himself than to Farrell. "If we hit the pause button, we don't know how long it'll be before we gear up again. I don't want to lose all the momentum that ACT has generated."

Farrell knew that this was what Baumgartner wanted from the beginning. The chief just wanted to make sure they considered all the options first. "Then we need a new sergeant," he said. "The problem, as you pointed out before, is from where? McGinn came from day shift patrol, and his corporal has been leading the team in his absence. But that's a veteran corporal who can handle it, even long term. Shorting another patrol team on top of McGinn's is risky. You start to spread the leadership thin, and then all we're really doing is transferring liability from one setting to another."

"Captain Hatcher is going to be reluctant to give up another sergeant to the team," Baumgartner observed. "Is she still pissy about the team falling under the Investigative Division?"

Farrell thought about how formal and brief, even curt, his interactions with Dana Hatcher had been over the last few months since the chief made the decision to give him command of the Anti-Crime Team. Not that he blamed her. The idea for implementing ACT had been hers in the first place. She'd presented it at a command staff meeting, where Baumgartner first rejected it, then handed it over to him. Hatcher was understandably upset. He'd feel the same if their positions were reversed.

"She's a little salty," he admitted.

"What about one of your investigative sergeants, then?" Baumgartner asked.

"We're even thinner than patrol. I've got eleven or twelve detectives under each sergeant. They can barely keep up with the paperwork, much less get into the field to help them out. I don't even have a sergeant for Major Crimes. Lieutenant Flowers is pulling double duty."

"All right. So tell me where we get a body, Tom? I can't just go to the sergeant store and pick one up for you."

"I've been thinking about this since I heard about McGinn," Farrell said, "and the only person I can come up with is Kelly Ragland."

"The admin sergeant?" Baumgartner pursed his lips in thought. "He's not exactly a barnburner."

"But he knows policy, and he follows the rules. That's what we need most with the Anti-Crime Team. They've already got solid cops on the team, and good intel support from Crime Analysis. They don't absolutely need a dynamic leader, even though McGinn was exactly that. What they do need is oversight and someone to make sure that policy is adhered to along the way."

"Someone to tap the brakes a little, huh?"

"Exactly."

Baumgartner considered the idea. "You think Barry will squawk about giving him up?"

Farrell tried to keep his tone neutral, even though he couldn't stand the administrative captain. Barry thought his position was the most critical one in the department. "Ragland doesn't fall under the administrative chain of command. He's still under patrol."

"The admin sergeant doesn't answer to the admin captain? That sounds like a joke."

"It's odd," Farrell agreed. "I think the position started out to manage the front desk, which is a patrol function, and it just never got moved."

"Makes sense, but we should probably fix that next time we revise the organizational chart. Meanwhile," the chief smiled mischievously, "that means you're still asking Hatcher for another one of her sergeants."

"Ask her? Why can't you just *tell* her?"

"I will, if it comes to it," Baumgartner said. "But ask first. Either way, though, Ragland is going to ACT, and Hatcher will have to deal with it. Make it happen."

"Yes, sir." Farrell stood and left the chief's office.

When it came to unpleasant conversations, he thought, there was no time like the present.

Chapter 3

Officer Ray Zielinski finalized his brief additional report for the Mulvaney arrest and hit the send button on the computer. He glanced over at Yang, who was still typing.

"How much can you write?" he asked. "It's basically a warrant arrest."

"With a foot pursuit," Yang said.

"That we weren't part of," Zielinski pointed out. "Thanks to Maverick and Goose."

Jun stopped, and turned to him. "That's the second time you've called them that. I don't get it."

"You never saw *Top Gun*?"

"Is that a western or something?"

Zielinski peered at her closely, trying to decide if she was messing with him. He didn't completely have a handle on who Jun Yang was, other than the fact that she was still a rookie, just a month out of the field training car. That made her presence on the Anti-Crime Team as much a mystery as his own, he supposed.

"You're serious?"

"I wouldn't lie to you."

Zielinski grunted. "Well, then your pop culture education is severely lacking."

"Really?" She arched an eyebrow. "Have you ever seen *Crouching Tiger, Hidden Dragon*?"

He shook his head.

"Me, neither," Yang said and turned back to her report.

He stared at her, still unsure what to make of the young woman he'd been partnered with for the last week. During the first couple weeks of the team, Sergeant McGinn had rotated the officers around so that everyone spent time working with everyone else. He'd taken the time to explain his reasoning to them. As a former SWAT operator, he was of the strong opinion that all team members should be comfortable with everyone on the team—you never knew who you were going to be next to when a fight broke out.

Zielinski hadn't argued the point, though he still adhered to the more traditional idea that longtime partners worked together in ways that were damn near telepathic. That kind of connection took time to build, and it was what might make the crucial difference in a case, or in a fight.

But he was also old school when it came to chain of command, and Sergeant McGinn was the boss. So he did a stint with each member for a week. Along the way, he put up with Stone's Dudley Do-Right posturing, and Garrett's cool public arrogance and surly aloofness while they were alone.

He actually enjoyed riding with Yang. She had a quiet confidence to her and seemed older than her rookie status would indicate. While she was friendly enough to Stone and Garrett, she didn't kiss Garrett's ass. He liked that about her.

Anyone who doesn't think Tyler Garrett is the second coming of Officer Jesus Christ Superstar is all right in my book.

When news of McGinn's tragedy broke a few days ago, the team hadn't missed a step in the sergeant's absence. Crime Analysis provided intel on which HPOs were out of jail and active, and ACT focused on them. If the hippo had a warrant, they went and snagged him. If not, they alternated between openly hounding them and surreptitiously following them. Zielinski had joked to Yang that he felt like the great white hippo hunter.

She'd actually laughed, which he also liked, instead of looking for some kind of racial element to what he said. Yang seemed secure in who she was, so he supposed he was lucky that once McGinn quit making the team assignments, and Garrett and Stone as partners quickly became a fixture, that left him to pair with Yang.

"I'm going to get a soda," Zielinski said. "You want anything?"

"Water, if they have it."

Zielinski rose and left the report writing room at the police substation. It was a short walk to the small kitchen, where he rummaged around the refrigerator. He found a Coke for himself and a bottled water for Yang. He was slipping a couple of dollars into the honor jar when his phone buzzed.

The number wasn't familiar. Zielinski pressed the green button on the ancient flip phone and put it to his ear.

"Zielinski."

"Ray?"

Zielinski scowled, not recognizing the voice. He only shared his cell number with a select few people. "Who is this? How'd you get this number?"

"It's Neil," the man said. "Neil Clemons. You gave me your card. After the traffic accident, remember?"

A cold wash went over Zielinski's torso.

About three months ago, he'd accidentally bumped into Neil's car with his police cruiser. He had been distracted, upset by a call he was responding to, and not paying attention to the traffic in front of him. There was no damage to either vehicle nor any injuries. Even so, policy dictated a collision report, as well as an internal investigation. Zielinski had known what the finding would be—a preventable collision. Since he was riding two Internal Affairs complaints at the time, he didn't want to add more to the pile. When Neil had suggested that they just forget about it—no harm, no foul—Zielinski took him up on it. He'd worried about it coming back to haunt him for several weeks, but that concern faded, especially after one, then the other, of his Internal Affairs complaints were resolved favorably.

Now, suddenly, he was concerned again.

"I remember," Zielinski said, his voice turning hard. "What's up?"

He half expected to hear how Neil had suddenly discovered he was actually hurt in the collision and now had no choice but to sue the city. That would result in a slow unraveling of Zielinski's life, because the only thing worse than doing something wrong as a cop was failing to report it or covering it up.

You lie, you die. Zielinski knew that when he made his choice, but it had seemed like the best option at the time.

Neil let out a long sigh. "I need your help with something."

"What?"

"It's a little messy. Can I tell you about it over coffee, or a beer?"

"No," Zielinski said firmly. He needed to get an idea what Neil wanted right away. "Give it to me now."

"Okay. Basically, I'm having some problems with my ex-wife's new boyfriend."

"What kind of problems?"

"The kind that make a guy call a cop for a favor," Neil said. "The rest would be easier to tell you in person. Will you help me?"

Zielinski hesitated. He didn't want to get involved in any *problems* outside of work, but he owed Neil, and the guy knew it. At the very least, he decided he should hear the man out.

"I'm not sure when I'll be off work tonight," Zielinski told him. "But I'll call you. How late is too late?"

"No late is too late," Neil said. "Call whenever, and I'll meet you wherever."

"All right," Zielinski said, and snapped the phone shut.

He brought Yang's water back to the report writing room. She was still typing, so he set the bottle next to her.

"Thank you," she said, without looking away from the screen.

Zielinski sipped his soda. "What are you still writing about?"

"I'm putting in the information we got from the fence we arrested earlier, in case we're able to develop probable cause later on," she said.

Zielinski grunted.

"Even though he's in jail," Yang added.

"He'll be out again. You know why?"

"No."

"Because hippos bounce."

She gave him a dubious sideways glance. "That makes about as much sense as your western movie references."

"It's not…never mind."

Yang stopped typing and hit the send button on her report. Then she swiveled her chair toward Zielinski. "You think we should get some flowers for Sergeant McGinn?"

Zielinski nodded. "Good thinking."

"Do you have his address?" Yang twisted the cap off her bottle and took a drink.

"No, but dispatch can look it up for us."

Yang swallowed before asking, "We should include the whole team, right?"

Zielinski thought about it, then shrugged. "If you want to ask them, ask them."

Yang stared at him for a few moments, looking as if she was going to ask him another question. Then she screwed the cap back on her water bottle and rose from her chair. "I'm ready to roll. You?"

He stood without a word, and together, they headed out to the car.

Chapter 4

Detective Wardell Clint shuffled his bare feet on the mat in the police station's exercise room. He regulated his breathing, and envisioned his opponents attacking him as he went through the moves of the aikido kata. Normally, this was executed with a partner, but Clint didn't have anyone available, so he improvised. He saw with precision where the blows came from and exactly how he intercepted each one, before turning the force back upon his imaginary opponent.

While he moved, his mind was blissfully empty, focused solely on the elements of each motion. Footwork. Stance. Movement. Flow. It took all his concentration, and he willingly gave it.

As soon as he completed the final technique, however, his ever-busy brain started firing again in a staccato rhythm, a barrage of non-sequitur thoughts that represented his daily life.

Which of his cases demanded his immediate attention?

How secure was the Human Resources computer system at city hall? He didn't want his personal information to be at risk, and he knew those pencil pushers couldn't care less about it, or maybe they couldn't know less.

Sooner or later, Lieutenant Flowers was going to come down on him for the decrease in his case clearance rate. Sure, his was still better than most of the Major Crimes detectives, but Clint knew he got singled out for these things despite that. He didn't suffer fools or kiss up, for one thing. And for another thing, his skin was the wrong color for this pale bastion of the Pacific Northwest.

Clint slipped his socks and shoes back on. He tied the first shoelace, then the second. When the second was uneven and didn't match the first, he untied and then retied it so that it did. Then he dabbed his forehead and neck, getting rid of the light sheen of sweat there. He needed to get some water, but first he slid his gun back onto his belt and clipped on his badge as well.

At the fountain, he took several long drinks. He left the small gym without speaking to anyone.

His brisk pace dried off the last of the sweat from his face. As he walked, he refolded his towel. Meanwhile, his mind continued to whir.

Why hadn't he managed to get any dirt on Tyler Garrett yet? It had been months since Farrell made the ill-advised decision to put the officer on the Anti-Crime Team. Clint had urged him not to do it, warning him that it would only make catching the man more difficult. Farrell pressed ahead with his plan anyway, in typical brass-knows-best fashion.

And what happened? Exactly what I said would happen, that's what.

Since the team started operations three weeks ago, Clint's efforts to keep an eye on Tyler Garrett had become progressively more difficult. Whereas he used to have to worry about one set of eyes spotting him as a tail, now there were two sets, as Sergeant McGinn had the officers in two-man undercover vehicles.

That made it harder, too. A marked police car was easier to watch from a greater distance than a nondescript undercover rig. Even though Clint was more than familiar with the old Chevy Caprice dubbed the Gray Ghost, it was still easier to lose in traffic than a black-and-white with a light bar on top.

The worst part, though, was that since Garrett was partnered with another cop, he was far less likely to do anything criminal. That made watching him on-duty a waste of time, a conclusion that Clint reached about three days into ACT's existence. He was already spending his personal time watching Garrett during the officer's off-duty hours.

Essentially, instead of ACT working a trap for Garrett, it had given him greater security. And with all the high-profile arrests, guns and drug seizures, Garrett's reputation as the model exemplary cop was only being cemented.

Farrell. What a fool.

The captain was the only other person in the police department who knew the truth about Tyler Garrett. He and Clint had discovered it all in the beginning, two years ago, then had been sideswiped by events and the politics that followed, forcing them to keep their knowledge quiet.

For now, at least. The detective had no intention of letting this go on forever.

When he'd objected to Farrell's plan, he'd been characteristically blunt.

"This is not going to work the way you think it is," he told the captain. "Trust me."

He still remembered how Farrell's jaw muscles clenched and unclenched as he struggled to keep his temper. "We have to try. Nothing else is working."

"This will make it worse."

"I don't think so."

Normally, he might have considered holding his tongue due to Farrell's rank, but after all they'd been through, Clint thought he could cut through decorum to the heart of the matter. "You're an idiot," he told the captain.

At that point, Farrell lost his cool. "What have you accomplished, Ward? Huh? Tell me that."

"My name is Wardell," Clint reminded him, keeping his composure.

"I know your name!" Farrell snapped, his face flushing red. "I also know you've been at this for almost two years, and you've got jack to show for it. So I'm going to try something new."

"It will fail."

"Well, you already have, so deal with it!"

Clint had glared at him then. "I have *not* failed," he said in a low tone.

"Yes, you have."

"If anyone's failed," Clint told him coldly, "it's you. You're supposed to be a leader, but all you've done is make one mistake after another."

Farrell scowled at him. He opened his mouth to answer, but Clint beat him to the punch.

"And now you're about to make another mistake by putting Garrett on this team."

"It's our best option!" Farrell yelled back. He glanced at the closed door, then lowered his voice. "It's the best way to flush him out. If we plant an eye inside the group—"

"You want to bring more people into our circle? That's even stupider than putting Garrett on the team."

"We can't do this alone anymore," Farrell said through gritted teeth. "We need help."

"The only thing you'll accomplish by bringing in someone else is get us both fired, or even sent to jail."

"Damn it!" Farrell growled. He paused, looking up at the ceiling, trying to maintain his composure. "Why do you have to be so difficult every single day?"

"If you listened to reason, things wouldn't be difficult at all," Clint said.

That was when Farrell finally snapped. Clint had seen it in his eyes, a volcanic anger that seemed to take every ounce of the captain's self-control to keep it from exploding. "Maybe you're the problem. Maybe you're why we haven't caught him red-handed yet."

Clint shrugged. "And maybe you're afraid to do anything that actually puts you and your captain's bars in jeopardy."

"You're done, Detective," Farrell snarled. "You're off this case. Get out of my office."

Clint hadn't wanted to talk inside the captain's office in the first place, since he remained suspicious that all the offices on Mahogany Row were bugged. So he was fine with leaving. But off the case?

No. Farrell didn't have the authority to take him off the case. Bringing down Tyler Garrett was completely off the books. Rank did not exist in this arena. Clint didn't care if Farrell sanctioned his actions or not. And when he eventually brought the hammer down on Garrett, it wouldn't matter.

After their meeting, the only thing that changed for Clint was that he stopped giving Farrell updates on what he did, when he did it, and what he saw. If anything, the development made his work easier.

When he reached the Major Crimes division, he put his towel in a drawer of his desk, then went to find Detective Marty Hill. Hill was attached to the Anti-Crime Team, but he was coming off a knee surgery, so he was office-bound. Still, Clint imagined he could get some decent intelligence from the detective.

He found Hill at his desk with one leg propped up on a chair while he read through a file. When Clint approached, Hill glanced up. The veteran detective gave him an easy smile. "Hey, Wardell. How's it going?"

"Fine," Clint said. He long ago learned that was the easiest and best answer to this opening conversation salvo. It allowed him to move past pleasantries and into the business at hand without appearing unduly rude. He knew some level of chit-chat was necessary for most people, and Hill was more of a people person than most. Clint pointed at Hill's propped leg. "It seems like a long recovery from that surgery."

Hill's expression became a little chagrined. "I was doing fine, right on schedule, and then I reinjured it."

"How?"

"I took the brace off too soon."

"That's all?"

Hill chuckled ruefully and shook his head. "No. Then I tried to keep up with the ACT kids on a warrant arrest. I came off the steps a little funny, tweaked my knee. Doctor says I added about three weeks to my recovery, at least."

"I'm sorry," Clint said, knowing it was the right thing to say even though he didn't understand why people said it. He was glad Hill brought up ACT, though. It gave him an easy segue. "How's that going?"

"The knee? I just told you."

"No, the Anti-Crime Team."

"Oh." Hill seemed to shrug and nod at the same time. "Pretty good. They're kicking plenty of doors while I sit here on my fat ass."

"They're making a lot of arrests?"

"Definitely."

"Guns? Drugs?"

"Plenty of both," Hill said, a trace of pride in his voice. "They're a wrecking machine. Especially Garrett."

"Especially him?"

Hill must have caught something in Clint's voice, even though he was trying to keep his tone even. A flicker of suspicion danced in Hill's eyes for a moment, then was gone. "You know how he is. High speed, low drag, like always. Shouldn't be a surprise to anyone."

"No," Clint agreed. "I suppose not. How about the others?"

"They're doing fine. Stone is gaining confidence, which, if we're being honest, the guy probably needed. He's smart but I don't think he's spent much time in the trenches."

He's a cake-eater. "Interesting that they put a veteran like Zielinski on the team."

"I guess they wanted some experience to balance out Stone and Yang, especially with her just barely out of the training car." Hill eyed Clint carefully. "Was there something that you wanted, Wardell?"

Clint shook his head. "Not really." He thought for a moment, then said, "My therapist said I should be more social, and that I should start with people I like. I don't like a lot of people. So here I am, talking to you."

Hill leaned back in mild surprise. "Wow. You've got a therapist?"

"No," Clint said. "Actually, my barber said that."

Hill laughed out loud. Clint tried to smile along with him.

"Look at this," Hill said, still laughing. "Wardell Clint is making jokes at my desk. Wonders will never cease."

"Don't get used to it," Clint said.

"Oh, don't worry about that," Hill said, laughing even harder.

Clint waited until Hill's mirth subsided. Then he said, "With your injury, if you need any help on any of your cases, let me know. Interviews out in the field, or errands. Anti-Crime stuff, whatever you need."

"Okay," Hill said. "Thanks. I appreciate it."

Clint tried to read the detective's expression, but Hill had always been good at masking his thoughts. It was something Clint admired about him, though at the moment, he wished it weren't so. He didn't want to tip his hand.

"What's all this laughing?" Lieutenant Dan Flowers asked as he rounded the corner of Hill's desk.

Flowers was a lean and compact man. Clint distrusted him, but he mistrusted most people. Especially the brass, which, as a lieutenant, Flowers was. Clint knew a climber when he saw one, and Flowers was looking to make captain if he could.

"Wardell is doing stand up," Hill told him.

Flowers raised an eyebrow. "I doubt that."

"Then you'd be right," Clint told him.

"He's funny if you give him the chance," Hill said, trying to draw out the moment.

"Uh-huh," Flowers said. "Well, here's something I think is funny. Clint is the only cop left in the entire city still driving a Crown Victoria. How's that for a laugh riot?" He looked at Clint expectantly.

Hill fell silent in the face of the mood shift.

"I like my ride," Clint said evenly.

"Oh, I know. But as they say, all good things must end."

Clint stared at him. The administration had been trying to get him to turn in his aging Crown Vic for the last couple of years. He'd delayed, bargained, and outright refused, and so far, his tactics had worked. His exemplary case record gave him some latitude, and he supposed it also helped that most people found his personality difficult. Bumping him to the bottom of the list probably ended up being the easiest route, and supervisors and garage mechanics alike always seemed to ultimately opt for that.

"I think I'll hang onto her for a little while longer," Clint said.

Flowers shook his head firmly. "Nope. Yours is the last one, and it is time for it to be mothballed. This is coming from the garage and the fleet commander. They want this car off the books and you in a new Impala like everyone else."

Clint wasn't surprised. He knew the new cars were likely outfitted with GPS, so they could track his movements. In addition to that, Impalas were gutless. He didn't have to drive fast often, but he'd like to be able to call on a V8 when the time came. You didn't have to be good at math to know four cylinders wasn't going to be quite the same in those situations.

"I'll make an appointment," Clint said, figuring that ought to buy him some time. Maybe in the meantime they'd forget about it for a while.

"Already done," Flowers said, handing him a slip of paper. "It's Thursday. Get it done."

"What if I'm too busy on Thursday?"

Flowers unclipped his lieutenant's badge and held it up. "What's that say, Detective?"

"Spokane Police."

Flowers scowled at him. "Below that."

"Lieutenant," Clint read.

"That's right. And as *your* lieutenant specifically, I'm telling you that you're *not* going to be too busy on Thursday. You're going to be on time for your appointment, and you're going to turn in that beast. If you don't do exactly that, you'll be in violation of a direct order, and you'll be reprimanded."

"Can I take the reprimand and keep the car?"

"No." Flowers clipped the badge back onto his belt. "Nice try. Get it done, Wardell. I'm serious."

Flowers turned and walked away.

"He *is* serious, isn't he?" Clint said, glancing down at Hill.

Hill gave him a half smile. "If that was supposed to be a joke, that makes two today. Which has to be a Wardell Clint record of some kind."

"The joke's on you," Clint said. "Because I wasn't fooling about any of it."

Chapter 5

Captain Tom Farrell knocked on the frame of the opened doorway to Captain Dana Hatcher's office. She looked up at the sound. When she saw him, her features darkened slightly. "Yes, Captain?" she asked.

Farrell resisted the urge to sigh. He wished he could rewind the clock and find some way to repair the damage to their relationship. He liked it better when she called him Tom.

"You have a minute?" he asked.

"Barely."

That was better than nothing, so Farrell took it. He stepped inside the office and sat in the chair across from her desk before she could object. "We need to talk about ACT."

"*Your* Anti-Crime Team, you mean?" she asked coldly. "The one with all of *my* patrol officers on it?"

Farrell did sigh then. "Yeah, that team. Look, Dana, how long are we going to go on like this?"

"Like what?"

"Like this. With you being mad."

"You're right," Hatcher said flatly. "I should probably just get over it."

Farrell watched her, trying to gauge her sincerity. She stared back, impassive. He decided to let it lie. Feuding with her was the last thing he needed. Between his clash with Clint over the Anti-Crime Team, Baumgartner's pressure to keep the team producing, and his anguish over how to push Garrett into a situation where he finally revealed himself, he was juggling plenty of balls at once. Fighting with Hatcher was a luxury he couldn't afford, even if he wanted to. Besides, in the end, they both knew she was right to be angry.

"You heard about McGinn, right?" he asked.

"Of course. He's one of my people. I take care of *my* people."

"I know," Farrell said. "And if there's anything he needs, the chief has made it clear he'll make it happen."

"Good to know," Hatcher said coolly.

"With McGinn out indefinitely, that leaves ACT without a sergeant. We need to figure out a replacement."

"*We?*"

"As in you and I."

Hatcher looked at him a moment. Then she said, "I figured you'd just do like you did before and tell me who you were taking from my command. Are you telling me I have a choice this time around?"

Farrell felt the warmth of anger creeping up the back of his neck. "Do you have any suggestions?" he asked.

"No. But I don't want to lose another sergeant. I'm running short as it is."

"We all are."

She gave him a patronizing look. "It's different for Patrol. Investigative supervisors spend most of their time pushing paper. Patrol sergeants are out in the field, a resource to the officers. When we run short, cops are waiting around for booking approvals, or scenes that need a supervisor sit stagnant until one can break free to get there. Then the situation dominoes, and calls stack up. When that happens, cops cut corners to try to clear the screen, and when cops cut corners, they can get hurt. I can't spare a sergeant from Patrol."

Farrell didn't argue. "I don't want a patrol sergeant."

"Who, then?"

"Kelly Ragland."

Hatcher looked mildly surprised. "My admin sergeant?"

"I think it's the best solution. It won't put Patrol down another sergeant, but ACT has to have a supervisor."

Hatcher considered for a few moments. Then she said, "No."

Farrell raised his eyebrows in surprise. "No?"

She stared at him with that same flat gaze she'd worn when talking with him over the past two months. "Did I stutter, Tom?"

Farrell clenched his jaw. *Sure,* now *she calls me Tom. Great.*

"Why not?"

Hatcher reached up to her uniform collar and pulled it out slightly. She looked down appraisingly. Then she turned back to Farrell. "According to my collar, I'm a captain, just like you. In fact, I'm the captain of Patrol, and you're trying to steal one of my sergeants… *from Patrol.* My decision is no. Since I don't work for you, I don't need to explain my decision to you."

Farrell was quiet for a few seconds, considering his options. He didn't see many, and none of them ended well. Finally, he said, "The Anti-Crime Team needs a sergeant. The chief and I gave this considerable thought and assigning Sergeant Ragland has the least amount of impact on any other units."

"Especially to Investigations, right?"

"And to Patrol," Farrell said.

"Oh, it impacts Patrol," Hatcher shot back. "As usual. We're supposed to be the backbone of the department, but anytime some special project comes along, where do the bodies come from? Ripped from Patrol, that's where."

"ACT was *your* idea!" Farrell said, and immediately regretted it.

Hatcher's eyes held a quiet fury. "I know," she grated. "But somehow you ended up with the team."

He waited for her to add *and the credit,* but it never came.

Instead, she added, "Didn't you?"

Farrell didn't want to rehash the chief's earlier decision. "How does taking Ragland impact Patrol?"

"He schedules the front desk rotation, for one."

Farrell shrugged. "He can keep that duty while he's assigned to ACT."

Hatcher wasn't assuaged. "He's my safety valve. I'm already down McGinn because of your team. What if I lose another sergeant to injury or God knows what? Ragland is who I would plug into that team whenever it's needed."

Farrell was incredulous. "So I'm supposed to go back to the chief and say that you won't agree to fill an existing need because you want to have an asset in reserve to fill a need that doesn't exist yet?"

Hatcher blinked at his convoluted argument. Then she shrugged. "You act like patrol shortages never happen. They happen constantly, and we're already understaffed, even before you stole five bodies for your team."

"That's not fair, Dana. You were fine with reassigning those officers when it was your plan."

"It *still* is my plan. You're just getting credit for it."

And there it is. He leaned back, weary and frustrated. "Let me put it to you like this," he said wearily. "The chief has authorized this move. Ragland is going to ACT. It's a done deal."

Hatcher nodded slowly, as if she'd expected that. "If you already had daddy's permission, why didn't you lead with that? It would've saved us both some time."

Farrell stood. "Thank you, Dana," he said as pleasantly as he could, and headed back to his own office.

He needed some Rolaids.

Chapter 6

It surprised Gary Stone how easily the Anti-Crime Team detained Harlin Schmick.

Schmick, a lanky white man with an overgrown mohawk, had been sitting on the front steps of a dilapidated house in the worst part of Hillyard, Spokane's poorest neighborhood. He was enjoying a cigarette with his eyes closed, listening to loud country music blasting through the open front door. His head bounced and swayed to the rhythm of the song as he mumbled along with the chorus.

When he opened his eyes and saw four officers approaching, his smile faded.

Ray Zielinski led a procession of officers toward Schmick. Jun Yang was slightly behind him while Gary Stone was on her heels. Tyler Garrett brought up the rear.

Harlin Schmick nonchalantly looked back over his shoulder into the house then crushed out his cigarette. When he stood, he raised his arms slightly, showing his palms. His conduct made it obvious to Stone that this wasn't his first police contact and that he expected them to arrive at some point.

Schmick wore a red Spokane Chiefs hockey jersey, blue jean shorts, and black Converse high-tops without socks. Even though he was in his late twenties, he had considerable acne and was missing several front teeth.

As he approached the surrendering man, Zielinski stated, "Harlin Schmick." Stone imagined it was more out of habit than any question as to the man's identity.

Stone and the rest of the team knew Schmick by sight as they had studied his picture prior to leaving the department.

Detective Marty Hill had developed probable cause to arrest Schmick and obtained a signed arrest warrant. Schmick was another hippo, a high-profile offender, due to his proclivity for breaking into people's homes. Hill had classified him as something less than a professional burglar, but more of a high-end amateur.

Schmick grunted something in response to Zielinski's statement, not bothering to lie or conceal who he was.

Zielinski grabbed the man's right hand and quickly twisted his arm behind his back. "You're under arrest for First Degree Burglary," Zielinski said. Yang assisted him in handcuffing the man while Stone moved with Garrett to the front door of the house.

The country music continued to blare, and Stone spotted another white male moving inside. He was singing along to the music as well.

"Hey!" Stone yelled.

The man turned to look at the officer. He was holding a paper plate with a sandwich on it.

"Spokane Police! Come outside!"

The man hesitated and looked at his sandwich.

"Now!" Stone yelled.

"And turn that music off!" Garrett hollered. To Stone he said, "What is it with loud, terrible music today?"

Stone didn't look at Garrett but kept his eyes on the approaching man. The guy put his sandwich next to the stereo and clicked the music off as he exited the house. He wore a black tank top, baggy cargo shorts, and untied red high-tops.

"Anyone else inside?" Garrett asked.

"Just me," the man said as he walked down the stairs.

Garrett remained at the front steps, watching the interior of the house.

As he motioned for the man to step away from Garrett, Stone said, "Let's see your driver's license."

"I don't have one."

"What about an ID card?"

The man shook his head.

"You don't have a driver's license or an ID card?" Stone asked.

"No," the man reiterated.

"Typical Stat-five," Garrett muttered, his eyes still focused on the inside of the house. A Stat-5, or Status 5, was department slang for a suspicious person. The term had come from the 10-code system used in decades past. Even though the codes had long been phased out for radio use, a few of them remained in the department's lexicon.

"What about a name?" Stone asked. "Got one of those?"

The man pulled his lips back as he thought, revealing several rotten teeth. "Wayne," he said finally.

Stone rolled his eyes, hoping this was not the start of the name game. "What about your *last* name?"

"Cattage."

"Wayne Cattage?"

"Uh-huh."

"Got a middle initial?"

"No."

"What's your date of birth?"

Cattage rattled off a date, including birth year.

"How old are you?"

"Twenty-six," Cattage replied immediately.

Stone did the math, and it was correct. Either the birthdate was the real deal, or Cattage was adept at playing the game. With his three-week baptism of fire back onto the streets, Stone was getting better at quickly discovering a person's true identity. With Cattage's information, Stone called into dispatch and ran the man's name, checking him for any current wants.

While dispatch checked Cattage's background, Stone eyed Garrett who was still observing the front of the house. The officer was on alert in case someone appeared and suddenly posed a threat. Stone felt confident working with Garrett. The man was a full-time professional and knew how to handle anything that happened on the street. When Stone first came onto the department, Garrett was his patrolman role model, the type of officer he wanted to become. Garrett didn't know that, and Stone wasn't likely to tell him.

He'd recently come to terms with the fact that Garrett released information to the newspaper that had gotten him removed from his old position. Initially, he suspected as much, and Captain Farrell even intimated it. He never imagined he would get past his anger. However, when Stone confronted Garrett about it on their first ride-along, the senior officer admitted doing it.

"Whether you choose to believe it," he said, "I was looking out for you."

Stone couldn't believe the boldness of his statement, but Garrett continued.

"Sometimes we can't see the path we're on, so others have to help us find our way. I didn't mean for you to get caught up in a giant hassle. I'd never have wanted that for you. I'm sorry. I truly am. But Gary, coming clean about what the city and the chief were doing was the right thing."

They both agreed that the department had been wrong to cover up the details surrounding a young woman's suicide for the benefit of a councilman. The senior officer then stated that he'd been a victim of a city and department cover-up and that's why he wouldn't let a teenage girl's death be handled the same way.

When Garrett presented it that way, Stone saw the nobleness of what the man actually did. He risked not only losing Stone as a friend, but getting fired, labeled a pariah, and possibly facing a criminal charge for interfering in an investigation.

Stone felt slightly ashamed at that moment because he realized he hadn't considered the other victims whose stories were brought to light by what Garrett did. Even though Stone felt the cover-up was wrong, he didn't have the courage to stand up and do something about it. Instead, he went along with it.

Only Garrett had the courage to take action and do what was right.

There was a silver lining to the release of the information, though. Had it not happened, he would never have ended up being assigned to ACT. Since joining the team, his admiration for Garrett had only increased.

His eyes drifted to Zielinski and Yang, who were interviewing Harlin Schmick. Stone wanted to like the older cop, but Zielinski had once referred to him as the Chief's Bitch because of the administrative role he had been assigned. Stone wasn't going to easily forget that. Still, Zielinski was a good cop and someone he appreciated working alongside.

Yang was a good officer, too. Although slightly younger than him, both in life and on the department, she seemed more confident than him. He knew she had prior law enforcement experience in the military and perhaps that was where her poise came from. It showed in the way she carried herself. He wondered if it was the military training that had gotten her onto this team while still a rookie.

Harlin Schmick suddenly seemed agitated and he danced around with his hands behind his back. Yang grabbed him by the elbow in an attempt to hold him in place.

When Stone's eyes returned to Cattage, he realized the man had been studying him. Stone scowled at Cattage who didn't respond except for possibly blinking slower.

"Tango-fourteen," the dispatcher said.

Stone keyed his portable radio. "Go ahead."

At that moment, movement occurred inside the house. A woman briefly appeared, saw Garrett and Stone, then turned back inside.

"You in the house!" Garrett yelled.

Stone instinctively stepped back to get a better angle to see the woman.

Garrett shouted, "Come outside."

The dispatcher said something, but Stone missed it in the

commotion of movement and yelling.

"Do you need help?" Zielinski hollered to Garrett, who in turn held up a hand for the other officer to wait where he was.

Harlin Schmick suddenly yelled, "I wanna talk with your supervisor."

Stone lifted the portable, his eyes still on the interior of the house, and distractedly said to the dispatcher, "Tango-fourteen, please repeat."

From the corner of his eye, Cattage seemed closer to him than before. Stone thought he had moved back from the man.

The woman stepped around the corner again.

Garrett removed his Glock and pointed it at the woman. He yelled, "Let me see your hands!"

"Your supervisor!" hollered Schmick.

"Shut your pie-hole," Zielinski shouted at his detainee.

Stone again didn't hear the radio transmission over the other officer's shouts as his focus was on the woman. She had something in her hands, but he couldn't see what it was.

"Let me see your hands!" Garrett yelled again.

"Police brutality!" Schmick screamed. "Police—"

"We're not touching you!" Zielinski bellowed.

"Relax!" the woman inside the house shouted. "I'm comin' out. Gimme a second."

"Now!" Garrett demanded.

The woman turned her hands over to reveal a pack of cigarettes in one and a lighter in the other.

"Get out here!" Garrett ordered.

Schmick, his eyes on the front of the house, suddenly seemed to calm down.

Zielinski and Yang were intently watching Schmick.

"All right! I told you I was comin' out," the woman said.

Stone let out his breath, unaware that he had been holding it from the moment Garrett drew his gun.

The woman stepped out of the house toward Garrett. She was medium height, with long, dirty hair. She had on a man's blue T-shirt and ripped jean shorts. She wore black flip-flops on her dirty feet.

"Repeating for Tango-fourteen," the dispatcher said, "Wayne Cattage has—"

But Stone never heard the end of the transmission as Cattage shoved him then, causing him to stumble several steps back. Wayne Cattage sprinted from the yard.

Since he still had a gun in his right hand, Garrett snatched the woman by the upper arm with his free hand and yelled to Stone "Get him!"

Harlin Schmick tried to run with his handcuffs behind his back, but both Zielinski and Yang quickly grabbed him and wrestled him to the ground.

Stone regained his footing then dashed after the man. Cattage didn't have much of a lead on him and, for that, he was thankful. It was embarrassing that the man had given Stone the slip while standing right in front of him.

Cattage was now on the sidewalk running down the block, his red high-tops noisily smacking the concrete, the shoestrings whipping wildly about.

Stone was already tired from the chase earlier in the day. He still carried his portable radio in his right hand and, if the chase went much further, he would call in the foot pursuit to ask for additional help. He was sure that he would catch Cattage, though.

They crossed Lee Street and entered another yard. Cattage raced toward a six-foot cedar fence. When he jumped at its top, his body banged into the wooden wall. His feet scrambled helplessly to get him over the top. As he struggled for grip on the fence, his left shoe fell off, then his right. Clad only in white socks, Cattage hopelessly tried to lift himself over.

Stone made it to the fence as Cattage had his belly on the top of the fence. To be free, all the man had to do was either swing a leg over or just fall headfirst to the other side. He was too slow, though. Stone grabbed Cattage's left foot with his left hand and pulled him back away from the fence.

Cattage kicked back with his right foot, hitting Stone in the chest.

This angered the officer, who still held the man's left foot. Using the butt of his portable radio, Stone clubbed Cattage in his left calf. In that moment of anger and frustration, the act of striking Cattage felt so good that Stone did it again. Almost as quickly as he hit the man, Stone realized what he did was wrong, but there was no time to consider those actions.

Howling in pain, Cattage kicked at Stone with his free leg.

Stone dropped his portable and caught the right foot under his arm pit when Cattage attempted a third kick.

"Son of bitch," Stone muttered.

He clung to Cattage's feet as the man frantically tried to pull himself over the other side.

The officer yanked several times, dragging Cattage's belly back across the top of the fence, but the man did not let go. Finally, Stone leaned back, letting his own weight work against Cattage's arms. It took several moments, but the criminal's arms finally extended to their fullest, his hands clinging to the edge of the fence top.

With a final jerk from Stone, the man lost his grip and fell. The officer stumbled several feet backward but retained his hold around the man's feet. Cattage landed face-first onto the ground.

Stone clambered onto the man's back then and handcuffed him. Triumphantly, he sat there for a moment, catching his breath and resetting his wits. In a moment of self-realization, Stone understood that if someone took a video of this altercation, it would not look good for an officer to be sitting astride a suspect now that he was under control. He rolled off and knelt next to Cattage. He listened to the man breathing heavily for a moment.

Finally, Stone turned Cattage over and lifted him into a seated position on the curb. The criminal's mouth and chin were bloody.

He found his portable radio and picked it up. "Tango-fourteen," he called.

"Fourteen," dispatch said.

"One in custody," he said, through breaths of deep air. "Advise a supervisor."

Cattage bent forward, his head bowed. He spat a glob of blood into the street.

Stone sat next to him. "Why'd you make me run, man?"

Cattage shrugged. "Seemed like a good idea at the time."

The comment made Stone smile slightly. "Didn't quite turn out like you planned."

"Nope," Cattage grunted. He contorted slightly, trying to wipe his mouth on his jersey front. Due to the handcuffs, he couldn't quite reach. Stone grabbed a handful of the material and lifted it closer. Cattage smeared it with blood and mucus.

"Thanks, man," he said.

"No problem."

They sat quietly for a few seconds as each caught their breath. Finally, Cattage inhaled deeply and said, "Well, hell. This is what I get for hanging out with idiots, I guess."

Stone didn't reply. He could sense an odd sort of camaraderie growing between him and Cattage, as if they were just two blue-collar guys doing their respective jobs, enjoying a moment's respite. He'd heard about this from veteran officers, but the strangeness of it still struck him.

"You mean Harlin?" he asked, cautiously.

"Yeah, Harlin, the dumb idiot. And who knows what Kenny would do if you arrested her."

"Kenny is the woman?"

He nodded.

"You worried about her?"

"Yeah," he said.

"Why?"

He smirked. "'Cause she's stupid and Harlin gets that way too when she's around."

Stone knew building rapport with a suspect was important, so he continued to engage him in conversation. "That happens when women are around."

"Not like this."

"How so?"

"Dude, she's so far up his nose he can't think straight."

"Like how?"

Cattage rolled his eyes. "Like when we did this job last week in Five Mile. Great potential but guess what she does?"

Stone's pulse accelerated. The man was actually confessing a crime. "What'd she do?" he asked, careful not to let his excitement show in his voice.

Cattage moved his jaw around as if he was feeling for something broken.

Stone wanted to repeat his question but forced himself to be patient. If he was anxious, Cattage might pick up on it and stop talking.

The man licked his lips, smearing blood across them. "We were supposed to be looking for things we can easily carry, things we can sell, but she gets distracted by a DVD collection."

Stone relaxed once the man was talking again. "DVDs?"

"That's what I'm saying." Cattage spat another glob of blood into the street. "She starts flipping through these movies, picking the ones she wants to take home. Me and Harlin, we're running from room to room looking for things that will put food on the table and she's pulling *Mrs. Doubtfire* out, asking if we've ever seen it."

"I've never seen it," Stone admitted.

"Me neither and I ain't never going to watch it now, just out of spite."

"She didn't carry her weight is what you're saying."

Cattage shook his head. "It got worse when she started yelling for Harlin to grab a toaster."

"A toaster?"

"Yeah, a frickin' toaster. And the stupid idiot did it. Stopped looking for things we could sell to go grab her a toaster. That set her off on a shopping list, like we was at Target or something."

"The toaster had to be the worst of it, right?"

"Know what an Instapot is?"

"No."

"Neither do I, but she's got one now." He shook his head ruefully. "I don't know why I work with the morons."

"If they're unreliable, why hang with them?"

"Stupid bitch is my sister and he's been my best friend since my first trip to juvie."

"You said this job was in Five Mile?"

Cattage turned his head and eyed him. His expression hardened. He hocked up another glob of blood and spat it on the concrete. "I said enough."

Stone could barely contain his excitement. He'd just gotten a confession about a break-in. He'd be able to take it to Marty Hill and, once the detective found that original burglary report, they could tie it back to Cattage and his small crew. Stone had solved a burglary on his own.

He smiled to himself and patted Cattage on the shoulder. "Let's head back."

They walked the block and half back to the dilapidated house. Cattage had a noticeable limp from where Stone had struck him in the calf. He wondered if he should report that or just say that the man injured himself in the fall from the fence.

When they arrived back at the house, there were two patrol cars waiting to transport the arrestees. The ACT cars were not equipped to take anyone to jail. Stone handed Cattage off to a waiting patrol officer.

When Garrett approached, he said with an approving grin, "Two foot pursuits in one day, and you got 'em both. That must be a personal best."

"It is," Stone said. He then looked to Zielinski and Yang who were searching Harlin Schmick next to the open door of a patrol car. "Pretty good bust."

"Not bad," he said, "but I drew the short straw."

"What do you mean?"

"The woman, Kendra Cattage, has a history, but she came

back clean. No reason to arrest her." Garrett sighed. "I wish we had something to get us inside that house."

"We do," Stone said and then relayed Cattage's admission.

"No lie?" Garrett said. "The man admitted to another burglary? Just like that?"

"I prompted him a few times, but he kept on talking."

"Nice work, Stoney." Garrett clapped him on the shoulder. "Really."

Stone observed Officer Yang standing next to Harlin Schmick as he sat in the back of patrol car. She was reading from a small card, causing Schmick to lean forward in resignation.

The Miranda warning, Stone thought. He looked to Cattage who was now sitting in the back of the other patrol car.

"Damn," Stone muttered to himself.

"What's wrong?" Garrett asked.

"I didn't read him his rights before we started talking then I kept asking him questions. He was already in custody, so none of it will be admissible. We won't be able to get a warrant."

Garrett studied Stone for a moment, then looked to Cattage. "So? Read him his rights now."

"But it's too late."

"It'll be fine," Garrett said. "Read him the card and ask him about the admission he made."

Stone considered the senior officer's words then pulled his notebook out of his back pocket. He tugged a Miranda warning card loose and walked over to the patrol car where Cattage was detained. He opened the back door and said, "Wayne, I need to read you your rights before I ask you some follow-up questions."

Cattage leaned his head back on the car seat. "No."

Reading from the card, Stone said, "You have the right to remain silent. Anything you say—"

"I don't need you to read them. I know my rights and I'm not saying anythin' to you."

Stone frowned. "But we already talked about the break-in on Five Mile."

Cattage rolled his head to the officer. "You hit me, man. Then you beat me up. I don't know why I told you all that other stuff."

"That's what I'd like to talk to you about. I just need to read you these rights."

"You hit me!" Cattage yelled. "You made me talk!"

Stone jerked his head up to see Zielinski and Yang now looking at him. The other officers present were also watching him as Cattage continued to yell.

"You assaulted me! You violated my rights! I'll have your badge!"

Tyler Garrett walked up to Stone, pulled him slightly back, and slammed the door shut on Cattage. The man continued to holler inside the car, but his volume was severely muted.

Stone hung his head and muttered, "Damn it."

"Lift up your head, Stoney."

"What?"

"Lift up your head and look directly at me."

Stone obeyed.

Garrett looked intently into his eyes. "Don't ever let anyone see you doubt yourself."

Stone started to look around.

"Pay attention to me and listen to what I'm about to tell you."

Stone's brow furrowed, but he stared at Garrett. The man's eyes bored into him.

"You paying attention?"

"Yes."

Garrett spoke slowly and deliberately. "You did it in the right order."

"What?"

"You did it in the *right* order. Do you understand? You arrested the man, you read him his rights, and he confessed to the crime."

Stone pulled back slightly, but Garrett grabbed his arm to stop him. "If they see you doubting yourself, no one will believe you. Do you understand?"

He slowly nodded.

"Do you want him to get away with the burglary? The one you *know* he did."

Stone's eyes slid to Cattage who continued to scream profanities at him from the back of the patrol car. He spat on the window in the middle of a string of vulgarities.

Garrett didn't seem to notice. "Or do you want to remember it the way I do? This will be another rock star bust for you. Don't let it be wasted due to some ridiculous technicality."

"It's the law," Stone said quietly. "He has rights."

"What's more important?" Garrett asked. "The rights of a confessed, piece-of-crap burglar, or the rights of the decent citizens whose house he broke into?"

Stone didn't reply, but he saw the logic. And Cattage *had* admitted to the crime…

"You did your job, Stoney, and you did it well. Write your report that way. I'll back your play, then we'll get inside *his* house. What do you want to bet it's full of stolen property?"

"I know it is."

"So we're on the same page?"

Stone took a deep breath, nodding. "We're on the same page," he said.

Garrett smiled. "You're going to like this, then. Follow me."

They walked over to Kendra Cattage who sat on the front steps of the house. She eyed the officers with suspicion.

Garrett thumbed toward the car where her brother was currently throwing a fit. "Your brother admitted to a burglary up in Five Mile. He said you and your boyfriend were part of it."

Kendra's eyes widened then narrowed. "You're lying."

"He rolled," Garrett said. "Deal with it. We know there's a…what's in there, Stoney?"

Stone ticked them off with his fingers. "A *Mrs. Doubtfire* DVD, a toaster, and an Instapot."

"Instant Pot," Kendra corrected, and looked away. "Those things are mine," she muttered unconvincingly.

"Got a receipt for them?" Garrett asked.

"Who keeps receipts for anything? Do you?"

Garrett's smile grew as he watched her. The woman eventually looked away from his gaze.

"So here's where things stand," Garrett said. "Either you let us search your house for that stolen property—"

"I'm not going to do that," she blurted.

"Or we're going to get a warrant to search it."

"You can't do that," Kendra almost whispered.

Garrett leaned into her. "We're going in one way or another."

"It's not fair," Kendra mumbled.

"Fair's got nothing to do with it," Garrett stated flatly. "The only difference is how you come out in all this."

"What's that mean?" she asked.

"If you give us permission, you need to stay while we search. If we gotta go get a warrant, you'll walk away right now."

"I don't understand," Kendra said.

To be honest, neither did Stone. As his mind whirred, he watched Garrett.

"Give us permission to search and you stay right there," the senior officer said, pointing to where Kendra sat. "Or refuse to let us search, and you can leave right now."

Kendra's face brightened. "I'm not giving you permission."

"All right." Garrett was unruffled by the refusal.

"Then I'm free to go?"

Disbelieving of what he heard, Stone's mouth dropped open.

Garrett glanced to Stone then back to Kendra. "You're free to go, but you can't go back into that house."

She stood quickly and walked away, not bothering to shut

the door to her house. She didn't look back at the officers nor did she glance at her brother or boyfriend. She kept her eyes forward as she hurried toward freedom.

Tyler Garrett put his arm around Gary Stone's shoulders. "And that, my friend, is how you start building your own network of informants."

"You're just letting her go?" Stone asked as he watched Kendra almost break into a run as she left the property.

"Why not? We know who she is and by the time were done searching this house, we'll have a warrant for her arrest later. We can pick her up whenever we want and leverage her to get something better, always dangling the warrant over her head."

"But a warrant is a judge's order, right? We're supposed to take a person to jail whenever we find someone with one."

Garrett looked at him as if he was talking to a child. "They tell you that because it's simple. It's easy. That's how the politicians want to pretend the game should be played, but we can't always do it that way." Garrett tapped the side of his temple. "We need to be smarter than the criminals. We need to operate differently."

"And letting her go accomplishes that?"

"You could tell she's a woman who would do anything to avoid jail, right? I know you saw that. You're smart."

Stone nodded cautiously. "I saw it."

"So why waste that by dragging her ass down there right now, today? Let's remember her, keep tabs on her, and twist her later. We'll get more from her tomorrow than we would today. We've already got a home run with the two maggots over there. There's no profit from arresting her now."

"Is that our job? Deciding how and when to leverage an informant? That sounds like what detectives are supposed to do."

Garrett whispered in Stone's ear. "Detectives are spoiled children. They're overrated. They only work as hard as they have to. If they're given a hard case, they won't work it. They want low-hanging fruit, something we've already done all the work on. Don't look up to them, man. You'll only be disappointed."

Stone's brow furrowed.

"Stoney, here's the truth. You play chess, right? Well, on the street, as in life, you're either a pawn or you're a king. Which do you want to be? Because I want to be a king."

Stone smiled. "If I said I want to be the queen, would you think I'm gay?"

Garrett howled with laughter.

Chapter 7

Jun Yang closed the door to the patrol car, shutting Harlin Schmick in the rear. She stepped back and surveyed the scene.

About forty feet away, Wayne Cattage continued to yell in the back of a different patrol car. He bounced up and down in his seat as he threw his tantrum. If this display continued at jail, the staff there would not tolerate it for very long. They would strap him into a chair until he calmed down. Yang knew it wouldn't be a pleasant experience, but it was effective in keeping order. That's how many things in life were.

The woman with the stringy hair, Kendra Cattage, hastily walked away from the house. She looked as if she was about to break into a sprint, but she held herself back, her pace uneven at times.

Tyler Garrett had his arm around Gary Stone's shoulders, whispering something into his ear, as they watched the Cattage woman hurry away. Stone smiled before both men laughed. They were clearly enjoying this moment.

The two officers bothered Yang, but for different reasons.

She didn't trust Garrett, but she couldn't put her finger on a single reason why. She'd come across his type before while in the Army—hyper aggressive and highly effective, yet beguiling when put into social situations. Those men were always on the hunt for a new kill, either literal or figurative. However, that wasn't the only reason she didn't trust Garrett. It had to do with the way Captain Farrell watched him with weary eyes—the way a cop watches a criminal.

Stone, on the other hand, was a follower, a man who molded his personality to those around him. When they had ridden together in the first week, Stone was quiet and reflective. She thought he might have been a kindred soul. She no longer believed that. Since becoming Tyler Garrett's full-time partner, Stone appeared to be changing into something she wasn't sure she liked. He was quickly adopting mannerisms related to aggression and cockiness. Even some of his speech patterns reflected Garrett's. If this had happened in a just over a week, what would happen in a month? Or a year?

"Waiting for an invitation?" Ray Zielinski said.

Yang turned to him and raised her eyebrows.

Zielinski's drooping mustache made it seem like he wore a perpetual scowl. "Can we go or is there something else you want to do here?"

"We can go," she said.

Zielinski led the way back to their car, his shoulders rolled slightly forward, a man carrying an unknown weight.

He was a burnout, she thought. She'd also seen this in the Army, but mostly from career men and women. Those who stayed too long after they lost their initial reason for being a soldier. There was no doubt that Zielinski was a smart cop. The man knew the law and was keenly aware of officer safety protocols. Yang felt adequately prepared for the street with him as her partner.

He even tried to lighten the mood at times by either making a joke or referring to some old movie. She appreciated those attempts to be more engaging.

However, it was clear he no longer had a love for the job nor the people he was sworn to protect and serve. He frequently complained about the work. He grumbled often about his ex-wives. In fact, he groused about a lot of things. Why did he continue to show up and be unhappy? Why didn't he just quit and go do something he would enjoy?

Yang knew she had a habit of pigeonholing people and maybe she was doing that with her teammates. Her intuition was often correct, but it wasn't infallible.

For example, she initially thought Captain Tom Farrell to

be an intelligent man with a keen sense of fairness. That early assessment was based upon her sole interaction with him at her academy graduation dinner.

After she finished her full rotation with her field training officers, though, the captain sought her out one evening after roll call. They had a private conversation about a new team, one that he was forming to focus on career criminals, one that he wanted her as a member.

She was flattered, of course, but she had to know why she was chosen above so many other officers with much more experience.

"It's because of who you are, Jun," he said.

"What's that mean?" she asked.

"Your military police record was exemplary," he said. "Also, the incident in the academy spoke volumes about who you are, not as only as a person but who you would become with the badge."

Yang didn't respond to Farrell then. Instead, she chose to remain quiet. She preferred not to talk about "the incident." Too many people wanted to weigh in on something they had cursory knowledge about.

"I want someone," Farrell continued, "who won't be afraid to report something if she sees it as wrong or unethical. I need a woman with a distinct moral compass on this team."

They talked for several minutes longer as Farrell described the Anti-Crime Team. She was new to the department and didn't believe she had the right to challenge the assignment. Farrell was pleased that she accepted, and he walked away confident and happy. Unfortunately, he had no idea how Yang felt.

What remained with her since that interaction were two things.

First, the only reason Captain Farrell wanted her on the team was because he believed she had the moral courage to report another officer for doing something wrong. She had done it while at the academy. He was not concerned with her ability to investigate crimes nor her ability to fit in with a small unit. Captain Farrell only cared that she was okay with being a rat.

Second, and this one irked her the more she thought about it, he never asked how she was doing. He just assumed she was doing well and that she would want the assignment. This proved him to be like every other officer she'd met so far. They talked about themselves first, not inquiring about others until they ran out of things to say, often hoping to bring the conversation back around to them again. They placed their needs above the needs of others. It was something she was disappointed to see in Farrell. It was something she hoped she would never develop in herself as her experience as an officer grew.

"Hey," Zielinski asked, "did you order those flowers for Sergeant McGinn?"

"Garrett did it before I could. He signed the card from the team."

Zielinski stopped walking and closed his eyes, his face reddening.

"I thought it was a nice gesture," Yang said.

The senior officer opened his eyes and muttered, "Of course, you would." He walked away, shaking his head.

Jun Yang watched him drop into the old Ford Maverick and slam the door. She glanced back at Garrett and Stone, who were still smiling and laughing.

In the Army, she was a vital part of an organization where people relied on her and trusted her. Here she was purposefully placed on a team to spy on them, although no one ever officially stated that. She was smart enough to know that she was the designated tattletale.

Did the rest of the team know her role?

It was then she had a sad realization. She didn't *feel* like a police officer.

Instead, she felt like a woman *pretending* to be a police officer. She hated feeling that way.

Chapter 8

"Kelly!" Farrell said to the uniformed sergeant ahead of him. "Hold up."

Sergeant Kelly Ragland paused at the west doors of the police department. He gave Farrell a look of mild surprise. "Can I help you, Captain?"

"I need to talk to you for a minute."

The two men exited the building and walked a few yards to the left of the doorway, out of earshot of anyone coming or going from the Public Safety Building. Since it was the employee entrance, Farrell wasn't too worried about who might walk by, but then again, they didn't need to hear his business.

Glancing at his watch, Ragland asked, "What's up?"

"Have you spoken with Captain Hatcher today?"

"No. Why?"

"I've got a great opportunity for you," Farrell said.

Ragland didn't look especially thrilled at the prospect of adventure. He said nothing and waited for Farrell to continue.

"You know about the Anti-Crime Team, right?"

Ragland nodded.

"Well, McGinn was leading the team, but he had to take emergency family leave. So right now, the team is without a sergeant."

"I don't want the job," Ragland immediately interjected.

Farrell paused, a tickle of irritation in the pit of his gut. *Just once, it would be nice if something went smoothly.*

"Look," he said, keeping his voice even, "this is a specialty team. It's a chance to make a difference, to do something meaningful."

"So, what I'm doing has no meaning?" Ragland snapped. Then he added, "Sir?"

"I didn't say that. This is a different kind of opportunity. More of a direct impact."

"I feel like my work has a pretty significant impact around here."

"It does." Farrell tried a different tactic. "Kelly, a team like this needs a strong supervisor. The cops on the team are hunters, focused on finding the prey. That's good, it's what they're supposed to do, but we need a sergeant on the team who can make sure that other considerations don't fall by the wayside."

"Like what?"

"Policy, for one. Proper procedure. Keeping the team focused, and not forgetting the overall mission."

"You don't need me to do that. Any sergeant can."

"In case you haven't noticed, we're a bit strapped for sergeants these days."

"So promote some more."

"I wish I could, but that's up to city hall and the chief." Farrell looked Ragland in the eye. "These teams tend to perform really well, and this specific team is no different. They're kicking ass out there. But these teams can also go astray."

"What are you talking about?"

"I'm talking about cutting corners. Making poor decisions in the name of making good arrests. Deciding that the ends justify the means, then the means get farther and farther away from true north."

"You mean noble cause corruption," Ragland said.

"That's exactly right." Farrell smiled. "I'm glad you know about that."

"Yeah, I read that book for my promotional exam." He shook his head. "I think it's mostly academic crap, if you want the truth, Captain."

Farrell stared at him, a little surprised. Then he said, "It's happened before, plenty of times."

"In Chicago and Los Angeles, maybe. But not here."

Farrell couldn't decide for certain if Ragland was being naïve or passive aggressive. Then he decided he didn't care. "Maybe you're right," he said. "But if it doesn't or won't happen here, a big part of the reason why is the vigilance of our sergeants. And that's what I need you to be on this team, Kelly. I need you to be vigilant."

Ragland seemed to think about it for about fifteen seconds. Then he shook his head slowly. "I really don't want the position, Captain. My days of running and gunning are behind me. I took this admin job because it's structured, and it gets me home every night on time for dinner. So thanks for thinking of me and all, but I'm going to have to say no."

Farrell had had enough. He forced himself to keep an even tone as he spoke. "You mistake me, *Sergeant*. I'm not requesting anything. I'm advising you of your assignment change. Effective tomorrow, you're the interim squad leader for ACT."

Ragland clenched his jaw and gave Farrell a hard stare.

The captain tried to soften the blow. "When McGinn returns to duty, he'll take back the position. Until then, it's yours."

Ragland remained quiet for a few seconds. Then he asked, "Will that be all, Captain?"

"That's it, Sergeant."

Without a word, Ragland spun on his heel and stalked away.

Farrell watched him go, feeling more alone by the moment.

Chapter 9

Gary Stone stood at the podium in his black suit, white shirt, and blue tie. While the rest of the team prepped a search warrant on Harlin Schmick's house, he went home to prepare for this briefing. He showered and changed into the suit he hadn't worn in months. His hair could have used a slight trim, but it was perfectly combed. He even shaved for the second time that day.

This was his first time seeing any of the councilmembers since his humiliating removal from city hall. Prior to that moment, he was a confidant—a person any of them could count on in the event they ever needed a friendly ear in the police department. Since that moment, however, not one of them ever inquired about him. To be honest, he hadn't reached out to them either. The whole incident was just too embarrassing.

The initial Anti-Crime Team briefing was supposed to have been Sergeant McGinn's responsibility, but due to his absence, Captain Farrell assigned it to Stone. Even though they only had three weeks of data to share, the briefing had to be now as the next two council meetings were scheduled to be at neighborhood centers. Those meetings were limited in their scope due to the size of the venues.

Despite his protests, Farrell wouldn't let Stone bow out of delivering the report. The captain said he wanted a team member in front of the microphone and believed Stone to be the best suited for the task. He also said he wanted the officer to face up to his demons and no longer be worried about those in city hall. Stone thought the captain oversold the whole thing as if he himself did not want to get up in front of the podium.

After being announced by Council President Phillip Crandall, Stone had walked confidently to the microphone and introduced himself. This was a formality, but he took it seriously. He wanted to make sure he represented the department the best he could. A mistake now would follow him for at least the next seven days as the council meetings were broadcast live then replayed throughout the week on Channel 5.

The usual nine council seats were missing three members— a fallout from recent scandals which prompted an upcoming special election at the end of the summer.

On the two large monitors, one at each end of the council dais, the Anti-Crime Team's arrest statistics appeared.

Stone cleared his voice and dived into the report, "Councilmembers, over the past three weeks, SPD's Anti-Crime Team has executed nineteen new arrest warrants and six search warrants."

He looked up at the councilmembers. All six of them except Councilwoman Margaret Patterson were following along with the spreadsheet; she was intently watching Stone.

The officer returned his attention to the numbers.

"Pursuant to those warrants, ACT has also made nine additional arrests and charged a total of forty felonies."

There was a murmur of surprise in the crowd attending the meeting. Stone felt a swell of confidence at the noise. He knew that they'd rightfully charged most suspects with multiple felonies, so the actual number of physical arrests was considerably less than the number of charges, but any way you cut it, forty was an impressive number in just three weeks.

"We also made fourteen unrelated warrant arrests—by the way, those are warrants that were previously outstanding, but the person had not been located—"

The crowd murmured its approval.

"—and we recovered three stolen handguns and seven stolen cars."

He looked up from the report, wondering if he should have

come up with a way to lengthen it. It went fast, he realized, too fast. The councilmembers were going to blast him for not giving enough information.

Council President Crandall smiled then. He had a round face and his bald head appeared as if it was recently sunburned. "Nice and efficient, Officer Stone. Good work, especially filling in on such short notice."

Councilwoman Lani Pierce leaned forward to speak into her microphone. She was the youngest member of the council, just past her thirty-second birthday. Her hair was cut in a bob and her eyes widened as she spoke. "We heard about Sergeant McGinn's tragic loss. Our thoughts and prayers go out to his family."

The rest of the council nodded in agreement with her pronouncement except Margaret Patterson, who continued to study Stone with intense scrutiny.

Pierce approached her microphone once more. "Officer Stone, do you believe this is making an immediate impact on calls for service?"

"Yes, ma'am, definitely," Stone said, "but right now we can only report anecdotally as it's still too early to provide an actual trend analysis. We're getting feedback from patrol officers and detectives that the team is making a difference."

Stone didn't know if the last part was true, but he felt that he wouldn't get in trouble by adding it. In his mind, it wasn't a lie. It was puffery and marketing agencies did it all the time.

"Does anyone have further questions for Officer Stone?"

Councilman Robin Allen leaned forward, indicating a question. As a black man, he was often seen as the council's leading proponent for fair housing and social justice issues. He glanced at the spreadsheet and spoke. "Officer Stone, I'm concerned that there is no ethnic or gender breakdown for those that ACT has arrested. Was that purposeful or an oversight?"

Stone frowned. "Councilman, I take full responsibility for that and assure you that it was indeed an oversight."

It was not an oversight, though.

The initial report format had been prepared by Sergeant McGinn and Crime Analysis a week prior and was given the blessing by both the chief and Captain Farrell. However, Stone knew the council did not need to know that as this briefing was about managing their expectations. "I will go back to Crime Analysis and ask them to update this report. When it's done, I will email it to you."

Councilman Allen nodded his approval then leaned forward. "Please email it to the entire council, Officer."

"Yes, sir."

The council president smiled again as he leaned forward to say, "If there are no further—"

With a slight scowl, Margaret Patterson interrupted, "I have a question." Even from the podium, Stone could see the American flag pinned to the lapel of her green jacket.

He thought about responding to her with a simple, "Yes, ma'am?" in an attempt to be a peacemaker, but he didn't know why she was so obviously angry. He remembered Garrett's words from earlier in the day—"you're either a pawn or a king." Because of that, he chose to remain silent.

"Officer Stone, how did the ACT team develop?"

"I have no idea, ma'am."

"You don't know who came up with the idea for the ACT team?"

"No, ma'am. ACT was fully formed when I became a member."

Councilwoman Patterson pursed her lips. "Well, then, who invited you to be on the team?"

The way she phrased it made the question feel like a trap, like she was directing him the way a detective leads a suspect into a confession. Stone bet she was dragging him into a game of politics, which left him only one answer. "The chief," he said.

"Excuse me?" Patterson said, slightly surprised by his answered.

"I was invited to participate by Chief Baumgartner."

"I'm not sure how these questions are helping," Council President Crandall said.

Patterson held up her hand to silence Crandall. "Who selected the officers to be on the ACT team?" she asked.

"Ma'am?"

"Let me change the question. What are the qualifications to be on the ACT team?"

Stone took a deep breath, delaying his response to give him time to think. "I wasn't part of the selection process, so I can't be certain. All the members are officers of the Spokane Police Department and were selected by the chief of police like I was. Other than that, you'll have to take up the selection process with him."

Patterson shook her head in disbelief. "You're telling me that the chief created the team? That he selected its members?"

Officer Stone made eye contact with the other councilmembers before returning his focus to Councilwoman Patterson. "It's his department, ma'am. I think the ultimate responsibility is his, no matter what team we're talking about."

Patterson dropped back into her chair and crossed her arms.

Stone felt perspiration running down his back then. He wondered if his forehead was sweating.

"Any further questions?" Council President Crandall asked. When no one spoke up, he dismissed the officer.

Stone gathered his notes and headed toward the lobby, wiping wetness from his forehead. As he walked up the aisle, he made eye contact with Margaret Patterson's newest assistant and his friend, Jean Carter. She winked at him.

In the lobby, the rest of the team was there, still dressed in the blue jeans and T-shirts from their work shift.

"Way to go, partner," Tyler Garrett almost yelled with enthusiasm. "Sergeant Run and Gun couldn't have done it any better."

"Yeah," Ray Zielinski muttered, "nice work." He looked like he was about to say more but he abruptly closed his mouth.

Marty Hill playfully punched Stone in the shoulder. "I loved how Patterson kept calling it the ACT team." He shook his head and chuckled. "The Anti-Crime Team team. Classic."

Yang remained silent but smiled. She nodded her approval.

Stone beamed at his team's adulation. "It seemed like she had it out for us, didn't it?"

"She's a rabid dog," Garrett said, "but you smacked her on the nose." Garrett mimed whacking a dog on the snoot. "She backed up after that."

The door to the council chambers opened and Jean Carter stepped out. She wore gray slacks and a blue blouse. Her dark hair was pulled back. The guys moved out of her way as she went directly to Stone and hugged him.

"You did great, boy-o!" she said. "Really great."

"I don't know, Jean. You think so?"

"Of course, I do."

He grabbed Jean by the elbow and turned her to face the others. "Jean, this is the team. You already know Ty, but that's, well, this is the rest of the team. Guys, this is Jean."

Garrett put his arm around Stone's shoulders. "We're going for drinks, Jean. Come join us."

She politely smiled at Garrett. "I would love to, but I have to get back inside. It's going to be a long one tonight." She turned to Stone. "See you tomorrow?"

"Of course," he said.

Jean squeezed Stone's arm before returning to the chambers.

"Okay, boys and girl," Garrett said, walking backward toward the stairs, "let's get our drink on." He spun and headed up the stairs. Marty Hill and Ray Zielinski slowly made their way up next.

Stone watched Jean until she was about to sit. She looked back and waved to him. He waved to her then turned to leave, bumping into Jun Yang who was near him.

"She seems nice," Yang said. "Is she your girlfriend?"

"Jean? She's my best friend."

"Huh."

Stone started toward the stairs. "Why do you ask?"

"No reason," she said, falling into step with him.

Chapter 10

Detective Wardell Clint watched from his car as he waited for the Anti-Crime Team to emerge from city hall. He'd been listening to the council meeting on the radio and had heard Stone's report to the council. It was typical political tripe, full of data that may or may not mean anything. All that most politicians and bosses cared about was having beans they could count, not what the actual results were. They focused on output instead of outcomes. That was the reason things never got solved.

When Stone dodged the questions about overall calls for service, Clint wasn't surprised. The way he dealt with Councilwoman Patterson caught him a little off guard, though. Maybe Stone wasn't quite the cake-eater he'd pegged him to be, at least not anymore. Maybe he was changing.

And I wonder why that is?

As if on cue, first out of city hall was Tyler Garrett. The man's stride was confident, but Clint thought he saw him cast a wary glance left and right while he waited for the others. This was par for the course. Some of the vigilance was bred into him as a cop. His stint on the SWAT team no doubt amplified it. But Clint was sure that the biggest factor for his heightened awareness was the dirt the man had been doing for at least the last two years.

Ironically, Clint realized that Garrett might be the only officer on the department who believed in vigilance as much as he did himself. The thought didn't accompany any sense of kinship for the man.

Detective Marty Hill and Ray Zielinski exited the building next. Despite being veteran officers of about the same seniority, and being roughly the same build, the two men were a study in opposites. Clint knew Hill's body was broken from football in his early years and a long SWAT career. But even though he walked with a pronounced limp due to the knee brace, Hill's movements had an easy energy to them, and his actions seemed almost buoyant. In contrast, Zielinski seemed to be in slightly better shape and had no nagging injuries that Clint was aware of, yet the veteran officer plodded heavily, and seemed to constantly slouch. His expression tended toward sour, whereas Hill's was almost always open.

Clint suspected that part of the reason for Zielinski's stance and demeanor was that he harbored some suspicions about Tyler Garrett. He'd said as much to Clint on more than one occasion, fishing for validation from the detective. Clint wondered if Zielinski's time on the team was strengthening those suspicions or weakening the man's resolve.

Stone finally came outside, followed by Yang. Clint watched Hill say his goodbyes, waving at most of the team, but clapping Garrett on the shoulder. As he walked away, he pointed at Stone in what looked like a congratulatory manner.

The rest of the team walked the short block to O'Doherty's, an Irish pub. From where he sat, Clint watched them go inside. He debated waiting outside but decided there was no sense in sitting around while they drank. Besides, it had been a long day already, and he could feel how tired he was right down to his bones.

Clint started his car and headed home. As he approached the Monroe Street Hill, he decided to make a detour. He hadn't been past Garrett's old house in a couple of weeks. Angela Garrett still lived there along with the kids, and Clint made a point to keep loose tabs on them as part of his surveillance of Garrett. Farrell had been of the opinion that Garrett might worm his way back in with his wife, especially after he received a large settlement from the city for the events following his officer-involved shooting. But Clint had seen them interact, and it was clear that Angie Garrett knew or strongly suspected what Garrett had done. He sensed the steel in Angie Garrett's spine, and never thought for a moment that Garrett stood a chance of winning her back.

Still, those were only his thoughts, not established facts. Even if he believed something was a dead end or unlikely, he still checked it out. His years as an investigator had ingrained that need for verification into him.

Angie Garrett lived on the Five-Mile Prairie, a flat expanse of land on top of a huge bluff in north Spokane. Most of the houses were at least upper-middle class, and the ones on the edges of the bluff were luxurious. The Garretts lived in one of the more modest homes, though still very nice. As a matter of course, Clint had reviewed the tax records to see what they paid for the home, and its current value. It cost more than he had expected, and its value had almost doubled in the eight years since they purchased it.

Knowing what he did about Garrett, Clint realized that the house was right in the perfect bandwidth. It seemed like something a cop and a nurse could afford, so it didn't raise suspicion. But a closer look at the numbers made him suspicious. Sure, there was enough money there to cover the mortgage and the two cars. But Angie and the kids dressed nicely. He bet there was a big TV and a game console in the living room, maybe even another in the boy's bedroom. And with Garrett now living separately, how exactly did they afford it all?

Clint had toyed with the idea that Angie Garrett was complicit in Garrett's crimes. In the end, he decided against it. He didn't think Garrett was above using accomplices, but doubted Angie was involved. What convinced him was her throwing him out on his ass. If they were in it together, why would she do that? Besides, even though a look didn't constitute hard evidence, the expression on her face whenever he'd seen her deal with Garrett was telling.

Of course, he'd keep digging to be certain. But his gut said her only complicity was turning a blind eye after the fact, and

Clint suspected she did that for the good of her children.

He pulled onto Garrett's street and slowed his car to a crawl. Immediately, he noticed a vehicle in the driveway that he didn't recognize. It looked like an Audi or a BMW. Clint stopped at the curb a few houses away. He dug into his field bag and removed a small pair of binoculars. He quickly verified that it was an Audi and jotted down the license plate number.

Did Angie have a new car? If so, why not park it in the garage, like she usually did?

Clint wished again that his car was equipped with a mobile data computer so he could run the license plate. He could call dispatch, but that would be too memorable. It was bad enough that the system would capture his license search and archive it forever. At least that record was only available if someone went looking for it. Calling a chatty dispatcher raised the profile of the license check significantly.

He had long desired a way to run name checks and vehicle licenses anonymously. If he could create a shadow login, that would be perfect. Clint had considered using a retired or fired officer's credentials, but that was difficult. The username was always the officer's badge number, so that wasn't a problem, but it still required knowing the officer's password. He'd tried a couple, using common passwords such as "password" and "SPD123456," which he knew were defaults set in place until the account was activated. None of his efforts panned out, though, and he was wary of trying too many times. That kind of activity was likely tracked as well.

How much did a new Audi cost? He made a note to check the internet when he got home. This was one of the few times he saw the value in having a smart phone, but the convenience was not worth the risk. The GPS in today's phones was accessible to far too many people, and he suspected there was plenty of spyware funneling data about everything a person did to people who had no right to it. Clint refused to be exploited in that way. His antiquated flip phone was questionable enough as it was.

He spotted some motion at the front door of the Garrett home. The door was open, and someone was exiting. Clint raised his binoculars and adjusted the focus. Angie Garrett's attractive face came sharply into view. She was smiling at the man now on the porch. He said something that made her laugh and look away shyly for a moment. Then she looked back at him and leaned forward to kiss him.

The kiss lasted a few seconds and seemed more romantic than passionate. Still, Clint sensed some familiarity to the action. He wondered how long this had been going on.

When the kiss ended, there were smiles again, then the man made his way to the Audi. He waved to Angie before he got into the car. She waved back. She waved yet again when he'd pulled out of the driveway and started up the street, away from Clint's location.

Clint kept his eye on Angie Garrett. She watched the departing car for several seconds before turning and heading back inside.

He lowered the binoculars and realized his lips were twisted into a near smile. So far, for the last two years, everything had broken Garrett's way. He'd been in a questionable shooting, and later exonerated, then paid a settlement by the city for the way they handled the situation. Although the rest of the world was unaware, Garrett had been responsible for the deaths of two SPD detectives, Butch Talbott and Justin Pomeroy, who he'd partnered with in the drug trade. On top of that, he killed his drug supplier and the other three people in the house, all to cover his tracks. Through it all, he played the golden child card and he played the race card, and he dealt both from the bottom of the deck.

And it worked. Garrett had won at every turn.

But not with Angie, and that gave Clint a certain, grim satisfaction.

He wondered how Garrett was going to react when he discovered his ex-wife had already moved on. And with a white man, no less.

Clint drove home. He felt like he might sleep a little better tonight.

Chapter 11

Tyler Garrett raised his beer mug. "Another toast," he said.

Zielinski frowned. Garrett was such a glory hound. Even sitting at a pub having drinks, he had to be a showboat. But everyone else raised their glasses, so he reluctantly did the same.

"To Stoney bitch-slapping Patterson on public television," Garrett said. With his free hand, he mimed the same gesture he'd made right after the presentation, smacking an imaginary puppy on the nose with a rolled-up newspaper. "*Shmack!*"

Stone laughed loudly, but Yang smiled slightly at Garrett's animated display.

Zielinski just grunted and drank. After he swallowed, he wiped foam from his mustache.

The foursome sat and talked. Zielinski didn't add much, even though he was justifiably proud of the team's accomplishments. He sipped his Guinness and watched how the team members interacted. Yang sat quietly, slowly drinking her bourbon, a choice that had surprised him. He hadn't expected her to go with an Asian beer or anything like that, but bourbon had been unexpected.

What hadn't been a surprise was that Garrett and Stone were both drinking Bud Lights. The way Stone emulated Garrett seemed to be increasing as the two rode exclusively together. It was a character trait that not only irritated Zielinski, but he found weak.

Zielinski glanced at Garrett. The man gave him a cool look in return, only turning away to chuckle and then comment on something Stone said.

I know you're dirty.

At least, he thought so. He couldn't prove anything, and that bothered him. If he was wrong about it, then he was condemning a brother officer unfairly. Maybe he just didn't like Garrett.

Zielinski frowned. That wasn't it. He'd always liked and respected Garrett when they'd worked together on power shift. It was only after the man's questionable shooting that Zielinski's doubts began.

"One dog and pony show down," Garrett was saying, "a thousand more to go."

"Not for him," Zielinski said.

All three sets of eyes turned to stare at Zielinski.

"Why not him?" Garrett asked. "You don't think he did a good job?"

"He did a great job. It just isn't *his* job. It's the sergeant's."

Garrett smiled broadly. "In case you haven't been keeping up on current events, our sergeant is on the sidelines. So Stoney is gonna have to be our man until he's back."

"They'll find us another sergeant."

"Where? Special order from the sergeant factory?"

Stone laughed, but Yang remained silent.

"I've been around this place a long time," Zielinski began.

"Maybe too long," Garrett cut in. His tone was light, but his eyes were hard.

Zielinski scowled. "I'll decide that for myself, so mind your own business."

Garrett held up his hands in a peaceful gesture. "Easy, Z. I'm just having a little fun. It's all friendly, right?" He looked to Stone and Yang, then back to Zielinski. "Lighten up, man."

Zielinski fumed for a few quiet moments but decided to let it go for now. "All I'm saying is that they'll find a sergeant for us soon. No way will they let a team like this run around unsupervised."

"We don't need supervision," Garrett said. "We're not in kindergarten."

Stone softly chuckled at that, and Yang tilted her head.

"All we need to do," Garrett continued, "is keep making arrests. Put guns and drugs and money on the table for the white shirts to show the media. Rack up the stats and they'll leave us alone to get the job done."

"You're wrong about that," Zielinski said.

Garrett shrugged. "We'll see."

"I guess we will."

An uneasy silence settled around the table. Celtic rock played through the bar's speakers. The hum of conversation around them seemed louder to Zielinski now that no one at their table was talking.

Finally, Stone said, "Did you guys see Cattage try to get over that fence today?"

Garrett grinned. "He looked like a starfish." He spread his arms and wobbled. Stone laughed at the imitation, clearly enjoying the attention. "It was a good catch, man," Garrett added.

Zielinski remained quiet, finishing his beer while the others talked. When he'd drained the last of it, he pushed it away and stood. "I'm out," he said.

"What?" Stone asked. "One round? Come on, Ray. Stay."

Zielinski shook his head. "I've got some personal business."

"More like a personal booty call," Garrett said with a mischievous smile.

"That's not it."

Garrett held up his hands. "No, man, it's cool. We get it. Don't let the team stand between you and a piece of ass."

Slightly embarrassed, Zielinski glanced at Yang. The officer didn't appear bothered by the exchange, however. He looked back at Garrett, who had an amiable expression, even though Zielinski could sense the barb beneath his words. But if he lashed back, he'd be the one to look like the unreasonable jerk.

"It's not a booty call," he finally said. "Just some family stuff."

"Sure," Garrett muttered.

Stone and Yang both waved to him as he left.

Outside, he walked to his car, glad for the fresh air. He was still bristling at Garrett's antics, and he saw them for what they were. First, the officer had carved Stone away from the rest of the group and made him into a partner and ally. Now he was trying to draw Yang into the fold and isolate Zielinski.

But why?

You know why.

Zielinski stopped at his car door and took a deep breath. Was he right?

Maybe. But he didn't have time to figure it out tonight. Tonight, he had other things to attend to.

He took out his phone and called Neil. "You still want to talk tonight?"

"Definitely," Neil said.

Zielinski had been hoping the man might change his mind. "Meet me at Rick's Ringside in fifteen minutes."

On the drive to the bar, all Zielinski could think about was how smooth Garrett was. It was as if he could project the image of confidence and good humor to the rest of the world while letting only Zielinski see the veiled sarcasm or bite to his words. The smarmy element was barely detectable, and invisible to everyone else, but it was unmistakably there. Such an ability was impressive, even if it was wrong.

At Rick's, Neil waited for him in a corner booth. Zielinski sat and noticed the man had a black eye. He didn't say anything about it, though. Instead, he ordered another Guinness. This one came in a bottle, unlike the draft at O'Doherty's. Neil drank Coors.

"Tell me what's going on," Zielinski said.

"It's my ex-wife," Neil said.

Zielinski frowned. "No story that starts that way ever has a happy ending."

"She's dating a scumbag."

"Do you two have kids?"

"No, but what does that matter?"

Zielinski lifted the Guinness to his lips and drank. Then he said, "My experience with ex-wives is that they all suck. If you don't have kids with the woman, you're lucky. You can just move on with your life and never have to see her again."

Neil looked pained. "I still love her."

"No, you don't. You just think you do."

Neil shook his head. "You're wrong there. I didn't want the divorce, she did. I wanted to work things out. I still do."

"Sounds like she's got everything already worked out, and that you're not part of the equation."

Neil scowled. "Are you going to listen to me or what?"

Zielinski shrugged. "Go ahead."

Neil hesitated, taking a drink of his beer. Then he plunged ahead with his story. "She started dating this guy a few weeks ago. I don't know, maybe longer. Either way, a few days ago, I found out he was hitting her. I told her to go to the police, but she won't do it. She said…" Neil stopped, swallowing hard before he continued. "She said she loves him, and it was her fault. That she pushed him to do it."

It was a classic domestic violence scenario. Zielinski had seen it a hundred times. The circle went from an abusive incident to apology and a honeymoon phase, during which time the victim made excuses for the assault. Then the tension built back up until another abusive incident. The victim suffered psychologically and emotionally as much as physically, or so he'd been taught. If he was being honest, it always baffled him why so many women didn't just leave.

Zielinski pointed to Neil's black eye. "And that?"

"When she wouldn't leave or call the cops, I knew I had to do something. So I confronted him."

"Where?"

"Outside her house."

Zielinski shook his head.

"What?" Neil asked.

"Confronting him wasn't the greatest of ideas, and in front

of her house, too?"

Neil looked down at his beer. "He caught me by surprise and basically knocked me on my ass. Then he laughed at me. When I got up, I saw her standing in the window. She saw the whole thing."

"What's her name?"

"Sheryl."

"What is it you want from me?"

Neil twirled his beer glass slowly. "The guy is all tatted up, and he looks like a hard case. I was hoping you could find out if he's some kind of ex-con or criminal, or not. If the guy is just a poser and he got in a lucky shot, so be it. I'll handle it myself. But if he's some kind of badass…" He trailed off.

"If he's some kind of badass, what? You want me to do something about it?"

Neil shrugged. "I'm not a wimp or anything, but if I'm being honest, I'm just a regular guy. I just want to know what I'm dealing with here, that's all."

Zielinski considered for a little while. Then he asked, "What's this guy's name?"

"Darold Barden."

Zielinski grunted. Darold was a stupid name, but he'd seen a lot of stupid names in his career. With a name like that, he figured the guy was either black or a redneck. Not that it mattered either way to him.

"I'll check into it," he told Neil.

TUESDAY

Corruption is like a ball of snow,
once it's set a'rolling it must increase.
—Charles Caleb Colton, cleric and writer

Chapter 12

Tom Farrell walked down the corridor of the police station. He'd hoped to touch base with Sergeant Ragland, but when he reached the administrative sergeant's office, the door was closed and the lights off.

That was good, he thought. It meant that despite his reluctance, Ragland had made the adjustment. Now Farrell would have oversight on the team's daily actions, and he'd have Yang's inside eye, as well. He made his way toward his own office, his steps a little lighter. Things were looking up.

On the way, he wondered if he should reach out to Clint. Their blow up was almost a month ago now, and Farrell's anger had subsided since then. For a long time, he and Clint were the only two doing anything to expose Garrett's dark side. Now, it was just him. Even though he had agents in place, none of them knew what Farrell knew. Clint had been a true confederate.

But he was so damn impossible.

Farrell shrugged off the thought. Between Ragland and Yang, he had active assets in place. Zielinski might be a possibility, too. Regardless, at some point, he'd definitely pull Stone into the fold. The officer was rock solid in terms of his ethics, a fact he'd proven to Farrell during a difficult time a few months ago. Stone took his lumps, getting removed from a cushy office job as a liaison to city hall, and remained loyal to the chief. Farrell knew he could trust him when the time came.

He didn't need Clint. Not for this. Not anymore.

As he turned the corner, he was surprised to find Sergeant Kelly Ragland standing outside his office door. He was accompanied by Union President Dale Thomas.

Farrell's heart sank. He tried to hide his disappointment as he greeted the two men.

"Good morning, Kelly," he said, then nodded to Thomas. "Dale."

"Can we have a word, Captain?" Thomas asked in a tone that sounded more like a directive than a question.

"Sure," Farrell said, keeping things agreeable as long as possible. "I've got a few minutes before I need to check in with the chief."

He unlocked his office door and went inside, turning on the lights as he did so. The fluorescent bulbs in the ceiling fluttered to life. Farrell sat in his chair and waited for the two men to take the seats opposite him. It was times like this that he wished he had a small conference table in his office like the chief did. It didn't seem as adversarial as facing each other across his big desk.

"I'll get right to it," Thomas said. "This is about you illegally changing Sergeant Ragland's work assignment."

"Illegally?"

Thomas shrugged. "It's a term to delineate an action outside of the scope of the collective bargaining agreement."

"It has a much different connotation in the police world."

"If it'll make you more comfortable, I'll rephrase. We're here to talk about your improper reassignment of my member."

Farrell thought carefully before replying. He longed for the old days, before the union hired an outside attorney to serve as full-time president. Back then, members served as union officers, and it seemed like it was much easier to reach an agreeable solution to any situation. Now, almost everything seemed to become a grievance and end up in binding arbitration. That was costly, in time and money. Of course, Farrell suspected that was exactly what Thomas wanted. It didn't hurt his bottom line one bit.

"Captain? Do you have a response?"

"Honestly, I'm trying to figure out why this is a problem. Kelly is a patrol sergeant, subject to changes in shift based on department needs. The department has a need for him to supervise ACT, so his shift is being adjusted. How is that improper?"

Thomas shook his head. "First off, his shift isn't being *adjusted*, it's being radically changed. He's going from a nine-hour day shift with an unpaid hour lunch to a swing shift that doesn't start until eleven o'clock and goes to an indeterminate end of shift."

"I don't know how accurate that is," Farrell said.

"I got it straight from one of the team members," Thomas told him. "He specifically told me that they worked from quote, 'eleven to whenever it takes,' unquote."

"Who said that?"

"I'd rather not say, but I can ask payroll to provide work records to validate it, if you want. I'm sure the overtime cards and the team pay sheet will match."

Farrell shook his head. *Garrett. It had to be.*

That son of a bitch.

"Just with the start time alone, that's a four-hour change, not to mention the mandatory overtime. By the letter of the contract, a change like that needs to be bargained."

"I don't know that I agree with that interpretation," Farrell said, "but let's say I do for just a second. Let's bargain, then."

"You're not the chief."

"I am his designee in this situation. I have the authority to bargain on his behalf."

"It doesn't matter. At this time, we're not willing to bargain on this point. It's too big of an issue and is something we'll bring up during contract negotiations."

"How about a nonbinding, non-precedent-setting, temporary agreement?" Farrell asked.

Thomas smiled thinly. "Nice try, Captain, but we know how easily those turn into binding, permanent agreements that serve as precedent. No, thank you."

"Then we have a problem. I have a special team that needs a supervisor. I don't have anyone else to fill that hole."

"That does sound like a problem."

Farrell felt warmth at the base of his neck. The patronizing tone of Thomas was starting to get to him. "So how do you propose we solve it?"

"That's not for me to say," Thomas told him. "That's the administration's problem. My job is to make sure the rights of my members aren't violated, and that the city adheres to the collective bargaining agreement. It's your job to figure out how to solve staffing needs and still remain within those boundaries."

The heat flooded up Farrell's neck and into his face. He hated the union stance of *not our problem, you figure it out* while they stood around with their hands in their pockets. It was like they had no vested interest in the success of the police department or the community.

"The chief has the authority to move anyone in the department anywhere he deems necessary in the case of an emergency," Farrell said, his voice measured but tight.

"Are you calling this an emergency? Because it seems more like a routine staffing issue."

"It's not routine. It's a proactive, aggressive team that needs a leader."

"Well, it's not for me to say," Thomas said, "but maybe that's the real problem."

"What do you mean?"

"Maybe you need to shut the team down if you can't properly staff it."

Farrell blanched, his mind flashing back to his conversation with the chief the previous morning. He shook his head. "They're succeeding at exactly what the police are here to do—catching bad guys and interdicting crime. We're not shutting them down."

Thomas shrugged. "As I said, it's not for me to say. It's your problem. I just know that you can't reassign my member like you did."

"It's already done," Farrell said. "Effective today."

Thomas gave him a disappointed look. "You realize we *will* file a grievance, right?"

It was Farrell's turn to shrug. "Do what you have to do. In the meantime, I expect Sergeant Ragland to perform his directed duties with the Anti-Crime Team."

Thomas pursed his lips. "Is there anything I can do or say to change your course of action in this matter?"

Farrell had heard this line from Thomas before. He knew it was a seed the lawyer liked to plant, hoping it would bear fruit later in arbitration as a testament to how reasonably he had negotiated with the administration.

"No," Farrell said.

"Then I believe we're done here." Thomas rose from his chair and headed toward the door. Ragland stood to follow. Farrell noticed the sergeant's expression looked strangely pleased. He almost commented on it but resisted the urge. He let them both leave in silence.

Farrell leaned back in his chair and tried to process what had just occurred. The spark of irritation threatened to derail his thinking, so he tried to stamp it out. He took a deep breath and released it. When that didn't immediately work, he spun in his chair and looked at the pictures on his wall. In comparison to the chief's "all about me" display, Farrell's décor was sparse. He had a picture of his academy class, one of his wife Karen, and his college diploma.

The diploma was hard won, and he had Karen to thank for pushing him to complete his degree. The photograph of her was his favorite. She had a light, slightly mischievous smile playing on her lips. But this morning, it was the academy shot that caught his eye, full of young bright faces. He picked out the ones who were still on the job amidst those who hadn't made it through probation or had since retired. Besides himself, only three members of the class remained in law enforcement. That number surprised him, reminding him that he had been at this job for a long time.

He took another deep breath and let it out slowly, staring at the photograph.

People at his stage of their career often worried about legacy. What would they leave behind? Would anyone remember them? Farrell realized that while he'd never thought in exactly those terms, his crusade regarding Garrett would ultimately define his career. It would be his legacy.

A pang of sadness replaced the irritation he'd been feeling. Could any of the brash young men in that photograph have imagined such a convoluted destiny? He didn't think so. Farrell hadn't. All he'd been thinking about was chasing bad guys and being a hero.

Farrell let the somber moment linger. It was easier to think through sadness than anger. His mind clearer now, he closed his eyes, and considered the situation with Sergeant Ragland and Dale Thomas.

In a few minutes, he'd check in with Baumgartner and let the chief know a grievance was coming. The chief had become inured to such events as they became more common over the past few years, so he didn't expect an overly negative reaction.

Farrell wasn't entirely certain he had the right read of the situation, at least with regard to the letter of the contract, but he didn't care. He knew how long a grievance would take, especially once the chief denied the initial stage of it. He hoped that McGinn's situation would stabilize before then and the sergeant would return to duty. That would solve everything.

It was a gamble, but then again, when it came to his career, Tom Farrell had been gambling a lot in the last two years.

Chapter 13

"You really think I did well at the council meeting?"

"Yes, boy-o, I already told you that. Is your ego that fragile now?"

"No," Stone said then sipped his plain latte. "I just like hearing it."

They were at the Nordstrom Espresso Bar, the small coffee stand near the department store's entrance inside River Park Square, the downtown shopping mall. Soft music played in the background and the occasional hiss of the coffee maker reminded them that they were indeed at an open-air coffee bar.

The meeting location was a quick walk for Jean, just outside city hall and across Spokane Falls Boulevard. She could be there in two minutes.

For Stone, however, it was a bit of a pain, driving into downtown for a fifteen-minute coffee break with his friend. However, it had become tradition since he was removed from the Special Police Problems position at city hall. While they worked together in the same building, he didn't realize how much he had grown accustomed to being near her. Now, working back at the department, he missed the daily routine they had built. She was his closest confidant and the hassle of finding a daily parking spot was more than worth it.

Jean tore a piece of her croissant free and stuck it in her mouth.

Stone took that as a signal to keep talking. "I thought I spoke way too fast. I mean, there wasn't a lot of information to share in the first place since we only had three weeks of statistics to go on, but still, I should have figured a way to stretch it out."

Several tables near them were filled with other city hall employees taking a midmorning break. Stone knew them by sight and avoided making eye contact. A few tables away, a homeless man sat alone staring off into the distance. Stone occasionally eyed him, though. He was the one who didn't belong inside the trendy mall.

Jean grabbed her drink—Stone didn't know what it was as she'd ordered it before he arrived—and took a sip.

Her movement brought Stone back to the conversation. "And Patterson was up my butt from the jump-off," he said. "You saw that, right? Something got stuck in her craw. She was going to use me to prove a point. I don't know what it was, but I stopped that noise by smacking her on the nose." Stone mimed the same action Garrett had done the night before.

"You think she's a dog?"

"What?"

"A bitch, maybe?" Jean asked, her look clearly disapproving.

Stone blinked a couple of times.

"Listen, boy-o, Patterson's got an agenda, that's clear, but they all do right, especially right now. Three seats are empty, and Crandall is on his last term as council president. It's her time to shine and she's going to take every opportunity to do so."

"You think that's what she was doing? Just trying to shine?"

"I don't know. She doesn't talk to me about these things. Besides, she's carrying a bunch of extra duties with those empty seats. I can't wait for the special election to get here. Have you heard the latest predictions?"

Stone checked his watch. He still had a couple hours before the team's shift was supposed to start. Ty Garrett had invited him to work out at the northside Planet Fitness if he wanted. Stone usually used the department's gym, but when he told that to Garrett, the man teased him about working out in the ghetto. Stone knew the department's equipment was old, the treadmills were beat to hell, and the place looked like a dungeon, but it was free. He used to think that if it was good enough for a bunch of other cops, it was good enough for him. Except now, he was thinking about joining Garrett for a pre-shift workout at the brightly lit Planet Fitness, full of brand-new equipment.

"Earth to Gary."

"Huh?"

He looked up to see Jean impatiently staring at him. "Did you hear any of what I just said?"

"Sure."

Jean put her hands on the edge of the round table and straightened in her chair. "What did I say?"

"C'mon, Jean," Stone said, with a disarming smile.

"You zoned out, didn't you?"

"Yeah," Stone lied. "I'm tired. I didn't get much sleep." That was a lie as well. The team had only had a couple drinks after the council meeting then everyone left. Stone went home and went to bed. He actually felt great.

"Well," Jean said, "what I had said was that I saw some of the early polling data."

"Don't they show that on the TV news?"

Jean rolled her eyes. "Yeah, but I got to see some of the actual reports courtesy of Patterson."

"And?"

"It looks like two women will definitely be elected."

"And the third?"

"Gary, you just ignored the fact that there will be two more women on the council. That's huge."

Stone politely smiled. "Sorry."

"You okay? You seem distracted lately."

"I'm fine. Who's the third you think?"

"Cody Lofton."

"That figures. He's the one with the name recognition." Lofton had been the mayor's chief of staff a couple of years prior but resigned in the aftermath of Garrett's shooting. He'd recently lost an ill-advised run for mayor. His running for an interim council position seemed to Stone to be a desperate cry for attention.

"It's exciting stuff to be around," Jean said.

"Yeah," Stone replied, checking his watch. They should be done with coffee soon. If he hurried, he could make the workout with Garrett.

"Are you late for something?" Jean asked.

"What?"

"You keep checking your watch."

He shrugged. "I'm supposed to meet Ty for a workout."

Jean studied him for a moment then picked up her coffee and what was left of her croissant. "I need to get back to the office." As she stood, her chair scraped on the concrete floor.

"Wait. Don't you have a few more minutes?"

"It's okay, Gary. You need to go, and I need to get back. We'll meet up tomorrow."

"You sure?"

"Yeah. Should we meet a little earlier? If you're going to work out again, I mean."

Stone considered her offer. "That would be good, yeah."

Jean nodded a couple times, then walked off without saying goodbye.

Gary Stone checked his watch once more and smiled. He now had plenty of time to get to the gym.

Chapter 14

Detective Wardell Clint waited in the parking lot of the sleepy urgent care on the north side of Spokane until he saw her step out of the side door for a cigarette. Then he exited his car and walked directly toward her.

Angela Garrett didn't notice his approach until he was only a few feet away. When her eyes landed on him, it took a moment before recognition settled in. Then her gaze narrowed, and her face tightened.

Clint was used to that reaction.

"A nurse who smokes," he said. "That's some cognitive dissonance."

Angie blew smoke out her nostrils. "Not as much as you might think."

Clint understood. Stressful jobs bred smokers, even in today's world. "I'm glad I caught you on a break," he said. "I've been meaning to talk to you for a while."

She eyed him suspiciously. "About what?"

He gave her a knowing look. "You know what."

Angie took a deep drag on her cigarette and exhaled the cloud of smoke. "Detective, I'm in the middle of a twelve-hour shift, and the doctor on duty has an ego the size of Mount Rushmore. I don't have time for riddles."

This was one of the ways Clint had imagined this meeting might go, but he had decided it was worth trying anyway. In his estimation, he couldn't lose. If she was willing to tell him something, that was a win. Even if she refused and told Garrett that he talked with her, it was still a win. It kept the pressure on Garrett, and if the officer went whining to his command, then maybe that was how things all came out into the light.

Just about every scenario Clint envisioned represented a positive outcome.

He gave her an easy shrug. "Fair enough. I'm here because we both know something about your ex-husband that most people don't."

"So what? You want to start a club or something?"

Clint twisted his lips into an approximation of a smile. "That's funny. I didn't realize you were so sardonic."

Something flashed in her eyes in that moment. Clint couldn't identify the emotion for certain, but he sensed it was sadness. There was nothing sad about her tone, though.

"There's no reason you should know anything about me at all," she said. "And the only interaction I have with my ex-husband revolves around our kids."

"I'm sure that's true," Clint said. From his surveillance over the past two years, he knew it was. "But you know that he's into some dark things."

"No, I don't."

"Then you suspect," Clint said, his tone matter of fact but not accusatory. "A wife realizes things about her husband. My guess is that's why you showed him the door."

Angie tapped ash from her cigarette. "Do you spend a lot of time trying to figure out why other people's marriages fail, Detective?" Her eyes flicked to his left hand. "Maybe that explains why you're not married yourself."

"My reasons go much deeper than that."

"I'll bet." She shook her head slightly. "I don't get you. When Ty's shooting went down, you were there trying to help him. Now it sounds like you're out to get him. What happened?"

"You're right. I believed in him, and I tried to help him. And then I found out the truth. Just like you."

Angie lifted her foot and balanced expertly on one leg while she ground out the cigarette, twisting it against the sole of her shoe. "You may think you know things, and you may think you know me, but you're wrong."

"I'm very seldom wrong."

She gave him a cold smile. "Then aren't I the lucky one, to witness such a rare event?"

"Angie—"

"Don't presume you can call me by my first name. We are *not* that familiar." She slipped the cigarette butt into her smock pocket. "And I've got nothing to say to you, Detective. So leave me alone."

Angie brushed past him, used her identification badge to open the secure side door, and went inside.

Clint stood still, staring after her for a moment until the door clicked shut. Then he turned around and headed to his car.

Chapter 15

Chief Robert Baumgartner leaned back in his large chair, smiling at Farrell. "You're doing a great job, Tom. I'm pleased."

"It's not me. It's the team that's doing all the work."

Baumgartner nodded. "The line guys always do the heavy lifting. But leadership can either get *in* the way, get *out* of the way, or do what you're doing—make it easier for them to get the job done by giving them everything they need."

"Thank you, sir," Farrell said. "But what they need now is a sergeant, and that's been a struggle."

Baumgartner waved away his comment. "You got Ragland. So what if the union files a grievance? He'll do the job while it all hashes out, and that's what we need."

"It feels a little unethical," Farrell said. He hadn't felt that way when he spoke with Thomas and Ragland earlier in the day, but once he had a few moments to reflect on it, he started to reconsider.

"You think the union doesn't resort to gamesmanship to accomplish their goals? That they don't exploit the process for their own ends?" Baumgartner asked. "Trust me, they do."

"My mother used to say that two wrongs don't make a right."

"*My* mother used to say shut the hell up and eat your broccoli."

Farrell blinked in confusion and cocked his head at the chief. "I don't get the point."

"The point is stop worrying about it and move on," Baumgartner said. "You did your part, and if it becomes a labor issue, I'll take lead on it. That's my job. You keep your eye on the ball, Tom. Keep the Anti-Crime Team on the tracks.”

“Yes, sir.” He allowed himself a small smile. “They *have* been tearing it up.”

“We knew they would.”

“I know, but I think they’re exceeding expectations.”

Baumgartner nodded. “I think so, too.” He handed a sheaf of papers across the desk to Farrell. “Those are atta boy emails from the mayor and several city council members, along with some citizen feedback from the department website, too. Share them with the team. They deserve to know how well they’re doing.”

“They know.”

Baumgartner opened his hands in agreement. “What I mean is, they deserve to know that other people feel they’re doing a great job. Tell them I’m proud of them, too.”

“I will.” Farrell leafed through the papers. “Nothing from Councilwoman Patterson?”

Baumgartner smiled darkly. “That woman is on the hunt, and I get the distinct feeling that she sees me as the big game.”

“When she tried to go after Stone at the council meeting last night, that was all about ACT being Hatcher’s original idea.” Farrell knew that Hatcher and Patterson were close friends.

“Of course, it was.”

“She’s right, though. It *was* Dana’s plan.”

Baumgartner gave Farrell a disdainful look. “Tom, you’ve been pounding that drum since day one. Let it go.”

“I just don’t want it to look like this is some kind of a good old boys’ club. She should get proper credit, that’s all.”

“Proper credit, huh?”

Farrell nodded.

Baumgartner leaned forward. “Let me tell you how I see it. One of my captains brought forward an underdeveloped version of a plan for a specialty team that is common in most medium to large police departments across the country. I rejected the plan. Do you remember why?"

"You were concerned about the team getting corrupted at some point."

"Exactly," the chief said. "Hatcher's plan had a lack of direct leadership. She was going to run the team herself from her office. No boots on the ground. That would leave those four officers to their own devices, and no matter how good the cops you start with are, that's a recipe for disaster. Someone will eventually decide to do the wrong thing for a very noble reason, and then the wheels come off."

"I know."

"I know you do. That's why you have the team under your command. When you suggested the changes to her plan, it made the thing viable."

Farrell shifted uncomfortably. "It still feels like I stole her work."

"You need to get over that."

"I'm trying."

"Look, you want to drop her name at every opportunity as being the genius who came up with the original idea, be my guest. I don't care." He tapped his thick fingers on his desk. "What I care about is that the outstanding numbers Gary Stone reported to the city council last night happens every month. So keep that team dialed in."

"Yes, sir."

Chapter 16

Ray Zielinski slipped into the report writing room at the police station and was relieved to find it empty. He still had twenty minutes before the Anti-Crime Team met for their informal roll call. Plenty of time.

He sat at one of the data terminals and logged in. Then he typed in the name Darold Barden. Even though Zielinski didn't have Barden's date of birth, the man popped up in the local criminal database. He selected the name, and a surly photograph of Barden appeared.

"A redneck," Zielinski muttered. "Great."

Next to the mug shot, the entire page filled with entries. He read down the list. Barden had multiple arrests for domestic violence, including two previous restraining orders, and several other assaults. There were a few drug entries as well, and a smattering of traffic offenses. He was listed as Status-5, which used to mean an intelligence want. Either a specific detective or unit wanted information on the subject, or there was a general directive to complete a field interview report any time he was contacted. Zielinski still adhered to this protocol, but he knew that in recent years, "Stat-5" had become more of a slang for dirtbag than an actual status code.

"Nice work, Neil," he said to the empty room. *Way to pick a winner.*

Zielinski hit the print button, then logged off and collected Barden's sheet, folding it up and tucking it away in a pocket.

When he left the report writing room, he drifted toward the lounge area where the team held their roll calls. When he realized he'd be sitting in there for fifteen minutes, he decided to first stop by the detectives' division. Not only would it kill some time, but he could get a jump on anything Detective Hill might have for the team.

In the Major Crimes Unit, he found Hill's desk empty. He wondered if Marty was already up in the lounge, or perhaps conferring with Crime Analysis. On a whim, he wandered back to the rear of the bullpen. The cubicle walls made it seem like a rabbit warren, but he imagined the detectives needed some privacy to do their work. Or to goof off.

Wardell Clint was at his desk, fixated on the yellow notepad that he wrote on. He seemed to sense Zielinski before he saw him, and deliberately flipped the pad over before turning to face the officer.

"What do you want?" Clint asked.

Zielinski motioned toward Hill's desk. "I came by to see Marty."

"He's not here."

"I saw that."

"Then I guess you can leave."

No matter how much interaction he had with Clint, Zielinski could never get used to his abrupt nature. But he nodded, and said, "In a minute, yeah. Since I was here, I thought I'd say hello to you."

Clint gave him a strange look. "Why?"

"Just touching base," Zielinski said. "You know I'm working on the Anti-Crime Team now, right?"

"Of course."

"It's going pretty good."

Clint stared at him, expressionless.

Zielinski cleared his throat. "Anyway, if you ever need us to run something down for you, let me know."

"I carry my own water," Clint said.

"I know. Just if you ever need help."

"I won't."

Zielinski forced himself to keep from frowning. *This is why they call you Honey Badger.* "Call it an emergency option," he said. "A backup parachute. Something like that."

Clint continued to stare at him. Then, wordlessly, he flipped over his legal pad and pointedly angled his body so that Zielinski couldn't see his work.

Zielinski shook his head, wondering why he even tried. He turned away and headed back upstairs for roll call.

Chapter 17

"This car needs a radio," Tyler Garrett muttered, his eyes focused on the small house with the peeling white paint.

Stone absently pointed to the police radio hidden under the dashboard. He, too, was watching the same house as Garrett, but his thoughts were on their recent briefing with the new sergeant.

They were parked in a dented, primer gray 1979 Chevrolet Caprice. Nicknamed the Gray Ghost, it had been used by officers for years to conduct surveillance. Along with the Bronze Beast, the '77 Ford Maverick which Zielinski and Yang were in, the two vehicles were maintained by Fleet Services to run like original NASCAR stock cars even though they looked like rolling dumpsters.

"Not a police radio, dumbass," Garrett snickered. "A *radio* radio. For some music."

"Right," Stone said. He should have guessed that's what Garrett meant.

The house they watched was at the dead end of a T-section and they were parked several car lengths away. Zielinski and Yang were around the corner, without a clean line of sight on the house.

They didn't have a warrant for Russell Krug, but he was most definitely a hippo. A career criminal going back to when he was fourteen years old, Krug was suspected in a string of recent burglaries since his release from Geiger Correctional. There was no direct evidence tying the recent break-ins directly back to the man, except that his favorite method of entry was used—a crowbar on a back window—and his calling card was left—a turd left unflushed in a toilet. Other than that, though, no evidence had been collected to develop probable cause to arrest Krug.

He'd already been detained once by patrol officers and later brought in for questioning by a property crimes detective. Those contacts resulted in no evidence and no confessions.

If it was just the crowbar and the vulgar present left in the toilet, Krug would be considered a low-to-mid-priority offender, busy but unremarkable. However, what concerned the department was that he focused on households with elderly residents. He raided their medicine cabinets to steal whatever prescriptions he could find. Krug had never come into contact with a resident yet, but there was growing concern from the leadership that he was pressing his luck, and no one wanted to know how the man would respond in that scenario. This was what Marty Hill had stressed in their earlier roll call briefing—while this had been Krug's MO in his prior convictions, there was still no direct proof that he was indeed the man committing the recent rash of burglaries.

Hill recommended the team sit on his last known residence until they could get an eye on him. What they did after that would be dictated by the moment.

"Where's your head, Stoney?"

He glanced to his partner for a moment, then returned to watching for the arrival of their hippo. "Thinking about Ragland."

"What about him?"

"Think he's going to break us up?"

"We going steady or something?"

Stone's face warmed from embarrassment.

Garrett adjusted himself in the driver's seat and leaned forward, his arms resting on the steering wheel. "Ragland's not going to do anything but hide his head in the sand."

Stone turned slightly toward his partner.

"That fat bastard hasn't left the station in years except to go home," Garrett assured him. "Don't worry about him."

Stone leaned back against the headrest. Life seemed a lot

easier with Garrett around. The man understood how the department functioned in a way that no one else seemed to.

"So, tell me something," Stone asked.

"Hmm?"

"Why are we sitting around here yanking dick when we should have a warrant for this guy?"

A slow grin grew on Garrett's face and he turned to look directly at Stone. "Yanking dick?"

"You know what I mean."

Garrett turned his attention back to the house.

"What I'm saying is, how come Marty couldn't pull together PC for this guy?"

"You could?"

"I think so, yeah."

Garrett rolled his lower lip down as he thought. "Run it for me, Detective."

Stone leaned forward as he spoke. "Krug's a career criminal who got out of jail a week before several burglaries occurred with a similar MO that he used in the past."

"Can't use that to establish probable cause. A lot of burglars use a crowbar to break into a house. It's not exactly a specialized skill to lever a window open."

"Okay," Stone said, "but the timing is a building block for the case."

"That's for attorneys to argue. It's not an element of a crime."

"What about the feces in the toilets?"

Garrett's nose crinkled. "Still not PC."

"It could be."

"How do you mean?"

"If they tried to get some DNA from one of those turds, it could tie Krug to the scene."

Garrett pulled slightly away from Stone. "You'd reach into a bowl and take a sample of one of those?"

"Well...no."

"Then why would you expect another officer to do it?

Besides, no way is Forensics going to run DNA on a burglary case, no matter how high profile. They're backed up on murders and rapes as it is."

Garrett faced the front again and silence descended on the car.

Finally, Stone muttered, "Krug's a Stat-five maggot."

"So why didn't you lead with that?"

"Huh?"

"That's your PC," Garrett said, not bothering to look at him. "What more do you need?"

Stone studied his partner.

Both men fell back into a silence then, lost in their own thoughts. Several minutes passed until the radio broke the quiet. "Tango-eleven to Tango-thirteen, status check."

Garrett grabbed the microphone. "It's crickets over here," he said. They were using the car-to-car channel so Garrett's lack of radio etiquette could be forgiven.

"Copy," replied Ray Zielinski.

After he returned the microphone to its holder, Garrett said, "What do you think of ol' Yin and Yang?"

"They're okay," Stone said. "Especially Yang. She's kind of different."

Garrett fell quiet again and Stone let his own thoughts take over.

The thing with Krug bothered him. The guy was definitely a maggot, a career criminal who was breaking into the homes of elderly citizens and ripping them off. It was only a matter of time before one of them got hurt. He wanted to be the one to catch Krug. Not some other patrol officer. Not ACT, but him, Gary Stone.

Yesterday had been a good day for him, maybe the best he could remember ever having as an adult—two foot pursuits, both ending in arrests, capped off with the appearance in front of the city council.

By the end of the day, he'd gotten a lot of text messages from fellow officers and people he knew who worked in city hall. All the messages were positive and sent the same basic message—nice work, Gary.

He liked that feeling. He liked that people now noticed Gary Stone, *the cop*. Garrett helped push him past what he thought he could be as an officer.

In Special Police Problems, he had found a comfortable niche within the department, but he quickly stagnated. Other officers looked at him the same way he now looked at Ragland. That's not who he was going to be anymore. Captain Farrell believed in him enough to send him to surveillance school prior to ACT getting off the ground. Now that it was running full speed, Garrett trusted him enough to be his partner. Stone wanted to show everyone that he deserved their confidence.

Unfortunately, he tried too hard by telling Garrett that he could figure out the PC for Krug. That was stupid. If a veteran detective like Marty Hill couldn't find enough probable cause, who was Stone to think he could do it? Still, he knew Krug was behind the series of crimes. Everyone on the team did. It was like a foul-smelling dog had gotten into the house, but everyone had to politely look away, pretending it was something else so as not to hurt the dog's feelings.

Maybe that analogy didn't work right, but Stone didn't care. Krug stunk and he knew it. But knowing it and proving it were two different things, and it was in that gap where all the police work happened.

A late nineties Saturn S-Series pulled up near the house they were watching. Both officers leaned forward, and Stone reached for the clipboard where they had the suspect's picture taped. He lifted it up to the dashboard so they could both see the picture.

The driver exited the vehicle. He had long brown hair that surrounded a bald crown and wore a black T-shirt, dirty jeans, and clunky-looking boots.

"That's him," Stone whispered, dropping the clipboard.

"Definitely. No one would fake that haircut."

Russell Krug stepped to the rear door and opened it. He reached inside and pulled out a small blue gym duffel.

"You know there's dope in that bag," Stone whispered.

"There's always dope in the bag," Garrett said.

After Krug slung the duffel over his shoulder, he closed the car door and headed for the house.

Garrett quietly opened his door and stepped out.

Stone leaned over the driver's seat and looked up at his partner. "What are you doing?" his whispered.

"I'm going after him on your PC."

Garrett stepped away from the vehicle and moved into the street. Stone scrambled out of the car. He had to run to catch up to Garrett, who was now almost to Krug's car. The man was unlocking the front door to his house.

"On my PC?" Stone asked in a hushed tone.

"Do you want to get this guy or not?"

"But you said it wasn't enough."

"And *you* said it was. I'm putting my faith in you."

Krug had stepped into his house and was closing his door.

"Is he the guy, or isn't he?" Garrett asked.

"I know he is," Stone said, watching the door close behind Krug, "but we can't go into the house now. We need a warrant."

"No, we don't. We have exigent circumstances," Garrett said, before heading off, bent over and moving steadily toward the door.

Stone stepped behind him, keeping low. He pulled his Glock from his holster when he saw Garrett remove his.

As they neared the front steps, Garrett removed his portable radio, lifting it to his lips. "Tango-thirteen, he's running from us."

Zielinski returned the transmission. "Who? Who's running?"

Garrett kicked the front door near the knob, sending it inward with an explosion of splinters close to the lock. Stone was immediately behind Garrett as they entered the house.

In the middle of the front room, Russell Krug was on his knees with the duffel bag opened in front of him. Several bottles of prescription drugs lay around him.

"On the ground!" Garrett yelled.

"The hell!" Krug hollered.

"Police!" added Stone.

A patrol siren and a roaring engine sounded at the front of the house.

The man began to stand.

"On the ground!" Garrett yelled again.

"This is bullshit!" Krug bellowed.

Stone shoved his Glock into his holster, took a step, and dove at Krug, who turned at the last moment. His shoulder hit the man, but most of his force was wasted.

Krug then jumped onto Stone and snaked an arm around the officer's throat. The move pinned Stone's head under Krug's armpit. With his free hand, Krug punched the officer once on top of the head. It felt like a bomb went off on top of his cranium.

Stone was twisted sideways. His lower hand punched repeatedly at Krug's stomach, but bounced twice against an elbow. The one time he hit something soft, Krug hit him again on top of the head. Another bomb went off.

The two men struggled against each other, banging into the walls. Krug further tightened his grip around Stone's neck and once jerked the officer in hopes of throwing him to the ground.

As Stone's left hand now tried to pry Krug's arm free from around his throat, his right arm slapped Krug's back once, then twice. The second time Stone's hand landed in Krug's long hair and he quickly clenched his fingers into a fist. He twisted his hand as he pulled downward, which yanked the man's face into the air.

Suddenly, Krug's arm slackened around Stone's neck and the man fell to the floor with a heavy thud. Stone straightened and stared at the now silent Krug. Confused, he turned to Tyler Garrett.

Shaking his fist, Garrett said, "Say hello to the Sandman."

There was a commotion outside as footsteps rapidly approached the front of the house.

"Code-four," yelled Garrett.

Zielinski appeared in the doorway with Yang close on his heels. They stopped and stared at the big man lying on the floor.

"What the hell happened?" Zielinski asked.

"He ran from us," Garrett said.

Zielinski looked perplexed. "Why did you attempt contact?"

"If you had parked where I suggested," Garrett said, "you would have seen him arrive, too. Instead, you had to show us just how smart you were, Ray."

"Regardless of where we were parked, we were supposed to sit and watch. Why did you decide to abandon that order and go after him, risking the team, and our work?"

Garrett glanced to Stone. When both Zielinski and Yang faced him as well, he knew he had to come up with something.

"I saw prescription bottles in the bag," Stone lied.

"Those bottles?" Zielinski asked, pointing to the little orange containers strewn about the floor.

"Yeah."

Yang stepped around her partner to look at the gym bag that lay opened on the floor. She bent down and moved the bottles around with the tip of pen. "These are not his prescriptions."

"Great work, Yang," Garrett said.

She looked up at him with a furrowed brow.

Russell Krug moved slightly on the floor causing Yang to take a step back.

Stone bent down and cuffed the man. Krug mumbled, "Where's your search warrant, cop?"

When Stone stood upright, Zielinski leaned into him and studied his eyes. "Tell me again how you saw the bottles."

Garrett pulled Stone back. "Don't be a baby because you missed out on another bust, Ray."

Zielinski pointed his finger at Garrett. "Don't start."

Stone blurted, "He pulled some of them out when he got the bag from the trunk."

Zielinski eyed him doubtfully. "And you could read the prescription all the way from the front seat of the Gray Ghost, huh?"

Stone didn't answer. He knew Zielinski was right.

"They're orange prescription bottles in the hands of known burglar who is a suspect in a recent string of burgs where prescriptions were taken," Garrett rattled off. "Stoney's right, it's PC."

"It's weak."

"Well, since you didn't chase the guy down and catch him with his stolen pills, I guess you don't have to worry about it."

Zielinski glowered at him but said nothing.

Yang pointed at the gym bag. "You want us to put this on property?"

Zielinski said, "Let them deal with this mess. Marty has something else for us."

He left the three of them standing there as Krug regained more of his senses.

"I wanna talk to a supervisor," Krug mumbled.

Yang eyed the man on the floor before she turned to follow Zielinski.

Stone stared at the bag of drugs as Garrett put his arm around his shoulders. "Seems that your probable cause was spot on, Stoney."

He wasn't sure what to say at that moment because he knew what they did was wrong, but they caught a bad man in the process. Besides, his stomach no longer hurt, and it always ached when he was in Special Police Problems. Maybe what he was doing now was right and what he had always done before was wrong.

Garrett slapped him on the back. "Man, we've got a lot of a paperwork coming out of this."

Stone nodded. As Garrett had once told him, it was time for a CYA report.

Cover your ass.

Chapter 18

Ray Zielinski drove the Bronze Beast down Mission Avenue, fuming.

Jun Yang sat silently in the passenger seat, her attention focused on the scenery outside her own window.

In his gut, Zielinski knew that Stone had been lying about seeing the prescription bottles. His reaction when challenged told Zielinski that. But Garrett had come to the man's defense, rescuing his protégé. The explanation Garrett had spouted off was some weak-ass probable cause if Zielinski had ever heard any, but there was nothing further to be done. He'd already skirted the line of breaking the brotherhood code by arguing about procedure in front of a suspect. Zielinski liked to think that he only did it because Krug was halfway incoherent at the time, but he wondered if that were true. He'd been frustrated, even angry, and that was the more likely reason for his outburst.

Zielinski took in a deep breath and let it out. Without thinking about it, he reached into his shirt pocket and popped a Rolaids into his mouth and chewed. For a little while, his stomach issues had cleared up. He'd won a legal battle with his second ex-wife, so there was no more alimony going out to her. That somewhat cleared up his financial issues, though he still lived hand-to-mouth, it seemed. The bigger relief came when both of his outstanding Internal Affairs investigations came to a satisfactory close. He enjoyed a brief respite where all he had to worry about was normal life stuff, and of course, the perennial dangers of patrol. But he was used to both, so it was almost like a vacation.

Then Farrell came and sold him on the idea of the Anti-

Crime Team. "I need some veteran presence," he'd said. "Someone to keep the young bulls from running around recklessly."

Thoughts of Garrett filled his mind. It was bad enough that he suspected Garrett was dirty somehow. He'd come to believe it after the man's questionable shooting almost two years ago, and it was a feeling that haunted him. Now, Garrett had pulled Stone solidly into his orbit, and the effect on the younger officer was apparent. Maybe Zielinski hadn't thought much of Stone when he was working as the Chief's Bitch down at city hall, but he preferred that to the Garrett clone he seemed to be turning into. Garrett's effect was clearly toxic.

Zielinski had hesitated when Farrell made the offer, but eventually accepted. The flexible hours gave him a chance to try to see his kids more, and the overtime was more lucrative than the off-duty jobs he'd been taking to make ends meet. Besides, he knew Farrell could force the issue anyway, so better to volunteer than be volun*told*.

Most importantly, it gave him a chance to work more closely with Garrett, and he hoped that would either confirm his suspicions or quiet them.

So far, it wasn't very quiet.

Zielinski turned left on Cook Street and drifted into a residential neighborhood. As he cruised along, he watched the numbers on the houses, until he saw the address of Darold Barden. The house was a 1950s rancher with brown peeling paint. The grass was both overgrown and dying, and a tricycle with only two wheels sat on the porch.

"Look at that," Zielinski said, slowing down.

"Look at what?" Yang asked.

He pointed at the tricycle. "In this neighborhood, they even jack the wheels off trikes."

Yang smiled tightly but said nothing.

Zielinski took note that the house was dark, the shades pulled. No vehicles were in the driveway, and the small carport was empty except for an old couch.

He kept driving.

Barden was probably at Sheryl Clemons's house. Neil wouldn't like that.

He guessed it was also possible the man was at work, though it was just as likely his "work" was the same kind as Krug and Cattage's.

Zielinski narrowed his eyes in thought. He wondered if maybe he could find a way to get the team focused on Barden and solve the problem that way…

"Where are we going?"

He glanced over at Yang, his reverie broken. "What?"

"We're going to arrest Ron Bylsma on his warrant, right?"

"Yeah."

"We're headed the wrong direction." She pointed over her shoulder. "He lives in East Central."

"I know. I just needed to check on something."

"What, a broken tricycle?"

"No," Zielinski said, wishing now he hadn't pointed out the house to her.

Yang seemed to be waiting for further explanation.

"It's nothing important," he told her.

"It's not? Didn't Marty say Bylsma's mom called to say he was home? Missing him because you had to check on something isn't going to go over well."

Zielinski grunted then turned south on Smith and headed toward East Central. Beside him, he could feel Yang's suspicion, and he did his best to ignore it.

Chapter 19

Captain Tom Farrell buzzed into the jail booking area. He secured his gun in the nearby lockbox and headed into the officer's area. There he found Tyler Garrett and Gary Stone standing at the counter, each hunched over one of the small terminals.

Garrett spotted him first. He flashed his trademark smile, stood up straight, and gave Farrell a lazy salute.

"Attention on deck," he said jokingly.

"As you were," Farrell joked back. Despite his feelings about Garrett, he didn't want the man to know about his suspicions. He believed that Garrett was already aware of Clint's interest in him. Remaining in the shadows was one of the few advantages he still seemed to have in his quest to bring down the dirty cop.

Stone turned to him as well. Both officers waited expectantly. Captains didn't just happen into the booking area. They knew he was there for a purpose.

"Dispatch told me you were out at jail," he explained. "Who'd you get?"

"Russell Krug," Garrett said.

Farrell nodded. He'd read about Krug in the daily Crime Analysis intelligence flyer. The part about him likely running into one of the elderly homeowners at some point had worried him along with the rest of department's leadership.

"Good arrest," he said.

Garrett slapped Stone on the back. "It was all Stoney, sir. He spotted the maggot with the goods. Once he ran, he didn't stand a chance. My boy here is the white answer to Usain Bolt."

Stone blushed. "Krug wasn't that fast."

"Captain," Garrett said, "he's being humble. Yesterday, this guy ran down two different bad guys in one shift, and *then* went in front of the city council and knocked it out of the park." He held out his fist, and Stone bumped it.

"I heard your report to the council," Farrell said. "Nice work."

"Thank you, sir."

"In fact, that's why I came over." He handed Stone the sheaf of papers he'd received from the chief. "These are emails from the mayor, council members, and the public, all saying what a great job ACT is doing."

Stone's eyes widened slightly, and he looked through the stack, handing them off to Garrett as he finished each one.

"The chief wanted me to personally tell you that he's proud of you guys," Farrell added.

Stone glanced up, his eyes shining. "Thanks." Then he held up the papers in his hands. "You know, he could just forward these emails. He didn't have to print them off."

Farrell grinned. "The chief is old school. If it isn't on paper, it doesn't exist."

Stone nodded absently before returning his attention to the emails.

"Listen to this," Garrett said, reading from one. "'I love how this team is finally taking it to the creeps who prey on all of us good people.'" He looked up to Stone. "That's us, Stoney. Taking it to the creeps."

The two men laughed.

Garrett slapped Stone on the back again. "Welcome to the promised land, brother." He looked over at Farrell. "We got ourselves a bona fide meat-eater now, Captain."

Stone beamed.

Farrell nodded his approval, but concern rumbled in his gut. Stone's emergence as a more aggressive and confident officer was a good thing, but he'd brought him on board due to his ethics and loyalty. The influence of Garrett worried him. If he was going to eventually bring Stone into his confidence, he didn't want the man to struggle with conflicting loyalties.

"Anything else, sir?" Garrett asked him.

Farrell shook his head. "No. Just pass on the emails and the chief's message to the rest of the team, okay?"

Garrett nodded. "You bet. We'll let them know."

The captain thanked him and left the officer's area. As he retrieved his gun, he could hear their voices through the sliding glass door but couldn't make out the words. Their raucous laughter was unmistakable, though.

I don't have long, Farrell realized. *I have to make my move soon.*

He trudged back to his office, mulling things over in his head. Maybe it was time to reach out to Clint, after all.

Chapter 20

Jun Yang lazily dragged the mop across the black-and-white tile floor.

"You'd think with all that Army training you'd show a little more enthusiasm for mopping a floor."

Yang looked up at to find her younger brother, Xi-Wang, sitting atop the back of a plastic booth, his feet on its seat. He dropped a McDonald's hamburger bag on top of the orange table. Xi-Wang had just graduated from Lewis and Clark High School and was preparing to attend Central Washington University on an academic scholarship. He wore a Nike T-shirt, blue shorts, and flip-flops.

"It's precisely because of the Army that I lack the enthusiasm for this task. You, little brother, should be doing this."

"Ah…no," Xi-Wang said. "I get paid to do that."

Her brow furrowed. "Mom and dad pay you to work here?"

"What?" he said, running his fingers through his longish black hair. "You didn't get paid when you worked for them?"

Yang shook her head. It was yet another difference in the way her parents favored her brother. She wasn't entirely sure if it was because he was a boy, or because he was younger. Probably some of both.

"Sucks to be you." Xi-Wang bent over, opened the McDonald's bag, and extracted a hamburger. He held it out to her. "Want one?"

"No," she said and went back to her chore of mopping the floor.

Her parents owned Donut Make You Smile, a seven-day-a-week family business. They rented a twelve-hundred-square-foot building located in the much sought-after Perry District, a walkable neighborhood on the lower edge of the affluent South Hill. The family had been there since Yang was a little girl and the Perry District was sketchy. Now, it was hipster central and the little donut bistro attracted aficionados from the entire city.

She lifted the mop, dropped it into the bucket of water, then wrung it dry.

"You seem grouchy," Xi-Wang said.

Yang ignored him and instead slopped the mop onto the floor. She wetted the tiles with an ever-widening arc, removing the dirt and grime that had built up over the day.

She frowned. During the day, she removed the dirt and grime that stained the city's soul and then she came to her parent's store to mop it from their floor. Was she eternally a janitor?

Ugh, I'm turning into Ray.

Zielinski had told her that police officers were essentially garbagemen, collecting trash throughout the day and taking it to a processing center where it was to be recycled back onto the city streets. She needed to push those thoughts from her head. Thinking like Ray was a bad place for her soul to linger.

She wrung the dirty water out of the mop again before dropping it to the floor to collect the remaining wetness.

Ray may be a burnout—or perhaps still in the process of burning out, she was wavering on her earlier assessment—but something had gone on with him at the end of their shift. He was clearly on a side of town where they had no mission at that moment.

When Yang called him on it, he didn't even try to play it off. He had disrespected her by simply shutting down, forcing a wall of silence between them. That sucked because it was clear she was stuck riding with him for as long as she was on the Anti-Crime Team.

Garrett and Stone had quickly formed a tight bond and now rode together every day. Yang wasn't jealous of their connection. Unlike Ray, she wasn't even overtly suspicious of the two, but she remained wary of them. Something was off when they were together, a lurking danger.

When Stone was alone, he seemed like a nice, almost sweet man. When he was around Garrett, though, he became a different person, as if he had something to prove not only to the senior officer but to himself. Yang wondered what drove a man to behave that way. She'd seen some of that behavior before in the military, of course, but Stone seemed desperate to prove himself capable of the job.

As for Tyler Garrett, he was also different when away from the other man, but in a surprising way. When Yang rode with him, he seemed aloof, almost distracted. He spent most of the time with his phone, texting. She didn't feel it appropriate to inquire what he was doing as she was the younger officer. Garrett rarely engaged her in conversation and when he did, it seemed careful, as if the topics were always meant to be directed away from their personal lives. She never learned anything intimate about Garrett from their time together.

But when Stone was around the senior officer, Garrett spent extra time and energy building his confidence. It was as if Garrett was a training officer, but he was instructing him in something different than the policies and procedures of the department. What that was, Yang hadn't figured out yet.

"You missed a spot."

Yang looked up to see a grinning Xi-Wang.

She turned the mop handle toward her brother and poked him in the side with it. He fell into the booth.

"Ahh!" he cried from behind the hard plastic. "Police brutality."

"There's a clause in there for little brothers. I have amnesty."

Xi-Wang lifted his head above the booth. "Is there really a clause for that?"

Yang popped the end of the mop against the hard-plastic booth, forcing Xi-Wang to drop behind the seat back. "Leave me alone, brother! I'm doing your work for free."

His hand lifted above the table until he found the McDonald's bag and dragged it off to where he was hiding.

Yang continued mopping the floor and her thoughts returned to the team.

Zielinski, Garrett, and Stone. She was the odd person out. Not only was she a woman, she had barely gotten out of the training car and was technically still on probation before her assignment to the team. It felt as if none of them wanted her there. She wondered if that resentment was because she was female or because she was still a rookie. If it was because she was new to the department, she fully understood and sympathized. She'd been in similar situations while in the Army.

If it was because she was a woman, well, that was another matter entirely.

Xi-Wang climbed back to the top of the table and crushed a hamburger wrapper. "Work still good?" he asked.

"It's fine," Yang said.

"Anything exciting going on?" he asked, stuffing the sandwich wrapping inside the bag.

Yang slopped the mop back on the floor. "No."

"Is it fun?"

"Every job has its good days and its bad."

Xi-Wang crunched the bag, then tossed it in the air like a baseball.

"Is it what you thought it would be?"

"Yes," she said, as it was the easiest answer to give to her younger brother.

Being a police officer had been a childhood dream. She had gotten a taste of it while in the military, but she was an MP, not a cop. The hunger to achieve that dream had not been satisfied by enlisting.

"Are you happy that you came home for it?"

Yang ignored her brother and continued to pull the mop across the floor. When Xi-Wang tired of waiting for an answer, he got up and went into the back to begin washing the dishes. He knew that when Yang went silent, she wasn't going to answer further questions. After he left, she realized it was the same trick Zielinski had pulled on her. It's how she had dealt with her family since she was a little girl. Maybe she and Ray had something in common after all.

Her thoughts returned to her brother's question. Was she happy that she left the Army and returned to Spokane to join the police department?

At that moment, she couldn't answer the question, because she no longer knew how she felt.

Chapter 21

Tyler Garrett held the door for Tiana Kennedy as they left Steelhead Bar and Grill. When they were on the sidewalk, they headed south. It was warm out, almost eighty degrees, and the moon was half full.

"That was an excellent dinner," Tiana said.

Garrett slid his hand into hers. "It was."

They fell into a comfortable silence as they walked lazily back toward Tiana's condo.

"What a beautiful night, too," she said, resting her head on Garrett's shoulder.

They turned east onto Main Street. Tiana was now on the outside nearest the curb. A tricked-out Honda with neon lights under its body whizzed loudly by.

"You seem distracted," Tiana said.

"It's work," Garrett said. "but everything's fine."

Several hundred feet away, a Native American man turned at the sound of their voices. Even from this distance, he seemed tall. He was dressed in a baggy football jersey, jeans, and Timberland boots. He began walking in their direction.

"Did something happen with the team?"

"The team is fine," Garrett said.

Garrett released Tiana's left hand, stepped behind her, then grabbed her right hand. He was now on the outside, with her closest to the buildings. Since he was right-handed, this freed up his dominant hand.

The big man ambled toward them, his right hand was in his pocket, his left arm swinging naturally. Several more cars passed by.

"And Stone?"

"He's doing great."

The Native American man was almost to them when Tiana became aware of him. She gripped Garrett's hand tighter and he squeezed back.

The tall man's pockmarked face was passive, but his eyes were purposefully straight ahead. He never looked at either Garrett or Tiana. As he neared, the man pulled his hand from his pocket.

"Babe," Tiana whispered.

The big man never lifted his right hand and Garrett barely moved his.

Tiana looked over her shoulder at the tall man as he continued walking. "Weirdo," she mumbled.

"Here," Garrett said, handing her a thick wad of cash.

"What's that?"

"Work," he said.

"Oh," she softly said, grabbing the money and tucking it into her purse.

Chapter 22

Gary Stone sat on the edge of his bed, holding the printed emails in his hands. He had wanted to read them once more before turning in for the night. Nine citizens, four city council members, and the mayor—the *mayor*—had written Chief Baumgartner to share how excited they were about the reported Anti-Crime Team numbers.

The mayor's email was a big deal for Stone since he was the one who had personally kicked him out of city hall. To add further humiliation to the officer's exit, he had required a security detail escort Stone from the building.

If the mayor applauded ACT's success with Gary Stone front and center as the face of the team, then maybe no one really remembered why he was kicked out. He doubted that since it led to the downfall of a councilman, a threatened lawsuit from the family of a dead high school girl, and a three-day suspension for the chief of police.

Maybe, in the end, no one really cared because they had their own lives to worry about. That's what Captain Farrell said was likely to happen when he approached Stone about joining the Anti-Crime Team. Farrell had said that Stone would be dragged through the mud for a week, no one would remember him the week after that, and the public would be singing his praises in the third week.

The captain was off in his estimations, however. It took almost four months for someone to publicly praise him. But at least they were finally singing.

Stone looked up to the enlarged photograph that hung on the wall near his bed. A bison stood in a long-forgotten field as a heavy snow fell. He'd taken the picture years ago while on a trip to Montana.

The magnificent animal watched him as it stood unaffected by the elements. Large white flakes accumulated not only on the ground but on the bison as well. The animal's exhale of breath was evident in the cold. Even the effects of the wind, which Stone remembered from that day, could be seen in the flittering hair of the beast to the tall strands of bending grass.

Stone loved this picture and all it represented. When he took the photo, he could not have realized how much that simple moment by the roadside would have meant to his life. He sat here often, reminding himself to strive to be like the lonely animal braving the elements.

He should be calm when things occurred that he had zero control over.

He should be unfazed by the pressures of the outside world.

He should be unwavering in the face of adversity.

He tried to reach those goals, but often failed. He had failed miserably when he was removed from city hall. As outside pressures mounted, he questioned who he was, why he was a policeman, and doubted his worth to the profession. He wanted to walk away and give up the thing he'd worked hard to achieve.

Stone's eyes remained on the bison, but he clutched the printed emails tighter in his hands, crinkling the paper. Now, though, things were finally different.

He felt more alive.

He felt stronger.

He could stand anything life decided to throw his way.

Stone realized this new confidence was because he wasn't waiting for life to come to him, for it to bring the fight to his doorstep. He was now an active participant in his own existence.

The trouble at city hall was good for him in many ways. It had given him some political experience, but it also showed him something important—it revealed the man he no longer wanted to be.

For a moment, though, he wondered if he was becoming a good man, a man his parents would be proud of. He'd arrested a number of suspects now, stopping them from being able to hurt society, at least for a little while. But he knew he'd done things that weren't exactly right to make those arrests.

He hit Wayne Cattage with his portable radio. According to the department's Use of Force Policy, that strike was inappropriate. He chose to not write it in his report, which was a lie of omission. But he needed to get Cattage off the fence. Maybe he wouldn't get in trouble if someone saw him do it. There was a chance he could explain it away in the heat of the moment. Besides, when was the last time one of the white-shirt administrators who review those reports was actually out on the streets, fighting the good fight?

He had also failed to read Cattage his rights before questioning the man. There was no explaining that mistake away. But that man was clearly a criminal who needed to pay for his crimes. He'd stolen from a family that had worked hard for those items and he violated their home by his actions. Maybe Stone was not at his best when he forgot to read the Miranda warning or when he creatively wrote it into his report that he had, but his results spoke for themselves. Wayne Cattage was in jail and would not burglarize another home for the foreseeable future.

Russell Krug was no different. No, wait. That wasn't true. The man was worse for preying on the elderly. Should he remain free to victimize more helpless citizens of Spokane simply because Stone hadn't actually seen the drugs in the bag? What did it matter? He *knew* they were there. And Krug may not have run from him and Garrett, but he would have if he'd seen the officers. So what was the difference, except that he had to tell a slightly different story to get another dirt bag booked into jail?

There was no difference, he decided. Not one that mattered, anyway. Results mattered, and if he had to bend the rules a little to make justice happen, it was worth it.

He glanced at the papers in his hands. Hopefully, that was enough for his parents to be proud of him, for others to be proud of him. Stone wondered if Garrett ever doubted himself.

Probably not, he decided. *Garrett is too squared away for that.*

Stone put the emails on the nightstand and clicked off the lamp, darkening the room. He sat for another moment and sighed in contentment.

Then he lay in bed and went to sleep.

Chapter 23

Most of the Major Crimes Unit was dark and empty. Clint finished typing his summary report and a charging request on an assault case that Lieutenant Flowers had laid on him first thing Monday morning. He'd left it in Clint's box without explanation, something Flowers tended to do with straightforward cases, and this had been no exception. It involved a bar fight the previous Saturday night between two men. Once he saw the charge, the location, and the participants, Clint had known without reading the narrative that the odds were high that the reason for the fight had either been drugs or a woman. In this instance, it had been a woman. She went with one man, and the other took offense, following the couple out of the bar, where he smashed a bottle over the first man's head. The broken bottle left a nasty gash that required stitches. Worse yet, the stunned man fell to ground, striking his head on a parking meter on the way down, opening another large cut on his face.

Typical downtown Saturday night, Clint mused.

The case itself had taken minimal investigation. Patrol officers had interviewed both men and several witnesses, and he had to admit that the uniforms did an excellent job procuring all the necessary information. It was rare that Clint didn't follow up and reinterview everyone in the case, and even rarer that he chose not to talk to anyone at all, but this was one of those times.

The only leg work he had to do was to retrieve a copy of the victim's medical records for the file, and to confirm with the victim that he still wished to press charges. Beyond that, the case had arrived in his box almost gift-wrapped.

He wondered why Flowers was giving him a ground ball case like this. Usually, the lieutenant handed him the more difficult and convoluted cases because he knew Clint had a mind for sifting through the mess and getting to the truth. Was this purposeful? Or had it just come up when it was his turn to get a case?

Clint frowned. There was another possibility. Maybe Flowers was losing faith in him as an investigator.

That conclusion would be erroneous, he knew. But Flowers was like a lot of other people in the world—his conclusions were marred by emotion and prejudices. Clint was aware that people found him difficult to deal with, and many had emotional reactions to that, Flowers included. It wasn't a stretch to imagine that these emotions started to color the lieutenant's assessment of Clint's work.

Color. There was that, too. Clint stood out when it came to his work record, but even more for his skin color. Spokane was almost ninety percent white and barely above two percent black, and with numbers like that, there was no way to avoid standing out. Especially since he was the only detective of color in Major Crimes.

There were a few other things that were unavoidable, too, like the special brand of ninja racism he saw everywhere in this city. It was rarely overt or on the surface, but it lurked just underneath and manifested in insidious ways.

Clint kept typing as these thoughts flitted through his mind, making sure he included every witness statement and piece of physical evidence in his report. He had a reputation for being thorough, and it was deserved.

It was that thoroughness that took him up to Angela Garrett's workplace that morning. The interview may not have yielded anything of extraordinary value, but it was something he knew he needed to do, and unless she chose to complain to Internal Affairs or take some other radical, equally unlikely action, the outcome would be a win for him. As it was, he now knew exactly where she stood, which was exactly where he had expected her to stand.

Still, he wondered if that might not change over time. He wasn't willing to write off the possibility that she would inform on her ex-husband somewhere down the line. Maybe if the new boyfriend turned into a more serious relationship, she'd reconsider. After Clint ran the plate on the Audi, he did a cursory background check on its owner, William Cardwell. He worked in real estate, which Clint saw as a potentially dirty profession. But as best he could tell, Cardwell was an aboveboard businessman who did well for himself. He might be a person who gave Angela the level of security she needed to turn on Garrett.

Or hell, maybe all it would take would be for her dealings with Garrett to deteriorate. Things were already frosty, from what Clint could see. Perhaps some time was all that he needed.

Clint's frown deepened. Time wasn't his friend in this investigation. Every day that passed buried Garrett's misdeeds deeper and gave the man another opportunity to shine up his image.

He circled back around to Flowers and his choice of case assignment. He decided that the most likely explanation was pure chance. He got an easy case because that was the case that dropped when it was his turn. Flowers had no basis to doubt him or his work.

Or did he?

Clint stopped typing. He narrowed his eyes in thought. For the past two years, he'd been pursuing Garrett, following the officer, keeping him under surveillance, collecting data, and building a case against him. Was it possible that his other work had suffered? He hadn't been keeping track of his clearance rate lately, so it was entirely possible that it was off a few percentage points, but it couldn't be any more than that.

Could it?

Doubt was not an emotion Clint was comfortable with. Anger, sure. He kept a tight harness on his anger, but it was always there, and it fueled his suspicion. Suspicion was the emotional first cousin to skepticism, and that served him well as a detective. Doubt, though? That was a different matter. He rarely doubted his own analysis, or his own decisions. He was confident in them. And there were objective reasons that he should be, including his long track record of high performance.

Except in cracking Garrett, of course.

Clint realized he was clenching his jaw and forced himself to relax. Once his jaw slackened, he realized how tightly his shoulders and arms were tensed. He took a cleansing breath and willed his entire body to loosen. It took several breaths before he felt some of the tension seep out of his muscles.

In that moment, he had a small epiphany.

He was weary.

He was weary of Garrett.

With the exception of his visit to see Angela Garrett, he had done no work on the Garrett case that day. When five o'clock rolled around, he had elected to stay at his desk for several hours to catch up on paperwork and make calls to people at home from work rather than go out and try to follow Garrett and Stone around in the Gray Ghost to see what they were up to.

Why?

He still believed in Garrett's guilt. He'd seen more than enough evidence of that. But he was losing steam for this crusade, this marathon that felt like it had no end in sight. No one else was busting their hump to bring this man to justice. Even Farrell's weak attempts with the Anti-Crime Team looked more like the captain was trying to disengage from the situation in a way that insulated him.

Clint considered that last thought for a moment, then rejected it. He didn't entirely trust Farrell anymore, but he believed the captain still wanted to bring down Garrett. Farrell had even left a vague voicemail for him earlier in the day, saying he was, "Just checking in" and that Clint "should swing by." Clint deleted it without a second thought.

So, besides Farrell's lame machinations, he was the only person trying to do the right thing. The effort was taking its toll on him. Maybe, he realized, it was even affecting his other work, and he'd been blind to it.

He wondered if he should take a break. How much stamina did he have?

The idea was tempting. His life would be much simpler. If his case work had been suffering, that would certainly change by taking a break. He could join the rest of the sleepwalkers in the world and just go about his daily doings, unaware and unaffected by Garrett.

Except he wasn't unaware. He knew exactly what Garrett had done. And that affected him.

Clint began typing again, wrapping up the charging request on the ground ball assault case Flowers had given him. This case would be off his desk tonight and at the prosecutor's office in the morning, along with two others he'd finished today. That was the kind of detective he was. He believed he had a work ethic that was second to none. More than that, he knew that once he had his teeth into something, there was no letting go.

Clint had no illusions about who and what he was, or who Garrett was.

Garrett was a dirty cop.

And Clint wanted to be the man to catch him.

He hit send on his slam dunk report, shipping it electronically to Flowers for review. Then he reached up and switched off the desk light. Bathed in the sudden darkness of the empty Major Crimes Unit, he couldn't help but wonder if time was now on Garrett's side. Clint had been on this trail for two long years. Had he already missed his opportunity to bring the man to justice?

He hoped not.

But hope was not a plan.

WEDNESDAY

Responsibility for the Rampart Misconduct doesn't lie with a single individual, but with a relatively small group of renegade police officers whose misdeeds went unchecked as a result of a systematic failure of supervision and leadership throughout the chain of command. Ironically, it was the very effectiveness of Rampart CRASH that planted the seeds for its eventual corruption.
—Report of the Rampart Independent Review Panel, November 2000

Chapter 24

Captain Tom Farrell's morning started with a problem.

When he walked past Sergeant Kelly Ragland's office, he found the sergeant at his desk. Farrell stopped and stared through the open doorway in surprise. Ragland seemed to sense him and looked up.

"Captain?"

Farrell stepped inside Ragland's office. "ACT starting early today?" he asked.

"Not that I'm aware of."

That's what Farrell had figured. "Then why are you here?"

Ragland gave him an innocent look, but Farrell could see all the passive-aggressive ire beneath the expression. "This is when my shift starts, sir."

"I thought we discussed this."

"Oh, we did."

Farrell held out his hands, palms upturned. "Then I'll ask you again: why are you here? The Anti-Crime Team usually doesn't start until eleven or so."

"Captain, you told me I couldn't just drop all of my other responsibilities," Ragland said.

Farrell couldn't recall ever saying that, but he went along with it. "So?"

"So, it's going to take a few days for me to get everything in order before I can modify my shift."

"What is a few days?"

"A week or so."

"A week?" Farrell shook his head. "No, I need you on this team now."

"I *am* supervising the team, in addition to getting my other duties to a place where I can leave them on the shelf until Sergeant McGinn gets back," Ragland explained icily. "My shift still overlaps with theirs for half of their duty day, so I'm able to accomplish most of what you want."

Farrell stared at him, seething. Ragland had found an effective way to drag his feet on this assignment. If Farrell objected, he looked unreasonable. Ragland could point to his admin work as a reasonable delay, and Captain Hatcher would almost certainly support his assertion. Meanwhile, the clock ticked on the grievance timeline, and ACT was only marginally more supervised than in the complete absence of a sergeant.

Malicious compliance. That's what this is.

And there was little to nothing he could do about it.

"Are you up on the team's mission?" he asked Ragland, his voice tight.

"I think so."

"Tell me then."

Ragland scowled slightly. He was a veteran sergeant, albeit not a very dynamic one. Farrell knew he wasn't used to being talked to like he was brand new.

"Reduce crime through the interdiction of high-profile offenders," Ragland recited, "via the execution of existing arrest warrants, and development of new cases, including aggressive investigation of crimes likely committed by HPOs, and surveillance of same."

Farrell had to admit he was mildly impressed. That sounded like the team's mission statement, word for word. The sergeant had even used the phonetic *HPO* instead of the conveniently accessible slang term *hippo*. Ragland was smart. No wonder he knew the union contract so well. But he'd left out one important element with regard to the team. "Make sure that they continue coordinating with Crime Analysis," the captain said.

"Of course."

"How about the team members? Any questions about

them?”

Ragland shrugged. “It’s an interesting collection of cops. Not necessarily who I would have picked.”

Farrell bristled. “Each was selected for a purpose.”

“Like what?”

Farrell tried to keep the frustration out of his voice as he explained.

“Garrett is there because he’s a go-getter with a tactical background…”

And to fall into my trap.

“…Stone has political and media savvy…”

But mostly, to help me spring that trap.

“…Zielinski has veteran presence…”

He’s there in case I need an ally.

“…and Yang brings youth and a fresh perspective to the equation.”

And to keep an eye on all of them.

“Sounds like you got your rainbow team right there, Captain.”

“Listen,” Farrell grated, “I know you don’t want this assignment, but I’m telling you right now, you *will* be a professional and give it the leadership attention it deserves.”

Ragland glared back at him. “I wouldn’t think of doing anything different.”

“Good.”

“Is there anything else, Captain? Because every minute I’m delayed in closing down my admin work is another minute I’m not with your Anti-Crime Team.”

Farrell had a momentary vision of reaching out and throttling the corpulent sergeant, and he was certain the desire showed on his face. He pulled the emotion back inside and affected a calmer expression.

“I’ll leave you to it,” he said, and left Ragland’s office.

So help me, if I ever get the chance to hammer that sneaky, arrogant bastard, I will drop it like a sledge.

But he knew that was unlikely. Ragland played the game

well, and Farrell didn't have time for such diversion. He had to stay focused on the ball, and the ball was Officer Tyler Garrett.

Chapter 25

Ray Zielinski settled into the chair in the officers' lounge. Yang sat in another chair directly across from him. Despite the relaxed setting for roll call, she still had her pen and notepad ready. Garrett and Stone lounged on the couch, watching the TV on low volume. Detective Marty Hill stood off to the side, thumbing through some paperwork.

Sergeant Kelly Ragland trundled to the TV and looked around for the power button. No one offered to help him while he searched, first visually, then by running his fingertips around the flat screen. Finally, he turned to Garrett and said, "How do you turn this damn thing off?"

Coolly, Garrett picked up the remote from the small end table and pointed it at the TV, clicking off the power.

"Actually," Hill said, "I was going to hook my laptop to that, Sarge. I want to show the team some burglary trends that Crime Analysis put together."

"Why?" Ragland asked.

Hill looked a little confused at the question. "It's a six-week trend," he explained. "Three weeks before we started, and the three weeks since. I want to show the guys the impact we've had."

"Is crime down?" Garrett asked him.

"Yes."

Garrett held up his hands in a *there-you-are* gesture. "That's all I need to know."

Hill didn't appear bothered by the dismissal. He turned to Sergeant Ragland, offering him the packet of paperwork in his hands. "Do you want this?"

"Just the summary," Ragland said.

Hill handed him a single sheet of paper.

Ragland scanned the sheet, then said, "All right, listen up. These are the three targets we'll be pursuing over the next few days."

"Three?" Garrett asked. He glanced at Yang and then Zielinski. "Stoney and I will have three stuffed and cuffed by dinner. How are you two going to spend the shift? Maybe do a little shopping?"

Garrett and Stone bumped fists, chuckling lightly.

Zielinski gave Garrett a flat stare. "You know what I like about you, Ty?"

"How I make these raggedy ass undercover clothes look good?"

"No," Zielinski deadpanned. "I like how much of a team player you are."

Garrett's eyes narrowed slightly. "Team first, Z. Always."

"You guys want these names," Ragland asked, "or do you want to talk smack all day?"

"Lay 'em on us, Sarge," Garrett said. He nudged Stone and mimed writing something down. Stone dug for his notebook, pulling it out from under his vest. Then he patted his pockets for a pen, finding one after a few seconds.

Ragland waited impatiently until Stone clicked the pen top and sat poised and ready to take notes. "First up," he said, "is Alan Capehart. He's got a pair of res burg warrants."

"If we get him," Hill interjected, "I've got three more cases with similar MOs, so he's worth an interview."

"You want him in the box so you can go at him?" Garrett asked. "Or do you want us to chat him up in the field?"

"Your call," Hill said. "If you think he'll go for it in a field interview, take a shot."

"We'll swing by and read the other reports before we hit the streets, then," Garrett said.

That figures, Zielinski thought. *Garrett would think he's better at interrogating than Hill, despite all the detective's experience and specific training.*

Ragland continued. "Second target is Curtis Hiney."

Garrett let out a small snort, and a moment later, Stone giggled.

Children. I work with children.

"Hiney has nine warrants, three of which are felonies," Ragland said, ignoring their snickering. "His felonies are for burglary, fencing stolen property, and possession of narcotics."

"Let's get him before some patrol guy gets lucky and stops him for expired tabs on his license plate," Garrett said. "Those are our beans, not Patrol's."

The sergeant continued. "Last target is for equal opportunity purposes. A woman. Hanka Novakova."

Zielinski cringed slightly and glanced at Yang. She didn't react.

"The Russian Princess," Garrett muttered. "She steals cars like they're toilet paper."

"Eastern European," Yang said quietly.

"What?" Garrett looked over at her.

"They're not all from Russia," Yang said. "Some are from the Ukraine, or Georgia, for example. Or Poland and the Czech Republic. It's more accurate to call them Eastern European."

Garrett raised his brow. "Yeah. I'll do that."

Zielinski couldn't be sure if he was serious or not. He also didn't understand why Yang bristled on the overuse of the term *Russian*, and not at the sergeant's sexist reference. Maybe she just hit her breaking point.

"All of these targets come from Crime Analysis," Sergeant Ragland said, ignoring the banter. "They are supported by Detective Hill, who has several additional cases that each of them are likely good for. So hunt these three down first and foremost. If you finish, contact me here at the station for your next assignment."

Garrett raised a hand. Ragland nodded at him. "Sarge, what if we finish with these three after you've gone home? We work pretty late sometimes."

Ragland didn't appear to care much for the question, and it appeared Garrett asked it to needle the man. "Use your best judgment, *Officer*. That's why we hired you."

"Yes, sir."

Ragland turned to Hill. "Anything else?"

Hill shook his head. "Nope. I've got all the supporting documentation when you find any of the targets. I'll be here until six o'clock tonight, then I'm off. My daughter has a softball game."

The life of a detective, Zielinski thought sourly. *Pity if work ever got in the way of personal concerns.*

He tried to think of the last time he'd seen his daughter. It had been over a week, at least.

"All right," Ragland said. Without anything further, he turned and left the lounge, handing the single sheet of paper back to Hill as he walked past him.

Hill put the sheet with the rest of his paperwork. "Happy hunting," he told them, before limping toward the door. Zielinski could hear the creak of his knee brace with every other step.

Garrett slapped Stone on the leg while the man was still writing furiously. "You ready, Stoney?"

"How do you spell Novakova?" Stone asked.

"T-h-i-e-f," Garrett recited.

Stone started writing on the T, then stopped. "Seriously, I don't know how to spell it."

"Don't worry about it. I've already got her in my little black book of bad guys," Garrett told him. "Come on, let's hit it."

He and Stone rose together and strode to the door without looking back.

Yang clicked her pen top and slid it into her vest. "I guess we're riding together again," she said.

Zielinski lumbered to his feet. "Don't sound so disappointed."

Chapter 26

Wardell Clint heard Tyler Garrett's voice in the Major Crimes Unit. He listened carefully and pinpointed it at Marty Hill's desk. With a little concentration, it wasn't difficult to eavesdrop. Garrett asked about several burglaries and the MO of each, telling Stone to make notes as he and Hill discussed the details. It was clear that Hill suspected that one of the high-profile offenders Garrett and Stone were going after was also responsible for these other cases.

The entire conversation only lasted seven or eight minutes, and that included the time Garrett wasted chatting up Hill and bragging about Stone to him. Clint waited another half hour before purposefully walking past Hill's desk, pretending to be heading somewhere.

Hill gave him a nod. "Hey, Wardell."

Clint slowed, and then stopped at Hill's desk. "How's the knee?"

"Still hurts."

"Did you take something for it?"

"Ibuprofen. They gave me Oxy, but I can't take that and still work."

Clint nodded. "How much longer before you're back to full duty?"

"Doctor says six weeks. I say four."

Clint tried to smile, something he knew he wasn't good at. "Didn't that strategy have a bad result once already?"

Hill spread his hands. "A wise African American detective once told me that correlation doesn't equal causation."

"Sounds like a smart guy."

Hill chuckled at that. "When did you develop a sense of

humor, anyway?"

"I have a sense of humor. I just don't find much use for it."

That made Hill laugh a little more.

Clint pointed at his knee. "Once that's better, you can get out there with the Anti-Crime Team."

"Yeah, I'm looking forward to that. I miss being part of the fun. I haven't been this excited about taking doors since I was in SWAT."

"What kind of doors?"

Hill lifted a sheet of paper. "On the menu currently, we have Alan Capehart, and Curtis Hiney, burglars extraordinaire, and Hanka Novakova, prolific car thief."

Clint nodded his approval. Even though his case load revolved around assaults, rapes, and murders, he was familiar with all three names. "Well, at least you're picking their targets. That's something."

"Some of it's me," Hill said. "But I work with Crime Analysis a lot."

Clint kept his reply neutral. Crime Analysis was good at some things, maybe even great at those things, but it wasn't the silver bullet the brass thought it was. "Focused on HPOs?"

"Mostly," Hill said. "But not just the ones Crime Analysis comes up with. Garrett's been a great resource, too. He's brought several dealers to the table, and those have been good busts."

"Drugs? I thought your emphasis was on high profile offenders and property crimes."

"It is. But why do hippos commit all the crimes they do? Ninety percent of the time, it's to get money for drugs. So popping a few dealers along the way just seems to make sense. We don't go out of our way to target them, but when something falls in our lap, we can't say no to that."

"Makes sense," Clint allowed.

It did, too, though not in the way Hill and the others thought it did. If Clint's suspicions were correct, it was just as likely that Garrett was targeting specific dealers for a reason other than reducing crime, or amassing stats for the bosses. He had his own ulterior motives.

Hill was eyeing him curiously. "Why are you so interested in ACT all of a sudden, Wardell?"

"Excuse me?"

"You heard the question," Hill said. "I know you did. You hear everything."

Clint shook his head. "I don't care about ACT at all. I'm only asking about it because that's the work you're doing now. It's called making conversation."

"And that's all?"

"That's all."

Hill kept his gaze on him. Clint wondered if he was remembering how he'd lied right to Hill's face a couple of years ago, at the height of the Garrett incident, and the savvy detective had called him on it.

Clint tried another pained smile. "Barber's orders," he said.

Hill seemed to accept that, or at least wasn't ready to call bull on it. "Okay. Look, I gotta get back to work, Wardell. These guys don't mess around, and my bet is they'll have one of these three within an hour of hitting the street."

"I understand." Clint left and walked back to his own desk.

His fishing trip had been a success, as far as he was concerned. He'd learned that Tyler Garrett was getting the Anti-Crime Team to target specific drug dealers, ones he pointed them toward.

That, Clint decided, was a very interesting and telling fact.

Chapter 27

When Gary Stone threw Tarik Floyd into the home entertainment center, it collapsed sideways. This caused the loud, boisterous hip-hop music that had been playing to abruptly end. Also, the flat-screen TV with a rerun of *Miami Vice* playing fell from its stand, smacking the supine Floyd in the face. Stone froze since he was amazed at the destruction he caused by swinging the man free of him.

With the music stopped and the pressed-plywood furniture crumpled to the ground, everyone else involved in the melee suddenly paused.

The entire Anti-Crime Team was inside unit E302 of the Red Hawk Apartments in north Spokane. Tyler Garrett, Ray Zielinski, and Jun Yang each actively fought with someone until the rhythmic *thump-thump-thump* of the music was silenced.

For a second, both officer and criminal alike looked around as if unsure to continue their respective brawls.

Then Tarik Floyd hollered in pain from the blow to his head and shoved the TV screen away from his bloodied face. The group fight immediately began again.

The donnybrook originally started when the full team arrived to arrest Akiem Mack. A notation in his record cited a propensity for fighting with law enforcement.

Prior to pulling into the parking lot of the Red Hawk Apartments, the Anti-Crime Team had successfully arrested the three targets that Sergeant Ragland had assigned. In less than four hours, Zielinski and Yang located two of the three wanted individuals. Garrett and Stone found the remaining want, Hanka Novakova, in a rolling-stolen Subaru as she left her boyfriend's house. She was unaware that Garrett and Stone were following her in the Gray Ghost. They were about to request a marked patrol vehicle execute a high-risk stop when Novakova pulled into a 7-Eleven convenience store. They arrested her without incident as soon as she exited her vehicle and impounded the stolen car.

Akiem Mack was the special project Tyler Garrett had taken to Marty Hill after roll call. Upon a quick review, Hill greenlighted the grab if time was available after securing the three Crime Analysis HPOs. Once Garrett and Stone booked Novakova, the team still had half a shift and no sergeant to watch over them.

When Garrett pounded on the door, Mack opened it. His eyes were red and his lids droopy. Loud hip-hop music thumped from a stereo and the smell of marijuana wafted outside. Mack was in his late twenties with skin the color of coffee mixed with too much cream. He was a handsome man lessened only by tattoos that jutted out from under the collar of his T-shirt and ran around his neck.

Garrett said, "Hey, man, can I ask you about the incident on South Riverton?"

Stone, who stood slightly off to Garrett's right with a good view of Mack, had no idea what his partner was talking about. He'd never heard of an incident on Riverton and wondered if it was a ruse.

Mack's eyes drifted lazily to Stone then back to Garrett. "Whatever," he said and opened the door.

When Garrett stepped inside, he pushed the door fully open. Stone followed him in and saw three other black males in the apartment. Two were sitting on a ratty couch and the third was sitting in a low-slung chair. There was a haze of marijuana smoke and he noticed a couple of plastic bongs sitting on the coffee table in front of the couch.

Stone began to relax. Even in his short career, he knew guys who smoked marijuana rarely fought. Several senior officers had even mentioned this tendency to him.

On the entertainment center was a large screen TV showing an episode of *Miami Vice* with subtitles and no sound. Loud music continued to play.

Zielinski and Yang followed the first two officers in and turned to the two on the couch. The senior officer said, "Keep your hands where I can see them."

"Turn the music off," Garrett ordered Mack.

"Yo!" Mack said, ignoring the order and waving toward Zielinski and Yang. "The hell is this?"

The man in the chair stood then. He was slightly over six feet tall and had a medium-length afro. His green T-shirt was printed with *Property of the Green Bay Packers*.

"That's Tarik Floyd," Garrett told Stone, his eyes on the man near the chair. "Watch him."

Floyd's eyes slanted at the revelation of his name.

"I said turn it down," Garrett angrily ordered Mack.

"Man, I said you anna white boy could come in, but you brought more cops. Nah, no more. Get out."

Garrett looked to Zielinski but pointed to the men on the couch. "I don't know those two. ID them."

Tarik Floyd began to move his shoulders in a silent dance.

"You all right?" Stone asked.

Floyd nodded.

"Akiem Mack," Garrett yelled over the music, "you're under arrest for the possession of cocaine with intent to distribute."

Mack blinked. "What?"

Garrett grabbed the man's upper arms and spun him around. He then grabbed Mack's right arm and put it in a wrist lock before removing a set of handcuffs from a back pocket. When the sound of the first cuff ratcheting around Mack's wrist cut through the music, all hell broke loose.

Tarik Floyd jumped into Stone, grabbing him by the ballistic vest and pushing him all the way to the far wall. Stone flailed at Floyd's arms, trying to break his grip, but Floyd was too strong.

A plastic bong exploded against the wall next to Stone's head, causing him to flinch. Someone had thrown it in his direction.

From the corner of his eye, he saw the other officers were suddenly fighting as well and there was no help coming. The two men from the couch had jumped up and were now fighting with Zielinski and Yang. Akiem Mack had turned to fight with Garrett, the set of handcuffs swinging wildly from his right wrist.

Stone grabbed Floyd's arms then twisted and stepped to the side, spinning the man to the right and slamming him into the wall. Floyd didn't release his grip on Stone, though. Instead, Floyd twisted violently back and slammed Stone into the wall they had just been on. Stone maintained his grip and continued the momentum, accelerating the man's eventual flight into the entertainment center and collapse to the floor.

Floyd yelled in pain when the television hit him in the face. After he pushed it off, it revealed a large cut across his forehead that was already gushing blood. Floyd rolled over to his hands and knees, but Stone jumped onto his back, driving him to the ground. Floyd exhaled loudly. The man struggled to get away from Stone as if he was swimming wildly on the carpet. Stone struggled to secure one of the man's arms.

A loud crash happened next to him. Ray Zielinski had slammed his suspect into the coffee table, demolishing it. He now pressed his knee into the back of the man's upper shoulders to pin him. Stone saw Zielinski already reaching for his handcuffs. That motivated Stone as he did not want to be the last one to gain control of his suspect.

Stone climbed up Floyd's back and slipped his arm under the man's chin, moving in position for the lateral vascular neck restraint.

Floyd stopped swimming and grabbed the officer's arm. "I give!" he yelled. "I give!"

Stone didn't know what happened. He'd never had anyone quit fighting that quickly. Floyd must have been put to sleep by another officer at some time. He let go of the sleeper hold, grabbed Floyd's right arm and twisted it behind his back. The man howled in pain. Stone hadn't applied too much pressure, so he knew Floyd was acting.

"Get up," Garrett told Akiem Mack.

Was Garrett already done fighting, too? Stone wondered.

He then realized how quiet the apartment had suddenly become as he finished handcuffing Floyd.

"My shoulder!" Floyd yelled. "You didn't need to tear it out of the socket!"

Stone stood and announced with satisfaction, "You're under arrest for third assault. And you're fine. Quit whining."

When Stone turned to the rest of the team, they were all watching him, even Yang. Each of them had their suspects in handcuffs as well.

Damn, he thought. He'd come in last.

The four suspects were seated cross-legged, about twenty feet apart from each other, on the sidewalk in front of the apartment building. The team huddled up as they waited for patrol vehicles to arrive to transport the arrested men to jail. A paramedic unit had already arrived and was bandaging Tarik Floyd's forehead.

"We need to document the damage to the apartment," Garrett said. He turned to Zielinski. "You two want to handle that and we'll handle the booking?"

Stone smiled. He knew Garrett was trying to protect them from doing some crappy detail and get them back on the street as fast as possible.

Zielinski smirked, motioning toward Stone. "It was the young buck who did all that damage. He should enjoy the spoils of his actions."

Garrett started to argue but seemed to think better of it. He turned to Stone. "Well, Captain Paperwork, you just got outvoted by the senior officer."

"What?"

"You break it, you bought it," Zielinski grumbled before walking off to talk with an arriving patrol unit.

"But he broke the coffee table," Stone said, looking to Yang.

She only shrugged in response.

Garrett and Stone stood in the living room of the quiet apartment. It was filled with broken furniture, the evidence of their brawl. A corporal and a patrol supervisor had already been to the scene. The corporal photographed the scene for evidentiary value in case Mack decided to sue the city and the supervisor gave the city some authoritative validity that the team's response was appropriate. In reality, the lieutenant's presence was cursory, consisting of listening to Garrett's brief rendition of what went down, before nodding his approval and heading back to his car. The real review of their actions would come later in the formal use-of-force report they would submit to Sergeant Ragland.

Stone's notebook was filled with scribblings that he'd made so he could remember exactly what had happened in the apartment, what had been broken, and in what order. They had made the arrests legally, but this would require another CYA report. He was learning to write them pretty well.

"What now?" Stone asked.

"We secure the door and leave."

Stone tapped his notebook. "Sounds good."

Garrett stepped further into the apartment.

"Where are you going?" Stone asked

"To check the apartment and make sure no one is hiding out."

"What? Why?"

"We were downstairs a long time," Garrett said, "and we left the apartment open. Someone could be hiding in here. If we lock up and leave, all they've got to do is come out and burglarize the place. We'd get blamed."

"Oh." He'd never even thought of that.

"Let's go," Garrett said, turning down the hallway. "I'll check the rooms and you observe. Make notes of what you see."

The senior officer first stepped into the bathroom. The vinyl curtain was pulled back in the shower, so no one was hiding in the tub. He then opened the cabinet doors underneath the sink.

"You think someone could be hiding there?" Stone asked.

The senior officer raised his eyebrows. "I've found people hiding everywhere. Better safe than sorry."

In the first bedroom, the covers were a mess on the bed. Garrett yanked them up off the floor, tossing them into a ball on the mattress. He then got onto his hands and knees to look under the bed.

Stone held his notebook in his hand. "Anything?"

"No."

Stone couldn't be sure, but he thought Garrett sounded disappointed. Maybe it was because he was bent over with his head under the bed. That's probably why he sounded different.

The senior officer stood and checked the closet. Some clothes were hung, but most of them were strewn about the floor. Garrett kicked them to the side with his boot. When he turned around, he shrugged.

Stone made an entry in his notebook.

The second bedroom was in similar condition as the first. Garrett lifted the bedding that had slipped to the floor back onto the mattress. He then dropped to his hands and knees to look under the mattress.

"Anything?"

"Maybe."

Garrett reached his hand under the bed and pulled out a brown leather suitcase. He lifted it onto the bed, unzipped it, and flipped it open. Inside the case were several clear plastic bags of white powder. Next to the bags were multiple rolls of bills. More than ten, maybe as many as twenty.

"Wow..." Stone said.

Garrett pursed his lips and nodded. He hung his arm around Stone's shoulder.

"How much do you think is there?" Stone asked him.

"Money or dope?"

"Either?"

Garrett shrugged. "I don't know, but it's a lot either way."

"Yeah."

They stared at it for a bit. Garrett glanced at Stone then turned his attention back to the suitcase. He rubbed his chin, lost in his own thoughts.

Stone studied the cash and the dope. It was a good bust, one that would get them some more recognition, but they had a problem. They were sweeping the house for possible people, not searching for evidence. Legally, they could only look in places where a person might hide. Garrett might be able to convince a judge that someone could hide in a cabinet under the bathroom sink, but in a suitcase?

How were they going to make sure this evidence was admissible?

Stone looked over at Garrett. "What are you thinking?" he asked.

"I was thinking about Akiem Mack."

"What about him?"

"How's a guy like that get this much cash?"

"Drugs," Stone said.

"I get that, but don't you want to know how? I mean, it's not like he's working hard. We show up in the afternoon and he's sitting around smoking weed and watching TV. That doesn't seem like that hard of a life, does it?"

"I don't know, but I'm not that interested in smoking weed."

"What about that money?"

Stone picked up one of the rolls of bills and examined it. "I don't know if I've ever had that much money in my life." He tossed it back into the suitcase.

Garrett fell quiet again, his eyes drifted to Stone then back to the suitcase.

Stone watched him silently, knowing the senior officer was about to say something important. It had to be because Tyler Garrett never hesitated to speak his mind. He was confidence personified. The man knew what he wanted immediately and went after it. Hesitation in Garrett was something new and it intrigued Stone.

Finally, Garrett lowered his head and softly asked, "What do you say we put the drugs on property, and we split the cash?"

"What?"

Garrett's eyes bored into him. "The cash. Let's split it. You and me."

Stone's brow furrowed before a nervous smile played at his lips. "Are you…are you messing with me?"

Garrett didn't say anything but turned his attention back to the suitcase.

"It's not right," Stone whispered.

"It's not? Look how much is there. It's untaxed. How hard did Mack work for that?"

"He's going to jail for it."

"He's going to jail for some previous probable cause. He's made this money *since* then. Look at how much money he's making." Garrett grabbed two rolls of bills and held them up. "We're busting our asses, fighting guys like him, putting our lives on the line, but *they're* the ones making bank. Not us."

"It's not right," Stone repeated.

Does Ty really want to do this?

The senior officer clenched his jaw and closed his eyes. A moment later he began nodding. When he opened his eyes, he put his hand on Stone's shoulder. "You're right, Stoney."

Stone searched his partner's eyes, wondering what the other man was thinking.

Garrett grabbed his portable radio and lifted it to his mouth. "Tango-thirteen," he said.

Stone lifted his eyebrows questioningly.

"Tango-thirteen," the female dispatcher said, "go ahead."

"Thirteen, have the supervisor and the corporal return to our location."

"Copy, thirteen."

Garrett looked at Stone. "We need to get this on property, but I want a supervisor to see this and to get a corporal to photograph it. There's enough here for anyone to question this and we need to do it right, aboveboard all the way."

Stone nodded in approval. They still had to figure out exactly how the drugs and money would be admissible evidence, but he was confident they'd find a way.

"We need to do this right," Garrett muttered, staring at contents of the suitcase.

Stone patted his friend on the shoulder. "Zielinski and Yang are going to have kittens when they hear what we found."

Chapter 28

Captain Tom Farrell knocked on the door to the chief's office. A moment later, he heard Baumgartner's brusque voice bellow, "Come!" so he pushed the door open and went inside.

"Close the door behind you," Baumgartner said.

In years past, whenever a boss asked him to do that, it usually presaged some kind of ass-chewing. Since he'd asked for this meeting, he didn't think one was coming, but a stab of concern spiked in the pit of his stomach all the same. It was a feeling he was getting more and more used to these days.

The chief waited until he settled into the chair in front of the big mahogany desk before speaking. "What can I do for you, Tom?"

"I wanted to talk with you about ACT and Sergeant Ragland."

Baumgartner made an expression somewhere between a grimace and a smile. "A popular subject these days." When Farrell looked at him askance, he added, "I had breakfast with Mayor Sikes this morning."

"How'd that go?"

"Not as painful as usual." Baumgartner shook his head. "He couldn't stop talking about the Anti-Crime Team. He's getting a lot of mileage out of them. He even has a new slogan he's dropping at community meetings when it comes up."

"I'm afraid to ask."

Baumgartner raised his hands and made air quotes, affecting the mayor's smooth politician's voice as he recited, "'The time to *act* is now.'"

"Typical," Farrell muttered.

"It seems to play well."

"Good thing we didn't go with Strike Team for a name."

Baumgartner smiled slightly. "I'm starting to regret vetoing that idea." He leaned back in his chair. "Like I've said before, being in the mayor's good graces has its advantages. He is easier to deal with when it comes to other police matters, and he spends more of his time poking his nose into Utilities or Parks and Rec instead of us."

"That's a good thing, I suppose."

"It's a very good thing. When Sikes gets too focused on us, he tries to run the department from the seventh floor of city hall. Instead of fighting for what we need in terms of resources, I end up fighting to remind him that it's *my* job to run the department. It eats up a lot of time and energy."

Farrell nodded. He'd seen what the chief described firsthand.

"Luckily," Baumgartner continued, "ACT is the flavor of the month. With that and the issues on the city council, the mayor doesn't have time to meddle."

"What issues?" He remained concerned that there was a problem waiting for him.

Baumgartner gave him a surprised look. "You don't read the paper, Tom?"

Farrell shrugged. "Of course I read it. I wish I didn't, though."

"I could do without it sometimes, too. You know, in most cities, you end up with a major newspaper that dominates the market, and some kind of alternative that still has a pretty high profile. The two usually represent the two sides of the political spectrum, conservative and liberal. Which perspective is dominant and which is the loyal opposition depends on the prevailing views of the population in the region."

Farrell wondered why he was getting a political science lecture. "Your point?"

"My point is we have a conservative region, so the newspaper of record is generally conservative. Our alternative, *The Inlander*, is liberal. In most cases, conservative papers are pretty supportive of the police department, but we seem to have the one conservative, cop-hating paper in the entire country."

Farrell realized that there wasn't anything lurking in the tall grass of the chief's conversation. This was just another one of their frequent talks, which amounted to part briefing, part strategizing, and part shooting the breeze. "That might be a little overstated," he said.

"Maybe a little," Baumgartner admitted. "But I'm just saying, I can see why you don't like reading the newspaper."

"I still read it, though." Farrell thought for a moment. "Are you talking about the special elections, or something new?"

"No, it's the elections. The mayor is all wound up about them."

"He should be. All three of the vacant seats used to belong to supporters."

Farrell was still amazed at how quickly three different councilmembers had fallen from grace, one after another, just a few months ago. First, Justin Buckner came under fire for his relationship with his nineteen-year-old babysitter. He ended up lasting the longest of the three embattled councilors, but still ultimately resigned.

Patrick Armstrong's downfall was much seedier and involved him taking significant money in kickbacks for undue influence. Farrell wouldn't be surprised if formal charges eventually came in Armstrong's case, a concern that the mayor no doubt worried about, too. The mayor had been distancing himself from Armstrong steadily since the revelation of the councilman's dirty dealings came to light.

The final vacancy on the council came when Dennis Hahn resigned in humiliation after his affair with an underage girl was discovered. The girl, Bethany Rabe, had tragically taken her own life, adding fuel to the controversy. Hahn had likely been on the path to council president, and perhaps mayor, so the fall was a precipitous one. The police department's handling of the investigation had also been scrutinized, leading to a three-day suspension for Baumgartner and the removal of Gary Stone from his position within city hall. Fortunately, they avoided the worst of possible outcomes. Hahn's career, however, was destroyed for good.

Farrell didn't feel badly for any of the three departing councilmen. He hoped that whoever filled those seats was an upgrade but was skeptical that would be the case. He'd seen up close how politics worked.

"I'm glad to see all three gone," Baumgartner said. "Or I thought I was, until I started thinking about the possibility that we'd get someone worse to replace them."

"Is that what's happening? I haven't been watching the early polls."

Baumgartner sighed deeply. "How can you know?" he lamented. "Most of the candidates are political unknowns, so I'd be guessing based strictly on their backgrounds. That's an assumption that might not be entirely accurate."

"Is the mayor worried?"

"A bit. Two of the three seats look like they'll go to women candidates. If they join forces with Margaret Patterson, it'll make for a powerful voting bloc."

"And Patterson hates us."

"She hates *me*," Baumgartner said. "I think she'd be happy to find a way to get me fired. But hate the department?" He shook his head. "I don't think so. If I have her pegged correctly, it's not about hate or love for her. It's about what is most useful."

Farrell nodded. *Typical politician.* "Who's got the lead for the third seat?"

"Cody Lofton," Baumgartner told him.

Farrell's brow shot up in surprise. "The mayor's old chief of staff?"

"The very same."

"That's…interesting."

"Isn't it, though?" Baumgartner smiled slightly. "Sikes barely beat Lofton in the mayoral election, and now he might have to deal with him week-in and week-out if he's elected to city council."

"The fur will fly if that happens. I'd like to see that."

"The fur will most definitely fly," Baumgartner said. "I don't know how much of it will be in public, though. Lofton is pretty savvy. He'll do whatever's smart."

"I hope smart equals supporting the police department."

"So do I. If ACT keeps hammering bad guys and if the crime stats go down as a result, that goes a long way toward making it a smart move for councilmembers to get behind us and ride the wave, regardless of their politics." Baumgartner looked at him pointedly. "The team needs to keep stacking up felonies."

"I'm not worried about them doing that," Farrell said. "But I am worried about Ragland."

It was more than Ragland, though. He worried about whether he would be able to manipulate the pieces into the right place on the board so that he could claim checkmate on Officer Tyler Garrett. He worried about what Garrett might be getting away with every day he kept the team in play. He worried that taking down Garrett at some point also took down ACT and destroyed all the good work the team was doing. But he couldn't tell the chief most of that, so he stuck with what he could share.

"What's the problem with Ragland?" the chief asked.

"He's dragging his feet. He doesn't seem engaged."

"Is he hitting their roll calls?"

"As best I can tell, yes."

"Directing their activity?"

Farrell nodded. "Between Detective Hill and Crime Analysis, I think that piece is pretty solid."

Baumgartner shrugged. "Then don't worry about it, Tom. These guys are all good cops. They only need a light hand to keep them on the rails."

"Yes, sir." Farrell hoped his voice didn't betray his reservations. "I'd just be a lot happier if Sergeant McGinn were still running things. He was boots on the ground with this team."

"So would I. But we'll have to make do with Ragland until he gets back."

"I know."

Baumgartner considered him a moment. Then he said, "It'll be fine, Tom."

Farrell wished he had the easy confidence of the chief, but he didn't. Even as he tried to close in on Tyler Garrett, exposing the man or catching him dirty seemed further away than ever. He could feel control of the situation slowly but deliberately slipping out of his grasp.

"I'm sure you're right," he told Baumgartner.

Chapter 29

"Can I ask you something?" Jun Yang asked.

Roused from his thoughts, Ray Zielinski glanced over at her. They were headed to pick up one of the hippos that Marty Hill kept on the back burner for whenever the team zipped through their targets quickly, like they had today. As they drove, Zielinski had been brooding on what to do about Darold Barden. He had to help Neil, but he didn't see a safe way to do it, either. It was a problem. Whenever he managed to put that out of his mind, concerns about Garrett and Stone came flooding in. He needed a drink, and that wasn't a feeling he usually had during a shift.

"What is it?" he asked Yang.

"Why don't I ever get to drive?"

Zielinski considered the question for a few moments, then looked back at the road. "Are you old enough to drive?"

Yang snorted. "I'm twenty-seven."

"You look like you're still in high school."

"That sounds a little racist."

Zielinski shot her a quick look, but saw the slight smile playing on her lips, and so he relaxed. "You know what this team reminds me of?"

"Let me guess. *Top Gun*?"

"No. Not at all."

"I thought you were calling Garrett and Stone something from that movie."

"I was. Maverick and Goose."

"That's it. You know, I googled the movie. It's about fighter pilots."

"I know. I'm the one quoting from it."

"I tried to watch it, but I didn't last ten minutes. It was too macho—"

"Macho?"

"—and too corny."

"Yeah? Well, I tried to watch that crouching dragon movie you mentioned, and it sucked, too."

Yang looked at him suspiciously. "Did you really?"

"No."

"Well, I can't say much. I haven't watched it, either." They rode in silence for a few seconds. Then she asked, "What's the team remind you of?"

"Oh." Zielinski realized he'd lost the train of thought. All it took was a short trip down the Tom Cruise rabbit hole. "It's another movie you probably haven't seen. *The Breakfast Club*."

"Are you kidding? I love *The Breakfast Club*."

He looked sideways, trying to read her expression. "Are you busting my balls again?"

"No," she said. "I've seen it a bunch." She lowered her voice and sang, *"Don't you...forget about me..."*

"Hmmm," Zielinski grunted, mildly surprised.

"It doesn't strike me as your kind of movie, though," Yang said.

"I'm more complex than you think."

"Maybe," Yang allowed. "So you're saying we're like the kids in the movie?"

"Kind of."

"Who's the jock and who's the princess, then?"

Zielinski shook his head. "It's not a one-for-one thing like that. I just mean how we're all so different from each other."

"We're all cops," Yang asserted.

"Sure, but beyond that." Zielinski lifted his hand from the wheel and raised a finger to count.

"Will you keep your hands on the steering wheel, please?"

"I've got it," Zielinski said. He raised his left hand briefly, then grabbed onto the lower half of the wheel again.

"Two hands?"

"Relax. I was driving before you were out of diapers."

Yang gave him a light scowl. After a moment, it faded. She said, "Okay, you're right. The math works."

Zielinski raised his index finger again. "Back to the movie. We got a black, hot-shot SWAT guy—"

"Which is basically the jock," Yang interjected.

He stopped. "Are you going to let me do this?"

She motioned for him to continue.

Zielinski waved his finger again. "The black, hot-shot SWAT cop—"

"Jock," Yang said quietly.

He ignored her, raising another finger. "The white, former Chief's Bitch—"

"Who?"

"Stone."

"Why is he called—"

"Never mind."

"So what you're saying is Gary's the nerd."

"Basically." He raised another finger. "There's the old man..."

"Ooh," Yang said. "You're the cranky principal."

Zielinski eyed her.

"That's a character in the movie. He's the mess-with-the-bull, get-the-horns guy."

"I know, but I am *not* the principal."

"Says you. So who am I?"

"You're the Asian, rookie female."

"I get to be three things?"

Zielinski shrugged. "It is what it is."

"I don't think I'm the princess or the basket case...and, if you're not the principal, who are you in this scenario? The delinquent?"

No. If that's anyone, it's Garrett.

"I told you," he said. "It's not one-for-one. It's more of a concept match."

Yang shook her head. "I think you're the principal. What was his name?"

"Vernon, but I'm not like him."

"I could make a wardrobe joke that might change your mind."

Zielinski looked away, and returned his right hand to the wheel, feigning exasperation. "Forget I said anything."

"No, you brought it up. Let's see it through. Are you saying we need to come together like the kids did in the movie?"

Zielinski thought about it. Mostly, he'd just been making an observation, and the easy banter with Yang actually made him forget Barden for a few minutes. It even softened his concerns about Garrett and Stone, and the result was that his stomach quit hurting as bad. Now that it was moving from chit-chat to something serious, the joy of it left him.

"I doubt that'll ever happen," he said, his tone grim.

"Why not?"

"If you gotta ask," he said, "then maybe you aren't as smart as I thought you were."

The vibe in the car shifted with his comment. Yang stopped talking to him, and he could tell he'd made her angry. He tried to tell himself he didn't care, but he knew that wasn't true. He liked her and thought she had the makings of a good cop. But he also resented her naïveté. It had been a long time since he'd seen the world the way she seemed to see it.

As they drove in silence, his concerns about Garrett and Stone rose to the forefront of his thoughts again. Stone seemed to be turning into a Garrett clone. If he was right in his suspicions about Garrett, then that was a dangerous thing for Stone. He wished he could share his thoughts with Yang, but he didn't want to burden her. Besides, he wondered if she would understand. He was in the middle of it all and wasn't entirely sure *he* understood.

They turned onto Ostrander Street, parking a few houses away from the target address. Zielinski grabbed the clipboard between them containing the booking photo of Chad Hewitt.

Hewitt barely qualified as a hippo, but he always seemed on the fringes of several of the higher end hippos that Hill was investigating. The detective had suggested that Hewitt might be developed into a possible confidential informant, if he could be flipped. He had two charges for possession of stolen property (PSP) to use as leverage, so Zielinski and Yang's mission was to arrest the suspect and bring him down to the station so Hill could interrogate him.

Zielinski took a long look at the man's features, before he held it out to Yang. She glanced at it, then nodded.

Wordlessly, the two of them exited the Bronze Beast and made their way to the house. Ideally, they'd have another team or a patrol officer to watch the back door, but Hewitt had been deemed such a low risk that they decided to forego those measures. Yang took up a position at the corner of the house, her view of the side and part of the rear somewhat compensating for the lack of an officer at the back of the house.

Zielinski rapped authoritatively on the door. After a short time, it opened. He recognized Hewitt's wispy mustache and stringy hair. "Hey, Chad," he said gruffly, showing his badge. "We need to talk."

Hewitt hesitated. "About what?"

"Inside," Zielinski said, giving Yang a wave. He stepped forward, and Hewitt retreated into the living room.

As soon as all three of them were together in the room, Hewitt's attitude shifted. "What's this about?" he demanded.

"There's a detective who wants to talk to you," Zielinski told him.

"What detective?"

"Marty Hill."

"I don't know him."

"He knows you. So how about we go down to the station so he can take care of whatever business it is he needs to take care of, huh?"

Hewitt glanced from Zielinski to Yang and back again. "I

don't think so. In fact, I'd like you to leave."

"We're not leaving."

Hewitt pointed and shouted, "I want you out of my house, *now!*"

Yang drifted away from Zielinski, triangulating Hewitt. She moved smoothly, projecting no menace, but Hewitt still noticed her. He dropped into a crouch and lifted his hands. "Get out of my house!" he repeated.

Zielinski didn't want to fight again today. Although his adrenaline had kicked in at the apartment with the four suspects, there was no chemical reaction happening here. He felt almost bored and that, he knew, was dangerous.

"I don't want to fight with you," he told Hewitt evenly.

"Then get out of my house."

"I can't," Zielinski said, keeping that same easy tone in his voice.

"Sure you can. Just turn your fat ass around and leave." Hewitt looked sideways at Yang. "Both of you."

Zielinski held up his hands to placate him. "Unfortunately, Chad, I'm here now, and you've got a couple of warrants, so I can't leave."

"Warrants? That's bull!"

"It's true," Zielinski countered.

"For what?"

"Some chintzy PSP charge." Zielinski shrugged. "It's not a big deal, but it's still a warrant, and the detective wants to talk to you."

"I didn't do whatever it is you're saying I did."

"Okay."

"So the warrant's no good."

"It doesn't work that way. The warrant is signed by a judge, so for now, it's good. I can't just walk away now that I'm here, or I'm in contempt of court. I have no choice but to arrest you. The only question is which way it goes."

Hewitt eyed him suspiciously. "What do you mean, which way?"

"I mean, you can fight with us, if you want. Maybe you'll do okay, but if we don't start winning right away, we'll just call for more cops. They'll show up fighting mad, and no matter how long it takes, there'll eventually be a blue pile of bodies on top of you. That way, you go to jail with a beating and new charges. Or…" he trailed off.

Hewitt took the bait. "Or what?"

"Or you come peacefully, talk to the detective, see a judge in the morning, and get back here in time for lunch tomorrow." Zielinski gave him a passive look. "Up to you."

Hewitt seemed to consider it for a while. Zielinski waited patiently. Finally, the man's shoulders sagged, and he let out a sigh. "Fine," he said. "But don't make the cuffs too tight. I got sensitive wrists."

Zielinski handcuffed Hewitt without incident and searched him. Aside from a lighter, he found nothing. Per Hewitt's request, he left the lighter on the coffee table. The trio moved out onto the porch to wait for the patrol car to arrive for transport. He'd considered just putting Hewitt in the back of the Bronze Beast. He doubted the man would be any trouble, but the tactic was a policy violation. If Hewitt freaked out on the way to the station, there'd be hell to pay, and Zielinski didn't need any trouble right now. Not with the Barden problem hanging over his head.

The patrol response seemed to take an inordinate amount of time. When the uniform finally arrived, it was a younger officer with an irritated expression. Zielinski didn't recognize him, but his nametag read Sonntag.

"What's up?" Sonntag asked, his lip curling as he spoke.

"We need you to take Chad down to see Detective Hill," Zielinski said.

"What am I, a taxi?"

Zielinski's eyes narrowed. "Some days, yeah."

Sonntag snorted. "Do you know how many calls are stacked up on the screen right now?"

"No."

"Lots. And they'll keep stacking while I'm ferrying your guy down to the station. Meanwhile you ACT prima donnas get to run around and play."

Zielinski gave Sonntag a hard look. If the officer had more than five or six years on, he'd be surprised. He was way too young to be this salty. "I don't know what to tell you. The Bronze Beast doesn't have a shield."

"Then maybe one of your teams should drive an unmarked instead," Sonntag said. "That way you'd be self-sufficient."

Zielinski started to answer how it would be hard to run surveillance that way but decided not to continue the argument. "I'll bring it up," he said.

"Yeah, I'm sure you will," Sonntag replied, the sarcasm in his voice unmistakable. He motioned toward Hewitt. "Come on, bozo. Let's go."

Hewitt glanced at Zielinski. "Can he call me that?"

Zielinski shrugged. "He just did."

Sonntag tugged on Hewitt's arm. "I said, let's move it."

The officer escorted Hewitt to the marked patrol car where he was searched again before being placed in the back seat. Sonntag got behind the wheel and drove off without glancing toward Zielinski or Yang again.

There was no need for them to follow with any haste. Marty Hill would take some time to interview Hewitt before he and Yang would have to walk the man over to jail and book him on his warrants. Zielinski decided that he'd go through a coffee stand on the way to the station. There was plenty of time for that.

Plenty of time to worry some more about Barden again, too. Or Garrett and Stone.

His stomach twinged in pain. He reached into his pocket and withdrew a roll of Rolaids. Expertly, he flicked his thumb and popped a chalky tablet into his mouth.

"Hey," Yang said. "You mad at him?"

Zielinski shook his head, chewing. "Nope. He's got a point. We ought to consider having a unit with a shield in it."

"Maybe." She hesitated, then asked, "If you're not mad at him, what's bugging you?"

"Nothing," Zielinski said.

He stepped off the porch and headed back toward the Bronze Beast. After a few moments, Yang followed.

Chapter 30

The money was stacked in hundred-dollar increments. Each row had ten stacks, equaling a thousand dollars. There were twenty-two rows. Twenty-two thousand dollars.

Tyler Garrett's hand hovered over the bills.

"Want to take a picture before we package it?" Gary Stone asked. "Sort of like a trophy."

Garrett glanced at his partner. "Like hunters do?"

"I guess."

Garrett turned his attention back to the cash. "I'll pass. Feel free to take a photo for yourself."

"That's okay," Stone said. "I don't need it." Disappointment was evident in his voice.

The senior officer didn't care, though. He grabbed one of the sequentially numbered, clear plastic evidence bags and labeled it with a case number, his name, and officer number. He then put one thousand dollars into it and pulled the self-adhering strip, securing it closed. When he was done, he passed the bag to Stone who dutifully logged it onto the property sheet.

Garrett quietly filled several of these bags, his mind working through different problems. For his part, Stone remained silent as he completed his paperwork.

"Doesn't seem right," Garrett finally muttered.

"What's that?" Stone said as he entered another bag onto the evidence log.

"We take all sorts of risks protecting the city and its citizens and the union has to fight for us every couple of years to get us a two percent raise and protect our benefits from being eroded away a little at a time."

Stone muttered, "Uh-huh."

"Then guys like Akiem Mack," Garrett lifted a stack of bills, "make this kind of money hardly taking any risks at all."

"He's going to jail," Stone said. "That's a pretty big risk."

"You think so?"

Stone stopped writing. "Don't you?"

"If he thought it was that big of a risk," Garrett said, "wouldn't he do something else?"

"Maybe he doesn't see that he has many options available. I think he does, but maybe he doesn't think so."

The senior officer shook his head. "That's not what I meant. Look at it this way, a contractor is building a new tower downtown and a piece of machinery breaks. Oops. That happens. A guy walks off the job. Okay, hire a new man. Hell, a guy could get killed. Stuff happens. It's the cost of doing business, right? Going to jail is the same thing to these guys."

"I don't think you can equate that to selling drugs."

Garrett stuffed a stack of bills into a clear bag and sealed it. When he passed it to Stone, he said, "You're probably right. It just irks me, is all."

Stone dropped the bag onto the table and entered its info on the property sheet. "I get it, Ty. I really do."

Garrett didn't want to think about the money any longer. They still had several stacks to pack and log, then they would move onto the drugs. He wanted to talk about something else. "What's going on with Jean?"

"What do you mean?"

"Is there something between you two?"

Stone smiled but kept his eyes on the paper. "We're just friends. Have been for years now. She's the best."

Garrett turned to look at him then. Stone remained smiling as he wrote, probably thinking about Jean. He wanted to ask further about her but decided now wasn't the time. There would be an opportunity later to probe that subject. Garrett believed it to be another weak point for Stone, one that he would be able to exploit at another time. He would continue to watch Stone to figure out how to go about it.

For now, though, he needed to sit and wait. He'd already pushed too hard and too fast for today.

Now, things were in Gary Stone's court.

Chapter 31

Jun Yang stared into her coffee. She'd just left the department after finishing her shift with Ray Zielinski. Before leaving, though, she checked her department email account, a habit she'd gotten into doing after her first field training officer explained it was good practice.

Unfortunately, Captain Farrell had sent her an email requesting a coffee meeting after work. She had told her parents she would help clean the shop again. Accepting the meet would mean a late night for her.

She initially thought about ignoring the captain's email and telling him that she hadn't seen it until she arrived in the morning. That would have been a lie, though. While others believed little white lies were harmless, she didn't. They always led to something bigger.

For a moment, she wondered why so-called harmless lies were called *white lies*. She decided not to linger on the thought. She tried hard to avoid going down the rabbit hole of racism, even latent bigotry from generations past. If she lingered on it, she believed, she gave power to it. That was something she refused to do.

Instead, Yang had texted Farrell that she was available to meet as requested. He responded almost immediately and suggested they meet at the Perkins restaurant on Division Street. She arrived before him and ordered a coffee. Unlike most people, she didn't have a problem falling asleep after drinking caffeine late in the evening.

Motion at the front of the restaurant caught her eye. Captain Farrell walked in and glanced around. He wore a club shirt, faded jeans, and flip-flops. His normally perfect hair was slightly mussed. When he saw Yang, he lifted his chin in acknowledgement and headed her way.

He dropped into the booth and slid across. "Thanks for meeting me," he said.

She nodded once.

A server approached the table and asked Farrell if he wanted anything.

"A cup of decaf," he said. "That'll do it."

When the woman left, Farrell turned his attention to Yang. "How are things?"

"With me or the team?" she asked. There was more edge to her voice than she intended, and Farrell seemed slightly taken aback.

"Your choice," the captain said.

"The team is fine."

"You guys are getting lots of arrests. Making a big dent in crime."

"Yes," Yang said, slightly wiggling the handle of her coffee cup.

"Everyone is getting along well?"

The young officer stopped playing with her cup. "Does that matter?"

"Sure, of course it matters."

"The mission was to impact crime," Yang said. "and ACT is doing exactly that. We weren't mandated to get along."

Farrell's brow furrowed and he frowned. He was obviously displeased by her answer.

"Something wrong, Captain?"

"I've not had such a young officer be that disrespectful before."

Yang crossed her arms and leaned back. "I apologize if I came across as disrespectful. I didn't mean that. I was only trying to be matter of fact. Why would our feelings matter in this situation?"

"I'm worried about team cohesion. If the team fractures, things can fall through the cracks."

She considered what he said before answering. "Ray and I work well together. Ty and Gary work well together. When the four of us must work together, we do so. The results speak for themselves."

Her response seemed to intrigue Farrell and he cocked his head. "But there's something wrong with the four of you?"

"That's not what I said."

"Then I don't understand."

Yang inhaled deeply before answering. "Ray and Ty, they don't like each other. Whatever it is, Ray won't tell me, but it's there and it's obvious. And Ty tolerates me. Mostly I think it's because I'm new. Maybe it's because I'm a woman, but I doubt it. He doesn't treat other female officers the way he treats me."

"And Ray and Gary?"

"Ray called Gary the Chief's Bitch."

Farrell winced. "To his face?"

"No. I'm guessing it had something to do with his Special Police Problems position. I think Gary knows Ray doesn't really respect him."

"What about you? Do you like Gary?"

She thought about his question. She did like Gary, and, at moments, she liked him in a way that might be inappropriate for two officers on the same team to feel about each other. At other times, though, when Gary was basking in the shine of Tyler Garrett, she wasn't sure if she liked him at all. "Gary is fine."

The server brought Farrell's coffee and set it in front of him. She checked Yang's coffee and asked, "Need a refill, hon?" Yang smiled slightly and shook her head. The woman headed off.

"Have you noticed anything unusual occurring?" Farrell asked.

The young officer stared into her coffee cup and remained silent.

"Jun?" Farrell said.

She looked up.

"What is it?" the captain asked, an expectant look on his face.

"Why are we having this conversation here?"

"What?"

"Why aren't we meeting in your office?"

Farrell's eyes slanted briefly then relaxed. "Because I didn't want your teammates to see you talking with me."

"Why?"

"I want you to be comfortable speaking freely with me. If you were worried about the others seeing you, then you might hold back."

Yang's hand covered her coffee cup, feeling the little remaining warmth from the liquid inside. "Why me?"

Farrell watched her but remained quiet.

"Why did you put me into this role? Into this situation?"

"Because I knew you would be honest."

"You want me to be a rat."

"*Is* there something for you to rat on?"

Her smile was sad. "See? That's what I mean. I didn't leave the Army to become an informant, to join Internal Affairs."

"What do you want to be?"

"I want to be me, Jun Yang, patrol officer."

Farrell gave her an appraising look. Then he said, "Look, you're not on the team to tattle, Jun. I don't care about someone being rude to a suspect or parking in a handicapped slot."

"Then what are you worried about?"

"Bigger issues."

"Like what?"

"I don't know yet. Teams like this can take on a life of their own. That's why we need a dedicated sergeant to watch over them. With Sergeant McGinn on a leave of absence, things are looking a little dicey."

"Isn't this a conversation to have with your new sergeant?"

Farrell opened his mouth to answer then stopped to

reconsider his words. When he finally spoke, he asked, "You were a sergeant in the army, right?"

"I was, yes."

"Did you ever meet an NCO that was just waiting for retirement?"

She nodded. She'd met several noncommissioned officers who had mentally checked out early before leaving the service.

"So you'll understand this. I can't have a team that's full of hard chargers being led by someone who's retired-on-duty. Bad things are eventually going to happen. Understand?"

She thought he made a simple argument, but she didn't want to belabor the point any further. The donut shop floors still needed to be mopped before she could go home. "I understand," she said in hopes it would end the conversation.

"You're not on the team to spy, Jun. You're my safety mechanism, especially now that the sergeant is not a strong leader. Other than that, your job is to keep kicking ass and taking names."

Yang studied his face. He seemed earnest, as if he was trying hard to not only convince her, but himself as well. Regrettably, his words didn't help to alleviate that she felt like a fake.

Worse than that—a rat-in-waiting.

Chapter 32

Wardell Clint felt odd.

He knew why. He was a man most comfortable with routine. That was why he imposed it even upon the random chaos that was police work. It wasn't absolutely essential, but it gave him some measure of control, and that, in turn, brought him comfort.

But he'd broken his routine.

For the second night in a row, he'd gone home after work. He hadn't tried to tail Tyler Garrett and monitor his activity. He hadn't looked for ways to bring the man down, even though he deserved it more than any cop he'd ever personally known. Instead, he drove home in his Crown Victoria.

For the last time.

His police car seemed like a part of him. He'd had it for over six years, which was an eternity in a police fleet. The Crown Vic was more than just a car to him. It had been his only companion on many a late night, especially over the past two years. He had secreted his documentation on the Garrett case in a lockbox he kept in the trunk. Clint knew every inch of this car, and now it was time for him to turn it in to the barbarians at the garage so that they could issue him a damn Impala.

He tried to dredge up some resentment toward Lieutenant Flowers over the forced vehicle exchange, but he knew the man was only doing his job. If it wasn't him, it'd be someone else. The system was to rotate cars out of the fleet before the maintenance became cost prohibitive. He understood the reason. It was logical.

What wasn't logical was how sentimental he'd gotten about

the old car.

In the driveway of his small house, Clint turned off the engine. He sat in the driver's seat for a long while, soaking in the comfortable surroundings of the car's interior. Initially, he intended to take only a moment, but five minutes later, he was still sitting there.

This is stupid, he chastised himself. He grabbed his satchel off the passenger seat and got out of the car.

He'd cleaned out the interior earlier, before leaving the station. As it turned out, there wasn't much, and what he wanted to keep went into his satchel. Now, he slung that over his shoulder. At the rear of the vehicle, he unlocked the trunk and lifted the lid. Inside, he removed a larger bag with items he needed less often and set it on the ground. He reached deeper into the trunk and grabbed his camera. Deeper yet, his fingers found the cool metal of his lockbox. He flipped the latch he'd installed to keep it in place and pulled the box toward him.

The garage guys were going to wonder about that latch, he thought. Then he realized they probably wouldn't even notice it. They weren't big on detail, in his opinion.

Clint withdrew his pen light and shined it around the interior to make sure he'd left nothing behind. The trunk was empty.

He slammed the lid and slung the big bag over the same shoulder as his satchel. Next, he tucked the small lock box under his other arm and carried his camera bag with his free hand. Then he made his way carefully to his front door.

He had to put the camera down to unlock and open the door. Using his elbow and knee in tandem, he struggled through the doorway. To make it easier, he dropped the camera bag beside the couch, before closing and locking the door again. Then he put the big bag and his satchel on the dining room table that doubled as his case review location.

Lastly, he set the lockbox on the table in front of him and stared at it. He had a strong urge to open the box and review his notes again, but he knew that would suck him in, leading to a late night. That was something he couldn't afford. They were going to give him a new car tomorrow, and he needed to have a clear mind. There was no telling what special devices he might find on the Impala, hidden away by the brass.

That decided, Clint went to the kitchen and drank a glass of water. His mind was whirring, but that was normal. If he didn't land on one topic for too long, he might be able to sleep tonight.

Clint put the glass in the sink and went to the bedroom. He undressed methodically, brushed his teeth, and laid out his clothes for the next day. Then he turned back the covers of his bed and slid between crisp sheets. Finally, he snapped off the lamp.

But, as always, his mind continued to whir and sleep eluded him.

THURSDAY

Once you give a charlatan power over you,
you almost never get it back.
—Carl Sagan, astronomer

Chapter 33

"A pound and a half of cocaine," Gary Stone said. "Can you believe it?"

Jean Carter tilted her head. "A pound and a half? Is that a lot?"

"Are you kidding me? Some guys might go a whole career and not get a bust like that."

"Huh."

They were back at the Nordstrom Espresso Bar. They had moved their coffee time a little earlier today so that Stone would be able to join Tyler Garrett for a workout. Several of the tables around them were filled with patrons.

"Twenty-two grand plus that much coke," Stone said. "We're sure to get a commendation for it."

Jean sipped her latte. "And you fought the guy?"

"Oh man, Jean, I kicked his *ass*." An elderly woman looked in Stone's direction. He nodded at her but continued his story. "It was a crazy scene. The whole team was in a fight."

"With the same guy?"

Stone laughed at her. "No, not all. We were all fighting different guys. Four on four in a small apartment. It was wild. I threw my guy into an entertainment center, just demolishing it." He clapped his hands to add to the drama to his story.

"And you're proud of that?"

Stone paused, not comprehending her question.

Jean looked sad when she asked, "You're happy that you broke somebody's property?"

"We were fighting," Stone slowly said.

"I heard you."

"He was fighting with *me*," Stone said, tapping his chest,

"a cop."

"I know that."

"They were drug dealers, Jean."

"I get that, too."

"Then I don't understand what the problem is."

"The problem, boy-o, is that you're different."

Stone grasped it then. She still thought of him as the old Gary Stone—the friend she knew from college, the guy who worked at city hall. "I'm different, sure. But I'm also better. I'm not such a pussy anymore."

Jean cringed.

"I mean I'm not such a wimp."

She looked exasperated. "I always thought you were perfect the way you were."

Stone shook his head. "Of course, you would say that, but you weren't the guy getting walked on. I was. People never respected me, Jean." For a moment, the image of the bison flashed in his mind. "But they do now. No one pushes me around anymore."

She lowered her head and looked down at her coffee.

"Oh, man!" Gary exclaimed. "I almost forgot to tell you about this rolling stolen Garrett and I stopped yesterday. Freakin' hilarious. Wait 'til you hear this."

Jean checked her watch and said, "Listen, I've got to get back. Councilwoman Patterson needs a memo." She pushed her chair back and stood.

"A memo? I thought you had a few more minutes."

His friend looked as if she wanted to say something but was holding her tongue.

"What, Jean? Just spit it out."

"Okay, boy-o, I will. We've been here for ten minutes and do you know you never once asked how I was doing?"

Stone leaned back. "Yes, I did."

"No, you didn't because if you did, I would have told you that I was awarded city hall's employee of the month yesterday afternoon. It was kind of a big deal for me and I was excited to share it with you. Instead, all we've done is talk about you."

"I'm sure I asked how you were doing."

"No," Jean said, her voice stern, "*you* didn't. The old Gary would know he didn't ask and wouldn't try to convince me otherwise. I'm not sure what's going on with you, my friend, but you probably should take a hard look in the mirror and see if who you're becoming is worth the friends you're about to lose."

She turned and walked away.

"Jean!" Stone called as he hurried from his seat.

She stopped but didn't face him.

Stone ran over to her. "Hey, I'm really sorry. I didn't know."

Sadness washed over her face. "I know that."

"If I'd known, I would have asked about it. The award is a cool thing."

"I believe you. I really do." She was quiet for a moment, staring at him with a strange combination of knowledge and confusion in her eyes. "You've been my dearest friend for years, but you've changed. I would never have thought I needed to prompt you to ask me how my day was. Everything has never just been about you. Until recently."

He reached out and took her hand. "Want to sit down and tell me about it now?"

Jean shook her head. "Just call me after work. I'll tell you about it then."

"Okay," Stone said softly.

"Be safe out there, Gary."

As she left him standing in the middle of the mall, he just couldn't understand why she wouldn't like a new, more confident version of himself.

Chapter 34

Captain Tom Farrell walked into the restroom. The three-urinal, two-seater was situated outside of the detectives' division, and just down the hall from the command offices. He and the other senior leaders used it, along with the detectives. The chief had his own bathroom attached to his office, but sometimes he came down the hall, too. Farrell asked him why once, and Baumgartner told him that a lot of useful conversations started from bumping into people in the hallway on the way to the restroom.

As he stepped inside, he saw one man already at the far-left urinal. Instinctively, he took the far right. Once he'd gotten his business started, he glanced over and saw it was Officer Ray Zielinski.

Zielinski had his eyes closed and seemed to be working hard at what he was doing, so Farrell didn't say anything. He thought to himself that Baumgartner's theory had some validity, though. Running into Zielinski was fortuitous.

After a little while, Zielinski flushed. As he moved toward the sink, he noticed Farrell and gave the captain a bare nod. "Sir," he grunted.

Farrell nodded back. He finished and joined Zielinski at the sink. "How're things going?" he asked, washing his hands.

"Good."

"You guys are crushing crime, that's for sure."

Zielinski said unenthusiastically, "We're making some good arrests."

"What are you doing down here?"

The officer motioned with his head. "Getting some intel from Detective Hill before we head out." He shut off the water and moved to the towel dispenser.

"That's good." Farrell turned off his faucet and shook his wet hands into the sink. "How's the new sergeant working out?"

Zielinski didn't reply. He worked the lever on the paper towel dispenser several times and tore off the towel to dry his hands.

Farrell waited. Clint had told him about Zielinski's suspicions of Garrett, but the officer didn't know about the operation Farrell was running to bring down Garrett. So he wondered if his hesitation was more about a natural distrust of the brass, or something more.

When Farrell moved to the dispenser, Zielinski racked the lever a couple of times, exposing some paper towel for him. "Thanks," Farrell said, tearing it off. He dried off his hands, still not pressing for an answer to his question.

Eventually, Zielinski said, "I'm not too high on Kelly Ragland, if you want the truth."

"No?" Farrell opened the door, and he and Zielinski stepped out of the restroom. For the moment, the hallway around them was empty. "Why not?"

"He's not…very in charge."

Farrell nodded that he understood. "Is the team handling that all right?"

Zielinski gave a short shrug. "We make it work. You know how it is. We're cops."

"Adapt and overcome?"

"Exactly."

"How about you, Ray? Everything good with you?"

The officer looked slightly startled at the question. "Uh, yeah. I'm fine."

"And the new girl, Yang?"

Zielinski seemed to relax a little as the focus shifted from him. "She's solid."

"Garrett?"

"Garrett's Garrett." Zielinski's tone was clipped.

Farrell decided not to push further. "How about Stone?"

Zielinski hesitated. His expression shifted, as if he found the question distasteful. Or maybe it was his answer that he didn't like. Farrell waited to hear something tangible but was disappointed when Zielinski spoke. "Gary's doing all right. He's getting a little badge heavy, but he's…he's okay."

"Badge heavy?" Farrell asked. "In what way?"

He thought about the interaction he'd seen between Garrett and Stone at jail and wondered if Stone was being drawn too deeply into Garrett's sphere of influence. Was that what Zielinski meant?

Zielinski appeared to regret his choice of words. He stroked his mustache and cleared his throat. "Maybe badge heavy is the wrong way to put it. He's being more aggressive. He's just stepping up his game, I guess."

The captain waited for him to continue.

Zielinski shifted uncomfortably from one foot to the other. "There probably weren't a lot of opportunities to do real police work in Special Police Problems, so he's pretty eager, that's all."

Farrell stared at him, disappointed. At one time, he'd considered bringing Zielinski into his confidence, especially after Clint reported that the officer had come around asking about Garrett and expressing doubts about the man. He'd put Zielinski on the team in case the possibility of recruiting him to their cause became an option. Now it was apparent to him that the man was coolly keeping his distance, not sharing his true thoughts. Maybe he'd been wrong about Zielinski.

"I gotta get going, Captain," Zielinski said. He motioned toward the door leading to the Major Crimes Unit. "Hill has our marching orders, and everyone's waiting on me."

"Sure," Farrell said. "Thanks, Ray."

Farrell watched Zielinski walk away. He believed he was looking at a decent man, and a good cop, which explained the sinking feeling in his stomach. Zielinski hadn't exactly lied to him just then, but he hadn't been forthright, either. He'd hoped for more from the veteran officer. It was disheartening, and not what he'd expected from Zielinski.

He still had Yang, he thought. And maybe he could bring Clint back into the fold, though he wondered if the two of them would be enough. They had to be, he told himself, because he was risking everything, and failure wasn't an option he could afford to consider.

Despite that sentiment, Farrell couldn't shake the notion that the cards he was currently holding might not be strong enough to win.

Chapter 35

ESPN's *SportsCenter* played on the television in the officers' lounge, highlighting action from the previous night's Seattle Mariners game. The sound was off, but both Gary Stone and Tyler Garrett watched the replays.

"Nice catch," Garrett muttered as a fielder snagged a potential home run just over the left outfield wall.

"Very," Stone agreed. "The M's are playing some great defense this year."

"One game out of first. Their pitching needs to step it up, though, or it'll be the same ol' story."

When the highlights switched to the Yankees game, Stone glanced to Garrett. "Should we touch base with Marty now?" The detective was preparing a search warrant and had told them to wait in the lounge until he was done.

Garrett checked his watch. "He'll call us when he's ready. Relax, man. You're getting paid to watch *SportsCenter*. What more do you want?"

Stone leaned forward. "I'm anxious, I guess."

"There'll always be more bad guys to catch, Stoney. Be patient."

Stone dropped back in his chair and crossed his arms. He didn't want to watch television. He wanted to be outside in the sun, chasing criminals, putting them in jail. Even if they didn't have a warrant, they could go scare up someone noteworthy. Garrett had an uncanny ability for finding where they hid, and Stone wanted to learn how to duplicate the man's talent.

"Hey," Garrett said.

Stone rolled his head on the back of his chair so he could see Garrett.

"I'm sorry for losing it last night."

"What do you mean?"

Garrett glanced around before he said, "When I said the stuff about the money, it was wrong."

Stone didn't know what to say, so he just nodded.

"My wife is cleaning me out with her divorce attorney."

"Damn," Stone said. "I didn't know that."

"It's got me…it's got me all messed up in the head." Garrett turned his attention back to the television. The senior officer seemed embarrassed by the admission and Stone studied him closely.

From the moment of weakness of asking to keep a drug dealer's cash to now hearing Garrett's confession of how badly his divorce was going, Stone saw his patrolman role model through different eyes. Tyler Garrett wasn't just the best high-speed/low-drag cop on the department, he was a man who was hurting. Garrett is like the rest of us, Stone realized.

"I'm sorry," Stone muttered.

Garrett nodded. "I appreciate what you did. That's what a partner is supposed to do. Be by your side when things get sideways. Help keep things in perspective, you know? You were a real friend, Gary, and I'll never forget that."

A swell of pride grew inside Stone. He had helped Tyler Garrett in a moment of need. Not many people could claim that. "You can count on me," he said, his voice thick with emotion. It sounded corny when he said it, but he meant every word.

Garrett playfully punched Stone in the leg.

They sat in silence for several minutes, watching more highlights. Stone wondered what would have happened to Garrett if he hadn't been there to help the man. Would he have made a bad decision, or would he have seen the error in his thinking before it was too late?

The senior officer had done so much for him recently, helping him gain a new level of confidence and happiness that he didn't think he would ever get to repay him. He felt fortunate that life had given him just such an opportunity after walking through the fire created by his removal at city hall.

"We should hang out tomorrow night," Garrett said. "Maybe watch a game, drink a couple beers."

Stone brightened. "That would be great."

"All right. Let's do it."

"If you want, we can do it tonight. I don't have anything going on."

Garrett's smile was kind, almost apologetic. "I can't. I've already got plans, but tomorrow for sure."

"Yeah, no, tomorrow night. That sounds great."

"Will Jean be there?" Garrett asked.

"Jean? No. Why?"

"Just wondering."

Stone was about to ask why Garrett had been asking about Jean so much lately when the man asked him another question.

"Have you asked her out yet?"

"No. I told you, she's my friend."

"In that case, would you mind if I do?"

Garrett's eyes remained on the television. Stone didn't understand why his face suddenly warmed. Why was he bothered that Garrett wanted to go out with her? Would he be bothered if Jean said yes to the date? Jean and he were just friends, right?

"What about Tiana?" Stone asked, his voice suddenly sounding weak and whiny. "Aren't you still going out with her?"

Garrett nodded. "Yeah, sure, but Jean's cute. Almost librarian hot, if you know what I mean. If she said yes, who knows where things would lead to? I owe it to myself to chase that down."

Stone was bothered that Garrett wanted to go out with his friend. Jean was a nice girl. Hell, so was Tiana, for that matter. Why should Garrett get to have both girls?

"If you don't want me to, Stoney, you can just say so."

"No, man," Stone heard himself say. "It's cool. Ask her."

What the hell is wrong with me?

"Beautiful. I'll give her a ring later."

"You already have her number?" Stone asked, slightly surprised.

"Of course," Garrett said, a slight smile playing at the edges of his lips. "If I like a girl, I get to know all about her before I make a move."

Stone stared at the television, experiencing something he'd never felt before about Jean.

Jealousy.

Chapter 36

Clint listened attentively while the mechanic, a stocky man with a long salt-and-pepper beard whose nametag on his gray overalls read *Ike*, walked him through the features of his new police Impala. It wasn't the patrol car, so there weren't many differences from a stock model. A police radio under the dashboard and the red-and-blue lights in the grill was about it. The entire walkthrough took less than ten minutes.

When Ike had finished, he asked Clint if he had any questions.

"Where's the GPS?" Clint asked.

The mechanic shook his head. "There's no navigation system in this model. Only the new patrol vehicles have—"

"No," Clint interrupted. "I mean the GPS transmitter."

"I'm sorry?"

"So the brass can track where the car is in real time," Clint explained. "Where is it located? The trunk, or under the hood?"

Ike's look was strange. "There's no transmitter on this car, man."

Clint frowned. "I'm going to find it. Why don't you save us both some time, and just tell me. At least that way, you get your transmitter back. I find it, it's going into the river."

Ike spread his hands in surrender. "Man, if you find a GPS transmitter on this car, you can sell it on Craigslist, for all I care. But there ain't one, so good luck."

"Uh-huh." Clint remained unconvinced. Maybe the transmitter was in the police radio. A mechanic like Ike would be unaware of it if that were the case.

"You get everything out of your old car?" Ike asked.

Clint held up his satchel. "Traveling light today."

"Say your goodbyes?"

"It's a car," Clint said. No way was he going to admit sentimentality to a garage monkey.

Ike shrugged. "It's a classic, and that was the last one in the fleet."

Clint made a noncommittal sound.

"Too bad it'll get auctioned off and end up being driven by a half-assed security guard or some high school kid," Ike lamented.

"Or a drug dealer," Clint said.

Ike chuckled and held out the keys to the new car. "All right, man. It's all yours. Enjoy."

Clint took the keys without a thank you. He slid behind the wheel and dropped his satchel onto the passenger seat. The engine started right up and was almost silent in comparison to his old model.

He noticed Ike still watching him, so he put on his seat belt and drove away.

The interior still had that new car scent. He'd forgotten what that smelled like. The car felt foreign to him, but surprisingly nice. The seat was comfortable and once he'd adjusted it, fit perfectly. He experienced a strange buzz of energy, like a renewed confidence. Was this how it was when he first got behind the wheel of the Crown Victoria?

No. Unlike this one, he didn't get that car new. It had been handed down from some white-shirted brasshole, probably as soon as the new car smell wore out.

But this one was his from the very beginning. The thought of that was oddly satisfying.

Clint reached out and punched the buttons to the stereo, tuning into his favorite jazz station. The sounds of Chris Botti's signature trumpet filled the cab.

"Huh," Clint grunted, pleased. Even the speakers were better in this new car.

Maybe change wasn't as bad as he thought.

A crooked, almost grudging, smile creased his lips. Botti's notes punctuated his feeling of momentary joy. He rode the emotion for a few measures, an uncommon respite for him. Then he came back down to Earth.

Don't get caught up in what doesn't matter.
There's still work to do.

Chapter 37

"Is this going to be us now?" Jun Yang asked Ray Zielinski.

They were in the Bronze Beast, headed over to arrest a prolific thief named Shane Hunsicker at his girlfriend's house. Garrett and Stone were right behind them in the Gray Ghost. Even the sergeant was coming on this one, which had shocked everyone on the team.

Detective Hill got both an arrest warrant for Hunsicker and a search warrant for the house based on information Zielinski had gathered from a confidential informant. The CI was the girlfriend's sister, who hated Hunsicker and wanted him out of her sister's life. She was able to give them enough details to establish that Hunsicker lived at the residence, which made it much easier for Hill to obtain the search warrant.

"Us?" Zielinski asked her.

"Yeah, us." She pointed back and forth between them. "Is this the way it's going to be from now on? You brood all shift long and I suffer in silence? I mean, I'm just asking, so I can be prepared."

Zielinski considered her words. Had he been brooding lately? He decided she probably had the right of it, though he hadn't realized it had been so prominent. Garrett and Stone were getting on his nerves, and now he had the captain of Investigations grilling him about the Anti-Crime Team when all he wanted to do was take a leak. And then there was the thing with Neil Clemons and Darold Barden still hovering in the background, waiting to be resolved.

"I'm sorry," he told her. "I haven't been great company today."

"I don't care about company. I'm your partner. If

something's bothering you, tell me. Maybe I can help."

Zielinski glanced at her. For a moment, he was tempted to tell her everything. It seemed like Farrell had been fishing about Stone, even more than about Garrett. Did he think that Stone was dirty? If so, why?

More to the point, if Stone was dirty, along with Garrett, was he going to get dragged down with the two of them when things finally came to a head?

Yang's open expression was inviting, but Zielinski resisted. She didn't understand department politics. She was still a green rookie. Maybe not a fresh-faced, brand-new rookie, but a rookie all the same. Not only wouldn't she understand the nuances of what he was dealing with, but the blue code said it was his job as the senior officer to protect her from crap she didn't need to be involved in. She wasn't even off probation yet.

Her stare continued until he realized he had to say something. So he told a partial truth.

"I'm just frustrated with Garrett and Stone," he said. "They're acting like a couple of hot shot jerks."

"Okay," Yang said, her voice not betraying her thoughts. "Are you talking about a specific instance or just in general?"

"Both, but if you want specific, how about this? During the briefing for this warrant, the two of them were joking around, and acting like what I had to say wasn't important."

Yang half shrugged. "Yeah, I guess they were, a little."

"A little? It was nonstop. And the sergeant did nothing about it." It was fairly typical of Sergeant Ragland, but it still irritated Zielinski. "It's like they think the only police work that matters is the work *they* do. I'm getting sick of it."

Yang didn't answer.

Zielinski wrapped up his tirade. "We're not a team. It's them and it's us, and that's not the way it's supposed to work."

"You're right about that," Yang whispered.

"I know." He glanced up in his rearview mirror. The Gray Ghost was no longer there. Stone and Garrett were probably just taking a different route to the staging area, but the plan had been to caravan there. Garrett didn't think the rules applied to him, even for something as simple as driving somewhere as a team.

"So what do we do?" Yang asked.

Zielinski shrugged. "I have no idea. Hope it gets better, I guess."

"It will, when Sergeant McGinn comes back."

"Whenever that'll be."

They drove in silence the rest of the way to the staging area, an elementary school parking lot two blocks from Hunsicker's house. Zielinski parked and turned off the car. A moment later, Sergeant Ragland's marked car pulled in beside him.

Garrett and Stone were nowhere to be seen.

Zielinski sighed and exited the car. He took up a position at the back, leaning against the trunk and crossing his arms. Yang joined him there. Ragland stayed in his vehicle.

Less than two minutes later, the Gray Ghost whipped into the lot with Garrett behind the wheel. It lurched to a stop nearby, and Garrett and Stone piled out of the car, sauntering easily toward them.

Zielinski glared at Garrett. "What, you had to take a last-minute leak or something?"

Garrett flashed a malicious smile. "Easy, old man. Not everyone has to pee every five minutes."

"Then where were you?"

Garrett stared back, his expression unruffled.

Sergeant Ragland got out of his car and joined the group.

Zielinski wasn't letting it go. "We were supposed to caravan directly here. Where were you?"

Garrett made a show of looking at Zielinski's shirt sleeve. "Hunh. I was right, no sergeant stripes there. Guess I don't answer to you, Yin."

"What did you call me?"

Garrett just smiled.

"We did some recon," Stone said, his tone wavering

somewhere between reconciling and contentious.

Zielinski's gaze snapped to him. "Recon?"

"We checked out the target house. Maybe see if Hunsicker's car was there, that sort of thing."

The senior officer shook his head in disbelief. He held up his phone. "The sister texted me thirty minutes ago when she left the house. He's there, sleeping on the couch. The girlfriend is still home, too."

"That's old intel," Garrett said.

Stone glanced at Garrett, then back to Zielinski. "We wanted to get a tactical picture of the house, too."

"Tactical picture? It's a house."

Garrett wagged a finger at him. "See, if you were ever SWAT, you wouldn't spout nonsense like that."

"Oh, screw you and your black pajamas, Ty."

Garrett's eyebrows shot up. "Black pajamas? What the hell?"

"This is my op," Zielinski said, his jaw clenched. "My CI, and my plan. When it's your plan, we do it your way. But this is my plan, so you better start doing it my way."

"Or what?"

Zielinski glanced over at Sergeant Ragland. "You want to jump in here at some point?"

Ragland looked put out. "This squabbling is useless, and it doesn't matter. Let's review the plan and get this guy. I have some work back at the station I need to finish by close of business."

Zielinski shook his head in disgust. So much for counting on leadership.

"Yeah, Z." Garrett's tone was light and mocking. "What's your brilliant plan again?"

"It's simple," Zielinski said, scowling. "You two stage at the back. I stage at the front. The sergeant sits off in his marked unit around the corner. We send Yang up to the door with a ruse to get his girlfriend to answer the door. Once the door's open, Yang and I go in. At the same time, you two come through the rear, and the sergeant pulls up out front with his lights on so that the neighbors don't call nine-one-one on a home invasion or something."

"You're right," Garrett said. "That is simple."

"Simple is best."

Garrett shrugged.

"Any questions?" Zielinski asked.

No one spoke.

"Then let's go," he said.

Everyone got back into their cars. Zielinski drove the two blocks to the target address, parking several houses away. He waited until he heard Stone's terse transmission, "In position." Then he and Yang got out and made their way to the house. Zielinski cut through the neighbor's front yard and hid off to the side of the front door. Yang, wearing an oversized EWU sweatshirt to camouflage her ballistic vest and cover the police gear on her belt, approached the front door.

They'd devised a simple ruse that Yang was out looking for her lost dog. Alongside the *I just hit your car and I'm sorry* trick, it ranked as the most used and most successful to flush criminals out of their homes.

Before Yang could even knock, Zielinski heard a crashing noise from the back of the house and shouts of "Police! Down on the ground!"

Zielinski cursed. Garrett and Stone had jumped off early.

Yang's surprised expression was already fading as she reached beneath her sweatshirt for her gun. Zielinski nudged her aside and drove his foot forward hard, striking near the doorknob. The thick wooden door shuddered on its frame but held.

Behind him, he heard Yang speaking into her radio, advising Ragland of what was happening. Zielinski took a half step backward, reloaded and kicked again, this time putting all his weight into it. The doorjamb cracked and the door sprang inward, swinging out of sight. Drawing his pistol as he strode through the doorway, Zielinski scanned the living room. He spotted Hunsicker facedown on the carpeted floor, wearing flannel pajama bottoms and a T-shirt, Garrett's knee already pinning him face down. The officer snapped on the handcuffs while Stone covered a white woman huddled in the corner.

Garrett looked up at Zielinski. "Two kicks, huh? You could have waited ten more seconds, and I would have opened it for you, old man."

Zielinski stared at him with open anger but said nothing. Instead, he pulled his portable radio from his back pocket and keyed the mike. "Come inside, Sergeant."

He waited while Ragland took what seemed like forever to pull in front of his house with his overhead lights on. Then the portly sergeant got out of the car and ambled into the front room.

"We good?" he asked.

"No," Zielinski said, his rage bubbling up. "Not even close."

Garrett stood, motioning toward the prone Hunsicker and his girlfriend in the corner. "You guys want to watch these two while Stoney and I sweep the rest of the house?"

Zielinski nodded. He didn't trust himself to speak to Garrett at this point without exploding.

Garrett turned to Ragland. "Sarge, you wanna play?"

Ragland hesitated, then shrugged and drew his Glock. "As long as I'm here, might as well."

Garrett made eye contact with Stone, and the three of them began to search the remainder of the ground floor for any more suspects. Zielinski didn't believe they'd find anyone, based on the intelligence from his CI, but he knew it was protocol to check.

He switched his portable to the main north side channel, listening for a few moments to make sure he wouldn't step on any important transmissions. When the air seemed clear, he lifted the radio to his mouth. "Tango-eleven on channel one."

"Go ahead, Eleven," replied the dispatcher.

"I need a shield for transport."

"Copy," the dispatcher said.

Zielinski took a deep breath and looked around the ground floor of the house. The big living room and connected dining room were littered with empty beer bottles, old pizza boxes, and clothing. Interspersed with that were a few of the items listed in their search warrant: DVD players, a pair of laptops, even the bicycle Hunsicker had stolen from the garage of a young couple a few blocks away.

He should feel good about the arrest, and in knowing they'd hit on at least some of what they were searching for. It was a good bust and made another dent in exactly the type of crime the team had been formed to attack, but Zielinski couldn't revel in the success. He could only think of one thing.

Garrett.

Yang moved to the chair situated next to the couch. She checked it quickly to make sure there were no weapons hidden beside it or beneath the cushion, then motioned to the frightened woman crouched in the corner. "Come here," she said. "Sit down."

Cautiously, the woman rose and walked toward Yang. She gestured toward the chair to encourage her, and the woman sat down.

"What's your name?"

"Summer."

"Keep your hands on your knees, Summer."

The woman clapped her hands to her knees immediately.

"What about me?" Hunsicker said from his belly.

"Lay there," Yang instructed.

"Why does she get to sit, and I have to stay on the floor?"

"Because you're under arrest and she isn't."

"That's a stupid reason."

"Then how about this?" Yang said. "Because I said so. Now shut up."

"Screw you, you gook bitch."

Zielinski felt something snap within him. He took two huge strides toward Hunsicker. Yang moved forward to intercept him, but she wasn't fast enough. Zielinski loaded up to kick him in the ribs as hard he could, but something stopped him in the last moment. His toe skidded to a stop just in front of his other foot. Instead, he reached down and grabbed Hunsicker by the arm, jerking the man upright.

Hunsicker stared at him defiantly, inviting him to do something. Summer stared on in shocked surprise, her mouth hanging open.

"Ray!" Yang's voice was low and intense. "It doesn't matter."

"It *does* matter."

"He's going to jail," she said. "That's what matters."

Zielinski knew she was right, knew his rage at Garrett was channeling right into this new offense, increasing it exponentially. Still, his fingers dug into Hunsicker's arm and his free hand twitched as he imagined punching Hunsicker hard enough to blast that smirk right off his smug face.

He took a deep breath and brought himself under control. Or something close to it, at least. Next to him, he could sense Yang relax.

"Pussy," Hunsicker hissed at him.

Zielinski pulled Hunsicker's arm. "We'll wait outside for the transport."

"Ray—"

"It's all right," he told her. "I'm fine."

She looked at him appraisingly, but finally nodded.

"Come on," Zielinski said, tugging on Hunsicker. They started toward the door.

"Oh, I see how it is," Hunsicker said. "She's your girlfriend."

"Shut up."

Hunsicker glanced over his shoulder at Yang. "No, man, I get it. I like a little yellow trim once in a whi—"

Zielinski walked Hunsicker into the wall next to the door, giving his own hips a twist at the last moment. The face-first impact cut off Hunsicker mid-sentence. He let out a surprised, pained grunt.

"The hell?"

"Stop trying to get away," Zielinski said coldly.

"I'm not!"

"The way you're talking, it sure seems like it."

Hunsicker gave him a dark look but closed his mouth.

Zielinski escorted him outside. They waited next to the sergeant's patrol car in silence. The senior officer searched Hunsicker, but it was a rote gesture, given the man's attire, and the fact that the transporting officer would inevitably search him again. These were the officer safety protocols that they lived by, and Zielinski adhered to them. Unlike some of the more inane policies he'd seen come down from the bosses over the years, these protocols served a very important purpose.

They kept cops alive.

A dark red unmarked patrol car came around the corner and slid to a stop a few feet behind Ragland's car. Zielinski knew there were a half dozen or so of these patrol cars scattered throughout the patrol fleet. Fully equipped on the inside, the vehicles lacked all the standard police markings on the outside, sporting a solid color instead. With the black push bar and the large whip antenna, though, there was no mistaking it as a police car.

Officer Sonntag exited the driver's side, bearing the same sour expression he had the last time Zielinski had seen him. Zielinski was in no mood for his attitude, so he kept his interaction brief.

"He's got two warrants for Second Degree Theft," he said, without any other greeting. "Just book him on those. I'll come down later and tack on the additional charges."

Hunsicker broke his silence. "Additional charges? What the hell are you talking about?"

Zielinski ignored his question and pulled him toward Sonntag.

The patrol officer took Hunsicker by the arm and walked him to the back door of his own car, where he began to search the man. Without turning around, he asked Zielinski, "You want to swap out his cuffs?"

"No. Just leave mine with the booking officer. I'll get them when I add charges."

"What charges?" Hunsicker whined. "You have to tell me."

Zielinski turned away and headed back into the house. By the time he reached the door, he could hear Sonntag depositing Hunsicker into the back seat of the patrol car.

"He has to tell me the charges," Hunsicker complained.

"Shut up," Sonntag told him.

Inside the living room, the sergeant and the other three ACT members were assembled and waiting. Zielinski couldn't contain his frustration any longer.

"What the hell was that cowboy bit?" he snarled at Garrett.

Garrett wasn't fazed. "What are you carping about now?"

"You were supposed to wait until we gave the signal to go," Zielinski said, his voice low and mean. He pointed at Yang. "She was going to make contact, and *then* we go in. You guys jumped off early."

"Relax, man," Garrett said, but his tone was more dismissive than placating.

"I won't relax! Why'd you go off plan, damn it?"

Garrett stared back at him.

"We had no choice," Stone interjected. He pointed to Summer. "She saw us out the kitchen window."

Zielinski scowled. "You let her see you?"

Stone shrugged. "There's no good places to hide back there."

The senior officer turned to Summer, who was shrinking back into the chair. "Is that true? Did you see them out the window?"

Summer leaned as far away as she could, then drew her knees to her chest, careful to keep her hands on them as she did so. She looked at Zielinski and shook her head. Then she glanced at Garrett and changed the motion into a firm nod.

"Will you let it go?" Garrett said, sounding bored and

exasperated at the same time. "Things happen in the field sometimes. No plan survives contact with the enemy. You adapt, and that's what we did."

"This is bull," Zielinski fumed.

"Why're you so mad?" Garrett said. "You got Hunsicker. You got your stolen property. Hell, wait till you see all the crap in the back bedroom. There's more DVDs and CDs than I've ever seen outside a pawn shop. This guy's got to be the number one vehicle prowler in the city. So be happy, Z."

Stone and Yang looked at him while Garrett spoke, and he read agreement in their eyes. When he glanced over at Ragland, he saw no help there. The best thing to do right now would be to just drop it.

But he couldn't.

Zielinski pointed a meaty finger directly at Garrett. "Stop acting like you're the leader of this team, Ty. You're not."

Garrett shrugged. "Never said I was."

"But you act like it."

"What I act like is a cop who wants to put bad guys in jail. Isn't that what you want?"

"You know what I want?" Zielinski asked.

"A discount membership to the AARP?" A smile played on Garrett's lips. Beside him, Stone chuckled.

"No, smart ass. I want you to stop with all these cowboy antics. It's dangerous, and it's gone on too long. Someone is going to get hurt."

"Only thing hurt around here seems to be your ego, pops."

Zielinski turned to Ragland. "He's going to get a cop killed," he said. "Are you just going to stand there and let that happen?"

Ragland didn't react. "You people need to simmer down and act professional." He motioned with his head toward Summer. "We don't argue in front of civilians."

"She's a collar," Zielinski snapped.

"That doesn't matter, and you know it." Ragland gave Zielinski a cool stare. "Now get yourself under control,

Officer. You've still got a lot of work to complete here."

Zielinski shook his head in disbelief but closed his mouth. This was going nowhere. He could see that now.

"Conduct your search," Ragland continued. "Seize whatever evidence you're going to seize and book it onto property. Make sure you leave a copy of the executed warrant on the premises."

Zielinski didn't answer. He knew how to handle a search warrant. He didn't need this house cat of a sergeant to tell him the way it worked.

"I'll be at my office," Ragland said. "Call if you need me." *Fat chance of that.*

Sergeant Ragland turned and left the house, leaving the four of them standing awkwardly in the living room, staring at each other.

Summer raised her arm tentatively. When Zielinski glanced over at her, she asked, "What's a collar?"

Garrett broke into a deep laugh, joined by Stone. Then he slapped Stone on the shoulder. "Come on, Stoney. Let's head over to the property room. We're going to need the transport van for this one. There's too much to haul in our rigs."

Without looking at Zielinski again, the two of them walked out the front door.

And once again, Garrett makes the decision for the team. Zielinski flexed his fingers, trying to force himself calm. If he stayed this angry, his blood pressure was going to cause his head to explode.

Yang had been quiet throughout the entire exchange. When he met her gaze, he noticed a concerned expression there. Before she could say a word, Zielinski said, "I'm fine."

Yang pursed her lips, not answering.

"Uh…" Summer said, her arm still raised in the air. "Seriously, what's a collar?"

Chapter 38

Captain Tom Farrell stood at Wardell Clint's empty desk. The sterile desktop was clean and completely empty, as if it were unused, but he knew that all of Clint's files were locked safely inside the cabinet or the drawers. The detective himself was nowhere to be seen. He'd hoped to pull Clint aside and mend fences with the prickly investigator. With Zielinski seeming like he wasn't an option, and Yang's newfound reluctance, he could feel his control over the situation slipping. He knew he couldn't do this alone, and he needed allies. Despite his hard-headed nature, Clint was still his best option.

That alone should tell me how screwed I am.

He was so deep into the woods now, though, that continuing through was almost certainly the shortest way out. Besides, now that he'd had some time to consider, maybe Clint's attitude about the Anti-Crime Team had changed.

Farrell smiled at the thought. He doubted it. But he'd learned that despite his rigid opinions, Clint was very much a pragmatist. Perhaps even if he didn't agree with Farrell's approach to ensnare Garrett using ACT, he would accept the plan now that it was underway. Farrell could use Clint's mind to complete the mission. The detective frequently had a different take than his own, and he valued his analysis, even if it came in a frustrating package.

He can't still be mad, can he?

Farrell left Clint's desk and wandered to the personnel board outside of Lieutenant Dan Flowers's office. The door was closed, though Farrell didn't know if that meant Flowers was gone or just wanted privacy. Either way, he was glad, because it helped him avoid explaining his own presence.

Most of the upper brass stayed on Mahogany Row and didn't mingle with the worker bees. He had the cover story of having conferred with Detective Marty Hill about ACT, but all the same, he didn't want to arouse any suspicion.

The personnel board had all of the detectives listed, as well as a magnetic button for each name. An IN and an OUT column appeared right next to the name list, but a glance made it clear to him that no one used that feature. Every detective showed IN, and he knew that wasn't the case.

Farrell left the Major Crimes Unit and walked down the hall. He moved as slowly as he could, wanting to avoid the upcoming meeting with the chief. A snatch of Shakespeare suddenly came to him, probably the only poetry he remembered from high school. Something about a freshly scrubbed schoolboy creeping like a snail, unwillingly, to school. That was how he felt now. He didn't want to report to the chief about how many arrests ACT continued to rack up, or how Crime Analysis was reporting the beginnings of a downward trend in property crime and even a slight drop in certain categories of calls for service. Sure, it was all good news, but it hid a deeper, painful truth.

He was failing.

Instead of trapping Garrett, he seemed to be increasing the man's legend and providing him with more armor. Zielinski was turning out to be of no help, and Yang was questioning her role. With McGinn out of the game, and Clint on the bench, that left him with no one to help bring things to a head.

Farrell considered that for a moment. He realized it wasn't exactly true. He had Stone, didn't he? After all, he was the one who assigned the officer to the team, who kept him from resigning after he got bounced from the city hall position. Stone had to feel some measure of loyalty for that. In no small way, he saved the man's career.

The scene he'd witnessed at the jail worried him, though. How much of an influence had Garrett managed to develop over Stone? Was Stone still the same man he'd rescued from the city hall debacle?

He had to be. Like Yang, he'd chosen Stone because of his ethics. Ethics don't just go away overnight.

Farrell stopped outside the closed office door of Captain Dana Hatcher. For a moment, he considered talking with her again, to try to patch things up, but decided against it. He didn't want to fail at one more thing today.

Besides, what explanation could he offer her? The only reason he'd let Baumgartner assign him the team was because he realized that it was the perfect trap for Officer Tyler Garrett.

Maybe it still was. On the Anti-Crime Team, Garrett was surrounded by good cops. By good people. Stone had shown his loyalty and good ethics in the incident with city hall. Yang had shown hers when several of her classmates at the academy cheated on an exam. Zielinski had a long history of being a solid cop. The pieces were all in place. The only thing that was missing was them knowing the truth about who Tyler Garrett really was.

Revealing that dark fact had been Clint's biggest objection to Farrell's plan. Nevertheless, he was starting to realize that it was a risk he had to take. Things were slowly going off the rails with ACT. They were still making arrests, but without a strong sergeant, the team was rudderless. Hell, it was more of a group of four officers than a team. Hill had told him that they were arresting suspects and executing search warrants on more and more drug houses, from leads developed by Garrett, and neglecting leads that came through Crime Analysis. The detective hadn't been bothered by the development, citing how interwoven drugs and property crimes were, but Farrell could sense some mission drift, and it worried him. Between that and Garrett's charismatic, strong personality, he stood a real chance of losing this team.

He had to decide who to bring into his confidence. And soon.

Repatriate Clint? Or tell an ACT member? Who?

Zielinski.

Yang.

Stone.

As a leader for the last eleven years since he became a sergeant, Farrell had become accustomed to making hard decisions. But this was going to be the biggest decision of his career, and at the moment, he was completely unsure which move was the right one.

Farrell ran his hand through his thinning hair and crept slowly up the hallway toward the chief's office. Willing or not, this freshly scrubbed schoolboy had a report to make.

Chapter 39

Zielinski parked a couple houses away from his destination, under a burnt-out streetlight. The events of the day still hung on him like a bad smell. He hoped a few drinks might clear the air, so to speak, but he still had something to take care of, and he couldn't be drunk for that.

Neil Clemons had only texted him a couple of times since their initial phone call, but Zielinski could sense the impatience behind his polite check-ins. There was always the unspoken element that he owed Neil for not saying anything about their fender bender. He wondered if that was all, or if there was an implied threat, too, that it wasn't too late for him to report the collision to the department. He didn't want to believe that a guy like Neil would resort to that, but people disappointed him all the time.

That led him back here, to the home of Darold Barden. The busted tricycle had been brushed off the porch and lay askew in the overgrown flower bed next to the steps, and Barden's Dodge Charger was parked in the driveway, but everything else looked the same.

Zielinski didn't want to be here. He wanted to be two drinks in already, and then sleeping away his frustration. But he couldn't risk leaving this thread hanging.

He knocked loudly on the front door, standing off to the side as much as he could on the small concrete porch. Inside, he could hear the muffled sounds of a television. When the door opened, the soundtrack from a superhero movie flooded out.

Darold Barden was smaller than he'd expected. His criminal record listed him at five foot seven, but Zielinski had been estimating height and weight on people for a decade and a half. If Barden broke five foot five, he'd be surprised. Someone must have made a mistake during an early arrest, and once something was in the system, it stuck.

Barden eyed him suspiciously. "Yeah?"

Zielinski flashed his badge. It wasn't something he wanted to do, but he couldn't see any way around it.

Barden looked at the badge, then back at Zielinski. "So? My TV ain't that loud, so the neighbors can go screw themselves."

"This isn't about your TV."

"Then what?"

"You want to talk out here where all your neighbors can hear?"

Barden looked around at the surrounding houses. "What do I care? They're too busy with their own little lives."

"Or I could slap cuffs on you, and we could talk down at the station," Zielinski said, bluffing.

Barden sighed. "Fine. But you can only go in the living room. Nowhere else."

That pinged on Zielinski's radar, but he reminded himself this wasn't about making an arrest. He'd looked for that angle and hadn't seen any way to bring Barden to the attention of ACT. He didn't appear to be doing a whole lot of crime at the moment. He wasn't listed as a suspect on any recent reports, at least. Besides, Garrett was taking up all the team's time with his leads. He'd been lucky to get them to work Hunsicker and look how that turned out.

No, he was there for one purpose only. To pay his debt to Neil and close the book on it.

In the living room, Zielinski saw a beer and a bag of Cheetos on the coffee table. The latent smell of marijuana hung in the air. A movie blared on the big screen TV, but Barden dutifully paused it. He dropped the remote back on the table and crossed his arms. "Now what do you want?"

"You need to lay off hitting Sheryl Clemons."

Barden looked surprised. "Sheryl sent you?"

"It doesn't matter. What matters is that I'm here, and that you understand the message. Don't hit her again."

Barden stared back at Zielinski, processing. "I never hit her," he said. "Not once."

"That's not the information I have."

"From who? Her?"

Zielinski didn't answer.

Barden smiled slightly. "From the ex, huh?"

"Like I said, none of that matters. Just don't hit her again."

"I never hit her in the first place."

"You said that. I'm not here to take you to jail for whatever happened in the past, so you can stop denying it."

"There's nothing to deny."

"Just don't do it again," Zielinski said.

"Or what?"

Zielinski gave him a hard stare. "Or you'll go to jail. Via Sacred Heart Medical Center."

Barden nodded, as if he understood. Then he asked, "Why aren't you wearing a uniform? And where's your backup? Cops never go anywhere alone."

"Again, none of that matters. You need to focus—"

"Are you a real cop, or just some dipstick friend of Sheryl's ex?"

Zielinski stepped forward menacingly, holding up his badge again. "I'm a real cop, and this is a real badge. If you want to try me, we can make that trip right now."

Barden held up his hands peacefully. "No, it's cool. I believe you."

"Are we clear on this Sheryl thing?" Zielinski asked.

"Yeah, I get it."

"Then we're done here."

When Zielinski turned to go, Barden charged at him.

The action took him mildly by surprise, but years of training to react to the unexpected kicked in. He pivoted and sidestepped as Barden swung his fists, and the man stumbled past him into the TV. The huge screen rocked on its stand, and Zielinski thought for a moment it was going to fall on top of Barden and kill him, like a tipped vending machine. But the wobbles dissipated, and the TV remained upright.

Barden rose to his feet and charged again. This time Zielinski was ready. When Barden was in range, he lashed out with the heel of his palm, striking the man on the forehead. The blow reverberated down his arm as Barden stepped into it.

With a grunt, Barden crumpled to his knees, his eyes unfocused.

Zielinski took him by the arm and hauled him to his feet, before dumping him unceremoniously onto the couch. He waited while Barden shook his head to clear his senses.

"That was dumb," Zielinski said.

"No kidding," Barden muttered. "Wow, that was some real kung fu moves. My head hurts."

Zielinski didn't respond. He didn't know kung fu, but the palm heel strike was one of the basic martial arts techniques that the police defensive tactics instructors taught at the academy, and he liked it. He could get some serious force behind it, it didn't break his knuckles, and it tended to leave far less in the way of bruises.

"Are we learning anything?" he asked.

Barden worked his jaw. "Oh, man, my ears are popping."

"Hey!"

"Yes!" Barden replied. "Okay, I get it."

"Tell me."

"What?"

"Tell me what you get. I don't want there to be any room for confusion."

Barden closed his eyes for a moment. Then he said, "I ain't never hit Sheryl, okay? But I get that you're saying I shouldn't start. So I won't."

"Won't what?"

"Hit her." Barden rubbed his temples with his thumbs.

"Man, I think I have concussion."

"That'll be the least of it if you beat on her again," Zielinski said.

He turned and left the house, closing the door behind him. Once he was in the car and driving, he made a call. The phone picked up on the second ring.

"Hello?"

"Neil, it's Ray. It's done."

"Yeah?"

"Yeah. I talked to him and he's going to keep his hands to himself."

"That's great." Neil sounded relieved. "Thanks."

"You're welcome."

"That worked slick. I should have asked you to make him dump her altogether," Neil said. "Then maybe I'd have a chance to get her back."

"Who she's with is her choice," Ray said. "Him hitting her is his choice. I only talked to him about his choices."

"Well, thanks for that. Maybe Sheryl and I are done. I don't know. But if that's how it ends up, at least I'll know she's safe."

Zielinski didn't answer. He'd investigated plenty of domestic violence cases over his career. Sometimes the victim moved on and lived a normal life. Sometimes they found a new abuser. But he wasn't going to tell Neil that. The guy might try to appoint him as Sheryl's guardian angel for life or something.

"Thanks, Ray," Neil said. "I appreciate what you did."

"It's probably better for us both if we remember it as I didn't do anything," Zielinski suggested.

"Huh?"

Zielinski remained quiet, letting him work it out.

It only took Neil a few seconds. "Oh…yeah, of course. But thanks all the same. I mean it."

"I owed you," Zielinski said. "And I'm glad I got to repay the debt and make things even."

"Me, too."

"Good night, Neil."

"Good night."

Zielinski hung up, hoping that this chapter of his life was now officially closed.

Chapter 40

Gary Stone rubbed the tips of his fingers into his sore chest muscles as he stood in front of his mirror.

He'd only been working out with Tyler Garrett for a week and his body was aching in ways he hadn't felt since the academy. It was a good feeling as Stone knew that his friend was pushing him to lift more and get stronger than he would on his own. Stone begrudgingly admitted to himself that he had the habit of going light, using less weights, so it wouldn't hurt too much. He'd never achieve his full potential by taking it easy on himself. Garrett was the type of person who perpetually pushed himself and he needed that presence, that example, in his life.

Stone stood in his white underwear, having just taken an after-work shower. The evening was warm, and he didn't have air-conditioning in his home. Some of the moisture on his skin started to dry, cooling him.

He pinched a bit of fat that was around his stomach. Stone wasn't chubby, but he'd grown a bit of a paunch since the academy. Garrett teased him that it was because he was riding a chair while in city hall and that they needed to get him back into fighting shape.

Stone moved away from the mirror and stretched. As he felt the warm pull across his chest muscles, his eyes drifted to the bison picture that hung on his wall. Stone knew he hadn't been like the stoic creature today. He'd been quite the opposite, in fact.

When Tyler Garrett asked about Jean Carter, Stone whined like a schoolboy, even asking Garrett if he was still dating Tiana Kennedy.

Stone closed his eyes and shook his head. "You're an idiot," he muttered.

He remained that way for several moments, replaying the embarrassing conversation in his mind.

When he opened his eyes, he relaxed the chest stretch. He put both arms behind his back, grabbed his hands, and pushed downward, feeling yet another stretch.

If Garrett wanted to see two women at the same time, what business was it of Stone's? Plenty of guys in the department had girls on the side. It was such a common occurrence there was slang for them, some of it incredibly derogatory—chips, chippies, badge bunnies, holster sniffers. He didn't figure Garrett to be one of those guys, though. Stone always thought of him as being singularly focused on Tiana. He hadn't met Angie, his soon-to-be ex-wife, but he imagined Garrett had been committed to her in much the same way.

His eyes returned to the bison photo as he relaxed his stretch. When Garrett said he wanted to ask Jean out, Stone told him to go ahead and that he was cool with it. The whole thing was a lie, though, and Stone didn't want to lie to his partner.

He didn't want Garrett to go after Jean.

She was *his* friend.

If anyone was going to make a move on her, it should be him. They had an easy connection. It was as if they were already going out. Without the physical contact, of course. Hell, they could almost finish each other's thoughts and it was clear how much they cared about the other.

Stone bent over to touch his toes, stretching his hamstrings.

At that moment, he even envisioned her laughing at various things he said. The more he thought about it, the more he realized that she had probably harbored some feelings for him all along. It just made sense for him to ask her out. He'd been dense not to see it all these years. Jean was probably already attracted to him.

Stone slowly rose from his stretch, his eyes meeting those

of the bison. That was it then. He was going to ask Jean out.

But Garrett was going after her first.

What if he's already called her?

Stone's heart raced. Garrett was attractive and charming. If he'd already talked with Jean, she might have said yes. If that happened and then Stone was to ask her out, it would seem like he was competing with Tyler. He would look weak in comparison, maybe even pathetic.

He needed to stop Garrett if he hadn't called her yet. Stone grabbed his phone from the bed and began texting. He stopped midway through his second sentence.

Texting? he thought.

Don't be a pussy.

Almost immediately he corrected himself. *Don't be a wimp.* Jean had cringed when he used that term earlier. It was a word he'd have to be careful using around her in the future, so it was best to not even think it.

He dialed Garrett and his friend answered on the third ring.

"Stoney?"

"Hey, Ty. What are you up to?"

"Nothing." Garrett's voice was flat, and Stone could hear other male voices in the background.

"Is this a good time to talk?"

"You're fine."

"Hey, about our conversation about Jean?"

The other voices faded in the background, as if Garrett had moved away from them.

"Yeah?"

"I think I do want to go after her."

"Really?"

"So I'd appreciate if you wouldn't ask her out. I'm not sure if you already have, but if you haven't, would you mind hanging back?"

"Yeah, Gary, sure," Garrett said.

Stone felt a rush of relief.

"What the hell was that?" Garrett asked, his voice away

from the phone speaker.

"Ty? Hello?"

Garrett ended the call.

Stone stared at the blinking call-ended notice on his phone. His eyes lifted to the bison and he smiled. It was decided. Jean was his.

Gary Stone tossed his phone to the bed and turned to the mirror where he flexed. He sucked in his gut and smiled.

Tomorrow was going to be a great day.

Chapter 41

Detective Wardell Clint was *back*.

He sat in his new car, parked a half block away from Tiana Kennedy's condo. Garrett was inside, and he wasn't sure how long the man would be. Maybe he was there for the night, maybe just for a pit stop. He'd wait it out and see. As long as the light in the window of Kennedy's condo stayed on, he knew it could still go either way.

Clint drummed his fingers on the steering wheel, then forced them still. An energy hummed through him that had been lacking for a while. The new ride was an unexpected shot in the arm. He'd resisted the exchange for so long, holding on to his Crown Victoria until the last possible moment, but now that he had the Impala, he wondered why he'd fought so hard against it.

Of course, he'd done his due diligence. After the garage issued him the vehicle, he drove it to the massive empty lot where a discount grocery store used to be and gave it a thorough examination. The vehicle manual that he downloaded assisted him in his careful search. In the end, though, he found nothing suspicious. This left him feeling oddly empty at first—like his railings against the administration and their frequent overreaching might be unjustified. When he accepted this as a positive turn of events, he became happy, even optimistic. It was a strange and unfamiliar feeling for Clint, especially since his Garrett crusade began.

He had to admit that the feeling wasn't bad. It buoyed him as he sat outside Kennedy's condo, waiting around while upstairs Garrett was undoubtedly making the beast with two backs.

Let the man have his fun. His time is coming.

Clint rotated his attention between the front door of the condo building, Garrett's black Lincoln Nautilus in the fenced parking area, and the book he'd brought along. He'd seen the book, *Personality Types and the Criminal Mind* by Ingrid Cain, reviewed in one of the trade journals that he studied each month. By reading it, he hoped to shore up one of his weaker skillsets.

Every detective had certain aspects of the job where he excelled, Clint knew. And every detective had a weak spot or two. Knowing those abilities was the first step toward playing to the strengths and improving the weaknesses.

Some detectives could read a scene well or assemble disparate facts into a cogent picture. Clint could do both, and he thought Marty Hill was pretty good at them, too. Other detectives were crack interviewers and interrogators. Clint had to admit Hill was great at that part of the job, too. His own skill in that area was satisfactory, but his weak point was finding the right way to empathize with the witness or the suspect. He could play the bad cop easily enough and manipulate an interrogation into a confession if it were a contest of logic, or if he and the suspect were trading punches and counters.

If the emotional approach were required, Clint knew his game was weak.

He once asked Hill how he approached these types of interviews. Hill had seemed surprised that he was asking for advice, but eventually shared his simple approach. He tried to understand how the other person thought, how that person saw the world, and that told him how the person might feel. Once he knew the emotion in play, and how the other person related to that emotion, the right strategy would be clear.

Logically, it made sense to Clint, even if empathy seemed slightly out his grasp. Since understanding how other people think seemed to be the crux of Hill's equation, he got himself a copy of Cain's book. It helped pass the time while he sat off on Garrett, and he was learning a few new things in the process. For instance, he was starting to believe that Garrett was at least a sociopath, and quite possibly a psychopath. His narcissism, lying, and lack of guilt were all classic symptoms.

Clint glanced up to see Garrett striding confidently out of Kennedy's building.

Speak of the devil.

He watched Garrett get into his rig and exit the private parking lot. Clint slid into traffic and followed him from a safe distance. Garrett drove like a cop, his casual disregard for minor traffic laws evident. Usually, it was difficult for Clint to keep on him due to these habits. Additionally, once Garrett became aware that he was being tailed, he took active measures to lose Clint.

Clint didn't like to admit it, but Garrett was actually pretty good at those evasive tactics, and he'd lost track of his target multiple times over the past year.

Tonight, though, Garrett didn't appear interested in shaking his tail. Aside from his slightly boorish driving manner, he took no actions designed to break free of surveillance.

He's driving like he's just going home for the night.

But if that were the case, Garrett was heading in the wrong direction.

Clint followed him for another five minutes before he realized what was happening.

"Ha!" Clint shouted into the car's interior, slapping the wheel.

It was the new car. Garrett hadn't associated the Impala with Clint yet. Another good outcome to exchanging the old Crown Vic.

Garrett exited Francis Avenue on Cincinnati Street and pulled into the parking lot for Snoop's Saloon. Clint knew the establishment as a working-class bar, almost a dive. Garrett slid into a parking space next to a green Taurus.

Clint drove past, then swung around and pulled to a stop alongside the road. From his vantage point, he could see

Garrett conversing with another man as the two stood between their cars. A few other men milled about nearby, a couple of parking stalls away. Clint couldn't tell if they were part of the same group, or unrelated customers, so he focused on Garrett and the other man. They looked to be engaged in easy conversation, but neither of them was animated. It had the sterile look of a business meeting. In the dim light of the parking lot, the other man was difficult to make out, though he looked black.

Garrett held up his finger to the man and lifted his phone to his ear. The man turned toward Clint's car, as if to give Garrett privacy by looking away.

I need photos.

Clint froze. His satchel rested on the passenger seat, but he hadn't been home yet with the car. His supplemental bag and his camera were still inside his house.

Thinking quickly, he pulled out his flip phone. It didn't have the high-quality camera of a smart phone, but he knew it took video. Carefully, he aimed the phone so that Garrett and his accomplice were framed on the small screen. Then he moved his thumb to the record button.

The phone clicked and a brilliant light flashed inside his car. For a brief second, Clint wondered if he'd been shot at. Then he realized what had happened.

He didn't take the time to utter a curse, but immediately pulled the lever next to his seat cushion. The driver's seat dropped backward, and Clint let himself fall with it so that he was below the line of the window. If anyone looked now, they'd see an empty, nondescript car.

With city plates, Clint realized.

"Son of a… *bitch*," he muttered, hoping Garrett didn't look too closely at his vehicle.

When he heard the chirp of tires, he lifted his head and peeked out. He caught the profile of Garrett's Lincoln turning right onto Francis. He glanced over at the parking lot where the green Taurus had been. It was turning onto Cincinnati and heading toward Francis as well. Clint read the license plate and recited it to himself while he reached for something to write on.

At Francis, the Taurus turned left, heading in the opposite direction, away from Garrett.

Clint adjusted his seat again to his comfort level, shaking his head in disgust while he wrote. A rookie mistake, forgetting to have the right equipment. Worse yet, blowing his cover like that with the photo flash from his phone, which likely burned his car, too.

At least he had the picture, though.

Clint peered at the tiny screen on his phone, calling up the photo gallery. He selected the most recent and looked at it.

And cursed aloud.

The windshield had reflected the flash, overexposing the shot. All he could make out were a few blurry shapes on the fringes of a complete whitewash.

Clint snapped the phone shut and clenched his jaw.

Now Garrett not only knew for sure that he was still being followed, but he also knew what Clint's new car looked like. So much for the element of surprise.

But at least Clint had one tangible lead to go on. He had the license plate of the Taurus.

That is, if it wasn't a stolen car, a stolen plate, or some other dead end.

Clint put his car into gear and headed home. A frown settled onto his face as he drove. There was no more he could do tonight.

FRIDAY

*The reality is that we do not wash our own laundry
—it just gets dirtier.*
—Frank Serpico, former police officer and whistleblower

Chapter 42

"Why didn't you hit me back last night? I called a couple times."

Jean Carter sat on the concrete park bench overlooking the Spokane River. They were in Riverfront Park near the Spokane Carousel. Gary Stone had texted her suggesting they meet there today and that he would bring the coffee.

She wore a yellow printed sun dress. Even though it was midmorning and the temperature was nearing the mid-eighties, Jean also had on a light sweater. Her dark hair was tucked behind her ears and sunglasses hid her eyes.

"I was…busy," Jean said.

"I was hoping to hear about your award."

Jean brought her coffee to her lips but didn't sip. Instead, she lowered the cup and put it on the bench next to her. "It's okay, Gary. It's wasn't that big of a deal."

Stone drank from a plastic protein shaker that he brought from home. He'd skipped getting himself a coffee that morning. "It *is* a big deal, Jean. You're employee of the month."

"Everyone wins it sometime," she said, her voice filled with melancholy.

"That's not true. Not everyone."

"Unless they're complete screw-ups, everyone is going to be employee of the month sometime in their career."

"I know you, Jean, and this award meant something."

She stared ahead. He couldn't see her eyes, but he imagined she was watching the ducks that floated in the water near the sitting steps. People often tossed bread or other food into the water, so the birds always hung around in hopes of getting fed.

Stone kicked back the last of his shake, tapping the bottom of the plastic container with his free hand. When he lowered it, he wiped his tongue across his teeth, removing the grit and film the protein drink had left behind.

"Are you working out with Tyler before shift?" Jean quietly asked.

"Yeah. I'm already starting to get some definition in my chest and arms. You should see it."

"I trust you."

Stone lifted his face to the sun. "Do you have any plans for the weekend?"

"Not really. Maybe go to the library for a bit."

"The library?" he asked, suppressing a laugh.

Jean faced him. "What about it?"

"Nothing."

"I like the library. It's something I look forward to doing."

"I know," Stone said, defensively.

They both turned to watch the ducks for a bit. After a minute, Jean grabbed her coffee and sipped it.

"Anything else?"

"What?" Jean asked.

"Are you doing anything else besides the library?"

"Probably. I don't have anything planned, but something will come up."

Stone nodded. "Yeah, something will come up."

Jean put her coffee down then faced Stone. "What's wrong with you, Gary?"

His face scrunched. "Nothing."

"You seem like something's wrong."

"Nothing's wrong."

"If you've got something to say, then say it, because I can tell when you're holding something back. It ticks me off when you do that."

Stone smiled. See, he thought, she was perfect for him. She could read him like an open book.

He reached out and grabbed her free hand. Jean's brow

furrowed. He knew it was because it was unlike him to touch her.

"Jean."

"Gary?"

"We should go out tomorrow night."

"And do what?"

She began to pull her hand back, but Stone held on to it.

"I mean, we should go out on a date, you and me."

"What?"

"Yeah. I've been thinking about it and I think we're perfect for each other."

Jean yanked her hand free from his. "What the hell are you talking about?"

"Isn't it obvious? We should be together. We're like total best friends. Everything about us being together just makes sense."

Her mouth lowered.

"Going out is like…well, it's obvious. I already said that, but I'll keep saying it. It's obvious."

Jean's frown deepened. "You're an idiot."

Stone pulled back.

"I am not interested in you like that, Gary."

"But you care about me like no one else. Doesn't that mean we should—"

"Whatever you think, Gary, it's wrong. We're great friends, but we should never go out together. Period. I thought we figured that out a long time ago."

"Yeah, but that was then, and—"

"How did you even arrive at this conclusion?"

He remained silent.

"*Tyler,*" Jean said, almost spitting the word.

"He had nothing to do with it."

"Right."

"I swear. I just thought we would be perfect together."

"Wherever your head has been lately, you need to have it examined. This isn't you."

Jean stood and Gary reached for her hand again. "Jean," he said, his voice almost whining.

She stepped back from him. "Stop it, Gary. Seriously, what happened to you? Where's my friend?"

Jean Carter turned and walked toward city hall, the little yellow dress lightly blowing in the wind.

Stone watched her go, his face warming. He turned to look at the ducks and absently flicked his hand in her direction.

"Whatever," he muttered.

Chapter 43

Ray Zielinski sat stone-faced during the morning briefing for ACT. Sergeant Ragland was wasting their time reading a patrol memo that had nothing to do with them, and from the expressions on the other faces in the room, he wasn't the only one tuning out the supervisor.

His mind kept returning to his encounter with Darold Barden last night. He'd thought that taking care of the favor for Neil would put the situation in his rearview mirror. But after he got home, all he did was worry. Even having a few drinks didn't quell his concerns, and this morning, his stomach hurt like it hadn't in months. Most of his negative thoughts since joining ACT were filled with frustration and anger. This morning felt like his old situation again, with money problems and IA hanging over his head, and his angst came with a familiar emotion.

Dread.

He shouldn't have fought with Barden. Maybe the guy didn't give him much of a choice, but he should have found a way to avoid it. If Barden decided to report the incident, things would unravel quickly for Zielinski. His actions last night would not stand up to any scrutiny, and he'd get hammered by any internal investigation. The outcome would be a suspension at best, termination at worst.

The possibility made his stomach ache.

Maybe he'd get away with it. Barden didn't know his name or his badge number. He might not even be sure the guy who showed up at his door was even a real cop. Anyone he reported it to would have the same suspicion.

A moment later, he rejected the idea. Internal Affairs was

thorough. They'd show Barden pictures of police officers until Barden picked him out.

It didn't stop there. Once Barden identified him, his connection to Neil would come to light. Even if he didn't confess to the reason he felt beholden to the man, he didn't think Neil would hold up under any questioning. The facts surrounding the on-duty collision would come to light, and all the weight from not reporting it would fall on Zielinski. If he was fortunate enough to only receive days off for the Barden fight, progressive discipline would come into play for the unreported collision. The best he could hope for would be a lengthy suspension, but in today's world, Zielinski feared that termination was more likely.

Why had he done it? Neil was nothing to him, just a guy who once did him a favor. Sure, it seemed like a big favor at the time, but the way things eventually worked out, right now he'd much rather have a preventable crash on his record than be dealing with this.

I should have gone to a sergeant.

He wished McGinn were still with the team. He was a leader Zielinski could have talked to about this before he confronted Barden. If the sergeant were still here, Zielinski felt like he could have approached him even now.

But Sergeant Ragland?

Zielinski watched the fat sergeant drone on about a patrol uniform policy change that could have been summarized in two short sentences. Ragland seemed like the kind of sergeant who would start dinging his officers for violations of this new policy on day one, instead of using the first few violations as a way to remind everyone of the change. How would he react to an unreported collision? An off-duty fight while he was doing a favor for the guy who helped him cover up the collision?

Damn.

The hole he'd dug for himself just kept getting deeper. And he seemed unable to stop himself from wielding the shovel. It was going to cost him his career, if he didn't find a way to stop the madness.

Worse yet, he knew that if Barden talked to a lawyer, even some half-assed hack with a law degree from a diploma mill, they'd find a way to sue him personally. A lawsuit would wipe him out in legal fees alone, much less a judgment since the department would not stand by him in this action.

Zielinski grimaced, and reached into his pocket for his antacids.

Sergeant Ragland wrapped up his rambling with a warning to pay attention to the uniform policy changes when the team members returned to patrol.

"When is that going to be?" Garrett asked him.

"Whenever you stop being the bright and shiny new toy for the brass," Ragland told him. "Now," he continued, "let's talk about assignments." He motioned to Detective Hill.

Hill threw out a couple of names. Garrett seized on one right away, and Hill made that the team's first priority.

"Now you're talking, Marty," Garrett said. "That guy needs to go to jail."

Zielinski didn't care. Let Garrett run the show. He could have the glory, and the liability that came with it.

He glanced over at Stone, expecting the officer to be yukking it up with his hero. Stone's smile was small, almost forced, and his expression seemed distracted.

Probably wondering how to grow a goatee that looks exactly like Garrett's.

Zielinski listened to the rest of Hill's rundown of suspects. He didn't object when Garrett suggested reordering the top three. Anything beyond those three was likely to get pushed to tomorrow, or fall off their plate entirely if newer, bigger hippos made the hit list.

Whatever. I just need to get through this day.

A sharp twinge lanced through his stomach, and he winced, resting a hand there.

No one seemed to notice.

Chapter 44

Clint glanced left and right, then pulled up the photograph he'd taken last night using his desktop computer. The result filled his monitor. The washed-out picture was a worthless mess. The only discernible image was part of the steering wheel at the bottom of the screen.

He'd hoped that looking at the photo on something larger than the tiny display on his flip phone would reveal something useful. But all he got was a bigger blob of white overexposure.

Clint deleted the file from his computer and emptied the recycle bin as well. Then he leaned back in his chair.

The photo would have been strong evidence. Showing Garrett in an off-duty meeting with a criminal was damning. It wasn't enough to bring down the entire house of cards, but it was a good start.

He was making an assumption, of course. The license plate he'd recorded last night came back to an Aurelia Ellis. She was a seventy-one-year-old woman with no criminal entries. But she was listed as a theft victim many years ago. The suspect was a man named Earl Ellis. Clint couldn't be certain from their respective birthdates if Earl was her son or grandson, but one or the other was the most likely possibility.

The theft complaint Aurelia had made against Earl Ellis was eventually dropped. It remained one of the few property crimes on Earl's record, which dated back to when he was a juvenile. The majority of his criminal record consisted of drug-related offenses, including several trafficking charges. None had resulted in a felony conviction, however, and the charges themselves were spaced out. In some cases, he'd gone years without so much as a traffic ticket. Clint had checked to make sure he wasn't in prison out of state or something but found nothing on Ellis outside of Washington State.

That told Clint the man was smarter than the average crook. He probably didn't use dope, or only did so recreationally. If Garrett was going to partner with a drug dealer, Earl Ellis was exactly the kind he would choose.

Clint fished around in his new file and pulled out a mug shot of Ellis. He couldn't tell for certain if it was the man he'd seen talking to Garrett last night, but the features looked about right. The booking photo was only a year old, and from a warrant arrest. The warrant stemmed from a charge filed two years prior to that. Ellis had eventually pleaded guilty to a misdemeanor and received a suspended sentence. Although that irked Clint, it wasn't what interested him most about the situation. What caught his eye was who had arrested and subsequently booked Ellis for that warrant.

Patrol Officer Tyler Garrett.

Now he had proof that the two knew each other. Sure, Garrett could say in his defense that he arrested and booked hundreds of people in his career. He could even claim not to remember Ellis, and the assertion was plausible. That's what made Clint's photographing blunder from last night worse. If he could have attached evidence of an off-duty, clandestine meeting between the two alongside the warrant arrest, *that* would have been a nice building block.

Still, there was time. Garrett wasn't going to stop what he was doing. The man was too sure of his own superiority to do that. That meant there would be other opportunities to capture the two of them on camera. Now that all his equipment was stowed in his new car, he was properly prepared to take advantage of the chance when it happened.

Clint rubbed his chin and was surprised to find stubble there. In his haste to get started on this new lead, he'd hurried through his morning routine. Skipping the shower was a conscious decision, but he hadn't realized that he'd also forgotten to shave.

It didn't matter.

What mattered was that he had a lead, and confirmation that Garrett was up to his old tricks.

Clint gathered up all his case materials, locked up his desk, and headed out to his car. It was time to find out more about Earl Ellis.

Chapter 45

Tyler Garrett sat on the trunk of the Gray Ghost, typing a text message into his cell phone.

He looked up as Gary Stone hurried toward him. Garrett quickly finished his message, hit the send button, and slid off the trunk. "What took you so long?"

"Ragland," Stone said. "He caught me coming out of the john and said I need to report to Captain Farrell."

"Farrell? The hell for?"

Stone shrugged. "Ragland didn't know. I just came out to tell so you wouldn't think I fell in." He turned and headed back toward the Public Safety Building. "I'll make it as quick as I can," he called over his shoulder.

Garrett watched his partner disappear into the building

What the hell does Farrell want with Stone?

Maybe it's nothing. Garrett climbed into the front seat of the Chevy Caprice. He left the door open and put his foot against it, letting the sun shine on him. Stone was now the team's official public face following Sergeant McGinn's departure. Maybe the captain was lining him up to do another dog and pony show for some city hall dignitaries.

He leaned back against the headrest and rubbed his goatee. If it wasn't some sort of public information blitz, maybe Farrell was following up on one of their reports. Since they'd been partners, Stone had written the bulk of the paperwork. The man was a natural talent at quickly stringing words together. Anyone reading their combined reports would know which parts were his and which were Stone's.

But Garrett didn't believe that's what the captain was after. He knew Farrell was working with that looney tune,

Wardell Clint. There had long been gossip within the department that every payday Clint not only bought a box of ammunition, but he also purchased a bar of silver, both of which he buried in his backyard. Rumor had it that Clint was preparing for the fall of the US government and would be prepared to fight back against interlopers and barter with those who had supplies. Garrett didn't know if it was true or not, but the rumor had legs because it seemed like it *could* be true.

Garrett first caught Clint following him almost a year and a half ago. Since then he'd made a game of it, losing the man when he needed to and letting him follow along when Garrett wanted to show him something. Clint never got close enough to see anything Garrett didn't want him to see.

What Clint didn't realize, though, was that Garrett had followed *him* occasionally, just to see what the man was up to in his free time. That's when he discovered the secret meetings with Captain Tom Farrell, the architect of the Anti-Crime Team, the guy who was pulling everyone's strings.

Farrell was the one who had assigned Garrett to ACT, making him the only team member to earn that designation.

Gary Stone had been *asked* to the team. He'd told Garrett as much on the first day they rode together. Farrell even sent him to a surveillance class prior to the start of the team, just to keep the man out of the limelight following his unceremonious removal from city hall.

Jun Yang, the academy princess, was the woman who ratted out four officers for stealing an answer sheet before the criminal law final. Garrett had more time in the men's locker room than she did on the entire department, yet she found her way onto a specialty team. *How?* Because Captain Farrell *invited* her to be on the team. She let that slip when they first rode together.

Ray Zielinski, the turncoat, barely said a word when they were forced to share a car. However, the man did admit one thing. That Tom Farrell *enticed* him to the team with the promise of overtime, something that serial-divorcee Zielinski needed to keep his ex-wives in check.

That meant only Tyler Garrett had the distinction of being *assigned* to the team. Except Captain Farrell hadn't even been man enough to do it himself. Instead, he sent Sergeant Christian McGinn to deliver the message.

McGinn came to his house and told him about the assignment. Initially, Garrett didn't want it, instead hoping to stay on power shift. McGinn said the assignment was nonnegotiable.

"It's from on high," McGinn said. "You're now part of the Anti-Crime Team."

"On high from who?"

"Farrell. The man was very specific that you were part of this team."

At the mention of the captain's name, Garrett immediately knew the team and its mission was suspect. Farrell must have figured McGinn's friendly face would lower Garrett's guard since he and the sergeant had been on the SWAT team together.

"What if I refuse?"

"I guess you can quit," McGinn said. "Other than that, I don't see any choice for you but to suck it up and come run and gun with me."

Accepting the assignment with ACT was like sliding into a pit of alligators, except they were all pretending he was the alligator. Only Garrett felt as if he was in constant danger.

Thinking about Farrell talking with Stone angered him.

He was already irritated from the previous night. Someone had taken his picture while he was at Snoop's Saloon. Whoever it was had been stupid and left their flash on, so he was lucky that he saw them. And he wasn't overly worried since he wasn't doing anything more than talking on the telephone to Gary Stone. However, someone had followed him to that location, and that bothered him.

He didn't know whose car it was as he'd never seen it before, but he had a pretty good idea of who the sneaky SOB was.

"Clint," he muttered then spat into the parking lot.

Garrett climbed out, slammed the car door, and headed toward the department.

Farrell and Clint. Clint and Farrell.

The two of them had made his life a hell since his shooting.

If Clint did get a picture of him, so what? All he would have is Garrett standing in the parking lot of a dive bar with a cell phone pressed to his ear. Yeah, Earl Ellis was in the parking lot, too. Again, so what? He doubted Clint knew Ellis. Besides, it was circumstantial. It didn't mean anything.

Garrett bounded the steps, pressed his ID card against the magnetic reader to release the door, and entered the building.

He was tired of the harassment and he was going to call Clint out on it.

What's the worst that could happen?

Clint could accuse Garrett of killing Detectives Butch Talbott and Justin Pomeroy, which would just make him sound like the crazy, conspiratorial idiot everyone already knew him to be. Besides, Clint had already run those stories up the flagpole and lost.

Detective Talbott had tried to ambush Garrett and he fired in self-defense. There were witness statements proving such, but they couldn't identify Garrett and he never owned up to it. He had initially called Clint and told him about the shooting, but he later recanted. There were no witnesses to his admission, therefore no evidence.

Then Detective Pomeroy committed suicide shortly after he told Clint about his drug dealing with Garrett and Talbott. Unfortunately for Clint, the medical examiner confirmed it was suicide. Thus, no one on the department wanted to hear his thoughts about how Garrett had forced the man to kill himself.

Was Clint now going to openly accuse Garrett of killing the drug dealer, Ernesto Ocampo? There had been no witnesses to that murder and there was no evidence to tie anyone to it, let alone Garrett. With little to go on, there was only one conclusion: Wardell Clint could go screw himself.

Garrett stalked into the Major Crimes bullpen, passing Detective Marty Hill's desk. Hill was reclined in his chair, both legs propped up on a second chair, as he read a report.

"Whoa, Ty," Marty said. "Who are you on the way to kill?"

He stopped suddenly and looked at the detective. "What?"

"You look seriously angry, man. I wouldn't want to get on the wrong side of you right now."

Marty Hill had been a long-time SWAT team member, who later served as an advisor to the team. He was the type of guy that Garrett could count on in a fight when the chips were down. If Hill was calling him out for looking like a psycho, then he needed to pay attention and calm himself—*fast*.

He glanced around before asking, "I look bad?"

"As my grandfather used to say, you're all horns and rattles."

Garrett's eyes drifted down as he thought up an excuse. When his eyes returned to Hill, he said, "The ex-wife, she's going after my deferred comp."

Hill's face flattened. "Ah, man. I'm sorry."

"What can you do? You marry them for love. They divorce you for money."

"Still, I'm sorry."

Garrett looked deeper into the Major Crimes bullpen. "Is Clint back there?"

"He left ten, maybe fifteen, minutes ago. Want to leave a message for him?"

"No," Garrett said. "It wasn't important."

His temper was calming now, and he realized he'd avoided a serious mistake. Had he walked back and yelled at Wardell Clint, he could have—no, he would have—created himself a problem that he did not want to have. It was better to not confront Clint head on. He was a problem that was always better attacked from an angle.

Garrett eyed Hill's knee brace. "How's the leg?"

"Still strong enough to kick your ass on the mat." Marty's smile was wide and genuine.

"Take care, Marty," Garrett said with a lift of his chin.

"You too, buddy."

He took a couple steps toward the hallway and stopped. He spun around and said, "Hey, Marty?"

"Yeah?"

"Did Wardell finally get rid of that old turd he was driving around? I thought I saw him in a shiny new Impala."

Marty smiled. "Can you believe it? The lieutenant was in here a couple days ago reading him the riot act about that old heap. Wardell was trying to negotiate to keep it. Funniest thing I've seen in a long time."

"Huh," Garrett said. When he turned toward the hallway, his shoulders slumped slightly.

Wardell Clint had gotten himself a new car.

Chapter 46

"The team is tearing it up," Farrell said.

"We're doing our best, sir." Stone sat stiffly on the chair in front of the captain's desk. Farrell could see that he was nervous and sought to put him at ease.

"Your work has been very noticeable." When that didn't get the reaction he wanted, Farrell pressed further. "I'm proud of you, and so is the chief. The mayor is, too, for what that's worth."

Stone grimaced slightly. "I'm glad you and the chief are pleased, sir."

Farrell noted the exclusion of the mayor in his response. *So there are still scabs on that wound.* "How are things on the team?" he asked.

"Fine," Stone said.

Farrell raised a brow. "In my experience, when you get four headstrong cops in the same car, a few sparks will fly."

"We're not all in the same car, sir. We ride double. Easier for surveillance and following a moving target."

"Of course." Farrell wondered if Stone had learned that in surveillance school. "Who do you ride with?"

"I ride with Ty." Stone's words held some measure of pride in them.

"Every day?"

"Pretty much."

"I'm surprised Sergeant Ragland doesn't rotate partners."

"McGinn did," Stone said. "He wanted us to be familiar with our teammates."

"And now you're familiar, so Ragland decided no more rotation?"

Stone shrugged. "To be honest, sir, Sergeant Ragland isn't super engaged with the team."

Farrell snapped his fingers, nodding. "That's one of the reasons I need you on this team, Gary. You aren't afraid to see things as they really are. And you're comfortable being honest with command staff about what you see."

"Thank you, sir." Stone seemed to appreciate the compliment, but Farrell didn't think it had the same impact it would have had on him a few months ago. Being around Garrett at such close quarters was definitely changing the man.

I hope I'm getting to him in time.

"I know your time at city hall was tough," he said. "Especially at the end."

"It was… a learning experience."

"What did you learn from it?"

"That I don't ever want to be a politician, or work with politicians, or watch politicians on TV."

Farrell smiled. "A good lesson. I wish I could live it." He leaned forward, lowering his voice slightly. "Gary, I need your help. And it's important."

Stone swallowed, looking slightly anxious, but he nodded. "What is it?"

"It's Garrett." When the officer's eyes slanted and he failed to respond, Farrell continued, "We're concerned about him."

Stone considered. "Ty's fine. I think he's put most of that shooting stuff behind him."

"That's not the concern."

"Then what?"

"I'm worried that he is engaging in questionable behavior," Farrell said, choosing his words carefully. "Have you seen anything that bothers you?"

Stone glanced away and shook his head. "No, sir. Nothing."

"Not a single thing?"

"No."

"It's okay for you to tell me," Farrell said. "In fact, I think we both know it's the right thing to do."

"If I saw anything, I would," Stone stated.

The officer's words seemed weak to Farrell. *He's lying.*

It had been years since Farrell had been in the box with a suspect, trying to extract a confession from someone who wouldn't even admit what city they were currently in, much less complicity in a crime. And while he loathed the idea of using those skills on a cop, a lie was still a lie, and it had to be broken. Cops were human, and just as susceptible to the same techniques as any witness or suspect.

The key, he remembered, was to get them to admit the lie by making it safe to do so. And while that sounded simple, it was often a complex dance.

Farrell took the first step. "Gary, the team is doing great work, and that matters. I know sometimes it takes a little ingenuity to get that kind of work done, especially day in and day out. Not every policy or every little rule always gets followed, and I don't care, if you want my honest feelings. I care about your safety, and I care about results. I'm not too worried…" Farrell flashed back to the words he used with Jun Yang, "if someone is rude to a suspect, or parks sideways in a handicapped slot. Make sense?"

Stone met his gaze and nodded cautiously.

"I also understand loyalty. Especially, loyalty to your partner. Someone makes a small mistake, you don't want to hang them out for it, particularly when all the good work they're doing counterbalances that mistake. Can we agree on that?"

"Yes." Stone's voice was quiet.

"I'm concerned about things bigger than that. Seven-forty-sevens, if you will. Not paper planes."

"Sir, there's really nothing. Ty would never do anything like that."

If that's true, and he's your hero, why aren't you mad right now?

"Do you remember what you told me when the Betty Rabe incident came out in the newspaper, Gary? About how the reporter got the information for her article?"

"Yes," Stone murmured. "I remember."

"You told me Garrett took pictures of your unfiled report with his phone when he was at your house. That he had to be the source, because it made no sense for anyone else who knew the details to leak it."

"I know."

"Do you still believe that?"

Stone squirmed. "I've gotten past that."

Farrell stopped short. "You've talked about it."

"Yes," Stone admitted. "He did it to help me."

"He did it to—" Farrell asked hurriedly, frustratedly, but stopped himself. He took a deep breath and asked a different question. "How did it help you? You got booted out of city hall because of it."

"Covering up—hiding why Betty Rabe killed herself—it wasn't right," Stone asserted. His voice reminded Farrell of a high school kid standing up to a parent for the first time—resolute but shaky. "We shouldn't have done that. I didn't have the courage to stand up for what was right."

"And Garrett did?"

Stone nodded.

Farrell let that hang in the air for a moment. Stone had been lying just a minute ago and now he was defending Garrett's action. A change in tactics was needed. The captain said, "He screwed you over."

Stone didn't respond and his face whitened. He stared at Farrell, blinking rapidly and shifting in his seat.

"Garrett isn't your friend," Farrell continued. "In fact, I think he's someone you need to be careful of."

"That's not true," Stone whispered.

"If I were to speak to Officer Zielinski or Officer Yang, what do you suppose they would tell me?"

"Ray hates Tyler. Who knows what Yang would say? All I know is that I haven't *seen* anything. I don't *know* anything."

"I think you do," Farrell said, his tone matter of fact. "I

think you've seen things that bother you, and that you're struggling with whether the right thing to do is let them go or to tell someone." He tapped the table with his index finger, an affectation he'd picked up from Baumgartner, and spoke in time with the hard taps. "You. Need. To. Tell. Me."

Stone swallowed, harder this time. Farrell spotted a few beads of sweat collecting on the man's temples. "There's nothing to tell," Stone said, without any force.

Garrett has his hooks into him good. He had to raise the stakes and get Stone's ethics to outbid his misplaced loyalty in Garrett. Doing that meant starting to show his hole cards, but Farrell saw no other way forward. If he didn't make his play now, he suspected Garrett's influence over Stone would only grow as more time passed.

"Gary, I'm not talking about procedural mistakes here or bad paperwork. I'm not even talking about not allowing some dirtbag suspect to give up on the backswing. It's more than that."

Stone was clearly rattled. "What... what do you mean?"

"We believe Tyler Garrett has committed crimes."

"What kind of crimes?"

"Serious ones."

Another silence descended on the room. Farrell stared at Stone, his gaze firm and level. Stone looked away, wiping a trickle of sweat with his sleeve. "I...like, what...?"

"Felonies," Farrell answered.

"Felonies?" Stone repeated.

"That's right. Dating back a couple of years."

Stone looked up. "His shooting?"

Farrell nodded. "That, and more. Continuing right up until today."

Stone drew a wavering breath, shaking his head in shocked disbelief. "I... I don't want to believe this."

"But it's true."

"Does anyone else know?"

"Yes, several of us."

"Then why are you telling me this? Couldn't you and the others—"

"Do you know why I put you on this team, Gary?"

Stone thought about it. "You said my media skills. And big picture thinking, too." His eyes narrowed slightly. "Was that not true?"

"No, it was very true. But there was one more reason, the most important reason of all." Farrell paused for effect, another Baumgartner trick. "Your ethics. I knew you were a man who would always do what was right."

Stone sank in his chair and lowered his head, deflated.

Farrell thought about bringing up the recent changes he'd seen in Stone but decided there was too much risk. Pointing them out would result in Stone embracing them rather than rejecting them. Instead, he said, "I need to know that you're still that person, that good man. I need to know that I can trust you."

Stone didn't move or speak.

"Can I trust you, Gary?" Farrell prodded.

Stone looked up slowly and stared back at him. Finally, he nodded.

Farrell felt a surge of electricity jolt through his system. Despite Garrett's charm and influence, he'd succeeded.

Stone was his again.

"Good," Farrell said. "Now, let's talk about our plan."

Chapter 47

Clint's car was tucked behind an aging green Honda, and next to an old willow tree with overgrown branches that hung over the edge of the street. City maintenance would likely cut back the overhang soon, but for now, Clint enjoyed the camouflage.

Earl Ellis had been busy so far today. Clint had observed him as he made five different contacts throughout the north side of the city. In two of the instances, he'd merely spoken with the other men, one black and one white. Clint snapped photos anyway. The three other meetings involved an exchange. Once it had been Ellis delivering a package to a short, stocky white female. Clint took photos, guessing the package most likely had product in it. On the other two meets, Ellis was the one receiving a package. The first was an envelope from a tall Native American male in a battered San Diego Chargers jersey, sweatpants, and Timberland boots. The second time, it was a ratty looking paper bag that Ellis didn't seem too pleased to be receiving from a skinny white male in a torn concert T-shirt. Clint wondered if it was just the container or if the money inside was a crumpled mess, too. Either way, Ellis gave the man a stern lecture. Clint couldn't hear the words, but the implication was clear: get your act together.

Now Ellis had returned to the house where'd he'd been living, presumably for lunch. Clint still hadn't verified if the woman on the mortgage was Ellis's mother or grandmother. He suspected grandmother, but he supposed it didn't matter. He had more pressing investigative questions to answer.

While Clint waited for Ellis to eat, he checked the photographs on his camera's view screen. The digital quality was high, definitely high enough for facial recognition software if he could think of a reason to get Crime Analysis to do it without arousing suspicion.

Elation was not an emotion that Clint experienced often. Grudging satisfaction was usually his high-water mark. But with the field work he'd done today, he felt a whisper of elation now. He was on his way to getting solid IDs on Ellis's associates, which would give him a clear flowchart of this criminal operation. From there, all he had to do was pick off whichever one was the weakest in the herd and get that person to flip on Ellis. One undercover delivery later, and he'd have Ellis by the short hairs. Then it would be time to get Ellis to name Garrett as an accomplice and wear a wire. Once he had Garrett on tape, he could lay that next to all the other evidence he had from the past two years of his investigation, and everything new from this stage, and that would be it.

Garrett was done.

The very thought of it gave Clint a sense of… well, elation.

"Still work to do," he muttered to himself. Things were coming along, and that felt good after such a long period of stagnation, but he knew there was plenty of road left on this trip. The fact he had investigative moves to make now was a welcome change, though. Action made him much happier than passivity.

Clint waited. He used the time to nibble on a few almonds and scratch out some notes. One of the men Ellis met with had been sitting on the hood of a car when they spoke. Maybe the car was his, maybe not, but Clint had photographed the license plate, just in case. Aside from the images on his camera, the plate was the only new tangible lead he had.

Though he cast more than a few cautious glances around as he travelled, Ellis still seemed unaware of his presence. That being the case, who knew what he might lead Clint to? If tailing Ellis stopped bearing fruit, he could start working on his underlings, too. He'd have to do that eventually, anyway. The point was, Clint now had options. He didn't have to follow

Garrett around exclusively, waiting for a man who knew he was being followed to make a mistake. These other members of his little empire would prove to be much more fertile ground for finding evidence and building his case. All of them were still unaware that Clint was onto them, and he suspected they weren't nearly as smart or as careful as Garrett.

It won't matter. All his smarts won't matter once I'm finished with him.

Clint almost grinned at that. Then he went back to his notes.

Chapter 48

"What did the captain want?"

Gary Stone watched the scenery slip by his window. "Nothing."

"Nothing?" Tyler Garrett asked while he drove the Gray Ghost. "A captain doesn't call you into his office for nothing."

Stone glanced toward his partner. Garrett eyed him, searching for the truth.

"I'm being investigated," Stone said, finally.

Garrett's eyes returned to the road, but his brow furrowed. "For what?"

Stone watched the scenery for a moment until Garrett repeated the question. "Stoney? For what?"

"For assaulting that piece of crap, Wayne Cattage."

"The guy that tried to jump the fence?"

"Yeah."

They were quiet for a bit and Stone leaned his head against his window. Finally, Garrett asked, "What's he saying happened?"

"Wasn't him. It's the jail sergeant," Stone said.

"The jail sergeant?"

"When I hit Cattage in the back of the leg with my radio, I must have torn his calf muscle or something. The maggot told the sergeant what happened, and they called in a doctor who confirmed it. The jail commander filed an assault report on me."

"Damn," Garrett muttered.

An uneasy quiet hung in the Chevy Caprice. Garrett reached over and purposefully shook Stone's shoulder. Normally, it would have cheered him up, but it wasn't doing so today.

Stone was bothered by how easily the lie sprang to his lips. Several months ago he'd been anxious about telling a small untruth to Chief Baumgartner. Now, he could lie to anyone, even his friend.

Three months. Ninety days. Is that all the time it took to darken his soul?

And why was lying suddenly so easy? Was it being on the Anti-Crime Team or was it something else?

"Keep your head in the game," Garrett sternly said.

"What?" Stone asked, facing his partner.

"You still have a job to do and there are people out here who will look to do you harm."

"I know that," he said, defensively.

"If you take your eye off the ball, for even a moment, you'll end up hurt, or worse."

"I'm okay," he said.

Garrett glanced at him while he drove. "I'm serious, Gary."

Not only his tone, but the senior officer's use of his first name demanded additional attention.

"If you want to mope," Garrett said, "do it at home. Call Ragland and request some time off. Or I'll take you back to the station. I don't need a partner who is a danger to himself and me."

Stone straightened. "I'm not moping," he said, his voice hardening.

"You sure?"

"I'm sure."

"Then who are we looking for?"

Stone smirked. "Dwight Poff."

"That's right. Dwight ever-loving Poff, scumbag of the highest order. Keep an eye out for a red Toyota four by four. A real pile. If he's home, it'll be in the driveway. If not, he'll be out running around in it."

"I heard all this in the briefing," Stone muttered.

"Yeah? Well, I'm reminding you, Stoney, because the man

has a history of guns. So stay alert. Yin and Yang have already grabbed one hippo today, so we need to get on the board. We can't have them sitting at the head of the class."

They were driving toward the Logan neighborhood near Gonzaga University and stuck in a long line of stalled traffic. Construction season was in full swing, so several arterials were torn up, slowing their progress. It was said that Spokane had four seasons—fall, winter, spring, and road construction.

While they sat in traffic, Stone's mind drifted back to the conversation with Captain Farrell. That took him to the moment in Akiem Mack's apartment when Garrett asked him if they should take the money.

If Ty was dirty, wouldn't he have just taken it?

Or wouldn't he have found a reason to get me to leave the room and then take it?

Why would Ty blatantly ask *me if we should take the money?*

His friend seemed disappointed when he said no, but Garrett didn't keep after him begging to take the money. Instead, he later thanked Stone for helping him keep his wits.

Sure, there were other incidents where Garrett told him to do things against policy but that was to put someone into jail, someone who had harmed others. None of those things actually enriched Garrett. In fact, they helped citizens he didn't even know. They were altruistic choices. Maybe someone like Farrell wouldn't see it like that, but it had been a lot of years since the captain had been on the street. Times had changed.

The traffic eased and they made it through the intersection of Division and Sharp.

The captain said there were several other people who knew about Garrett's supposed crimes. *Supposed.* He was giving Garrett the benefit of the doubt that the captain hadn't.

Why was a captain of the police department so eager to take down one of his own men?

And who were the other people?

Zielinski was the first one he thought about. The officer clearly hated Ty and was always bickering with him. That Zielinski used to call Stone the Chief's Bitch made it easy to hate the officer. But did that mean he actually suspected Garrett of being dirty? If he did, wouldn't Zielinski always be in his face? No, that seemed unlikely. It seemed more probable that he would be quiet and unassuming, watching and waiting.

Like Yang.

Yeah, Jun Yang. Fresh out of the training car, she was selected for one of the most coveted specialty teams. A lot of guys wanted to be on the Anti-Crime Team and somehow a fresh-faced rookie got the assignment. He knew why exactly. It was because of the reputation she'd earned in the academy for ratting out four other students.

Farrell had selected her to be a rat. *His* rat.

Stone then had a thought that sent a wince of pain through his stomach.

Farrell had selected him to be a rat as well, from the very beginning. That was obvious from the meeting he just had with the captain. Farrell wanted him to spy on Garrett.

And if the captain had selected Yang and him to be rats, then that meant Zielinski was probably the same thing. Another rat. Maybe that's why the man was so angry all the time. He didn't really want to be a rat.

Neither did Stone, but did he have a choice?

Did any of them?

A car honked at them as Garrett changed lanes.

Three rats, standing around Tyler Garrett, an actual bona fide hero in the Spokane Police Department. The man had earned the Medal of Valor, a Silver Star, and a Lifesaving Medal. Stone had never been awarded a medal and Yang was too new to even be considered. The only thing Zielinski had won was a Merit of Service award, which was essentially a time-in-grade pat on the head.

The Caprice turned northbound onto Astor Street.

"There!" Garrett yelled.

A rusty Toyota was in front of them, its tailgate missing. Garrett reached down and activated the Gray Ghost's emergency lights, which were located inside its grill.

The red truck immediately accelerated, its unmufflered exhaust roaring in protest. The Toyota turned eastbound, driving through the grass of the house on the corner. It bounced back onto Sinto Street, swerving wildly until its driver got control.

The engine of the gray Chevy Caprice whined in excitement as it careened around the corner.

"Call it in," Garrett hollered.

Stone grabbed for the microphone hidden under the dashboard. "Tango-fourteen," he said.

"Fourteen," the male dispatcher responded.

"Traffic stop at Sinto and Astor." Stone then rattled off the plate numbers. "The truck is running from us, eastbound on Sinto."

The truck accelerated again as a plume of exhaust belched behind it.

Before the dispatcher could respond, the truck collided with a newer Volkswagen in the middle of the intersection of Sinto Avenue and Standard Street.

Garrett slammed the brakes, bringing the Gray Ghost to a sliding stop. Both Stone and Garrett jumped from the car. Due to the positioning of the Caprice, Garrett was furthest away.

Dwight Poff was already out of his truck, running northbound. Poff wore an opened Hawaiian shirt, faded jeans, and leather sandals. His dirty brown hair trailed past his shoulders as he ran.

Stone was fifty feet behind the suspect when he yelled, "Police!"

Poff stopped suddenly and spun, his hand coming up from his waist band.

Stone hadn't seen the gun in time and he suddenly froze. His mind seized, forgetting everything except for one single thought.

I'm going to be shot.

In the next moment, he was hit by a freight train. His head snapped sideways from the force. Garrett landed on him as the man tackled him to the ground. His partner continued rolling and came up, somehow with his gun at the ready.

Poff hadn't fired yet. Instead, he stood staring at the gun in his hand.

"Drop it!" Garrett yelled.

Stone stared at Poff from the ground as his partner kneeled next to him, protecting him.

Poff hit his gun with a fist and stomped the ground in frustration.

"Drop it, Dwight!" Garrett yelled again.

When Stone realized he should have his gun out, he reached down and yanked it from its holster. Still lying on the ground, he pointed his weapon at the suspect.

Poff finally came to the slow realization that his gun had malfunctioned, and he didn't know how to fix it. Hitting it further wasn't going to make it work. His head lowered in defeat, and the gun slipped from his hands, clanking when it hit the pavement.

"On the ground," Garrett yelled as he stood.

Dwight Poff complied, dropping first to his knees, then to his stomach.

"Place your hands out to your sides."

Again, Poff did as he was ordered.

"You okay?" Garrett asked, his voice low and caring.

"Yeah," Stone said, rising to his feet.

"Good. Now, let's cuff that bastard. I'll cover you."

Chapter 49

As soon as Ray Zielinski and Jun Yang finished booking their suspect into jail, Ray told her, "I need to swing into the station for a few minutes."

"Why?" Yang asked, removing her Glock from the gun locker and sliding it into her holster.

"I need to see a captain."

"Farrell?"

Zielinski shook his head. "Hatcher."

Yang looked at him expectantly.

"She used to be my sergeant," he explained. "I check in with her occasionally."

"And she's okay with that?"

"Why wouldn't she be?"

"She's a captain. You're a patrol officer."

Zielinski buzzed out of the jail side door, holding it open for Yang. "You were in the Army, right?"

Yang nodded, stepping through the door.

The two of them fell into step as they made the short walk to the west doors of the police department. "It's not like that here. I mean, rank matters, but if there's a personal relationship, it's not absolute. You can talk, socialize, whatever."

"We called that fraternization," Yang said. "And it was strictly forbidden."

"Well, this is different. It's not the Army, it's police. Things are more civilianized." He thought for a moment, then said, "Think of us like you would the Air Force."

Yang laughed. "Okay, I think I get it."

"Dana's good people," Zielinski said. "She actually cares.

Near as I can tell, she still hasn't drank the Kool-Aid yet when it comes to being a boss." He didn't mention how he'd started to worry that she might be sipping at it, though.

They arrived at the west doors to the police department. "How long will you be?"

"Maybe ten, fifteen minutes."

Yang held out her hand. "Keys."

Zielinski didn't move.

Yang wiggled her fingers. "Keys," she demanded. "If I'm going to wait for you, I'm going to park the car in the shade under a tree and start this report."

He reluctantly pulled the key ring from his pocket. "You're going to hand write the report?"

"No, I have my laptop in my bag. We're in a city hot zone. Don't worry about it."

Zielinski sighed and handed her the key. "I guess I had to let you drive sometime, right?"

"Seniority only goes so far."

"Didn't used to be that way."

"Things change," Yang said.

"Unfortunately."

Zielinski touched his identification card to the sensor and the door unlocked.

"See?" Yang asked. "Progress."

"Whatever. I'll call you on the radio when I'm done."

"Just text me. I'll pick you up here."

Zielinski nodded and went into the building. He found Captain Dana Hatcher's office door open, as it usually was. He rapped lightly on the door frame. "Cap?"

Hatcher looked up. As soon as she saw him, she gave him a genuine smile. "Ray! Come in."

Zielinski stepped inside. Casually, he swung the door shut before he sat down.

Hatcher noticed his action. "Closed door talk, huh?"

"Is this a bad time?"

"Not at all. Talk to me."

Zielinski hesitated. For most of her career, Hatcher had been someone he could talk to. Rarely had she failed to understand what he was going through. During his first divorce, she'd been the only person who he trusted with his frustrations. He wanted to tell her about Barden but knew he couldn't do that to her. If he did, she'd be forced to choose between him and her duty as a captain, and it wasn't fair for him to put her in that position. Plus, he didn't like his odds when it came to which choice she'd make.

So he turned to the team instead. He described the change in dynamics since McGinn went on family leave, including his frustration with Garrett. He expressed his concern about Garrett's influence on Stone, as well. Zielinski could hear the anger in his own voice, and he knew he sounded as if he were on a rant, but he couldn't help it. All he knew was it was good to share it with someone he could trust.

Hatcher listened quietly. When there was a break in his tirade, she asked, "Is Sergeant Ragland doing anything about all of this?"

"Ragland?" Zielinski shook his head. "He's barely present. The man is retired-on-duty."

"Well…" Hatcher spread her hands. "He does a pretty good job handling admin stuff."

"That's about three hours of work a day."

"And you know this because…?"

"Because if it's a job Kelly Ragland would want, it'd have to amount to that little work." He looked at her, surprised. "Why are you defending him?"

Hatcher leaned forward. "Look, when I was a patrol officer, I thought the same thing about detectives and any admin position. They weren't patrol, so they didn't work. Or at least not as hard as we did. Since then, I've seen these kinds of jobs up close, and the work that goes into them. It's hard work, too."

"I find that tough to believe."

"It's not standing in the rain or going to a call with a stinky dead guy, I grant you. And the greatest physical danger most of them face every day is a paper cut or a stapler malfunction. But it's still work, Ray, and it's valuable."

"Maybe," Zielinski allowed. "But it doesn't seem that Ragland is doing much work when it comes to ACT."

"He has other duties, too. The whole world doesn't revolve around ACT. It just seems like it."

Zielinski took a deep breath and let it out. This wasn't how he'd expected the conversation to go. It was disintegrating into a repeat of his last serious conversation with her a few months ago. She hadn't understood his point of view then, either. Had she changed?

"As far as your concerns about Garrett," she said, "have you seen anything you need to tell me about? Anything outside of policy?"

Zielinski clenched his jaw and gave his head a single shake. "No."

"How about Stone?"

"Other than both acting like hotshot jerks, no."

"Well, what you've been describing so far sounds like some high-speed, low-drag alpha cops who are ratcheting up their macho quotient to match the situation."

"It's not that."

"It sounds like it."

"Maybe it is, but it's not *just* that."

"What else is it, then?"

Zielinski thought about it and realized he couldn't tell her anything more. He had nothing concrete, only suspicions. Besides that, she wasn't listening.

"I guess nothing," he said sullenly.

"You sound like my little nephew when he has to say something he doesn't want to say, even if it's true."

Now she's comparing me to a kid?

"Thanks for your time, Captain." He stood up to leave.

"Whoa, whoa." Hatcher raised her hands in a slow-down motion. "Don't be angry, Ray. I assume you came to me because you know I'll tell you the truth."

"I come to you because you listen."

Or you used to.

"I did listen and what it sounds like to me is some ego clashing. Garrett and Stone are racking up a lot of stats. They look like the varsity team. Are you sure you're not a little jealous of that?"

Zielinski was distraught. She was completely reading him wrong, and he could see that nothing he could say was going to change that. All he could do now was try to end the conversation gracefully, and not burn the relationship.

"You've given me something to think about," he said evenly.

"Good."

He motioned toward the door. "I gotta go. My partner is waiting."

"Okay. I'm glad you stopped by, Ray."

"So am I."

"My door's always open to you."

Zielinski pulled open the office door. "I know. Thanks again."

Hatcher smiled at him, and coupled with his disappointment, her smile seared his heart.

On the way out of the building, his chest burned with frustration and hurt. By the time he made it to the door, though, he'd put on his mask again. Showing that pain to the world wasn't going to do any good, and suspects read it as weakness.

He couldn't afford to be weak.

Zielinski pulled out his flip phone and laboriously texted Yang that he was ready to go.

Chapter 50

The boy ran ten yards out, cut to the right, his head whipping around as he did so. His eyes followed the blue football as it spiraled through the air until it landed in his hands.

"Nice catch, buddy," Tyler Garrett said.

Jake Garrett danced as if he just scored a touchdown.

"He's pretty good," Tiana Kennedy muttered. She sat on a checkered flannel blanket with Molly Garrett as the two of them played a game of Go Fish.

"He's getting there."

The four of them had gone to Riverfront Park for a picnic dinner. Tiana had made salami and provolone sandwiches for them, except for Molly who would only eat peanut butter and jelly. They had walked over from Tiana's condo and set out the blanket across the river from the Convention Center.

The grassy area was full of families and Jake saw some kid in ratty sweats and a dirty white T-shirt that went to school with him. Garrett couldn't remember his name, but he did recall that his father had been convicted twice for drunk driving. Jake trotted over to his friend.

"Go fish," Molly said with a giggle.

"You okay after what happened today?" Tiana asked Garrett as she drew a card.

Garrett watched his son show his friend the blue football. "The thing with the gun?"

"Yeah," Tiana said.

"Do you have any eights?" Molly asked.

"I'm good," he mumbled. "Part of the job."

In fact, he was good with the arrest of Dwight Poff. No one was shot and the man was arrested on Marty Hill's warrant.

They also tacked on the additional charges of Felon in Possession of a Firearm, Second Degree Assault, and Attempt to Elude. It was a great arrest.

It was two entirely different things that bothered him.

First, the more he thought about Captain Farrell as puppet master, the angrier he became. Farrell had allowed his harassment by Wardell Clint to continue for almost two years. No, he must have encouraged it.

Garrett caught Farrell and Clint meeting three times. One of those conversations was in the department's parking lot and that, by itself, wouldn't be a big deal, but the other two were physically away from the Public Safety Building.

Once was in a roadside chat behind the arena.

The other was at the Maxwell House, a cop bar for old-timers like Clint and Farrell.

Without the captain's support, Clint would just be running around like the conspiratorial fool he was, spouting ridiculous theories. He needed an audience to give his stories any credence and he found one in Farrell. Who was the most dangerous man in that relationship?

Clearly, it was Farrell.

The second thing that bothered Garrett was the revelation that Stone was getting jammed by the jail commander for the strike on Wayne Cattage. The turd deserved what he got, but some liberal-minded jailer was telling a cop how to act on the street. Not only did that anger Garrett, it now gave Captain Farrell leverage over Stone. Who knew what the captain would try to get Stone to do?

To save his partner and protect himself, Wayne Cattage would have to recant his story. How could he make that happen?

"Babe," Tiana said, "it's almost eight."

He nodded and yelled, "Jake! Time to go."

They packed the remnants of their dinner into a carry bag that Tiana slung over her shoulder. Garrett folded the blanket and tucked it under his arm. The family then began the short walk toward the giant red wagon where they were supposed to meet Angie Garrett, Tyler's soon-to-be ex-wife. She had been shopping at the downtown mall and said that they could do the exchange of the children in the park.

Tyler and Angie had signed the divorce paperwork and now it was just a waiting game. It took ninety days to finalize after filing it with the court. Garrett didn't know the exact date it would become official, but it was any day now.

Tiana held Molly's hand, giggling at some secret joke they shared.

Jake looked up at Garrett. "Dad?"

"Hmm?"

"When can I come live with you?"

Garrett put his hand on his son's neck and pulled him to his side as they walked. "Someday, buddy, but not today."

"Why?"

"Because that's part of the deal."

Jake fell silent after that. For several minutes, the only noise the family made was the giggling from Molly and Tiana.

She was standing near the wagon, searching the crowd for the faces she recognized. When Angela Garrett's gaze fell on her former husband, her eyes shifted to Tiana and they hardened. She crossed her arms as the four of them approached.

"You should probably wait here," Garrett whispered.

"Ya think?" Tiana whispered back. She bent down and quickly hugged Molly. The little girl kissed her on the cheek.

"C'mon, guys. Let's go to your mom."

Jake remained by his side as Garrett walked toward Angie. Molly ran ahead and clutched her mother's leg. When Jake was near, Angie said, "Kids, go play on the wagon for a few minutes. I want to talk with your father."

As the children climbed the ladder for the over-sized wagon, Angie laid into him. "You brought *her* out with the kids?" Her face contorted with disgust.

"She's my girlfriend," Garrett said flatly. "It's fine."

"Our divorce isn't even final and you're running around with some Beyoncé knock-off."

Garrett rolled his eyes.

She pointed a finger at him. "Don't you roll your eyes at me, Tyler Garrett."

He lifted his hands in surrender. "Hey, you were the one who wanted the divorce, Angie. Not me. You knew I still loved you, but you kicked me to the curb."

She clenched her jaw and anger flashed in her eyes.

"I moved on with my life because I had to," Garrett said. "Maybe it's time you did, too."

"I am moving on," she insisted.

"Sure sounds like it." He looked up at the kids who peered down from the big red wagon. They watched their parents with wide eyes.

"Good night, guys. I love you."

His children waved to him. Molly's wave was exuberant and joyful, while Jake's was more dejected.

Garrett waved back. Then he turned around and walked toward the beautiful woman who waited for him, a worry growing in his chest.

He was going to have to do something about Captain Tom Farrell.

Chapter 51

Jun Yang tucked the mop bucket into the storage closet and stepped back, closing the door. The shop was eerily quiet, but she liked these moments, as if she was the only person in the world. It was shortly after eight and the store had been closed for several hours.

After grabbing the two maple bars that her parents always kept safely hidden away for her and a bottle of milk, she sat in the booth furthest from the windows. The shop was dark except for the first row of emergency lights near the front.

Her parents were at home, probably preparing for bed. Due to owning a donut shop, they were asleep early every night so they could be back at the store by three a.m. It was a hard life, but one that they chose to give their children a better chance for success.

Xi-Wang was out, shirking his duties to the store. It was Friday night and the summer. He was heading to college next year, so this was his last opportunity to spend time with his high school buddies. Jun wished she would have done a little more of that, instead of being so focused on leaving Spokane to get started with her life.

She'd signed up for the Army while still in high school, using the military's delayed entry program. Upon graduation, she only had one week before she left for basic training. She didn't travel or hang with her friends. Instead, she worked at the store. Her parents were upset with her leaving them and the family business. Working that last week was the least she could do to make it up to them.

After basic training, she attended the twenty-week school for military police. She ended up at a small installation in

Panama for her first assignment. It was a radical change from Spokane, but she enjoyed it. The military allowed her to take college courses online and later, when she was in the States, attend in person at night and on the weekends.

It took her longer than her friends, but she achieved an AA degree in three years and was only ten credits shy of a bachelor's degree before she left the service at the end of her eighth year.

Yang took a bite of one of the bars, its sugary, doughy goodness doing little to brighten her thoughts.

The military had a level of camaraderie she grew to expect everywhere else in civilian life. She experienced it a little in high school with some of her fellow students, but the Army showed her what it was like to have true friends, people who would lay their lives down for one another.

Unfortunately, that wasn't true in the police department, which baffled her. They were in a fight against the evils of the world and should be like the brotherhood of soldiers, standing shoulder to shoulder in the struggle. Yet many of the officers seemed eager to tear each other down or pull each other apart.

The department was rampant with name calling, cliques, and years-old grudges. Officers had affairs with the spouses of other officers. Some officers coveted positions currently held by others and did their best to undercut their efficiency.

There was little respect for rank, and seniority only mattered to those who had it. The disregard for it all confused her. The Army prided itself on discipline. The police department paid lip service to the idea while demanding self-control of the citizens they patrolled. Ironically, the officers were sometimes the ones least in control of themselves.

She'd been on the job less than a year and had seen the ugliness of it all.

And it disappointed her.

A banging on the door broke her thoughts.

Outside, Captain Farrell stood with his hands cupped around his eyes, peering into the store. He wore an untucked

Polo shirt, jeans, and flip-flops. His hair was a mess, as if he had run his hands through it several times.

Yang dropped her unfinished donut onto a napkin and slid out of the booth. She walked to the door, spun the lock, and pulled it opened.

"A cop walks into a donut shop," Farrell said, stepping inside.

"What?"

"Sounds like the start of a joke, doesn't it?" His tone held no hint of humor, as if he were trying to force himself to sound casual.

Yang stared at him, her hand remaining on the open door.

"Got a minute?" he asked.

She wanted to tell him she didn't, but it was obvious she did.

"How are things?"

"They're fine."

"Everything's good?"

"Yes," Yang said, drawing out the single syllable.

Farrell ran his fingers through his hair. "Okay then. That's good."

"Is something wrong, Captain?"

"No, no. Just wanted to check on you."

"And we couldn't do this at the department?"

Farrell shoved his hands in his pockets. "I was just in the neighborhood. Thought I would stop in and see how you were doing."

Yang knew it was a lie. Something was wrong with the captain, even if he wouldn't verbalize it. "Everything is fine, sir."

"Anything happen with the team this afternoon?"

"What do you mean?"

Farrell shrugged. "Nothing. Just making conversation."

It was another lie. He wanted her to be truthful with him, but the reverse wasn't true. She wanted to ask him what was going on, but it was inappropriate. Junior officers did not question the motivation of superior officers.

"Okay," she said.

He noticed the donuts on the back booth and said, "Is that your dinner?"

"A reward for cleaning the store."

"Cops and donuts," he said. "Some clichés are true."

She remained silent until it grew uncomfortable for the captain. Finally, he said, "Well, I'll get out of your way."

"Have a nice night, Captain."

He hurried into the parking lot. She looked for his car but didn't see it. He disappeared around the corner. She wondered why he hadn't parked in front, especially if he was in the neighborhood and just wanted to check in on her.

Yang locked the store and returned to her booth. She stared at the donuts which now seemed unappealing. She picked them up, walked over to the trashcan, and tossed them in.

"Cops and their secrets," she muttered. "Some clichés are true."

Chapter 52

Ray Zielinski knocked on the door. He had to purposefully dial back the intensity of his usual power shift knock to keep it polite. A few moments later, Gary Stone answered the door. He looked mildly surprised to see Zielinski.

"Hey, Ray…"

"Thought I'd swing by and talk to you. You got a few minutes?"

After his disastrous conversation with Captain Hatcher, he'd decided that his best course of action was to deal with his concerns about the team in a more direct manner. There was little chance he could get through to Garrett, but maybe Stone would listen to reason. If nothing else, he could get a handle on how far under Garrett's spell the man was. That, at least, would let him know what he was up against.

"Okay, sure," Stone said. He held open the door to let him in.

Zielinski stepped through the door, thinking about how to start the difficult conversation. Then he saw Tyler Garrett lounging on the couch in front of the TV and stopped dead in his tracks.

"Look at who I found loitering at the front door," Stone said, his intonation sounding a lot like Garrett to Zielinski's ear.

"Hey, Z." Garrett greeted him easily, but his eyes were wary. "Whatchya doing?"

Zielinski shrugged. "Just out and about. Thought I'd stop in."

Garrett didn't reply, but the suspicion remained.

"We're watching the game and having a beer," Stone said.

"You want one?"

Zielinski didn't. His mission in coming here was scrapped by Garrett's presence. But he couldn't just leave. He was stuck. "Sounds good."

"I got Modelo in the bottle, and Coors Light in the can."

"Bottle," Zielinski said.

"Got it. Ty, another?"

"I'm good."

Stone went to the kitchen while Zielinski milled around the living room, waiting. Garrett studiously ignored him, watching the baseball game. Zielinski found his attention drawn there, as well. The two men watched in an uneasy silence.

When Stone returned with Zielinski's beer, he handed it to him and motioned to the couch. "Have a seat."

Zielinski settled into the far end of the couch, opposite Garrett. Stone sat in the chair next to Garrett's end. The three of them watched the game for a few moments without speaking. Zielinski sipped the cold beer and cast surreptitious looks at Garrett. He could tell the man was watching him in his peripheral vision, even though he was pretending not to. He'd seen the same *I don't notice the cop* look on plenty of suspects during his career.

The Mariners were playing the Cincinnati Reds in an interleague game. When Zielinski glanced at the score, he saw that Seattle was up by two runs.

"This pitcher," Garrett said, shaking his head.

"Yeah," Stone echoed absently. "This pitcher."

Garrett stared at the TV. "That's all you've got, Stoney? Are you even watching this game? This guy is painting the corners like he's standing in front of the plate. Our last two batters went down looking."

Stone cleared his throat. "That's what I mean. He's tearing us up. Gonna be another one we let get away."

"Maybe." Garrett took a drink and without looking away, he asked, "What do you think, Ray? Our boys gonna pull this one out?”

“I hope not.”

Both men turned to him in surprise.

“What, you don’t like the M’s?” Garrett asked.

“They’re fine. But I had a great-aunt who was heavy into baseball when I was kid. She was a Reds fan, going back to the Johnny Bench, Pete Rose days.”

Garrett nodded. “That was some sleazy crap what they did to Pete.”

“He was betting on baseball,” Stone said. “It’s against the rules.”

“Maybe. But he was betting on his own team to win. What’s wrong with that?”

Stone didn’t answer but seemed to be considering the logic. Zielinski didn’t join in on the topic, wishing he hadn’t shared anything about his great-aunt. He had good memories of her, and of watching a few games in her living room when she babysat him. Now those memories were exposed, and in Garrett’s hands.

Garrett was watching him. Zielinski sipped his beer and watched him back. He felt the animosity between them brewing under the surface, tamped down only by Stone’s presence.

A slow smile spread across Garrett’s mouth. “Hey, Z. You hear that Dayton, Ohio is trying to get a major league baseball team?”

“Nuh-uh.”

“The league said no. You know the reason?”

“No clue.”

“They said they couldn’t give Dayton a major league team because then Cincinnati would want one, too.” Garrett’s smile broadened, and he laughed.

Stone joined in, chuckling and shaking his head.

Zielinski didn’t react. He just glanced at the screen and asked, “When did the Mariners get called up from Triple-A again?”

Garrett's laughter subsided into snicker. "Weak sauce, Z. You've got no game."

Zielinski shrugged.

The inning ended with the Mariners batter grounding out to the second baseman. Even though commercials came on the TV, all three men kept watching. Zielinski stopped paying attention to Garrett and examined Stone. The man seemed edgy at times and slightly pale. Zielinski got the feeling that he was trying to pretend he was relaxed when he was actually tense. He knew the look—he'd worn it himself plenty.

Maybe he could get something out of this trip, after all. He just had to be more careful, with Garrett present.

"Everything okay with you, Gary?" Zielinski asked.

Stone glanced at him. Worry creased his face. He looked like he'd just been caught watching porn on his laptop. "I'm fine," he said. "Why?"

"You don't look so great, that's all."

Stone eyes fell and he shrugged. "I guess I'm feeling a little bummed. I didn't realize it was so obvious." He glanced up at Zielinski. "I missed a gun today."

Zielinski raised his brows in surprise. "On a search?"

"Not exactly. But I missed it, and it could have gone bad."

"Except it didn't," Garrett said firmly.

Stone nodded. "Because of you." He turned back to Zielinski. "Ty saved my life."

Zielinski listened, his heart sinking. He knew what something like that meant to a cop, how deep a bond it created. "What happened?"

"He's making more of it than it is," Garrett interjected, before Stone could answer. "Man had a penchant for carrying guns. We got behind him in the Gray Ghost and he tried to fly on us. He crashed into another car, but dude still managed to get out and run. You know these cockroaches, man. Almost nothing stops them."

"Who was it?"

"Dwight Poff. Know him?"

Zielinski shook his head.

Garrett grunted, as if he'd expected that reply. "Poff tears off running down the street from me and Stoney, and suddenly he pulls out his piece. I saw it. Stoney didn't. I had the better angle, that's all."

Stone shook his head. "Don't downplay it, Ty. You saw the gun, knocked me out of the line of fire, and still got him covered."

Garrett shrugged. "All in a day, right?"

"You saved my life," Stone said, his tone was reverent. After a pause, he added, "In more ways than one."

Zielinski watched the exchange, his dread growing along with his realization. He'd never pry Stone away from Garrett now. Not ever.

Garrett let the moment hang, then raised his beer in the air. "Here's to maggots with busted-ass guns that jam when they try to use them."

Stone raised his bottle, too, and Zielinski reluctantly joined them. Garrett and Stone drank, but Zielinski just lowered his bottle.

"I didn't hear about any of this," Zielinski said quietly. "Sounds like you two landed a big one."

"Poff's an alpha hippo, for sure. He'll do some time off of this."

"Anyone hurt in the crash?"

Garrett waved his hand dismissively. "Bumps and bruises."

"That's good."

Stone still seemed morose. The war story of their arrest of Poff didn't seem to diminish the emotion. If anything, it had deepened.

Garrett must have noticed, too. He reached out and shook Stone by the shoulders. "Cheer up, Stoney. You're alive, baby. And the Mariners are about to win this one."

Stone raised his beer again, then drank. "Go M's," he said, unconvincingly.

The conversation lagged after that, and they fell back into

the same uneasy silence as the eighth inning wound down. Zielinski finished his beer, then put the bottle on the table and stood.

"I'm going to take off. Thanks for the brew."

Stone looked up. "You don't want to stay and have another?"

"No, I've gotta go."

"You sure?" Garrett asked. "We wait around long enough, maybe Yang will show up and make it a true team party."

"Yang's coming?"

"I said maybe. How would I know what Yang's doing? Girl is her own thing, straight up." Garrett stood. "But I'll walk you out." He glanced down at Stone. "I left my phone charger in my ride. I'll be back in a few."

"You want me to pause the game?" Stone asked.

"Nah. You can fill me in." He headed toward the door.

Zielinski followed, walking through the open door that Garrett held for him. At the bottom of the porch stairs, he heard the *thunk* of the door as it closed behind them. It only took a few seconds for Garrett to fall in beside him.

"What's up with you, man?"

"What do you mean?" Zielinski asked, cringing at his own question. Maybe Garrett was right. Maybe he did lack game.

"I mean, you and me used to be tight back on power shift. Now, we're not."

Zielinski didn't answer. He just kept walking toward his car.

Garrett stayed with him. "I'm serious, Ray. I thought we were friends, but now all we do is bang heads. I don't like it."

Zielinski stopped halfway to his car. He turned to Garrett, his jaw clenched at the way the man was trying to manipulate him. "Maybe you should have thought about that the night you shot Todd Trotter."

Garrett stared back, his eyes hard. "That was a righteous shoot."

"You sure?"

"Screw you, Ray." He jabbed a finger toward Zielinski. "They investigated the hell out of it, and you know it. That was a good shoot."

"Maybe it was," Zielinski allowed. "But everything since hasn't been righteous at all."

Garrett held his gaze, a quiet fury in his eyes. Zielinski matched his stare. Now that this was out in the open between them, he wasn't going to back down.

"You're talking crazy," Garrett said, his voice low. "I got screwed over by the city, by the department, by everybody. Even you, Ray. You were supposed to be my friend, and even you turned on me. Why was that?"

"I didn't turn on you."

"You sure as hell didn't support me. And now, you're fighting me on every single thing we're trying to do with this team." He peered closely at Zielinski. "Why is that, Ray?"

Zielinski waited a beat before answering. He wondered if Garrett had always been who he was, even back when they worked together on power shift. Was it possible that he'd just missed it? Or had Garrett changed? If that were the case, had it been the shooting that did it? Or was Garrett always this man in front of him, just hidden behind a brilliant disguise?

"Why, Ray?" Garrett repeated. "Tell me."

"I already told you," Zielinski said.

He turned and walked away.

Chapter 53

When the front door opened, Tyler Garrett stepped inside.

"Everything okay?" Stone asked, emerging from his bedroom. While the other men were outside, he had taken an opportunity to stand in front of the bison photo. He needed a reminder to be stoic, to withstand the elements that were buffeting him. Zielinski had called him out about how he looked so he must have been doing a poor job of controlling his internal feelings.

Garrett pulled the door closed behind him. "Yeah, everything's cool."

The way he said it led Stone to believe that everything was not cool between the two men. He thought better of asking any further, though. If Garrett wanted to tell him more, he would.

"Did you get your charger?"

His friend looked at his empty hands then shrugged. "Forgot."

Stone walked to his chair and dropped into it. His friend took up his position on the end of the couch.

"Ray's tortured," Garrett muttered, reaching for his beer.

"What do you mean?"

"He was the first officer to respond to my shooting and it looked bad. You've heard all this, right? The ambush. The suspect I shot was hit in the back. The missing gun."

Stone nodded. He knew about the shooting, of course. He'd been on the department a few years when it had occurred.

"Ray was there. Not for the shooting, but close enough. The county assigned a couple detectives to investigate and then our department gave them a shadow, Wardell Clint. Have you met him?"

"No, but I know his reputation."

"Nut job, right?"

"That's the rumor."

"It's true," Garrett said. "Regardless, those three detectives investigated the hell out of my shooting and then turned it over to the prosecuting attorney who ruled the whole thing a justifiable homicide, a righteous shoot."

"So what's Ray's problem?"

"Every cop's problem when faced with an unsolvable puzzle."

Stone thought about it for a moment. "The missing gun?"

"The missing gun, right. But it doesn't matter, though. It was an ambush and rounds were flying from everywhere. He made a threatening move and I shot him. To this day, I swear he had a gun in his hand."

"Did they ever find them? The other guys, I mean?"

"No," Garrett flatly said then sipped his beer.

"So Ray thinks what…? That you killed the guy for some other purpose than survival…in the middle of an ambush?" Stone tried to understand what Garrett was saying, but he was confused. He could tell the subject bothered his friend and he wanted to be careful in what he said and how he asked his questions. This was some of what Farrell had told him, but it was nothing like the captain portrayed it.

Garrett shrugged. "I liked Ray. We used to be tight, but he's letting the tail wag the dog on this. Now, it's hard for us to be in the same room together. It's just sad."

Stone nodded and sipped his beer.

"So what's *your* deal, Stoney?" Garrett asked then took a pull from his beer.

"What do you mean?"

"Even Z saw it. Something's eating you and don't tell me it's the gun. You're tougher than letting that bother you."

Stone thought about telling Garrett about Captain Farrell's accusations. He wanted to know what his friend would say, but sitting with him now, he didn't have the courage to give voice to Farrell's allegations. They were too ugly.

"I'm mad about the Cattage thing," Stone said, hoping that his previous lie would again get him off the hook.

Garrett frowned. "Don't worry about that. Everybody gets a use-of-force complaint now and then. If you don't, then you're not doing real police work."

Stone feigned a smile.

"But that's not it," Garrett said. "There's something else eating at you."

His friend wasn't letting it go and Stone needed to give him something. Otherwise, he was going to be forced to talk about Farrell's claims and he hadn't even had a chance to process them yet. He needed another misdirection, but he didn't want to lie again.

"It's Jean," he said.

"Jean? What about her?"

"She hates me."

"She doesn't hate you."

"She does now."

Garrett blinked several times, taking in the severity of Stone's statement and the seriousness on his face. "How's that?"

"I messed up by asking her out."

"What do you mean? Was it *how* you asked her out?"

"No," Stone said, shaking his head. "It was that I asked her out at all. We had discussed it years ago. We're friends. Period. I should have known better."

"Then why did you do it?"

"I was jealous."

"Of me?"

"Yeah."

"Why?"

"Because if you went out with her, she wouldn't be my friend any longer. She'd be your girlfriend."

"I don't understand the distinction."

Stone shook his head. "You're Tyler Garrett—super cop.

What am I compared to that? Why would she want to spend time with me?"

Garrett chuckled. "You need to get yourself some confidence, buddy. You're Gary freakin' Stone. Look at the week you've had. Not many guys on this department have ever had a week like you've had. Ever. If Jean doesn't want to go out with you, then hell with her."

Stone's eyes softened. "No, she's great."

"Listen, I know that, and I don't mean any disrespect to her, but you don't have to be a pussy because she didn't want to go out. There are plenty of girls who'd dig a guy like you."

"I don't know, man."

"I'll tell you what. Join Tiana and me, tomorrow, for dinner and I'll introduce you to a nice girl. I know you'll dig her and better than that, I'll guarantee she likes you."

"For real?"

Garrett clinked his beer bottle against Stone's. "For real."

SATURDAY

If something can corrupt you,
you're corrupted already.
—Bob Marley, singer/songwriter

Chapter 54

Ray Zielinski poured himself three fingers of bourbon and capped the bottle. This was the third day in a row that he decided he needed a stiff drink. It was something he wanted to be careful about. Only a few months ago, he was drinking himself to sleep on a nightly basis. After some of his more pressing problems were resolved, he scaled back, tapering off to a few drinks a week. That was more along the lines of what a normal person drank, he figured.

With the Barden situation looming, he found himself needing something to bleed off all the anger and stress last night. He woke up slightly hung over and needing another drink. It was a bit early, but he figured what the hell, it was the weekend.

An image of Barden's smirking face hung in his mind. He didn't want to think about what had happened, or how it might cost him his job. At the moment, there was nothing he could do about it, at least as far as he could see.

He tried to convince himself that none of it mattered, and that he should just let it go. Let the Barden situation run its course and hope for the best. Do his time on ACT, keep his mouth shut, and collect his pension in a few years. Or the percentage of the pension that was still his, after his first wife took her piece, anyway.

Zielinski ground his teeth. He raised the glass and took a long sip.

Letting things go was definitely not his strong suit.

Good God, I'm turning into Wardell Clint.

That gave him pause. Clint had a deserved reputation for spinning conspiracy theories about the brass and their plans, as well as all of government. Everyone thought he was slightly crazy, and maybe he was. But all those same people acknowledged that he was smart and one hell of a detective. Zielinski knew Clint shared his suspicions about Garrett. He couldn't have worked that case so closely and thought otherwise, especially with his predisposition toward seeing collusion at every turn.

If Clint believed Garrett was dirty, there was no way the man would ever give up. So neither should Zielinski. And wasn't that bigger concern, really? If he was right about Garrett, the officer's crimes outweighed any of Zielinski's transgressions.

"I need to be more like Clint?" he muttered aloud. He spun his glass, staring into the rippling auburn liquid. "Are you kidding me?"

It wasn't that far-fetched, though. He and Clint were of a similar age, both in years and time on the job. And they shared a common trait in cops, the good ones at least—tenacity. Once they had their teeth into something, they didn't let go easily, if at all. Zielinski had always been that way on patrol, and he knew it was Clint's reputation as well. So he supposed he didn't need to be more like Clint, after all. He and Clint were already alike.

All of this went beyond his inability to let go of something just for the sake of it, Zielinski knew. He came on the job full of righteous vigor, like most young cops. And, also like most, that zeal had been beaten down and tarnished as the years passed. The seemingly endless supply of bad things happening to good people, the revolving door of the justice system, greater and greater restrictions on what the police could do to catch the criminals, and the collapse of two marriages all wore on him. His idealism faded to cynicism, his sympathy to annoyance. The belief that Garrett was getting away with being a dirty cop should have fallen right in line with all the other factors that ground down his soul. It should have passed right along, just like everything else.

Only it didn't.

It didn't because, despite all the contempt he felt for the system and his part in it, he still saw it as noble. It wasn't the bright and glorious thing he thought it was going to be when he first pinned the badge on his chest, even though he wished it to be long after he knew the truth. The truth was it was a dirty job. It was hauling garbage and shoveling crap, especially down in the trenches. People tried to pretend differently, especially the brass and the politicians, but that was the reality of it.

Yet, it was still noble. At least to him. Their efforts, *his* efforts, created the thin blue veil that kept society from crumbling. Yeah, maybe they did a poor job at times, even failed, but it was still far better than anarchy. It brought some measure of order in a chaotic world. That was a hard thing to do. As Zielinski saw it, though, it was a noble cause, and worth doing.

Which brought him to Garrett.

"Stupid Garrett," he grumbled, and took another drink. The bourbon burned all the way down, and the pleasant warmth in his stomach grew.

Keeping chaos at bay was hard enough as it was, but when a guy like Garrett pretended to be part of that when all he really was…

Zielinski hesitated, thinking. Then it came to him. Garrett was just a damn vampire, using his badge to bleed the system for his own personal gain. And that was messed up. It was wrong.

It wasn't something Zielinski could just let go.

He raised his glass. "Here's to crazy detectives and broke-ass patrol cops who can't let go," he said, his words a little thick even to his own ears. The bourbon sloshed in his glass, but he corrected it before it spilled.

Then he drank.

After a while, he decided to watch some TV. He turned it on, and the first thing he saw was highlights from yesterday's

Mariners game.

He snapped it off and dropped the remote. Instead, he sipped his bourbon and stared at the dark, flat screen.

Sometime later, his phone buzzed. He hadn't realized he'd been dozing, only recognizing that he'd slipped into sleep when the incoming call roused him. Zielinski set the glass down and picked up the phone. He stared at the name on the display.

Neil Clemons.

"What now?" he groaned.

He considered letting it go to voicemail but knew he'd only listen to the message and call Neil back, so what was the point? He pressed the green button.

"H'lo?"

"I thought you said you took care of this!" Neil's voice was full of frantic anger. "Do you know what happened?"

"No. It's my day off. What happened?"

"Barden beat up Sheryl."

Zielinski sat up straight. "Is she okay?"

"She's in the hospital. So… no, man, she is *not* okay."

"Neil, I… what happened?"

"I told you! He kicked the crap out of her, and then took off. I thought you had this handled!"

"I did. I talked to him. I… he attacked… he tried to tackle me…"

"Wait, are you *drunk*?"

"No."

"It's not even noon."

"I'm not drunk. I was just… I was taking a nap. I'm still waking up."

Neil was quiet on the other end of the phone. It went on for so long that Zielinski pulled the phone away to see if the connection was still there. When it was, he asked, "Neil?"

"She's hurt bad," he said, his voice low and angry.

"I'm sorry about that."

"I trusted you."

"I know." Zielinski rubbed his eyes with his thumb and forefinger. "Listen, did you call the cops?"

"I thought I was," Neil said, and broke the connection.

Zielinski stared at the phone for a long while. Then he picked up his glass and held it to his chest while he sat back, thinking.

Maybe this was something he could fix.

Chapter 55

"Chicken or spare ribs?" Karen Farrell asked her husband.

Farrell glanced up from the newspaper he wasn't actually reading. "Huh?"

"To barbecue," Karen said. "Aren't Bob and Darla coming over later? Or do I have the wrong Saturday?"

"Damn," Farrell muttered. The last thing he wanted to do this weekend was spend an evening with the chief and his girlfriend. "I forgot."

She gave him an odd look. "What's wrong? Do you want to cancel?"

"No," he said.

Karen walked over to him and pushed the paper aside. It dropped from his hands and fluttered to the floor as she sat lightly onto his lap. "Thomas Farrell, we need to talk."

He put his hand on her hip, where it always felt so comfortable to be. "If the chief's coming, better make it chicken *and* ribs. The man can eat."

"Fine, but that's not what I meant."

"What, then?" he asked, even though he knew what was coming.

"You know what, and don't pretend otherwise." Karen gave him a meaningful look. "You've been distracted for weeks, maybe longer. There's been more late hours at the office, too."

"I know. It's been busier than usual." It wasn't a lie, but he could hear how incomplete it sounded.

"Clearly. So busy that you have to go out after hours, too."

"Like I said."

"Except even though you say you're going out on police

business, you wear your civvies and don't drive your official car."

Farrell didn't have an answer prepared for that.

"Tell me, Tom, are you having an affair? Do you have a mistress?"

For a split-second, he thought she was serious. Panic slashed through his chest. If Karen thought he'd stepped out on her, she'd be gone in a heartbeat. He'd lose his marriage, and his best friend all at once.

Then he looked closer and saw her teasing, dancing eyes. She was doing what she had always done with him. He was too serious most of the time and didn't broach difficult topics easily, with her or anyone. Karen used light humor, laced with truth, to draw him out. She knew something was wrong, but she knew it wasn't an affair.

"I am," he admitted. "With three mistresses, actually."

She adjusted his hair with her fingers. "Tell me about all three of them."

"It's ACT," he said, and the words sounded true, because they were.

"I thought they were doing well."

"They are."

"They've been all over the news lately."

"So they have."

"What's the problem, then?"

For the thousandth time over the past two years, he wanted nothing more than to tell her. To take her back to that fateful night that Garrett shot Todd Trotter, and walk her forward with every piece of the puzzle. Garrett, Talbott, and Pomeroy, a veritable triumvirate of dirty cops. And he wouldn't forget Ernesto Ocampo, either. Three of the four ended up dead, not to mention three others caught in the crossfire. All killed by Garrett, he was sure. He just couldn't prove it.

Yet.

He longed to explain all of that to her. Hell, he *ached* to do it. She was the smartest person he knew. Maybe she could help him find the best way out of this, or through it. If nothing else, at least when she ran her fingers through his hair when she held him tight, she'd know what she was comforting him about.

He couldn't, though. To tell her would be selfish. It would make her complicit in something she didn't choose. And if all of the off-book investigations he'd directed Clint to do, and all of his own actions came to light before he had the proof against Garrett to justify them, he didn't want her to get hurt.

So he had to lie to her.

Which felt a thousand times worse.

"The sergeant," he told her. "Ragland. He replaced McGinn when he went on family leave."

"McGinn's the one who lost his wife and baby?"

Farrell nodded. "Ragland is doing a half-assed job with the team."

"But they're doing okay?"

"For now. But these teams run a certain kind of risk if there's a not a firm hand guiding them."

"Like yours?"

"No, not from an office. Boots on the ground. That's why I picked Christian McGinn. He's a hard charger but he plays strictly by the rules."

Karen thought about what he said. "You're talking about noble cause corruption, then."

He gave her a strange look. "Yeah, but how…?"

"Oh, give me a break, Tom. How many times did you test for promotion? Four, five times? That book was on every single one of those exams, and I was the one reading you flash cards when you studied your ass off."

"I remember." He squeezed her hip slightly. "It was the only way studying for promotional exams was bearable."

She kissed him on the nose. "Don't flirt. We still have to go to the store for chicken and ribs. Tell me why you're worried about this team."

Farrell sighed. "I don't want to see us become another

Rampart. The department doesn't need that. Not after everything else in the last two years."

Karen nodded that she understood. "So that's why the late nights?"

"That's part of it. Some of it's just having fifteen hours of paperwork to do in a ten- hour day."

"Well, I'll have to talk to Bob about that once I get some chicken in him."

Farrell laughed at that. "The last thing I need is my wife needling my boss about my workload."

"It is the last thing I'd ever do. I was only joking, babe."

"I know."

"What about the trips out after hours?" she asked. "That's ACT, too?"

He nodded because it was true. After a fashion. Checking in with Yang fell into that same category, he told himself. It wasn't exactly a lie.

"Doing what, exactly?"

"Checking up on them. Spot checks. If they don't know when the captain might show up…"

"It keeps them on the straight and narrow," she finished for him.

"That's the idea."

Karen considered his explanation. Then she said, "You should wear your uniform for that. It's more inspiring than a polo shirt and flip-flops. Or intimidating, if that's what you're going for."

"Both, really."

"Well, it works either way. And you'll have on your vest, in case something happens."

"Good idea," he said.

She smiled at him. "I don't want you getting hurt, all right?"

"All right."

She kissed him again, this time on the corner of his mouth. He smelled her skin, and her light, airy perfume. As always, it sent a charge through his body, like he was still fifteen and she was his first date. She hovered there for a second, then touched her forehead briefly to his, and climbed off his lap.

God, he hated these lies.

She took a couple of steps, then stopped. "Why three?"

He raised his eyebrows questioningly.

"You said three mistresses," Karen said. "With the sergeant, aren't there five officers on that team?"

No. There's an absentee sergeant, a dirty cop, and the three officers I put on that team to hopefully be my spies.

Farrell nodded slowly. "You're right. But I don't count the sergeant."

"Fair, but that still leaves four. Who aren't you counting?"

"Garrett, I guess," he admitted.

"Really? Why isn't he one of your mystery mistresses?"

He should be. He's the only one I'm actually trying to nail.

"Out of all them, he can take care of himself," he answered simply, hoping it was explanation enough.

Karen smiled at him. She held out her hand to him, and he reached out and took it. She gave it a squeeze. "You're probably right. He seems like a good cop."

Farrell didn't answer. He couldn't.

Chapter 56

"Then Gary throws his guy into an entertainment center—"

"Like the thing a TV sits on?" Tiana Kennedy asked.

"Yeah!" Tyler Garrett said, shaking Stone's shoulder.

Gary Stone was slightly embarrassed at the way his friend was telling the story.

They were seated on the patio of The Flying Goat, a craft beer and casual restaurant in the Audubon neighborhood. All the tables around them were full, lending itself to a festive atmosphere. Pop music played from hidden speakers.

Garrett had brought along Tiana's friend, Fia Woodson, a statuesque woman with skin the color of caramel. She wore a light summer dress that exposed her shoulders. She was leaning forward, her chin resting in her hands. Her brown eyes locked onto Stone's as Garrett continued his story.

"So the whole thing comes crashing to the ground and we all stopped fighting. Me and my guy, Ray and his, Jun and hers. All six of us just stopped throwing punches."

"Wait," Tiana said, "you were all fighting and then everybody suddenly stopped?"

Fia glanced at Garrett. "Why?"

"Because we had to see what happened. You should have seen the look on Gary's face. It was priceless."

"What were you feeling, Gary?" Fia asked.

"I was wondering if I would have to pay for it."

Garrett guffawed and the girls smiled politely.

"What happened then?" Tiana asked.

"Oh, the fight was back on," Garrett said, still chuckling. "It was a battle royale in that little apartment, but you could tell we all wanted to be the first one to get our guy in handcuffs.”

“So, who won?” Fia asked, her eyes still studying Stone.

Garrett’s hand went back to Stone’s shoulder. “My boy did. His guy put up a fight, but he didn’t stand a chance.”

Stone looked down at his beer, embarrassed at the lie Garrett told to make him look better. He was also a bit surprised at how Fia watched him.

Garrett continued with the tale. He was a natural storyteller when the spotlight was on him. That was fine as Stone wanted to be alone in his head. He had almost skipped meeting Garrett for dinner after spending the day alone.

He didn’t want to, of course. He called Jean Carter, but she never answered. He left a couple voicemails but never heard from her. He even texted her half a dozen times, a few of which were apologies.

For a while, he thought about going to her house, walking up to her door, and asking for forgiveness. He didn’t know if that would do any good, but he thought about it. He even went so far as to get into his car and drive toward her neighborhood, but he chickened out. She was mad and showing up uninvited might make it worse. It was clear she didn’t want to hear from him.

Stone stopped at a grocery store and went to the gift card section. He spent several minutes searching for the right card. He also bought a book of stamps at the checkout register and sat in his car for thirty minutes, thinking about the things he wanted to say.

In the end, he filled in all the white space on the card, first with an apology then with how much he loved her as a friend.

He knew what he did was wrong, and he wished that he could take it back.

If he could change that moment, he would.

His life was better with her in it, he wrote, and he wanted her to know that he missed her, that even a single day without her was a day too many.

He stopped by the post office and mailed the letter. He

resolved not to call her again until she was ready to talk with him. He had shared his feelings with her, so it was up to her now.

When Garrett stopped speaking, Fia asked Stone, "Hey, weren't you on TV? The news or something?"

Stone looked up into her deep brown eyes. "Hmm?"

"Didn't I see you on the news earlier this week?"

Garrett and Tiana turned expectantly to him.

"Probably. I gave a report to the city council on how our team was doing."

"I thought so," Fia said, a satisfied smiling spreading across her face. "That's why you look familiar. I've been trying to place where I'd seen you."

Garrett grabbed Stone's chin. "This handsome guy is going to be the face of the department someday, you watch."

Stone shook his head. "Not me. You maybe."

A waiter walked up to the table. "Another round?"

Garrett waved his finger in a circle. "Yes, please."

Fia looked to Garrett and Tiana. "Do you guys come here often?"

"This is one of our favorite places," she said.

As the three of them discussed the restaurant, Stone watched Garrett smile.

After he dealt with Jean, he was able to focus on his discussion with Farrell. The captain had said Garrett was suspected of felonies, but he wouldn't elaborate on what those felonies were. He kept those cards to his chest.

He said others also suspected Garrett of those crimes, but he wouldn't say who *they* were.

Stone believed that Zielinski and Yang had been brought into the Anti-Crime Team, the same way he had been—under false pretenses. Farrell was hiding things from him, or worse lying to him, yet wanting him to entrap Tyler Garrett, his friend and the man who had saved his life.

Stone went back and forth on how he wanted to handle the Farrell issue throughout the day. He'd only made up his mind as to what he was going to do just prior to arriving at the restaurant.

"If you'll excuse me," Tiana said, as she pushed back her chair. "I need to step around the corner."

Fia stood as well. "I'll join you."

As the girls walked away, Garrett touched his glass of beer against Stone's. "What'd I tell you? Fia's into you, man. She's a pretty girl."

Stone turned to him and leaned in slightly. "Farrell is setting you up," he whispered.

Garrett slowly lowered his glass, his eyes locking onto Stone's. For a moment, his friend didn't say anything. When he finally spoke, he only said one word. "Why?"

"I don't know," Stone said, still whispering. "He believes you committed some crimes—"

"Crimes?"

"Felonies. He wouldn't tell me what they were. He says there are others that believe you have as well."

"Who?"

"He wouldn't say."

Garrett's face contorted in anger. "That's a complete lie. I haven't done anything like that."

"I know," Stone said. "I don't believe what he's saying. You saved my life, Ty. You couldn't have done the things he's suggesting."

Garrett grabbed Stone by the back of the neck and pulled him closer until they touched foreheads. His eyes were closed, but his fingers dug into Stone's neck. It was a reassuring feeling.

When Garrett's hand relaxed, they parted, and his friend looked at him again. "This job, man. Sometimes it's harder to tell who your enemies are within the department than it is on the street."

Stone thought about the fights he and Garrett had recently been in. He envisioned Dwight Poff's twisted expression as he tried to shoot Stone with a malfunctioning gun. Then he recalled Captain Farrell in his office, telling Stone just enough information to get him to do what he wanted, and no more.

"Yeah," was all Stone said.

The girls emerged then from the inside of the restaurant, arm-in-arm and laughing. "Oh my God, the funniest thing just happened."

Tyler Garrett put his hand on Stone's shoulder and lightly squeezed. "Tell us," he said with a smile. "We could use a happy story."

Chapter 57

"Time is running out for you," she said.

"What do you mean?"

Jun Yang dipped a French fry into some ketchup and held it up for inspection. "College will start soon. Are you prepared?"

Xi-Wang dropped his hamburger onto its wrapper. "Seriously? I'm getting this conversation, now? We're supposed to be having fun tonight."

Her brother had convinced her to go out for burgers and shakes, a tradition that she did with him often while she was a teenager and he was in grade school. She rarely ate fast food now, preferring to eat a healthier diet to maintain her physical condition. Her reward donuts were her sole vice. They were at the Zip's Burgers in Spokane Valley. Only a couple other booths were occupied.

"Life is not always about fun," Jun said.

"But sister," Xi-Wang said, "you never have any fun."

Jun popped the fry into her mouth. "I have fun."

"Work is not fun."

"I wasn't talking about work."

Her brother crossed his arms. "You weren't? Then what is fun for you?"

"Racquetball. Racquetball is fun."

"I didn't know that. When is the last time you played?"

In the Army.

Xi-Wang smiled. "Been a while, huh? What else is fun?"

She used to like dancing, but that was when she went to the NCO clubs on the bases where she was stationed. She didn't go out to the bars in Spokane. Instead, she answered calls for service to those bars.

Xi-Wang didn't relent. "Taking college courses at night and lifting weights is not fun."

"Well, it can be," she said. She winced when she heard the defensiveness in her voice.

"It's not and you know it." He took a bite of his hamburger, watching her as he ate.

Dipping another fry, Jun said, "This was supposed to be about you."

"No, it wasn't," Xi-Wang said with a laugh. "It was supposed to be about us, about me and you hanging together on a Saturday night. I even pitched in and did my chores around the store so we could get out early tonight. I don't need a lecture on how to live my life."

"I only want the best for you."

"So do I."

"My advice is hard earned," Jun said. "I've been through things and am trying to help you achieve more, faster."

"I don't want the life you've had. No offense, but your life is sort of boring."

"Boring?"

"And lonely."

"It's not lonely," she said. Even as the words tumbled from her mouth, she felt a ping of loneliness.

"How many friends have you got? Not Facebook friends, real friends."

"I've got friends."

Xi-Wang leaned forward. "You mean work friends? They don't count."

She grabbed her shake and took a sip. She wanted to avoid answering his question because she knew the answer. She hadn't made any new friends since she'd come home from the Army.

The friends she had in high school were different than she remembered. They no longer had anything in common and she didn't want to be around them.

And she didn't have any friends on the department, especially now that she had been pigeon-holed into the Anti-Crime Team.

"What about a boyfriend?" Xi-Wang asked. "Got one?"

She'd had several while in the Army. In fact, she was often sought after. The male-to-female ratio in the military made her odds of finding a successful relationship greater than those in the civilian world. When she came home, her Army beauty faded into average civilian looks.

For a while, she thought that maybe Gary Stone would be an option, but he was too focused on chasing bad guys and being a Tyler Garrett protégé to notice her.

"See? Boring."

"Whatever," she said.

They ate quietly for a few moments and listened to the oldies music that played through the speakers that hung in the corners of the restaurant.

After a while, Xi-Wang softly said, "You seem different than when you first came home."

Her recent thoughts about her high school friends echoed in her head. "Different how?" she asked.

"Unhappy."

She picked up several fries and pushed them into her mouth, allowing her time for silence. Her brother was right. She was unhappy.

She'd left a military career that had been fulfilling to chase a childhood dream that now seemed tainted due to her assignment in the Anti-Crime Team.

But weren't those my feelings before I rotated into the team? Wasn't I already feeling this way before I got involved with Captain Farrell and his misguided boys?

That's when she realized it.

The Anti-Crime Team was not the problem.

Garrett, Zielinski, and Stone were not the issue.

Even Captain Farrell and his secrets were not the true problem.

No, when it came down to it, the real problem was her.

"What just happened?" Xi-Wang asked.

"What do you mean?"

"Your face relaxed. You look calm. Are you going to hit me?"

Jun Yang reached for another fry. "No, little brother, I just realized I've been looking at everything all wrong."

Chapter 58

Clint had enough photographs of Earl Ellis today that if he'd wanted to, he could create a photo album.

He had followed Ellis all day, and while he was convinced the man was a criminal and a drug dealer, he had to admire his work ethic. When Clint rolled into the East Central neighborhood where Ellis's grandmother lived early that morning, he passed the man coming the other way, already at work. There was no other traffic on the residential road, so Clint couldn't flip a U-turn without a high probability of being seen. He took a left and then raced around the block, the small engine of his Impala whining as he whipped through the neighborhood. He managed to get back on an arterial and spotted Ellis at a stoplight.

Clint fell in behind him. Throughout the day, he watched Ellis contact seven people, most of them men. Several Clint recognized from before, but he snapped pictures anyway. Others were new to him, so he took photos, and created a space for them on the makeshift chart he'd sketched on his legal pad.

He also took another photo of the woman he'd seen the day before with Ellis. Unlike the men who interacted with Ellis, the woman appeared tentative, as if her dealings with him were new. He couldn't hear the words Ellis said, but it appeared that he spoke gently with her. Almost as if he was speaking to a daughter. More than the men, Clint wanted to know who this woman was.

Ellis didn't give anything out on these stops, and he received something from each person, except for the new woman. It didn't take much for Clint to hypothesize what that meant.

"Saturday is pickup day," he mumbled, watching Ellis appear to give instructions to the man on this stop.

Of course, he'd seen Ellis pick up before, too. He considered how that might work. Perhaps every dealer messaged Ellis when they'd sold their existing stock, and he collected the money, rather than let it sit with the dealer, a constant temptation. Then, on Saturday, he always picked up, no matter how much was sold.

Waiting for Ellis to finish berating his flunky, Clint wondered how big Garrett's operation truly was in terms of dollars, but he knew that time would tell. He was only just beginning to crack this nut.

It felt good.

Ellis finished his business and got back into his car. Clint tailed him up Nevada and into the parking lot of an Albertson's, just north of Francis. There, he parked on the far end of the lot and met with someone. This man was new to Clint, and he zoomed in as close as he could with his camera while the two of them spoke. He noticed two things.

The first thing was that this new person, a white male with a shock of long black hair, had a scar from the corner of his mouth up to the middle of his left cheek. It reminded Clint of a one-sided Joker cut. He held on to the man's face for several shots to ensure he got the injury.

The second thing he noticed was that nothing passed between the two men. They spoke at length, but no one handed anything to anybody. This was different than Ellis's other meetings that day, and Clint wondered why. His mind raced through possibilities.

This could be a job interview of sorts. A first meet to feel each other out about a possible partnership of some kind.

Clint peered at the two of them through the zoom lens of the camera. They seemed too at ease with each other for that to be true. Both men watched their surroundings, but neither seemed wary of the other. This suggested familiarity to him.

So maybe this man with the facial scar was already part of

Ellis's operation. If so, what was his role? He could be a dealer, but if that were the case, why wasn't there any transfer happening?

Was he an enforcer?

Or maybe he was a lieutenant. If Garrett was using Ellis as a VP of operations to insulate himself, which Garrett suspected, perhaps Ellis was smart enough to do the same thing.

Clint bit his lip. That didn't quite make sense. If that was it, why was Ellis still collecting money?

Was this guy being trained to take over that role? He saw no direct evidence of this but supposed it could be possible.

If Clint were running the operation, he'd bifurcate the delivery of the drugs and the receipt of the money. It was a basic tactic that he knew many dealers used at the street level, but he thought it just as important at the higher levels. Maybe the scarred man was going to do the deliveries and Ellis would still pick up the money…

"I don't know," Clint muttered. There wasn't enough information yet to make a reasonable conclusion. But he was gaining more data every day, and at a much faster rate than he had been in the past year.

When the two men finished their palaver and returned to their cars, Clint was torn as to who he should follow. In the end, he stuck with Ellis. He still wanted to get a good photograph of him with Garrett. That would be a centerpiece to this part of the case. Maybe now that Ellis had the money, he'd take it to Garrett.

Ellis headed south, though, all the way home. He went inside, and even though Clint stayed there long into the night, the man never left.

He must have a safe.

But he has to take Garrett's cut to him eventually.

Clint's stomach rumbled. He reached for some almonds, but the bag was empty. He rubbed his weary eyes and scratched the stubble on his face. When all the lights in the house had been out for almost an hour, he finally went home himself to get a few hours' sleep before picking it up again tomorrow.

On the drive to his house, he turned on the radio and hummed along to Marvin Gaye's "I Heard It Through the Grapevine." He imagined what that photograph of Ellis and Garrett would look like when he took it. He saw the two of them glancing around to see if the coast was clear. Then Ellis handing Garrett a fat envelope.

Click, click.

Garrett accepting it, clutching it in his greedy hands.

Click, click, click.

Marvin Gaye's smooth voice spurred him to join in, but he made up his own lyrics to the end of the chorus.

"Oh, I gotcha by the throat now," Clint rumbled in time with the music. "Oh, I'm gonna take you down this time. Honey, honey, yeah…"

Chapter 59

Tyler Garrett stared at the white ceiling, which reflected the ambient lights from the neighboring buildings. They'd gone to bed with the curtains open, allowing visual noise to sneak into their bedroom. Tiana was breathing heavily next him, already in a deep sleep.

His mind whirred, filled with thoughts of recent revelations. Sleep had already eluded him for an hour. It was sure to evade him for some time further. He sat up, careful not to disturb his woman. When her breathing continued unaffected, he stood and walked to the window. He leaned against its frame and watched the activity below.

It was shortly after one in the morning and the sidewalks were still alive with revelers walking to and from the city bars.

Most weekends, he loved being on those streets, especially with Tiana. But tonight, he wanted to be away from everything. He wanted to be alone, to be inside his head, so he could determine where all the players stood on the board.

Down below, a man ran across the street, pursued by three other men. They disappeared between two buildings.

Everything in Garrett's life had suddenly changed. It was now life or death—his life, his death.

Gary Stone's revelation made that evident.

Captain Farrell, the puppet master, had orchestrated a play for his downfall. Zielinski, Yang, and Stone all played important roles, moved by the ever-present hands of Farrell. Every day at work, Garrett knew the captain was watching through the eyes of his fellow patrol officers.

He thought he had some control in the outcome, though, by working with Stone. The officer had come a long way in several weeks, further and faster than Garrett ever thought possible. Now, he realized the idea of control was an illusion. Unfortunately, he should have seen it sooner before he revealed any of himself to Stone.

At least he'd known he'd never get the academy princess to see the world his way and that Zielinski was so myopic he thought that police work was a righteous crusade when in fact the man was tilting at windmills. He'd kept a safe distance from those two.

Garrett went to work, mostly careful to never step too far out of line just in case one of Farrell's puppets might see and say something to their fearless leader.

Unfortunately for him, the favorite marionette was dancing off stage all the while, wreaking havoc. Wardell Clint might have discovered his relationship to Earl Ellis. That was unfortunate because Ellis was a dependable man and someone he would hate to lose.

There had already been enough men lost in this personal war with the constant hounding of the detective.

Garrett had to kill Detective Justin Pomeroy to ensure his silence. Clint had already talked with him and would have eventually broken the man, which would have guaranteed Garrett's incarceration. Pomeroy's partner, Butch Talbott, was a mean son of a bitch and it was unlikely that he would have rolled if pushed by Clint.

Talbott made the mistake of ambushing a younger and faster opponent. Both men died at the hands of Tyler Garrett. Talbott because he was arrogant; Pomeroy because he was weak.

Neither man was more valuable than Ernesto Ocampo, though. He had taught Garrett the importance of a network, how to recruit men, how to ship and receive drugs, and how to make new contacts. Garrett didn't kill Ocampo because of Clint directly, though. He had to kill the man and his crew because of the county detectives who were investigating his shooting into Todd Trotter. Clint was only a shadow in that investigation, but he would have found Ocampo sooner or later. Garrett couldn't risk that.

Down at street level, a police car raced by with its lights activated, the blues and reds bouncing off the nighttime glass of the surrounding buildings.

Skunk.

I almost forgot about him.

Ezekiel "Skunk" Hetzel. Garrett killed him because he knew Clint would find him. Skunk made a mistake and murdered a young woman that he was only supposed to threaten for Garrett. He had a five-cent head, but he was a decent drug slinger. If Clint ever got a whiff of Skunk, he would have pursued the man mercilessly.

All their deaths led directly back to Clint. Garrett had never intended on killing anyone, but the detective forced him to take those actions.

If he was looking at it critically, which he was trying to do, Clint's strings weren't in his own hands. They were in Captain Farrell's. He wondered if the ever-petulant Wardell Clint realized that the captain held him by the strings and, if the detective did know this, why didn't he try to cut himself free?

His mind continued to work the problem until he came to one unescapable conclusion—he had to resolve this issue. The Anti-Crime Team was built specifically to frame him, and it felt like they were getting close to accomplishing it.

Gary Stone had confirmed that earlier in the night.

That meant Farrell would continue to move the pieces on the board around him until Garrett was boxed in. As hard as it might be, though, he must be patient. A solution to this problem would come soon enough. It always did.

Captain Tom Farrell might have his pawns, but Tyler Garrett was the king. This game was built for him and Garrett knew there was always a winning move if he waited long enough to spot the opportunity to make it.

SUNDAY

What do you despise?
By this are you truly known.
—Frank Herbert, author
from the novel *Dune*

Chapter 60

When Gary Stone woke, he rolled over and found her already awake, staring at him.

"I was wondering how long you were going to sleep," she said.

He quickly replayed the remaining events of the previous night.

After another beer and the last of the pizza at the Flying Goat, they said goodnight to Ty and Tiana. Not wanting their night to end, the two of them caught an Uber downtown to The Globe where they had a couple more drinks and some intense conversation about life, dreams, and the universe.

She was a deeply spiritual person and wanted to discover what made Stone tick. At first, he tried to keep the cool persona he had worked hard to develop over the past few weeks, but as he drank more, he heard Jean's words looping in his head, "What happened to you, Gary?"

He dropped his guard and began sharing who he truly was. For whatever reason, that seemed to pique Fia's interest.

They took another Uber home to his house, opened a couple more beers, and he introduced her to Pink Martini, the band he held a secret affinity toward. They weren't halfway through the album before they were kissing on the floor of the living room. She never got to hear the last couple of songs.

"Long night," he said, flopping to his back.

She moved against him and rested her hand on his bare chest. "It was a fun night."

"Hmm," he grunted in agreement, his arm caressing her naked back.

"What's with the picture of the buffalo?" she asked, lifting her chin toward the photograph hanging on the wall.

"It's a bison."

"What?"

"Bison are in the Americas. Buffaloes are in Africa. And Asia, I think."

"Oh."

Stone nodded, his eyes slowly closing.

"So what's with the bison? Are you a hunter or something?"

He turned and stared at the photograph. "I took that picture. Several years ago, by the road, while in Montana. I've always thought it looked cool."

"It *is* cool," she agreed. "I really like its composition."

"The composition?"

"Yeah," she said. "It's how the light interacts with the snow and trees. How the wind is affecting not only the hair on the bison, but the grass and snowflakes as well. It gives a feeling of being there, of being cold."

"Huh. Composition."

Fia studied him. "It obviously spoke to you," she said. "So what did it say?"

He'd never told anyone about the photo, about what it meant to him, but based on their conversation about spirituality and personal growth, he thought she might understand. "It was about the bison."

"What about it?"

"He's standing there, amidst the cold, the wind, the loneliness, yet he's unaffected. That's how I want to be. When I feel like life is pushing me around, I think about this bison and I try to be like him."

Her smile was soft and kind. "You're sort of a romantic."

"Sort of," he said.

She lowered her head to his chest. "I like you, Gary Stone."

"And I like you, Fia Woodson."

Her hand rubbed his stomach. "You're different than I thought you'd be."

"How do you mean?" he said.

"When Tiana said she wanted me to meet a friend of Tyler's, I thought you'd be like him."

"Like what?" Stone asked, bothered by the way she said it.

"Not like you are." Her voice was dreamy, as if she was about to fall back asleep.

Stone lifted his head, moving her slightly so she'd look back him. "You thought I'd be like him, how?"

Fia lowered her eyes as she thought. When she looked up, she said, "Not nice."

"What? Ty's nice."

Her smile was soft. "No, he's not, Gary."

"How do you mean?"

"There's something…dark, I guess. I don't know. Can't you sense it?"

"Not really."

"His energy is off. Tiana doesn't see it, either. Maybe it's just me."

He fell silent for a moment, lost in thought. When he was about to ask her what she meant by dark energy, she climbed on top of him and lightly touched her lips to his.

Even in the morning, she still smelled wonderful.

Chapter 61

Wardell Clint wolfed down the breakfast burrito he'd bought at the convenience store where he'd stopped to use the restroom. He'd slept only a few hours last night and hurried out of the house this morning without packing any supplies, only to discover he'd already missed Earl Ellis. The man was clearly an early riser.

Clint spent part of his day checking out the locations that Ellis had previously met with his associates, and on the fourth one, he got lucky. There was nothing passed between Ellis and the pudgy man in a blue denim cap, but plenty of conversation. Clint made sure he snapped photos of the two of them together, and some more close-ups of each.

He managed to keep on Ellis for the remainder of the day. After stopping to talk to the Native American in Timberland boots, the dealer had a leisurely lunch at a Vietnamese restaurant. As soon as Clint saw his food arrive, he slipped away to the Circle K for relief and to grab something to eat himself. The burrito had the stiff and stale feel to it that convenience store food acquired when it sat too long under the heat lamp. Clint ignored the taste and chewed methodically. The burrito served one purpose; it was fuel for his body.

Ellis finished his lunch without anyone joining him. Then he slowly made his rounds again, touching base with his network one person at a time. This included the man with the odd fishhook scar, who Ellis spoke with at length. Clint wondered again who this man was, and what role he played. He hoped a computer search on Monday would turn something up, though the only thing he really had to go on that was at all unique was the scar. It might be enough, though.

Throughout the remainder of the day, Clint followed Ellis dutifully, but there were no real surprises.

And no Garrett.

Clint had hoped that Sunday might be a good day for Ellis to meet with Garrett. The Anti-Crime Team was scheduled Monday through Friday, so Garrett had the day off. He knew from experience that Garrett rarely had his kids on Sunday, and even when he did, it was only for a few hours. It was the perfect day for the two of them to conduct business.

But maybe it was also predictable. Clint realized this as the day went on and there was no sign of Garrett anywhere. One thing Garrett had done well over the past two years since his shooting, and probably before, was to remain unpredictable. There was no reason why that shouldn't extend to when and where he met with his underlings.

It didn't matter. They would meet eventually, and Clint planned to be there to memorialize the event. Once he had solid evidence to link Ellis and Garrett, he could start picking off the low-hanging fruit of their organization to build a solid case. He might not be able to prove some of the crimes Garrett committed in the aftermath of his shooting, but he could nail the dirty officer for what he was doing now.

By the time Earl Ellis finished for the day, Clint was hungry again, and he realized something else. With this breakthrough, maybe it was time to bring Captain Farrell back into the picture. When the prospect of nailing Garrett seemed bleak, it was easy for Clint to write off the captain's contributions, which had been admittedly weak. In addition, his plan to trap Garrett with the Anti-Crime Team was moronic, and Clint didn't want any part of it. All it served to do was make Clint's task more difficult.

Most of what Farrell could do for the cause came *after* the investigation, not during. Farrell was a captain, and that carried some weight, more than Clint's prowess as a detective. People who thought he was conspiracy-prone or called him Honey Badger would be skeptical of his claims, even with the evidence he hoped to bring to the table. Farrell's rank would give these findings, and the accusations that they led to, a certain degree of legitimacy that Clint could never achieve otherwise. It got people to stop doubting and to look at the evidence objectively. He needed that.

It was time to rebuild that smoldering bridge, he decided.

Chapter 62

Sundays were supposed to be for his kids. It had been that way for Ray Zielinski ever since the divorce from his first wife. But as his kids got older and strove for independence, they rebelled against that rigid structure. It started with the occasional skipped day for either the son or the daughter and evolved into a situation where he never knew what would happen. Sometimes he'd get to spend time with his son, other times it was his daughter who wanted to see him. In rarer instances, he had the two of them at once, which gave him plenty of teenage sullen angst to digest. More commonly, both begged off, giving excuses that were progressively less inventive and more dismissive.

He still dutifully called each Sunday morning at nine, as if he fully expected to be picking them both up at eleven. He knew that the one Sunday he didn't call, they'd both act as if he'd abandoned them, and that would become the new narrative. Besides, they were his kids, and he wanted to see them.

But when he called, Priscilla had told him R.J. was staying over at a friend's house, and Jody didn't feel up to visiting.

"Doesn't feel up to it?" he'd asked, a little annoyed.

"She's got her period," Priscilla told him.

"Oh." He knew his daughter had inherited her mother's unfortunate tendency of having difficult periods. "Well, tell her I love her, and I hope she feels better."

"She'll be fine in a day or so," Priscilla said, her tone neither brusque nor friendly. Their relationship had been a tumultuous one and the divorce ugly, but after Zielinski's second marriage ended, they'd come to something of a truce.

It didn't cost Zielinski any less money, but it was much easier emotionally.

They discussed a couple of financial and logistical issues, and then ended the call.

That left Zielinski free to work on his Barden problem. He had considered letting things ride, but the ache in his stomach that came with inaction was too much. So, he changed into his uniform and headed to a police substation. Once there, he logged into the computer system and brought up the Barden report. Due to the nature of her injuries, the hospital had notified the police, and Sheryl Clemons was interviewed by a patrol officer. Based upon that interview, the patrol officer had completed a warrant request. Until that worked its way through the system, Barden could be arrested on the officer's probable cause. At that point, he decided to spend the rest of his Sunday searching for the man.

With the PC for arrest in hand, Zielinski started checking locations based on what little he knew of the man. When Barden wasn't present at any of his usual haunts, Zielinski interviewed the people there, trying to develop further leads. Some of these led to dead ends, others to more people to talk to.

He discovered that a lot of people knew Darold Barden, and not all of them liked him. Still, most preferred Barden to the police, and so Zielinski had to find the right lever to entice these witnesses to talk. Sometimes it took the carrot and sometimes the stick, depending on a variety of factors. Zielinski usually guessed right on which to use and got information more often than he got stonewalled. A few pieces of info turned out to be bogus, but enough were legit that he was able to continue following the trail most of the day. He made a few quick stops into police substations to supplement his intel, hoping not to run into anyone there, especially a curious sergeant or lieutenant. The advantage of it being a Sunday was that most of them weren't working.

Eventually, he ended up at the third-floor apartment of

Alejandra Sanita, who one of the people Zielinski interviewed described as Barden's "sometimes girlfriend." The complex on Magnesium Road was at the northern fringe of Spokane. He rapped on the door, leaning more toward a polite tap than a power shift knock. An attractive Hispanic woman in her late thirties opened the door. Her hair tumbled down onto her shoulders and she wore flannel pajama bottoms and a pale blue T-shirt. As soon as she saw Zielinski in uniform, her eyes widened, and he knew he'd hit the jackpot.

"I need to talk to Darold," he said.

She started to glance over her shoulder, then stopped herself. *"¿Que?"* she said, her expression turning confused.

Zielinski shook his head. "Don't try that. I ran up your name, and I know you speak English." He was bluffing but given how long she'd lived and worked in Spokane, he felt like it was a safe one.

Sanita didn't say anything right away. Instead, she stared at him, as if contemplating her next move.

Zielinski didn't worry about Barden escaping out the rear of the place. The apartments didn't have balconies, and the drop from the third story window was precipitous. Plus the complex was built on a slope, so the back side fell sharply away. If Barden was inside, and Zielinski's gut told him that he was, then he was trapped.

"Look," Zielinski said, as he took a half step forward, making sure his foot was in place to stop the door if she tried to slam it. "This can go one of several ways. The easiest way is you invite me in so I can have my conversation with Darold and after that, I leave you in peace. The hardest way has your door getting smashed and lots people going to jail. There's about six other ways it can go, but most of them are closer to door smashing and jail than a peaceful Sunday afternoon." He shrugged. "I like easy myself, and I'm willing to bet you do, too, but I'm going to talk to Darold any way you cut it."

Sanita hesitated, mulling over his words. Finally, she nodded and stepped aside, opening the door wide.

"Alex, you stupid bitch, don't let him in!" Barden shouted, standing up from behind the couch and pointing at her.

Sanita tried to shut the door, but it was too late. Zielinski was already inside, and in three strides, he grasped Barden by the wrist and elbow and swept him to the ground. Barden grunted when he landed, and again when Zielinski dropped his weight onto him.

"Get off of me, you fat bastard!" Barden hollered, his words muffled and distorted by the carpet.

Zielinski ignored him, and pulled his handcuffs from his belt, where they hung in the small of his back. He ratcheted them onto Barden's wrists and clicked the double locks into place.

"Call the cops, Alex!" Barden screamed.

"Don't bother," Zielinski told her, pulling his flip phone from his pocket with his free hand. He dialed into call center, identified himself to the dispatcher, and gave his location.

"I have one in custody for DV assault," he said. "I need a shield for transport."

If the dispatcher found it odd that he was working on a Sunday or alone, she didn't show it in her tone. She advised him a patrol officer would be en route shortly, and Zielinski thanked her before hanging up.

"This is illegal entry," Barden said.

"She invited me in."

"You tricked her! This is illegal and I'm gonna sue you."

"Do you live here?"

"Yeah, man, I live here."

"Good. Then I can search the house incident to arrest." It wasn't true, and he had no intention of searching, but Zielinski was curious how much criminal law Barden really knew.

Barden was quiet for a few seconds. Then he said, "You can't search the place. I don't live here. I'm only visiting."

"Uh-huh."

"Let me up," Barden said. "You're hurting my neck."

Zielinski considered, then let up pressure with his knee that was across the prone man's upper back.

"It still hurts."

"Whatever."

"Come on, man. I had two vertebrae fused."

Zielinski suppressed a groan. "Fine," he mumbled. He shifted his positioning and helped Barden into a sitting position. With his hands behind his back, and Zielinski remaining behind him, Barden didn't pose much of a threat.

Sanita remained at the door, watching the whole scene unfold in surprised silence. That was fine with Zielinski. He was happy to wait for the patrol officer without speaking to either of these two again.

Barden had other plans. He looked over his shoulder and began to harangue Zielinski, insulting him in any way he could think of. Zielinski let most of it roll off his back, but when Barden called him a dirty cop, it tweaked him. Barden spotted the reaction and kept at him, badgering away at the point.

"That's right," he said. "You're dirty!'

I'm not dirty. I'm solving a problem.

"I'll have your badge," Barden told him.

"You couldn't carry it," Zielinski shot back.

"I'll have it," Barden said, "and then I'll wipe my ass with it."

Zielinski lashed out with his hand, cuffing Barden behind the ear with his palm. The man's head snapped forward with the force of the blow, his chin striking his chest. Barden yelped.

"You jerk! I bit my tongue!"

"Shut up."

"That's excessive force," Barden said.

"You want excessive?" Zielinski growled, staring at him.

Barden stared back. Then he looked away, spitting a bloody mess onto the floor before dropping into a sullen silence.

Zielinski glanced at Sanita, who was staring at him with the same surprised look.

He turned away.

I came here to make things right, and all I did was dig a deeper hole for myself. They all three waited without a word until a knock came at the door a few minutes later. Zielinski gave Sanita a stern look of warning, then jerked his head toward the door. She let in the patrol officer, a veteran named Sandi O'Brien. Zielinski knew her in passing from his time on day shift.

O'Brien took in the scene, then raised her eyebrows at Zielinski.

He pointed to Barden. "He's a collar."

She didn't ask any questions, and together the two of them helped Barden to a standing position and walked him out of the apartment. None of them spoke on the way to the marked police cruiser. Once there, O'Brien pulled a plastic bag from her uniform pocket and handed it to Zielinski. He held it open for her while she conducted a thorough search of Barden. He had a lighter, a few coins, his state identification card, and a condom. O'Brien dropped them all into the bag.

"Anything else?" she asked him.

Barden shook his head.

O'Brien popped open the back door of the police car and guided Barden inside. Then she closed the door and gave Zielinski an appraising stare. "You filling in on patrol today, Ray?"

He shook his head. "Still with Anti-Crime."

"I didn't think you guys worked weekends."

Zielinski swallowed. "We, uh, mix it up. Criminals don't keep Monday through Friday, nine to five hours, you know?"

"I do know," she said. "I'm working on a Sunday, after all." She pointed to his chest. "First time in uniform in a while, too, huh?"

Zielinski scowled slightly. "I figured it was better to fly the colors, since I was alone. Is there a problem, Sandi?"

O'Brien shook her head. "No problem." She reached for the driver's door. "But whatever you've gotten yourself into, Ray, make sure you don't get it on me."

He didn't answer.

O'Brien got into the car and drove away toward jail.

Great. Now I have to worry about her being suspicious of me.

He hoped the veteran officer would stick to the age-old cop mantra his own training officer had instilled in him. "On the street," he'd told Zielinski several times, "you need to be curious about everything. But where other cops are concerned, it's best you mind your own business."

Of course, none of that would matter if she got called into Internal Affairs as a witness.

Zielinski glanced up at the third-floor apartment. Alejandra Sanita stood in the doorway, her arms folded across her chest, an unreadable expression on her face. She held Zielinski's gaze for a few moments, then turned around and went back inside, closing the door behind her.

At least I kept my word about leaving her in peace. Despite everything, she should have a quiet Sunday from here on out.

He wouldn't, though.

Chapter 63

Tyler Garrett rested behind the steering wheel of his Lincoln Nautilus and studied the occasional cars that drove southbound on Highway 27. They rarely came.

No music played inside his vehicle. Besides taking it easy on his nagging headache, he wanted the quiet to think, to work through the thing he was now planning. The killings he had done in the past were quick, heated decisions and necessary for his continued freedom.

Now, he was coldly calculating the murder of a fellow cop, and he didn't know if the results would be what he hoped. There were too many variables and he worried that everything would tumble back in on itself, back in on him.

Once he would decide on a course of action, he'd step back and unmake it, choosing a different path. For the first time in a long while, Garrett felt something he was unfamiliar with—doubt.

After a restless night of sleep, he'd spent the day weighing his options, planning his future. He even thought about reporting to the department on Monday and quitting, walking away from everything he had built. In the end, though, he wouldn't do that.

The job was his life and it gave him power and access that no one else had. Walking away from it would be foolish. There was no doubt in that decision.

No, he chose to play this game. And no one forced him to push his chips into the middle of the table. It was time to see where the cards fell.

In the afternoon, when he could take no more of being restless, he dropped by the county jail to talk with a friend.

Afterward, he went to the department to develop a lead that he wanted to give Marty Hill on Monday morning. Sitting at a computer reserved for patrol officer use in the detective's bullpen, he found the person he was searching for and printed their record. He also found a Field Interview report that listed the individual living in an abandoned house. Garrett put the data sheet and the FI report on Marty's desk with a note that read, *Let's go after this guy.—Ty.*

As he walked by Wardell Clint's desk, he paused briefly. There was nothing on top except the man's phone. Garrett tugged on the drawers, confirming that each was locked.

"Figures," he muttered.

He stepped into the hallway known as Mahogany Row, unaccustomed to the weekend silence. Instead of heading for the exit, he moved deeper into the department. When he neared Captain Farrell's office, he grabbed the doorknob, twisted it, and stepped quickly inside.

Unlike Clint, Farrell locked nothing. All his desk drawers were easily accessed. However, there was nothing of value for him to find. He scanned Farrell's Anti-Crime Team file, but it was basic personnel notes. There was nothing to incriminate Farrell in a plot to frame Garrett. There was no smoking gun that he could grab and take to Human Resources or to the local newspaper. He closed the file, ended his search, and left.

Garrett then returned home to spend a restless couple of hours with Tiana before driving out to this meeting place.

When a Toyota Camry approached, Garrett stiffened, his eyes searching for any following vehicles. Seeing none, he relaxed. As the car left the roadway, Garrett slid out of his SUV and stood near the rear door. The Toyota pulled into the empty parking lot, passed by him, and continued to the end of the lot where it parked.

Garrett's eyes returned to the north horizon, the direction the Toyota had arrived from.

Satisfied that no one was following the car, he turned and crossed the parking lot. A tall man exited the Camry and sauntered toward Garrett.

He was a handsome man with striking features and a short haircut. His frame was trim, as if he spent time in a gym not to build mass, but to remain lean. He wore a sport coat, white shirt, blue jeans, and loafers.

"Why are we meeting way out here?" Earl Ellis asked.

They were in the parking lot of Freeman High School, located in the farming community of Rockford, south of Spokane Valley. It was forty minutes from downtown Spokane to the high school.

"Precaution."

Ellis laughed. "We're in Hicksville, in case you didn't notice. You and me, we stick out."

"I want to make sure you weren't followed."

"I wasn't. I've been checking, just like we talked about."

Garrett eyed Ellis's wardrobe. "What's with the threads?"

"I went to evening service with my grandmother."

"Didn't take you for the religious type."

"It's better than paying rent."

"Huh," Garrett said, his gaze turning back to the north. "Have you seen the Impala yet?"

"Maybe. I'm not sure. There's a lot of Impalas out there."

He turned back to Ellis. "If he's following you, don't stop until you get somewhere safe, somewhere clean. Understand?"

"You make him sound like he's the boogeyman."

"He is."

Ellis's eyes slanted.

"Listen, Earl. The man's been on me like a bad case of the clap for going on two years," Garrett held up as many fingers. "But suddenly he vanishes? I haven't seen him for days now. A dog like that doesn't give up a bone unless he's got something different to chew."

"You guess I'm the new bone?"

Garrett nodded.

"The night at the bar? With the flash?"

"It's the only thing I can figure."

Ellis's face grew grave. "What are we going to do about it?"

"I've got a plan, but you need someone you can trust…that we both can trust. Someone who will be hard to trace back to us. Most importantly, someone who can disappear."

Ellis turned his head and lifted his eyes as he thought.

Finally, he said, "I got the man for the job."

MONDAY

The streets were dark with something more than night.
—Raymond Chandler
From the introduction of the
short story collection, *Trouble Is My Business*

Chapter 64

Clint hesitated at the door, his hand already raised to knock. Under his other arm, he clutched his file on Tyler Garrett protectively. He realized his jaw was clenched. Reconciliation did not sit well with him, especially when the break-up was warranted due to the other party's stupidity. But he knew he had to do what was necessary, not what was pleasant.

He rapped on the captain's door, which was cracked open a few inches. From within, he heard a distracted bellow. "Come in."

Clint swung open the door and stepped inside. He closed the door before he looked in Farrell's direction. When he did, he saw a surprised expression on the captain's face.

"Wardell..." Farrell cleared his throat. "It's good to see you."

"Don't start with a lie," Clint said. "No one is ever glad to see me."

Farrell gave him an indulging smile. "But I actually am. I called you last week."

"I know. I deleted the message."

"Why?"

"I had nothing to say."

"*I* had something to say," Farrell said.

"Something different?"

Farrell hesitated. "Not exactly. More of an apology."

"Apologies are for politicians," Clint said. "I believe in pragmatism. Working together is our best chance to take down Tyler Garrett and both still survive the fallout. Everything else is just superfluous hogwash."

Farrell took a deep breath and let it out. "I suppose that's as close you get to saying you're sorry, huh?"

"I'm not sorry. You should be, but I don't care about that. I only care about finishing this."

"You want back on the case, then?" Farrell asked.

"I never left it."

Farrell's eyes narrowed. "You kept investigating after I ordered you to stop?"

"Of course I did. That's why I'm here."

"I don't understand."

Clint swallowed his first response, which was *I know*. Instead, he chose each word carefully, knowing it would hook the captain. "We have a breakthrough."

Farrell studied him. His expression waffled between angry, confused, and intrigued. Ultimately, anger and confusion melted away and curiosity won out. "What kind of breakthrough?"

Clint pressed the lock on the office door. The large metal knob clicked loudly in the room. Clint moved to the chair across from Farrell and slid it forward to the edge of the captain's desk. He set the file on the desktop and opened it. A photograph of Earl Ellis was on top, and he pushed it to Farrell.

"Last week, I followed Garrett to Snoop's Saloon on the north side. He met with this man in the parking lot. It was the first time I'd ever seen them together."

Farrell studied Ellis's photo. Then he looked up. "Who is he?"

"Earl Ellis. He lives in East Central with his mother or grandmother. I haven't confirmed which yet, but that doesn't matter. What does matter is that I spent the last few days following him." Clint spread out almost a dozen photographs in front of Farrell like a deck of cards. "He met with all of these people. A few times he delivered a package. More often, he picked up an envelope. Sometimes he just talked."

"So this guy Ellis is…"

"I think he's Garrett's lieutenant."

Farrell cringed. "Don't call him that. It sounds too much

like us."

"Fine," Clint said, unfazed. "Vice president of operations, then."

"That's better."

Clint tapped the photos. "I'm convinced that most of these are dealers. I got shots of several in action."

"And Ellis is running them?"

"Exactly." Clint turned a simplified organizational chart he'd created around for Farrell to see. "Down here at the bottom, you've got the dealers. I don't have solid IDs on them yet, but that should go quickly once I start working on it. Right now, I used their photos, likely role and physical identifiers as placeholders."

Farrell tapped one. "This guy with the fishhook scar has a question mark."

"I don't know if he's a dealer yet, or something else."

Farrell nodded and returned to studying the chart. "White male, Native American male, white female, black male…" he read, then looked up. "So this is definitely not a gang created along racial lines."

"It's not a gang."

Farrell gave him a slightly confused look. "What would you call it?"

"Don't you see?" Clint forced the frustrated edge from his voice. "This isn't the Eight Trey Crips or something. This is a business operation, and strictly about profit."

"And Garrett's the CEO?"

"I don't know for certain, but if he answers to anyone, I haven't seen it yet." He tapped the bottom tier of photographs, all of which had lines that linked directly to Ellis. "All of these people report to Ellis. Then the single line up to Garrett. This is their organization, at least what I have on it so far."

Farrell nodded, thinking. Then he paused. "Wait. You said you saw Garrett and Ellis together at a bar?"

"No. I saw them in the parking lot of Snoop's Saloon."

"Where's the photo of that?"

Clint felt warmth at the base of his neck. "I didn't have my camera with me. I'd just switched cars from my old Crown Vic, and the Impala wasn't completely outfitted yet."

"That's too bad."

Clint debated whether to tell Farrell about his mishap with the cell phone flash but decided not to. "I'll get a shot of them together," he said. "It's a matter of time."

"So, you don't think we have enough to bring Garrett in?"

"Not even close. Do you?"

Farrell considered, then shook his head. "All we've really got is you seeing them together. A photo would be better. And if we can work on some of his crew, get them to flip…"

"Exactly. My strategy is to get a couple of them to roll on Ellis and use that to get Ellis to roll on Garrett. Coupled with all of the circumstantial evidence I've collected over the past two years, that would give us enough to go to the chief and the prosecutor and blow this whole thing up."

Farrell looked down, then put his palms to his eyes and rubbed. "How is it that I can look forward to that day so much and still dread it at the same time?"

"It's called cognitive dissonance."

"No kidding." Farrell ran his hands through his hair.

Clint looked closer at the captain. The man seemed frayed at the edges. The stress of thinking he was the only one working to bring Garrett to justice must have worn on him over the past few months. One part of him concluded that Farrell got exactly what he deserved for dismissing Clint, but at the same time, he felt a small pang of sympathy for the man. He, too, knew the weight of Garrett.

I guess I have a little cognitive dissonance of my own.

He tried to offer Farrell some perspective. "The two things aren't mutually exclusive," he explained. "We'll take a risk when we tell the bosses what we've been doing, and that merits a large measure of concern. At the same time, it will be a relief to finally share it."

"Exactly," Farrell said softly. Then he sighed, "Do you

realize how messed up is it that you are literally the only other person in the world who understands that?"

"How do you think *I* feel?"

Farrell chuckled. "What's the timeframe to do the legwork on this?"

Clint considered. "A couple of months, at least. That's if everything breaks right for us."

"Meanwhile, we just keep everything rolling as it is?"

"Exactly."

"Including the Anti-Crime Team."

"Including that." Clint gave Farrell a careful look. He wondered if that was the source of Farrell's angst. "How is the team doing?"

"You don't know?" Farrell asked.

Clint shrugged.

Farrell took a deep breath and let it out. "The chief loves it so much he talked this weekend about making a second team. So far, they've made arrests, impacted crime, and put guns, drugs, and money on the table for the press conferences. On the surface, it's a smashing success."

"But underneath, it's something different."

"Yeah, unfortunately. I put three hand-picked officers on that team to surround Garrett in order to trap him. One's uninterested, one's reluctant to play the role I intended, and another one was falling under Garrett's spell."

"Zielinski, Yang, and Stone?" Clint asked, putting them in order.

Farrell nodded.

"Well, I don't think Zielinski's uninterested," Clint said. "He's approached me on several occasions, trying to get information. He thinks something is wrong with Garrett."

"Really? He gave me the cold shoulder."

"That's the brass effect, most likely."

"You're probably right."

"I know I am. Yang is pushing back?"

"A little."

"Maybe she doesn't want to be the designated rat."

Farrell frowned. "I'm not making her a rat."

"You can say that," Clint told him, "and you can say that Earl Ellis isn't Garrett's lieutenant, too. That doesn't change the truth about the roles of each."

"She's not a rat," Farrell insisted. "She's...a safety mechanism. A conscience. A watch dog."

"Captain, I don't have time to play the synonym game just to make you feel better about what we're doing. Tyler Garrett is a piece of garbage who has sullied the badge. *Our* badge, the same one we both wear." He pointed to the gold badge on Farrell's white uniform shirt. "If you have to put a rat on his team to get him there's nothing wrong with that, but call it what it is. Trust me, it makes things infinitely easier."

Farrell looked mildly nauseous and didn't reply.

"So," Clint continued, "Yang doesn't want to be the rat?"

"No," Farrell answered wearily.

"Will she come forward if she sees something?"

"She did during the academy."

"Lots of things happen in the academy that never make it to the streets."

"She's got a military background, too. A strong sense of ethics. She'll come forward."

"I thought Stone was your ethical ace-in-the-hole."

"He is."

"You said he's been infected by Garrett. That sounds like a loss to me."

"No," Farrell corrected, "I said he was falling under Garrett's spell. *Was*."

"What changed?"

"I intervened."

Clint gave him a concerned look. "Directly? How?"

"I brought Stone in and I told him about our suspicions regarding Garrett."

Clint stared at him in stunned silence. "You *told* him?"

"Yes. That was the plan all along, to tell him at some point."

"It was a stupid plan."

Farrell's expression turned defensive. "I had to act. Garrett's influence was getting stronger every day."

"That was a mistake."

"It was my only play."

Clint shook his head. "If you think that's the case, you ain't seeing the board, Captain."

"I see it fine, *Detective*," Farrell snapped back.

Clint ignored Farrell's tone. They were long past pulling rank. He'd only used Farrell's out of habit. "How much did you tell him?"

Farrell simmered for a few seconds before answering through gritted teeth. "Not much. Just that we suspect Garrett of some serious crimes."

"No way," Clint muttered.

"What?"

"That's the worst thing you could do. If Stone knows what we believe, then you put him at risk. He'll misjudge everything he does now."

"He also might see Garrett do things he would have missed before."

"I doubt it."

"You doubt everything."

"And I'm usually right."

"Stone could be the key to bringing Garrett down," Farrell insisted. "He's always been the lynchpin of this operation."

"That's why I was against the Anti-Crime Team plan from the beginning. I told you Garrett would never be stupid enough to be trapped like this. I'm sure he saw you and everyone coming from miles away."

"Then again," Farrell said, "it could be that Gary Stone will be the one to crack this case. He's a smart guy. Give him some credit."

Clint stared at Farrell for a tense few moments. He was convinced meeting with the captain was the right thing to do. For good or ill, they were in this mess together. More importantly, the meeting gave him a much more well-defined view of the bigger picture. Unfortunately, despite the man's command experience, it was also obvious to him that Farrell still didn't see it clearly.

"Maybe he will crack the case," Clint said. "That is, if he doesn't betray us to Garrett first."

Chapter 65

"Aren't we supposed to be heading east?" Jun Yang asked.

Ray Zielinski was behind the wheel of the Bronze Beast and they had just turned left onto Boone Avenue from Monroe Street.

His lips pressed tightly together, obviously frustrated by her question. He'd come into the department anxious this morning, wouldn't talk with her about what was wrong, and it appeared he was going to remain bottled up for the rest of the day. Zielinski looked like he wanted to say several different things to her, but he finally settled on, "I want to make a stop."

Yang pushed herself down in her seat and rested her head on its back. She hoped for Zielinski to tell her more, but when he didn't, she turned to look at her partner. "What is the purpose of this stop?" she asked, slowly and deliberately, hoping that her tone would not reveal any frustration.

"What is the purpose of this stop?" Zielinski sarcastically repeated, almost robotically. "C-3PO had more emotion than you."

She rolled her eyes then turned her head forward. He was being a dick this morning.

"Relax, all right? I want to check on a guy who was in a shooting with me. Can you be cool with that?"

Yang inhaled deeply then asked, "You couldn't do that on your own time?"

"What's your problem?" Zielinski snapped. "It'll be fifteen minutes at the most."

They turned north onto Maple Street, the engine revving as the car ran through a yellow light.

"Yellow means stop," Yang muttered. "Not accelerate."

"Are you kidding?" Zielinski said, glaring at her.

"What?"

"What crawled up your butt over this weekend?"

Yang set her feet on the floorboard and pushed herself upright. That did it. Whatever was bothering the man wasn't her responsibility. "You're really talking to me this way?"

"Uh, yeah. When you're acting crazy, I most definitely am."

"Are you implying something, Ray?"

He turned the steering wheel, whipping the Ford into the parking lot of a stout office building.

"I'm not implying anything," he said, as he parked. With a flick of the wrist, he turned off the car. It knocked for a moment before quieting. "I'm flat out saying that you're busting my balls."

"I am not *busting* your balls."

"You weren't just doing that about my driving?"

"We're cops, Ray. We're supposed to be an example."

"Look at this car," he said, spreading his arms wide. "Nobody even knows were cops." He slapped the steering wheel for emphasis. His anger over her comment seemed out of proportion.

"You're missing the point," Yang quietly said, hoping to lower her voice in an attempt that he would drop his.

"If it's not my driving," he said, his voice softening, "then you're giving me a hard time about checking on a friend."

"We have work to do," Yang said, again trying to maintain her calmness. She'd already lost control once and doing so again would make this situation worse.

"Are you the time-card police? Did Human Resources give you some new responsibilities I didn't know about?"

"We've got a list of hippos to chase."

"Don't worry about it. Those dirt balls aren't going anywhere."

She hated when he preached to her about the job. When he got on his soapbox, it sounded as if he was talking down to her, treating her as if she didn't know what she was doing. "You sound like a burnout," she said, immediately regretting that she verbalized her feelings.

"A burnout?" Zielinski said, his voice rising again. "You think I'm a burnout?"

Even though she wished she hadn't said those words, she wasn't going to back down from them now, especially since he was trying to bully her with his rage. She no longer had anything to lose. "Yeah, Ray, I do think that," she said, her words calm, purposefully mechanical. "You spend most of your days angry and complaining about how the department or someone is out to get you. And if you're not screwing off by meeting a captain or a friend, we occasionally get some work done. Good work, I might add."

He clenched his jaw several times before angrily pointing at the building in front of them. "There's a guy in that building who lost his leg in my shooting. Happened a few months back. Remember that?" His words were full of condescension.

"I remember that," she said, hating the way he was talking to her. "Everyone remembers that."

"Well, I was there when he got shot. I feel a certain responsibility to that guy, and I want to know how he's doing." Ray's face purpled as his voice rose. "Maybe you don't care about how people feel, but I do." He tapped his chest. "I still think of that as police work. It's not always about chasing bad guys."

"Maybe you should relax." She hadn't intended to push the senior officer so far into a rage that he might have a heart attack.

"Relax?" he seemed to be trying to whisper, but it came out as an exhale of fury. "You said I was a burnout. Well, screw you, princess, I'm not a burnout." Zielinski climbed out of the car, leaving the keys in the ignition, but leaned back in. "Wait here. I'll be back in fifteen minutes. Put a stopwatch on it."

He slammed the door.

Yang watched the senior officer stalk angrily into the

building. Whatever he was dealing with wasn't her fault, she told herself.

It didn't matter, though. It still felt bad. She hadn't intended to upset him.

After reaching peace with her decision on Saturday, she thought everything would fall into place. Instead, the world remained as disjointed as before. She needed to make an appointment with Captain Farrell soon.

She didn't know how many more days on the Anti-Crime Team she could take.

Chapter 66

"The brass are happy the team's doing so well," Marty Hill said, his hand resting on Tyler Garrett's shoulder. They were standing in the shadow of the Public Safety Building, the morning sun hidden behind the concrete behemoth. "We're making some dents in the crime rate."

Garrett nodded. "Making dents in criminals is how the crime rate is really impacted."

Hill's smile was disapproving. "One of these days, Ty, you're going to be old and slow. You're going to have to find a new way to do business. You can't keep banging heads forever."

"Wanna bet?" Garrett asked with a mischievous grin.

"If anyone could," the detective said, patting Garrett on the back, "it's you." Hill's eyes flicked to the piece of paper the officer held in his hand. "Good luck with him. Hope it turns out to be something."

Garrett lifted the data sheet. "We don't need luck with this one. He's as easy as your prom date was."

"My prom date was my wife."

"You were married in high school?"

Hill rolled his eyes. "Goofball."

The two men shared a casual laugh that petered out when the Gray Ghost pulled up to the front of the building. Gary Stone was behind the wheel.

"You're letting him drive?" Hill asked. "Must be a big day for the junior man."

Garrett smirked. "I let him fetch the car, Marty. Stone will never drive."

As if on command, Gary Stone slipped out from behind the

wheel, nodded toward Hill, and walked around the back of the car to the passenger side. "We going?" he asked.

"See ya," Garrett said with a nod toward the detective. He then walked over to the car and dropped inside. After setting the data sheet between him and Stone, Garrett slipped the Chevy Caprice into gear. The car sped out of the parking lot, bouncing onto Mallon Avenue.

"Where are we headed?" Stone asked.

"Dog Town."

Located in northeast Spokane, Hillyard was demographically the poorest section of the city. Within that area, though, was a neighborhood of residential and industrial buildings known as Dog Town. Garrett didn't know the origin of the derogatory name, nor did he care. It was likely that plenty of decent people lived and worked in the area, but he didn't care about that, either. To him, that part of town was a garbage pit and he only went up there for one reason—arrest bad men and take them to jail.

Stone picked up the data sheet. "Richard Van Pelt," he muttered as he read. "Fourth-degree assaults, fourth-degree thefts, a few malicious mischiefs." He looked over at Garrett, mildly confused. "And no active warrants. He's sort of small potatoes for us, isn't he?"

The Chevy raced north on Monroe, passing a slow-moving Porsche, its driver mean-mugging Garrett and Stone.

"Marty cleared the grab." There was no defensiveness in his voice.

Stone flipped over the data sheet. There was nothing there. "But why?" he asked. "Where's the juice?"

Garrett smiled. Stone *had* learned a lot in his few weeks. He wasn't looking just at the surface; he wanted to know the deeper justification for their actions. "A graveyard officer wrote an FI recently about an abandoned warehouse in Dog Town. Van Pelt's been seen around there several times by the officer."

Stone's brow furrowed as he considered Garrett's words.

"This sounds like a problem for a neighborhood resource officer, not us."

Garrett didn't respond as he slipped the Ghost past a stopped bus, then around a slow-moving clunker of a pickup, before picking up speed again as they continued northward.

"What's the hurry?" Stone asked.

"Yin and Yang have been out in the field for fifteen minutes longer than us. I want to get on the board before them and we've got to go far north to do so. Unless, of course, you don't mind being second place."

Stone shook his head. "By all means, drive faster. I don't want to be second to Zielinski."

"Me neither." Garrett glanced at his partner. "So, Van Pelt?"

"Yeah. What's the deal?"

"He's half-brother to William Schloss. Different moms, same dad, which is basically saying stupid runs in the blood line."

Stone scrunched his nose. "Schloss? Why's that sound familiar?"

Garrett accelerated and the Chevy ran the intersection at Garland Avenue as the light turned red. A car honked behind them. "Schloss is suspected in four home invasion robberies."

"That's where I heard the name," Stone said, snapping his fingers. "William Schloss."

"And his dim-witted half-brother, Ricky, is going to lead us right to him."

They drove for a few minutes before Stone asked. "Why didn't the officer grab Van Pelt when they saw him at the vacant warehouse?"

"He wasn't trespassing. He was on the sidewalk, later in the street. Public property. He had no reason to scoop him up. But since he'd seen Van Pelt in the area a few times, he wrote the report. Good police work, if you ask me. Now, we grab him and let Marty do his thing so we can get to his brother. His last known address is a few blocks from where the officer saw him."

"All right, man. If you think this is the play."

Garrett nodded. "This is definitely the play. Ricky will fold when Marty interviews him, and he'll give up Schloss. When we grab Schloss, we'll be on the front page again."

They fell silent as the Ghost sped northward. A black-and-white patrol car jumped behind them for several blocks. Garrett checked the rearview mirror, lifted his hand, and waved. The officer behind the wheel signaled recognition and the patrol unit turned onto a side street, disappearing into a residential neighborhood.

"I heard it went well with Fia," Garrett said.

Stone smiled. "I liked her. A lot."

"You going to see her again?"

"We're supposed to go out tonight."

"Yeah?"

His partner nodded.

"What do you do on a Monday night?"

"Dinner someplace nice, maybe walk through the park. I loved talking with her. She's really something, man." The smile on Stone's face revealed everything the man felt about the evening's prospects.

"Want us to join you?" Garrett asked.

Stone's smile melted away and he struggled to answer Garrett's question.

He let his partner remain uncomfortable for a few moments, then Garrett laughed. Stone turned to him, confusion on his face.

"It's okay, Stoney. We're not going to crash that party. Fia told Tiana she likes you, too. I'm glad you guys hit it off. We'll let you do your thing."

Stone's face relaxed and his smile returned.

They traveled in silence then. Garrett let Gary Stone drift away on his thoughts of Fia Woodson. He had enough thoughts of his own to deal with as he continued to grapple with how to escape Captain Farrell's trap.

The pieces were on the board and Garrett was moving them around carefully. Now, he needed others to do their part.

Chapter 67

Lindsay Wagner pushed his chair back from his desk when he saw Zielinski. Zielinski's gaze dropped involuntarily to the folded material where most of the man's left leg should be. He looked back up to Wagner's face, feeling embarrassed.

"It still hasn't grown back," the social worker said.

"Sorry," Zielinski said.

"Because I haven't sprouted a new leg?"

"No. For staring at it."

"I've gotten used to it." Wagner held out his hand. "How're you doing?"

Zielinski shook his hand. He sat in the visitor's chair next to Wagner's desk. "That's my line."

Wagner shrugged. "It's going all right. I'm working with a guy on a prosthetic, but it's a little more difficult because of how high up they had to go."

"That's good, though, right? You won't need your crutch anymore."

Wagner reached out and patted the tan crutch leaned against the cubicle wall beside him. "I like it. I might just stick with it."

Zielinski folded his hands on his lap. He'd done some reading after the shooting and knew that severe depression was common among amputees. Wagner didn't seem depressed, though. He seemed normal, in fact. His coarse hair was a little long, and he still wore a bushy, full beard. But the light blue collared shirt and dark slacks evened out his counterculture look.

"You seem okay," he told Wagner.

"I'm pretty good, all things considered."

Zielinski pointed to Wagner's beard. "You kept the Viking braids, I see."

"And you kept your cop 'stache."

"I guess it's just who I am."

"Same here."

"Are you able to do everything for your job?" he asked.

"They make allowances. I partner with someone, and we share a case load. She does all of the site visits with clients, and I do more of the paperwork to balance things out."

"No more going out into the field, huh?"

"For now. I hope to change that eventually, but it's a state agency, so they're worried about liability. I'm chipping away at it, though." Wagner smiled. "If I really wanted to speed up the process, I'd hint about filing an ADA lawsuit."

Zielinski blanched at the word.

Wagner looked at him in concern. "What's the matter?"

"Nothing," Zielinski said, pushing away thoughts of his encounter with Barden.

"I said lawsuit, and you looked like someone pointed a gun at you."

"I prefer a gun," Zielinski said. "It's more straightforward."

"And more final. Are you being sued?"

"No."

Wagner fell quiet, waiting. Zielinski wavered, then said, "It's a tough time at work, that's all."

"Aren't you on that new team, the one I saw on the news?"

"The Anti-Crime Team."

"Right. Inventive name, by the way."

"I didn't pick it. The brass did."

"I knew it wasn't you. If you picked it, it'd be the Get Off My Lawn Squad."

Zielinski grunted, but smiled a little at that. "Funny, my rookie partner was just telling me how grumpy I am, too. Actually, she said I was a burnout."

"I thought so, too," Wagner said. "When we first met."

"Yeah?" He thought back to his first encounter with the

social worker. He'd been facing down two Internal Affairs complaints and financial ruin was one misstep away. It didn't take much to imagine how gruff he'd seemed. "How about now?"

Wagner didn't reply right away, which surprised him. Then the man said, "You remember what I told you in the hospital, right? About how I heard your whole exchange with Lyle?"

Zielinski nodded. Lyle Bunney was the mentally ill man that had shot at them both, and whose bullet damaged Wagner's leg badly enough that it had to be amputated. "I remember."

"I meant what I said. I really was fearful that you'd shoot Lyle, even after he surrendered. But you didn't."

"No cop would," Zielinski said.

"Some might."

"No. That's just what cop-bashers want you to think."

Wagner made a slightly doubtful expression and lifted his hands a couple of inches but didn't argue Zielinski's statement. "Regardless, the point is that you did the right thing. To my way of thinking, a burnout would do something less than that. Or different."

Zielinski considered his words. He thought about all the rage he'd felt at the world in that moment he had Lyle in his gun sights. Wagner was right. He hadn't fired. But he was no saint. It hadn't been easy. Yesterday, he'd lashed out at Barden while the man was in handcuffs. That was definitely less than the right thing.

"It's hard," he muttered, looking down at his hands. "I never used to think it would be so hard."

Wagner nodded and pointed to the badge on Zielinski's belt. "That shield you're carrying is heavy. It's a burden."

Zielinski looked up at him.

"I never thought about it until what happened outside Lyle's house. What you had to do that day…it was harder than anything I'll ever have to face."

Zielinski cast a quick glance at the stub where Wagner's leg used to be. "Including that?"

Wagner shrugged. "Fair enough. Anything except that."

Zielinski nodded absently, thinking about what Wagner had said. "Doing the right thing is hard," he repeated.

"Of course it's hard," Wagner said. "If it wasn't, everyone would be doing it."

Chapter 68

The dumpy house was midblock, just north of Nebraska Avenue on Havana Street. It faced into a vacant lot that ran up into a wooded embankment. There were vacant lots on either side of it. No car sat in its small driveway and the narrow gravel-covered street left no room for parking out front.

Manufacturing and light industrial users had overrun the area in the post-World War II expansion that Spokane experienced. The little brown house was a holdover from that prewar period when antisocial types wanted to live on the fringes of society. Unfortunately for whoever originally built the home, the masses overran their dream of peaceful solitude and placed their dirtiest and smelliest businesses into their neighborhood.

Gary Stone disliked this part of town. The whole thing was just so disorganized. This was why cities needed growth management acts and planning departments. Otherwise, they became a hodgepodge mess like this.

The two officers sat in the Gray Ghost, parked more than a block away in the lot of an industrial building with the vague name of CaNoRo Manufacturing. What they built, neither man had a clue, but they weren't there to investigate the plant. Each man leaned forward in his car seat, straining to see any sign of movement of Richard "Ricky" Van Pelt within the small house.

"Do you think he's there?" Stone asked.

"I don't know," Garrett said, unenthusiastically.

They couldn't get an angle to see the house unless they got out of the car. Then they had the choice of moving directly toward the residence or up the hillside where they could look back down.

"Want to go up and knock?" Stone asked.

His partner shook his head. "Not yet. Let's wait and watch. There's no hurry."

"Unless Zielinski and Yang get on the board first."

Garrett raised his eyebrows. "You mean Yin and Yang?"

Stone shrugged. "Sure."

Garrett frowned. "He called you the Chief's Bitch, but you still don't call him Yin. Why is that?"

"I don't know," Stone muttered. "Two wrongs don't make a right? Sort of corny, but that's how I was raised."

A warm breeze blew through the Caprice.

Garrett leaned to his right to give him a better angle to look left. "Do you think Jean," he said, pausing as he considered something he saw, "will get jealous when she finds out about Fia?"

Stone smiled. "Not Jean. She'll be happy for me. We're friends."

Garrett straightened in his seat. "Men and women as friends, I don't see it. But you're a different cat than me."

"I don't think every guy and girl can be friends. It's sort of special what we have."

"Do you think Fia will understand?"

Stone nodded. "I already talked to her about Jean and I think she's going to like her. Fia's all spiritual and into how the universe brings people all together."

"Jean's into that?"

"Jean's sort of an atheist, but I think the two of them would appreciate how the other sees the world. They're both smart, you know what I mean?"

The senior officer shook his head. "All right, Stoney. Let me know how that works out."

"I've got to get Jean to talk with me first."

"She will. You're a good guy. She'll come around."

The made Stone smile. "Thanks, man. I appreciate that."

Garrett inhaled deeply and put his hands on the wheel,

straightening his arms, which forced his back into the seat. When he exhaled, he relaxed his arms and said, "I don't know, buddy. I think this might have been a wild goose chase."

"We should at least knock," Stone said, studying Richard Van Pelt's data sheet.

"Oh, we're gonna knock," Garrett said, climbing out of the car. "There's just no easy way to approach this house."

"At least if he runs, we're going to see him."

"You know I'm faster than you."

He glanced at his partner who was smiling. "In that case," Stone said, hooking a finger over his ballistic vest and tugging it into place, "I hope he runs."

As they approached the house, Garrett asked, "You want the front or the back?"

"I'll take the front."

"If he runs, I get the head start."

Stone chuckled. "If you need the head start, then I've already won."

Garrett laughed quietly and shook Stone's shoulder before moving toward the back of the house.

There was a window in the southeast corner of the house. Stone stood on his tiptoes to peek inside. Not seeing anything, he stepped toward the front steps. He carefully walked up the three stairs until he stood on the left side of the door.

He banged on the door with the flat of his fist. "Spokane Police!" he called. "Come to the door."

It sounded like movement inside, but he couldn't be sure. He waited several moments. When no one came to the door, Stone banged again. "Spokane Police. Ricky Van Pelt, come to the door."

"It's open," someone hollered.

"Come to the door," Stone yelled.

"My foot's broken. Let yerself in."

Stone rolled his eyes. If this was another Stat-5 maggot trying to get some sympathy it wasn't going to work. Still on the left side of the entryway, he reached across the door, twisted the knob, and pushed it open.

It was a tactical error known as entering the fatal funnel and there was no escaping it. His hand still held the doorknob and his body was stretched out as he stepped into the house. His lead foot never touched ground.

When he noticed the shotgun, it was too late.

The blast hit him in the lower part of the stomach and the groin where there was no protection from his ballistic vest. The force of it pushed him momentarily upright, back onto the leg that was still firmly planted.

Then as he crumpled awkwardly to the ground, twisting as if he'd been turned into a corkscrew, Gary Stone screamed in a voice he'd never heard from himself.

He couldn't see where he was hit. The pain of it was too excruciating. It felt like someone had driven a thousand burning knives into his stomach, his groin, and the inside of his legs.

The sound of a fresh shotgun round being racked pierced his screams.

His hands clenched into fists and his arms curled in on him, a hopeless attempt to protect himself.

The man with the shotgun hovered over him.

Gary Stone always believed that his life would flash in front of his eyes the moment before he died. Yet he didn't think of his mother or father, any other family members, or any beloved childhood memories.

He didn't recall the recently loved Fia Woodson nor how she made him feel, her scent, or how wonderfully soft her skin was to his touch.

He also didn't have a single memory of his longtime friend, Jean Carter, and all the moments of happiness they spent together, how she made him laugh, and how deeply sorry he was for hurting her.

Instead, the last thought Gary Stone would ever have was wondering why the man holding the shotgun over his head was not Ricky Van Pelt.

Chapter 69

Farrell literally bumped into Captain Dana Hatcher in the hallway near her office. He had his head down, staring at the latest crime statistics he'd retrieved from Crime Analysis, and he just barreled right into her.

Hatcher had been carrying coffee and the hot brown liquid flew through the air before splashing onto the tiled floor. Several of Farrell's papers fell from his hands and drifted into the coffee puddle.

The two captains stared at each other in surprise, frozen in position. Hatcher's arms were spread wide, her now-empty coffee cup in one hand and a phone in the other. Her shocked look of disbelief melted into anger a moment later.

"What the hell, Tom?"

"I'm sorry," Farrell said. "Are you okay?"

Hatcher rolled a shoulder, testing it, and scowled. "Yeah, I'm fine."

He held up his remaining papers. "I was looking at these, instead of where I was going."

Hatcher's expression softened slightly. She glanced at the phone in her hand. "I… was checking email." She looked back at him. "I guess it was my fault, too."

Farrell squatted down and pulled the dripping papers from the coffee. Then he looked at Hatcher. "ACT numbers," he explained.

Hatcher's look hardened again. "I'm sure they're stellar," she said tightly.

Farrell put the wet papers on top of the dry ones. It didn't matter if they were ruined, too. The hard copy report was for the chief, and so he'd need a completely new packet from

Crime Analysis now. "Actually, there's something I need to talk to you about."

"What?" Hatcher's tone was guarded.

"I met with the chief about the future of the Anti-Crime Team," he said. He didn't mention how the meeting had occurred over ribs, chicken, and beer in his backyard the previous weekend. Hatcher already fostered enough of a belief that he was part of Baumgartner's good old boys' club. "With the level of success they're having, he wants to expand the team."

"You want another one of my patrol officers?" she asked, her disapproval evident.

"No, he was thinking more along the lines of creating a second squad."

Hatcher's eyes narrowed.

"They'd work opposite hours of the existing team," Farrell explained. "That way, we'd have greater coverage."

Hatcher put her phone into her pocket and crossed her arms. "What about patrol coverage? We're already thin, and this would just make it worse."

Farrell motioned with the soggy mess of data he held. "Crime Analysis says calls for service have dipped two percent since the team started."

"That's not significant. And it's cyclical. It'll be up two, three percent next month."

She was right about that, but Farrell pressed on. "Property crime is down eleven percent. That *is* significant, especially in such a short period of time."

"One month is a small sample size and you know it."

"The team is doing good work," Farrell said. "The chief wants to capitalize on it."

"Well, then why don't we do this, Tom? Why don't we just disband patrol and make everyone part of the Anti-Crime Team? That should completely eliminate crime in about a week. Then we can all retire and go surfing."

Farrell frowned at her sarcasm. "Your original plan called

for a second team."

"I know what *my* plan looked like. But it's *your* team, under *your* command, so don't stand there and throw *my* plan in my face."

"If we add a second squad," Farrell said, "then I think it might be time to approach the chief about bringing the entire Anti-Crime Team over to your command."

He knew that he'd meet resistance with Baumgartner on this move, but he believed he could make it work. He also realized it would take a while, which gave him plenty of time to complete his plan to trap Garrett before transferring command of the team. All in all, it was a small risk, but if it mended fences with Hatcher, it'd be worth it.

The patrol captain remained unconvinced. "Don't try to bait me with empty promises," she told him. "I'm not biting."

"It's not an empty promise. Once there's a second team and we're through the summer—"

"See?" Hatcher interrupted. "Already another condition. What's next after getting through summer? The next mayoral election? Something as equally arbitrary?"

"Dana…"

Hatcher leaned in closer to him. "Why don't you come and take over patrol since you want it so badly?"

Farrell stared at her in surprise. "I don't want to—"

"Then if you want any more of my patrol officers," Hatcher interrupted, "you're going to have to come and take them."

When Farrell didn't reply, she turned and walked away, leaving him standing next to the puddle of coffee on the floor and holding the dripping crime reports.

Chapter 70

Tyler Garrett jumped at the shotgun blast.

Before he could yank his Glock from his holster, he heard Gary Stone's screams. Garrett hunkered down, his gun in both hands. "Gary!" he yelled and ran to the corner of the house.

He heard the distinct sound of a round being racked amid Stone's shrieks.

"Gary!" he yelled again as a second blast ended the screaming and the air was suddenly quiet.

Garrett moved toward the front of the house. From the bottom of the stairs, he eyed the man inside the door with the shotgun. The man lifted the shotgun and stepped from the line of sight.

"Hey!" he hollered. "It's me."

Garrett looked north and south along Havana Street. When he turned back to the house, he asked, "Is anyone else in there with you?"

"Besides the two dead guys?"

Garrett lowered his gun, walked up the steps, and entered the house. A man with a long fishhook scar on the side of his face stood with a shotgun dangling at his side. He blew out a long slow breath through his lips. Then he said, "Dude, you scared the hell outta me."

The officer lifted his gun and fired three times, hitting the man in the chest. He stumbled backward and fell. When he stopped moving, Garrett bent over him and searched his pockets. He was ensuring that the man had left his identification and cell phone with Earl Ellis. Not finding anything, Garrett stood.

Finally, someone did something right.

He stepped into the back room and found another body. Richard Van Pelt. Well, he presumed it to be Ricky as most of its head was missing courtesy of a shotgun blast.

A shotgun makes a mess, Garrett thought before returning to the living room.

For the first time, he paused and took in the scene.

Gary Stone was dead at the entry to the house, shot first in the pelvic girdle, exactly as Garrett had instructed. It was the only reliable way to take down a man in a ballistic vest. A head shot was too hard. The pelvic region was a bigger target and could immediately immobilize a man. Once a man was down, time could be taken with the second shot—the kill.

What a mess, he thought again, as he considered what remained of Stone's head.

Garrett felt nothing for the man he once called a friend. Gary Stone had proven to be unreliable and a liar, but the whole thing was Garrett's mistake. He realized it was his fault and nobody else's. He brought Stone in too close and too fast and revealed way too much to the man.

With Farrell manipulating everyone on the team and Clint discovering Ellis, there seemed to be only one choice left for Garrett.

Eliminate the immediate threat. There were more things to take care of, but he could only do one at a time.

Now comes the hard part.

He pulled his radio from his belt and took a deep breath. He let it out as he considered what he would say. He then pressed the button, held the microphone too close to his mouth in hopes it would distort, and yelled, "Charlie three sixteen!"

His old callsign. A good touch.

"Officer down! Officer down!"

Chapter 71

Jun Yang checked her watch for the third minute in a row. Eighteen minutes now. Three minutes longer than he promised. He even told her to put a stopwatch on it. She should have taken him up on that challenge.

She looked around and watched people casually entering and exiting the building.

Typical. He said he promised he would be out in fifteen, but he does what he wants. The rules don't apply to Senior Patrol Officer Ray Zielinski. His personal missions are more important than anyone else's life.

A piercing tone came over the radio then. Yang reached under the dashboard, turning up the radio's volume.

"All units respond," the female dispatcher said, "Havana and Nebraska. Officer-involved shooting. Officer down. Repeat. Officer down. Havana and Nebraska. All units respond."

Yang straightened. She felt like she needed to do something, but she sat quietly in the passenger seat, a submissive rider in Ray Zielinski's car.

Immediately, units across the city began reporting in. South side units, northwest units. Even county deputies jumped onto the city channel to report their response.

Where the hell is Ray?

She wasn't waiting anymore. Yang slid over behind the steering wheel, started the car, and backed it out of its parking stall. When she dropped the Bronze Beast into gear, she revved the engine.

C'mon, Ray!

The door to the office building burst open. Zielinski

sprinted out, saw Yang behind the wheel, and continued to the passenger side, yanking the door open.

"Go!" he yelled.

The car was moving before he shut the door.

The Ford Maverick careened onto Maple Street causing several cars to swerve out of the way. Zielinski reached down and flicked on the siren and the emergency lights hidden in the grill.

"Who was shot?" Zielinski asked, his head swiveling as he searched for oncoming traffic.

"I don't know," Yang said.

"Who?"

"I don't know!" she yelled.

Zielinski raised his hands in frustration. "We need a damn MDT in these cars!"

Yang shook her head. A data terminal in an undercover car was not only a dated reference, it was stupid.

Zielinski pulled his phone from his pocket.

"Who are you calling?" Yang asked.

"Dispatch," he said. "I want some answers."

A moment later he stabbed the red button on his phone. "No answer."

"They're probably getting flooded with calls."

"Or ignoring them," Zielinski said.

Yang spun the wheel as she made it to Wellesley Avenue, the little car's engine roaring in delight.

"Why aren't we hearing radio traffic from the shooting?" Yang yelled.

Ray glanced at her. Something occurred to him then and he reached for the patrol radio.

Yang slammed the brakes to narrowly avoid a teenage boy who jumped into the street with his BMX bike. Both Yang and Zielinski were restrained by their seatbelts. Zielinski's hand stopped inches from the patrol radio.

As soon as the boy returned to the sidewalk, she stomped on the accelerator, forcing them back into their seats. Zielinski threw his hands up in anger.

"Damn it," Zielinski snapped at Yang.

"What?"

He reached forward as his seatbelt relaxed and flicked the radio to the data channel, the one that ACT frequently used when they communicated with dispatch.

"Tango-thirteen, medics are en route," a male dispatcher said. The strain in his voice was obvious. "What's your status, Ty?"

Zielinski's face whitened as he turned to Yang.

"He's dead," Garrett said, his voice trembling over the radio.

"Thirteen, medics will be their shortly. Hang in there."

"He's dead," Garrett repeated. "It's too late."

Zielinski turned toward the front of the car, his face slackening. He made a strange, sad noise.

"Ray?" Yang asked.

Suddenly, the man punched the dashboard.

"Ray!"

Zielinski threw punch after punch into the dashboard, yelling guttural noises at the top of his lungs.

Yang lifted her foot from the accelerator and reached down to click off the lights and sirens. She continued driving but kept her eyes on the road.

When Ray tired, he sat in his seat, his chest heaving and spittle dripping from his lips.

"You done?" she asked.

"Yeah," he whispered. "I think so."

"Me too," she said, not bothering to look at the man.

Chapter 72

Captain Tom Farrell stood next to Lieutenant Dan Flowers at the hood of the lieutenant's car. Flowers made notes on his legal pad, talking while he wrote. "This is a mess, Cap. A giant, overflowing mess."

Farrell didn't answer. He stared past the yellow crime scene tape at the crumpled, bloody form in the doorway to the house.

Gary Stone.

They should cover him up or something.

He knew that was wrong. It was a human impulse to cover a dead body, though whether out of respect or so that the living didn't have to look upon the departed, he didn't know. Either way, all a blanket would accomplish would be to introduce foreign matter into the crime scene, and maybe destroy or alter the evidence on the body.

The body.

It wasn't just a body. It was a police officer. *His* officer.

Farrell looked away.

Leaning against another car, less than forty yards from where he stood with Flowers, he spotted Tyler Garrett. The officer held a water bottle and looked shaken. Somehow, Union President Dale Thomas was already present and standing with Garrett. Farrell's lip curled involuntarily. He knew Thomas was there to offer some comfort but mostly to protect his members.

Whether they deserve it or not.

He wondered how Thomas managed to get to the scene so quickly. Chief Baumgartner hadn't even arrived yet. For a crazy moment, Farrell considered the possibility that Thomas was in league with Garrett. He rejected the thought almost immediately.

He had to get his head straight.

"Tell me about this mess," he instructed Flowers.

The lieutenant finished writing something, then flipped back a couple of pages. "We've got one body in the doorway with massive gunshot wounds. Looks like a shotgun blast to the pelvis and then to the head." Flowers swallowed, his voice wavering momentarily. "The victim…we're almost sure it's Gary Stone."

"Almost?"

Flowers looked uncomfortable. "The head injury…it's bad. His face is gone. But he's wearing body armor, and the badge on the lanyard around his neck is Stone's badge. Besides, Garrett's debrief confirmed it was Stone."

Farrell nodded for him to continue.

Flowers glanced back down at his notes. "There's another DOA in the living room just inside the house. No ID on him yet. He appears to have been wounded in the chest several times and is holding a shotgun. Garrett's debrief was that this man was the shooter, and that after Stone was shot, he returned fire at the man." Flowers looked up at him. "And then it gets a little weird. There's a third DB inside a back room, with most of his head blown off. No solid ID on him yet, either."

"Does Garrett know who he is?"

"I didn't ask him. It's not part of the tactical debrief."

Like we can believe anything he says, anyway.

Farrell clenched his jaw and glanced over at Garrett again. Thomas had his hand on the officer's shoulder, consoling him. He looked away, and spotted Zielinski and Yang huddled together at their undercover vehicle. The two of them watched the commotion, both stone-faced.

"I talked to Detective Hill," Flowers said, "and he told me the team was headed up here to grab Richard Van Pelt for questioning. There's a good chance that's the third body."

"Van Pelt's a hippo?"

"Not really. But Hill said they hoped Van Pelt might give

up a bigger target, a William Schloss. They're half-brothers, apparently."

Farrell nodded. Everything Garrett did made sense because the man had planned it that way.

"We've got a good inner perimeter locked," Flowers went on, "and set a wide outer perimeter. That's the only luck we've hit so far—this house is secluded, and it's mostly industrial in this area. We've been able to set up barricades and tape quite a ways out, so we should be able to investigate without civilians or the media stepping all over things."

This house is secluded.

Of course it is.

"The media has staged in a parking lot over at an empty manufacturing plant a few blocks away. Their photographers have been angling around for a decent shot of the scene, but so far, they're keeping their distance."

"Good. They can wait for the chief. He'll give them a sound bite."

"Where is he?"

"On the way. He was in Cheney for a regional leadership meeting."

Flowers looked back down at his notepad and flipped the page. "As soon as you or the chief gives the order, I'll call county and invoke the Officer-Involved Shooting Protocol."

Farrell recalled how almost two years ago he had given the exact same order in the immediate aftermath of another shooting involving Tyler Garrett. Now, here he was again, about to turn over an investigation to an outside entity because the law enforcement world had decided that it was best practice. Objectivity and transparency were crucial to maintaining community trust, the thinking went.

At this point, the community's trust was political nonsense. He didn't need objectivity here. He needed someone supremely motivated to find the truth. And if that meant transparency had to take a hit, so be it.

But he knew he had to give the order. The protocol was

clear. One of his officers had shot someone. Another agency had to investigate. There was no way around it.

"Invoke the protocol," he said. Then, after a moment, he added, "Ask for Detective Harris, if you can. She did a good job on the last one."

Flowers gave him an odd look. "I think they use a wheel to determine who's up next, just like we do."

"You know your counterpart over at the Sheriff's Office?"

"Of course."

"Ask a favor, Dan."

Flowers appeared uncomfortable. "Captain—"

"Is what I said unclear?"

"No."

"Too hard for you?"

Flowers shook his head. "No, sir."

"Then just do it."

"Yes, sir."

"Did you call the mayor yet?"

Flowers blanched, which was the reaction Farrell wanted. In the previous shooting, Flowers had tipped off the mayor's chief of staff long before the chief had a chance to make the official notification. Farrell had covered for him when the chief found out. He wanted to remind Flowers of that, in case he had second thoughts about asking for Detective Harris. "No, sir. That's not my role."

Farrell moved on. "How about next of kin for Stone?"

"Chaplain is working on it."

"Good. Do we have—"

"Tom!"

Farrell turned to see Captain Dana Hatcher approaching. Her expression was livid. When she drew close, she asked in a severe voice, "What did you do?"

Farrell's eyes narrowed. "I didn't do anything."

She pointed toward Stone. "One of my officers is lying over there, dead. This is your fault."

"I don't have time for this," Farrell snapped. "If you want

to help, join the huddle. Otherwise—”

“Where was their backup?” Hatcher interrupted.

He motioned toward Zielinski and Yang up the block. “I haven’t gotten their reports yet.”

“This never should have happened.”

Farrell clenched his jaw. In the distance, he could hear another siren. “It should never happen anywhere.”

Hatcher pointed at him. “Is this how you run a team? Where was their sergeant?”

That was it. Farrell had heard enough. “He’s probably at the station doing paperwork for *you*.”

Hatcher’s eyes widened. “Don’t even try to blame this on me. You—”

“This is my crime scene,” Farrell snapped. “I don’t need your help, *Captain*. So do me a favor and piss off.”

Hatcher stared at him in disbelief. Then she turned and stalked away toward Zielinski and Yang. Farrell watched her go, knowing that this brief border skirmish probably signaled that the cold war between the two of them had erupted into a hot one. Zielinski spotted Hatcher coming and peeled off from Yang to walk toward her, which gave him an idea where the officer stood when it came to choosing sides.

He turned back to Flowers, who was looking at him, surprise etched on his face. “What?”

“Nothing,” Flowers said.

“Good. Anything else?”

Flowers looked down at his notepad. “No, I think that’s it.”

“Then call county and invoke the protocol.”

“Yes, sir.” Flowers turned to go.

“And Dan?”

The lieutenant looked at him expectantly.

“Cover the body.”

Flowers opened his mouth to object, then closed it. He gave a terse nod and hustled away.

As soon as the lieutenant left, Wardell Clint appeared at Farrell’s side. He hadn’t seen the detective arrive. Clint grabbed Farrell by the arm and spun the captain to face him.

"You did this." Clint pointed toward Stone's mangled body but kept his voice low. "You killed that man."

Farrell had heard enough of this kind of thing from Hatcher. He didn't want to listen to more of it from a detective. He tried to pull his arm away, but Clint's grasp was like iron. "Let go of me."

Clint's intense gaze seared into him, but after a moment, the detective released Farrell's arm. "You know as well as I do this stinks."

It reeks. And if I'm not careful, the stench is going to lead everyone right to me.

"I don't know that and neither do you," Farrell said, his voice lacking conviction. "You haven't even examined the evidence yet, Wardell. You're letting your feelings cloud your judgment."

"You're letting your guilt cloud yours." He motioned toward Stone's fallen form again. "Your little plan is lying in a heap over there, all because you didn't listen to me."

Farrell stared back at him. He had no answer.

"You screwed up bad," Clint said.

I know.

Clint watched him for a few seconds. Then he said, "We can still salvage this. I'm not next up on the wheel, but you need to get me on this shooting."

"I already invoked the protocol. County will be investigating."

Clint smirked.

"It's an officer-involved," Farrell said. "I had no choice."

"Then assign me as the shadow. I want this one."

"I don't know if I can do that."

Clint gave him a baleful look. "Really? Because you had no problem doing it two years ago."

"That was different. The chief ordered it. And I'm already pulling strings to get Detective Harris assigned from county. If I pull you out of rotation, it starts to look like I'm manipulating the investigation.”

“If you want to get to the truth, you’ll do it. And we both know what the truth is, don’t we?” Clint nudged his head toward a seemingly distraught Garrett up the street.

Farrell followed his gaze. He saw Officer Bo Sherman and another patrol officer he didn’t recognize standing with Garrett now. Sherman, a muscular black officer, pressed his forehead to Garrett’s, and clutched the man’s shoulder and the back of his neck reassuringly.

The siren Farrell had heard grew sharper and louder, punctuated by an air horn blast. Both men turned to see a large black police SUV pull up to the scene and lurch to a stop.

Chief Robert Baumgartner had arrived.

“You can do this, and you will, Captain,” Clint said, his tone resolute. “It’s the most important thing you’ve ever done. For all of us.”

Farrell didn’t answer. He watched Baumgartner spill out of his SUV and look around. As soon as he spotted Farrell, he strode toward him.

As Baumgartner approached, Clint walked away.

The chief didn’t seem to notice. His eyes bored into Farrell’s. “Is it confirmed? Is it Stone?”

Farrell nodded.

“Damn,” Baumgartner muttered. He raised his hand to his mouth and rubbed. “Gary was a good man.”

Farrell didn’t say a word. He just waited for the chief’s questions to begin, so he could brief him on the details Flowers had provided.

But the chief didn’t speak for a while. When he finally did, his words came after a wavering sigh. “This is bad. Another man on my watch. First, Talbott and Pomeroy.”

The comparison of Stone to these two men irked Farrell. “Talbott’s death was shady,” he said, keeping his voice low. “And Pomeroy was a suicide.”

Baumgartner glanced over at Farrell in anger and surprise. “That’s cold,” he said sharply. “Have a little respect for the dead, Tom."

Farrell stared back at him evenly. Then he said, "I respect Stone, sir."

Baumgartner let it go. "Did you invoke the protocol?"

"Yes."

"What about our shadow for their investigation? Who's the next detective up on the wheel?"

Farrell didn't hesitate. "Wardell Clint," he lied.

Baumgartner nodded absently, turning to look at a patrol officer draping a cover over Officer Gary Stone's still frame in the doorway of the house. "Good," he muttered. "Clint'll do a good job."

Chapter 73

Ray Zielinski sat on the curb across the street from the house where Gary Stone lay dead. After a brief discussion with Hatcher, which included an awkward hug, she'd left to check on Yang and other officers. Instead of returning to his partner, Zielinski settled onto the curb and watched the scene.

After his outburst in the car, he was a little surprised at the creeping numbness that had grown in him since they'd arrived. Now, it filled every corner of his being, and even crowded out his thoughts.

Mostly, he kept his eye on Garrett. For a while, the officer had stood with the union president, looking shaky but keeping it together. Then Officers Bo Sherman and Ken Norton showed up. He watched as the two SWAT members consoled Garrett. Sherman took him in a fierce embrace, his forehead mashed against Garrett's.

Zielinski turned and spat onto the pavement and absently wiped his mustache.

Norton was quickly pressed into service, as Lieutenant Flowers handed him a clipboard and pointed. Zielinski guessed he'd just been drafted to keep the crime scene log. A menial task like that wouldn't normally sit well with a meat-eater like Norton, but the man surprised Zielinski by not protesting.

That's good. Because I'm not doing it.

After a while, he turned to look at Stone's body, which someone had covered with one of the thin, yellow, plastic emergency blankets that all patrol cars carried in the trunk. They had replaced the wool blankets that had been in the cars when Zielinski started his career. He didn't understand how a thin piece of material like that could ever be warm, but they seemed to work.

When he returned his gaze to Garrett, he saw the man was now crying against Sherman's shoulder. The crying didn't look right to Zielinski. It looked forced, like Garrett was trying too hard. He wondered how no one else could see it.

On the curb next to him, Wardell Clint sat down. Zielinski looked over at the detective, who leaned forward, resting his forearms on his knees.

"Were you two friends?" Clint asked.

Zielinski thought about how he'd referred to Stone as Charlie Bravo, the phonetics for Chief's Bitch. "Not really. But he was a fellow cop who didn't deserve this."

"Nobody deserves that."

Zielinski snorted. "No kidding."

Clint didn't seem offended. "Where were you and Yang when the shooting happened?"

"I was on a citizen contact."

"Why didn't you back them on this?"

"We weren't told about the op."

"Is that normal for this team? Separate cars flying solo?"

Zielinski shrugged. "Lately, yeah."

Clint nodded, as if he'd already known that. He turned and studied the scene. Zielinski turned his head, too, and watched Garrett's weeping taper off. A few moments later, he saw Baumgartner approach the man and put a hand on the officer's shoulder. The chief's intense expression was a mixture of sadness and pride. He said something to Garrett, but Zielinski was too far away to even hear the chief's voice, much less make out the words.

Finally, Clint said, "This is all wrong."

"What's wrong?"

"This shooting. It should never have happened."

Zielinski turned to stare at him. Clint kept his eyes on the scene in front of him. Zielinski felt the beginnings of emotion again at the suggestion Clint seemed to be making. A whisper of anger brewed in his gut. "You got something to say, Detective, then damn well say it."

Clint didn't reply immediately. He seemed engrossed in the exchange between Baumgartner and Garrett. Then he turned to Zielinski. "I'm shadowing county on this investigation, so I'm going to be here a while. After I clear this scene, you and me, we need to talk."

Zielinski hesitated. Maybe he'd read Clint's statement wrong.

Clint patted him on the leg before he stood. "We're long overdue," he said, and walked back toward the crime scene.

Chapter 74

Jun Yang stood at the edge of the inner perimeter. A warm breeze blew from the northeast, rippling the yellow paper blanket on Gary Stone's body as it lay in the doorway of the house.

Her eyes swept the activity swirling around the crime scene.

Patrol Captain Dana Hatcher barked orders near the outer perimeter to patrol officers who ran to and from their cars. She had no idea why the officers ran as if someone's life depended on it. It no longer did.

An ambulance and fire truck were parked silently on the street. A half dozen firemen and a couple medics stood nearby all with solemn faces as they were rendered useless by the dead men inside the little house.

Do they need to be here? Was it a show of solidarity with Garrett, the man left behind? Or maybe it was a feeling of helplessness that caused the firemen and medics to remain, that one of their public safety tribe was taken from them and they couldn't do anything to aid him.

Wardell Clint and Ray Zielinski sat next to each other on the curb. If there were two men who were made for each other, it was those two. They were both angry at the world and suspicious of everyone. She caught them share a knowing look which quickly vanished.

Her eyes landed on Tyler Garrett. He suddenly appeared frail, not the man she had seen kick in doors and handle criminals by himself. Instead, he stood with a couple of officers and Union President Dale Thomas as Chief Baumgartner addressed him. They all seemed to be uttering words of support.

Away from everyone, Captain Farrell stood alone. Officers moved around him, but no one addressed him. She tried to determine what he was looking at, but she couldn't. It wasn't at the house. It wasn't at anyone in particular. He was simply staring off into the distance.

This wasn't her first dead body, and she knew everyone responded differently. Even those who had seen multiple bodies responded differently to each one.

She'd seen plenty of them as an MP, both abroad and while stateside on base. She'd responded to suicides of despondent soldiers and once helped investigate a base shooting where a gunman had killed several of his platoon mates at a practice range.

But this was the first time she'd ever known someone close who had been killed in such a brutal fashion.

The breeze kicked up again, causing the yellow blanket to slowly slide down Gary Stone's body and wrap around the toe of his boot. She glanced around for someone who was inside the inner perimeter to notice what was happening. She could have hollered out, but her voice felt stolen.

No one made eye contact with her so she couldn't signal that the blanket was about to blow away on the next gust of wind.

Jun Yang ducked under the yellow tape that boldly claimed Caution—Police Line—Do Not Cross and walked toward the house. No one called out to stop her.

She was focused on the flittering blanket wrapped around Stone's boot. Quickly, she ascended the steps, watching the fabric lose its tentative hold. As it finally released from his body and drifted away on a warm breeze, like a spirit finally set free, she caught it and pulled it back.

It was then that she saw the damage done to her friend.

Most of his head was gone. He no longer resembled anyone or anything she remembered.

She noticed blood and torn clothing in his mid-section.

He'd been shot there.

Oh my goodness.

For a brief second, Yang closed her eyes and imagined the horrible pain Gary Stone felt in the moments before his death.

Footsteps quickly approached, clomping up the stairs. "Hey, Yang! You're not supposed to be in here."

She turned to Senior Patrol Officer Ken Norton, her former field training officer. He held a clipboard with a log listing everyone who stepped into the inner perimeter. He'd been terrible to her while they rode together, a misogynistic jerk who barely contained his beliefs that women should not be police officers. None of that showed now, though. Only concern was in his eyes.

"The sheet," she said, holding it up. Her voice sound like it was coming from down a hallway. "I caught it when it blew away."

"Okay," Norton said, taking the yellow blanket. "Hold this," he said, handing her the clipboard.

She held it with two hands, like it was a baby that had just wet itself. It felt awkward and heavy.

Norton carefully lay the blanket over Stone's body. When he stood, he pulled the clipboard from Yang's tight grip. "You don't look so good."

"The blanket will just blow away again," she muttered.

"If it does, we'll get another. It'll be okay."

"We should watch it to make sure he's protected."

Norton grabbed her by the elbow and helped her down the stairs. "Listen," he said, directing her away from Stone's body, "maybe you should sit down."

Yang suddenly felt lightheaded. "Maybe I should sit down."

Norton said something else, but it didn't register. She let herself be guided out of the crime scene. Norton soon released her and wandered off to log someone into the perimeter.

For a moment, she felt herself sway side to side. When the moment passed, she turned around and watched through the open front door where several people were now studying the shooter. They seemed to be taking more interest in him than in Gary Stone. She wanted to yell at the officers and the brass to pay attention to their own, but her voice was weak after all the words with Norton.

The desire to sit alone overtook her. There was only one place she thought she could be by herself at this very moment. As she walked away from the crime scene, no one yelled for her to come back. When she approached the staging area for the press and non-essential personnel, she saw several familiar faces.

Mayor Sikes and Councilwoman Margaret Patterson stood at the yellow line of tape, both of their faces creased with concern, as Chief Baumgartner briefed them on the shooting.

Behind the councilwoman stood her assistant, Jean Carter. Tears streamed down her cheeks as she stared at the body lying at the bottom of the stairs.

Yang slipped under the yellow tape and stopped near Jean. She wanted to say something, anything, to comfort her. She knew Jean was looking at her, but she didn't make eye contact. There was nothing further she could give today.

Officer Jun Yang lowered her head and walked slowly to the Ford Maverick. She climbed into the passenger seat and closed the door. The summer's heat that had warmed the car felt oddly comforting.

There were no tears as she watched the living move about the dead.

Chapter 75

Clint walked around the inner perimeter of the crime scene, noting the structure and the grounds. He sketched a basic layout of the house's exterior as he did so. The most interesting thing to him about this house was its seclusion. It also made perfect sense for what happened.

He'd seen the weeping display that Tyler Garrett had made in front of his brother SWAT officers. It had been convincing, and he was sure everyone bought it. Why wouldn't they? None of them knew what he knew. Not yet, anyway. That time was coming.

When the chief of police consoled Garrett, Clint's stomach burned. He wanted to shout to Baumgartner that he was comforting a murderer and a drug dealer. But he couldn't. His evidence was still insufficient, and without a slam dunk case, it would be pointless to bring it forward. Sympathy for Tyler Garrett was running at an all-time high. The time wasn't right.

When he'd finished his exterior overview, he stood waiting at the yellow crime scene tape, debating about whether or not to go in before the county investigators arrived. Technically, his role was to assist and advise. The detective from the Sheriff's Office would be lead and that agency would supply a second, as well. He was the third wheel. Going in ahead of them was unlikely to be appreciated.

Normally, he wouldn't care. Ruffling a few feathers didn't bother him, especially since most of the feathers belonged to idiots. But on this one, he didn't need the extra tension. This one required some tact, he realized. Which included doing stupid things like waiting for the county detectives to arrive before entering the crime scene.

Then he caught a break. Officer Yang wandered under the perimeter tape, up the stairs, and stood at Stone's body in the doorway. The yellow sheet had blown almost completely off, and Yang seemed to want to replace it. But when she picked it up, she held it and stared down at Stone's body, frozen. Even from this distance, Clint could tell that the view was gruesome.

Officer Norton spotted Yang and moved to speak with her. Clint took advantage of the opening and ducked under the yellow tape. He walked confidently, holding his notepad prominently. It was amazing what a simple prop like a clipboard or a case file did when it came to legitimizing someone's actions.

Clint stepped past Yang and Norton, ignoring their conversation. He stopped at the sprawled body in the hallway just a few yards inside the door. Unlike Stone, the body remained uncovered, as was standard procedure. Clint looked down and saw a tight group of bullet wounds in the man's chest. His hand still lightly clutched the shotgun that lay alongside his body.

"Oh, shit," Clint muttered. His notepad slipped from his hand and thudded lightly next to his foot. He stared at the dead man's face, his eyes tracing the jagged fishhook scar that ran from the corner of his mouth up his left cheek.

I don't know your name.

But I know who you are.

Clint reached down and picked up his notepad. He took a few steps and glanced into the back room, where a third dead body lay. He didn't recognize the man, whose face had been obliterated just like Stone's.

He moved back toward the open front door, surveying events from the vantage point of the crime scene. Tyler Garrett stood surrounded by supporters, taking a drink from the bottle of water in his hand, looking appropriately shaken. All an act, Clint knew. As soon as he saw the scar on the dead suspect's face, he knew for certain that all of this was Garrett's doing. Carefully planned and coldly executed.

"Listen, maybe you should sit down," Norton said.

Clint glanced at him. Norton was escorting Yang down the steps.

"Maybe I should sit down," Yang repeated, sounding slightly dazed.

Norton spotted Clint and gave him a suspicious look over his shoulder. "You need me to log you in, Detective?"

Clint slowly shook his head. "No, I'll wait for county."

He turned and walked out of the house, down the steps, and took up a position on the edge of the crime scene tape again. Less than a minute later, almost on cue, he spotted an unmarked detective's car with county plates pulling up to the scene. At least he wouldn't have to wait long to get started. He turned back to look at the house.

Farrell appeared at his side. He didn't acknowledge the captain's presence but continued to stare at the disaster in front him.

"What do you think?" The captain asked, staring into the yard as well.

"There's a dead cop lying on the front porch of that house," Clint said. "I think someday we're all going to have to answer for that."

Chapter 76

Tyler Garrett stood at the window, looking down on the city street. The afternoon sun was still high above. He wore a tank top, gym shorts, and running shoes. Leaning his shoulder against the window frame, he folded his arms and crossed one foot over the other.

He was alone now. Tiana Kennedy hadn't returned to her condo yet. She would be home soon, as she left earlier to get something to make lunch. He didn't want to go out to eat and he didn't want to go to his house as he thought the press might know where he lived and be waiting for some sort of statement.

After the shooting, he had been driven to the Public Safety Building by his friend and former SWAT teammate, Bo Sherman, to meet the county investigator assigned to the case. When they arrived, the investigator collected Garrett's clothes. Garrett hid his surprise when he saw Spokane County Detective Shaun McNutt waiting outside the men's locker room. Along with his partner, Detective Cassidy Harris, Shaun McNutt investigated his shooting of Todd Trotter almost two years ago. The fact he was there now was too coincidental.

While Garrett undressed, Union President Dale Thomas stood silently by with Bo Sherman to witness the whole process. Garrett didn't speak as he removed each article, placing it into whichever brown paper bag McNutt pointed at.

He appreciated the detective's occasional kind expressions and his words of condolences, but Garrett didn't drop his guard. McNutt's notebook and pen were in his left hand, ready to record any slip he made.

As he changed into the dirty workout clothes that were in

his gym bag, Garrett said, "Sort of crazy to have you on another of my shootings."

McNutt rolled the top of one brown bag down, stopping any debris or foreign substances from possibly entering the bag. "We were jumped to the top of the list," he said, absently. He moved to the next bag to roll its top down.

Garrett bit back the single word he wanted say. He didn't need anyone to hear his response. He finished getting dressed and let Bo Sherman drive him to Tiana's home. His friend offered to stay, but Garrett assured him he was all right. He had Tiana, and besides, he wanted to be alone.

Now, as he stood watching the afternoon traffic move below the condo window, he could finally spit out that word, the one that continued to taste vile in his mouth.

"Farrell."

Maybe he had made a mistake in setting up the killing of Gary Stone. Perhaps he *should* have killed Tom Farrell instead. He had thought about it, of course. That was his initial intention, but everything he came up with looked like an assassination. He was sure Clint would be able to figure a way to point it back to him.

He heard the front door open and Tiana Kennedy stepped inside, a small bag of groceries in her hand.

"Hey baby," she said, her voice soft.

"Hey," he said, not bothering to look back.

She walked over and kissed the side of his face. "I love you," she said.

"I love you, too."

After rubbing his back for a moment, she headed to the kitchen. Garrett's eyes returned to the pedestrians moving about at street level.

Just like Tom Farrell, he also thought about killing Wardell Clint. No matter how he tried to position the man for it, though, it always seemed like a setup. And, truth be told, after two years of harassment, if the time ever did come to kill Clint, Tyler Garrett would be the man for that job.

For a moment, he even considered Ray Zielinski as a target, but the man was his own worst enemy. He presented a thorn in Garrett's side, but that wasn't worth killing him. If that was true, he would have killed Farrell and Clint years ago. Or countless other people. The world was full of people who acted as daily irritants.

When the Anti-Crime Team was formed, Garrett was under no illusions. He knew the team was some sort of scheme to entrap him. He also knew that he had some challenges with every person on the team.

Zielinski, his former friend, hated him now. The older man was not worth busting his pick on in trying to rebuild a relationship.

Jun Yang, the academy princess, had the built-in reputation of a rat. There was no way he was spending more time around her than necessary.

That left Gary Stone, the man he first befriended only months ago. Garrett first betrayed him by turning over information he'd stolen from Stone to the newspaper. It got the man removed from city hall and Garrett thought Stone would hate him forever. However, Farrell sent him to a surveillance school then put him on ACT.

Of anyone, Garrett expected Stone to be the hardest to get along with, yet they reconnected after Garrett told him he'd given the stolen information to the newspaper to help Stone. He was surprised the man believed the lie. If Gary Stone was anything, it was gullible, especially when it came to seeing the good in other people. It was that gullibility that Garrett hoped to take advantage of.

"Would you like an omelet and toast or an egg sandwich?" Tiana asked.

"The sandwich," he said. As an afterthought, he turned to her and said, "Please."

She smiled and went about the work of making lunch. He watched her pull a Keurig pod from the spinner, clip it into place, and start a cup of coffee.

Garrett turned back to the window and his thoughts returned to the fallen officer.

Stone seemed open to becoming a different type of cop. He no longer wanted to talk criminals into handcuffs. He wanted to stuff them into the cuffs. His new attitude was almost immediate when the younger officer began to mimic the way Garrett walked and talked and dealt with criminals. It was easy to spot, and Garrett was familiar with the old saying that imitation was the sincerest form of flattery.

That's where I made my mistake.

He liked the new Gary Stone and was moving him along too fast, too quick.

Garrett should have allowed the man more time before he began to try and show him the openings the job truly had for him. Garrett didn't suddenly understand how to grab an opportunity from a guy like Ernesto Ocampo. He had to make a lot of little discoveries along the way. Successes that he found himself.

His own impatience was the death of Gary Stone.

No, Tyler Garrett realized, that was not true.

Tom Farrell was the death of Gary Stone.

Captain Farrell was ultimately responsible for the murder of Stone. He should never have put the younger officer in a situation to lie. Stone was a terrible liar.

It was at dinner on Saturday when Garrett discovered the final truth. That's when Stone told him about Farrell's plans to trap him. He knew it already, of course, having figured it out on his own. Stone's revealing it, though, proved his earlier meeting with Farrell was not about an assault charge related to the Wayne Cattage arrest. That was his first lie and Stone was unable to keep to it.

To further confirm his suspicions, Garrett stopped by the jail on Sunday and spoke with a friend. It took a while to surreptitiously weave his way to the subject of Wayne Cattage, but when he did the jailer confirmed that Cattage was indeed fine and no complaint had been filed.

That meant Stone had lied to Garrett a second time, and the untruth originated from one of two places.

It could have originated at the direction of Captain Farrell, which meant Stone was a complete puppet of the captain. Therefore, everything Garrett had exposed to his partner now put his whole life at risk. Stone was suddenly the most dangerous man in his life. More than Farrell. More than Clint.

The second place where the lie could have originated was Stone's fear of being truthful with Garrett. This was as dangerous as the Farrell-directed lie. It meant he could never trust Stone, which was disappointing.

He would never have opened up and exposed who he really was if he thought Stone could have been a rat.

Or worse, a lying rat.

Tiana walked over and sat a plate containing a sandwich and a cup of coffee on the nearby table.

"Feel like talking?" she asked.

He wanted to tell her everything, but he had already made a mistake in revealing some of his true self to Stone. Tiana had seen parts of himself that he had never shown to his wife. He thought it would make him a freer man. He now saw the error of his ways.

"Let's talk later," he said, knowing he wouldn't say anything more then.

She rested her hand on his shoulder for a moment. "It will be okay, baby."

With his eyes still focused outside, he nodded. "I know," he said. "I know."

EPILOGUE

People don't get to change things. Things change people once in a while, but people don't change things.
—Lawrence Block,
from the novel *In the Midst of Death*

Chapter 77

It was the first time Jun Yang had seen the entire Spokane Police Department together. For most officers on the department, it was the first time any of them had ever seen it happen.

A gathering of every officer never happened for guild activities, presidential visits, or even school shootings. There were always parts of the city that needed to be covered or other crimes that needed response. There were officers who were on their days off or on vacation.

The murder of a cop changed everything, though.

That brought everyone out to pay their respects.

All officers, detectives, sergeants, and the brass were in attendance, their crispest uniforms on display. Officers came in from their days off. Those who were on vacation returned early. Everyone realized that this could be them.

Spouses were also present, either hugging or holding the hands of their officers.

Retired officers came in droves to pay their respects. Their faces held a guilty knowledge that they were lucky to have made it through an entire career and not faced this reality.

The mayor and city council stood dutifully nearby, their faces slack.

Elsewhere in the city, deputies from the Spokane County Sheriff's Office covered the city while Spokane's finest mourned one of its own.

While their deaths were slightly before her time, she heard Detective Butch Talbott's funeral had been dramatically less attended. He died under a cloud of suspicion, and the department convinced the family to ask for a small, private affair. A few officers attended Talbott's service on their own time. Most officers chose to work instead.

Detective Justin Pomeroy committed suicide while off duty, a day or two following Talbott's death. Since the two men were partners, the hint of suspicion also stuck to Pomeroy. Coupled with a contempt for suicide, this resulted in a sparsely attended funeral.

Unlike today, when almost three hundred officers assembled around the grave dressed in their dark blue uniforms, here to mourn a hero.

Tyler Garrett stood stoically amidst it all, his arm wrapped around his girlfriend's waist. He held the hand of another woman who cried and shook slightly as the chaplain read his eulogy. Yang wondered what his relationship was to the tall black woman. Was she Garrett's sister? If so, why did she have such an emotional reaction to Gary Stone's death?

Jean Carter stood with Councilwoman Patterson, and openly wept through the entire service.

Watching it all with dispassionate wonder was Jun Yang. She stood apart from her fellow officers and came alone. Instead of her uniform, she wore a long black dress and black sunglasses, her hair pulled tightly back.

When the honor guard fired the last of its three volleys, officers swarmed to Tyler Garrett. He moved away from his girlfriend and the other woman, leaving them to embrace each other. Even though Garrett appeared sad, he seemed to bask in the attention of his fellow officers. The fawning over the former SWAT hero bothered her.

Wardell Clint and a clean-shaven Ray Zielinski gravitated toward one another. When they met, their eyes locked onto Garrett as they spoke. The way the two men huddled together—hunched over, protecting their words from eavesdroppers—made them look like two thieves conspiring to rob a rich man.

Chief of Police Baumgartner stood between Captains Tom Farrell and Dana Hatcher as they addressed members of the city council. She didn't know why, but the chief looked like a man keeping peace between a divorcing husband and wife.

Every moment since she arrived at the little brown house on Havana Street felt like she was watching disjointed scenes in a movie. They made sense, but they didn't emotionally reach her.

She still hadn't cried.

Her mother told her the tears would come when they were needed. Her father shook his head scornfully at the idea. Even before this moment, she couldn't remember the last time she cried. Perhaps when she was a little girl and fell off her bike, skinning her knee.

Watching the actors in this un-filmed movie depressed her. She turned and headed toward the parking lot. No one stopped her to check on how she was doing.

Perhaps it was because she was a rookie. To them she was disposable because they hadn't formed an attachment to her beyond the badge she had barely worn.

Yang wondered if her murder would have brought the department out en masse like it did for Gary Stone.

"Excuse me," a woman's voice said.

She turned to see Jean Carter. She wore a high-necked black dress and a wide-brimmed black hat. In her left hand was a yellow greeting card envelope. It was unopened.

"You're Jun, right?"

"Hi, Jean."

Tears welled in the woman's eyes. "Can you tell me anything about the investigation?"

Yang shook her head. "I wish I could," she said. "But I don't know anything. They're keeping us in the dark." She was mostly telling the truth. The other part of the story was that Yang hadn't sought to ask—junior officers didn't do such a thing.

After Stone's death, the Anti-Crime Team was temporarily disbanded. Everyone was given a few days' leave. When they were able to come back to work, they were going to rotate back into their former patrol teams. Yang called and requested additional vacation days to avoid working.

Jean lifted the yellow envelope and looked at it.

"Are you okay?" Yang asked.

She shook her head. "No."

Yang thought about reaching out and touching Jean's arm, but it seemed too familiar. It wasn't something she would normally do.

"He sent me this," Jean said. "I got it the day after…" Tears ran down her cheek. "I haven't been able to open it to see what's inside. I thought maybe… I could do it here. I'm afraid to do it."

Yang thought about offering to be with her as she opened it, to see what Gary Stone wrote to her, but she didn't want to know. She didn't want any further hurt inside her heart.

"Then wait until another day," Yang said, the words sounding almost robotic even to her.

Jean stared at the envelope and sucked in a breath as she struggled not to cry.

Yang looked away at some children running in the nearby grass. It had been so long since she felt that way.

None of us would ever feel like that again, she realized.

Chapter 78

Ray Zielinski put the empty shot glass down on top of the envelope. As he swallowed, he stared at the jagged edge where he'd torn it open. Part of the single page inside poked out.

Margie appeared at his table. She'd been working at the Maxwell House Tavern for as long as he could remember, as much a fixture as the bar itself. "You doing okay here, Ray?"

"I'd be better if you'd hit me again."

She eyed the empty shot glasses already in front of him. "Maybe a beer?" she suggested.

Zielinski wavered in his chair a little while he looked at her. "You know what? I never realized what a truly beautiful woman you are."

Margie snorted. "You're going to force me to cut you off."

He raised his hands in surrender. "Sure, punish a guy for telling the truth." When his own words registered with him, he scowled. "Par for the course these days."

Margie gave him a kind look. "You want some truth?"

"I'd love some."

"You look good without the mustache."

Zielinski reached to his upper lip. The slightest trace of stubble was all he felt there.

"When did you shave it off?"

"Last night," he said, remembering. He'd been slightly drunk, but less so than he was now. Mostly, he felt dark, and that he needed to change who he was, how he felt. The mustache seemed like the right place to start. It was an offering to the gods, he supposed. The gods of change, the gods of truth, whatever gods may be.

"Well, I like it." Margie picked up his empty shot glasses

and retreated to the bar.

Zielinski didn't know if he liked it or not. Still barely on the good side of being sloppy drunk at the moment, he wasn't sure if now was the best time to decide, either.

He fingered the envelope. The letter inside was on heavy bond paper with the department letterhead. The message was terse but carried plenty of weight. Darold Barden and Alejandra Sanita had filed an official complaint against him for illegal entry and excessive force.

He didn't see this one playing out well for him. The process would take some time, but the facts were not on his side. The illegal entry element wouldn't stick, but there was no way around the fact he'd smacked Barden upside the head while the man was in handcuffs. Both Barden and Sanita would say so. His only option if he wanted to avoid the consequences was to lie.

And he was sick of lies.

Next to him, he sensed someone arriving at the table. He looked up, expecting it to be Margie with his beer, but saw Wardell Clint instead.

Zielinski glanced at his watch. "You're early."

Clint slid into the booth seat opposite him. "From the looks of it, I'm late."

Margie appeared at the table and slid a glass of beer in front of Zielinski. She looked at Clint, scowled, and didn't say anything.

"That looks good," Clint said. "And a shot of whisky, too."

Margie left without a reply.

Clint turned back to Zielinski. "I would have been here sooner, but I had to stop by the station to check on a couple of things after the funeral."

"It's been a hell of a day." Zielinski reached for his beer. "We went a long time without putting any badges in the ground. Now it seems like it's happening all the time."

"You mean Talbott and Pomeroy."

"And now Stone."

"Did you go to Talbott's funeral?"

Zielinski took a drink of beer and shook his head. Absently, he raised his fingers to brush foam from his mustache, then remembered he'd shaven it off. He dropped his hand to the table.

"Neither did I," Clint said.

"His wife said she wanted it to be small. Family only."

"I still wouldn't have gone."

Zielinski looked at him sharply. "Why not?"

Clint stared at him for a moment, as if he expected Zielinski to know the answer to that question already. Then he asked, "Did you go to Pomeroy's?"

"Yeah. There were a fair number of cops there, even though…" Zielinski trailed off.

"Even though he did himself, you mean."

"Yeah. Some guys still showed up for the service. Not many in uniform, though."

"Nothing like the big production today."

"No." Zielinski took another drink of his beer. "Not even close."

Margie arrived and clunked a glass of beer and a shot in front of Clint, leaving without another word. Zielinski looked after her, then back to Clint. "What's that about? She was in a good mood just a few minutes ago."

"It ain't you. She's still mad at me from forever ago."

Zielinski shook his head. "Jeez, Ward. Is there anyone you don't piss off eventually?"

"My name is Wardell," Clint said. "And as far as the rest, I don't give a shit."

Honey Badger, Zielinski thought.

Clint sipped the whisky, his expression unchanging. Then he said, "What I told you at the funeral, that you were right to think Garrett was dirty…well, here's the rest of the story."

Zielinski leaned forward to listen. As Clint spoke, Zielinski experienced a wide range of emotions. First came validation. His instincts to suspect the man had been correct. Then, as the list of offenses grew, that satisfaction at being right turned to disbelief. By the time Clint finished laying it out for him, disbelief had become outrage.

"If you've got pictures of his criminal associates, why isn't he in handcuffs?"

"I don't have enough to arrest him," Clint explained. He downed the last of his whisky. "I have to build the case."

"You need my help?"

"No."

Zielinski gave him a confused look. "If you don't want my help, why are you telling me all of this?"

"I didn't say that I didn't want your help. I said I didn't *need* it." Clint chased the whisky with a swig of beer. "But mostly I'm telling you this because I don't want to go to another dead cop's funeral."

Zielinski peered closer at him. He lowered his voice to a drunken whisper. "You really do think Garrett killed Stone, don't you?"

"I think he arranged it, yes."

"But why would he do that? Stone was his protégé. I saw it every day, on the team."

"Farrell messed up."

"What'd the captain do?"

"He told Stone about Garrett. He originally planted Stone on the team to trap Garrett, but when he tried to activate his sleeper agent, it didn't work. Stone must have told Garrett, and..." He turned up his hand. "You know the rest. I don't want you to end up the same way, so I figure you deserve a fair warning about what you're dealing with."

"So Garrett knows about you and Farrell?"

"I'm proceeding as if he knows everything at this point. If we're going to take him down, I think that's the only safe assumption."

"We?"

Clint took another drink of his beer, eying him over the rim of his glass. When he put it back on the table, he said, "Like it or not, you're armpit deep in this quagmire now. We might as well coordinate our efforts."

"And Farrell?"

"He's on board. He thinks he's in charge."

"He's a captain," Zielinski said. "That makes him in charge."

Clint shrugged. "I don't care. Hopefully, he won't mess things up again."

Zielinski sat quietly, his mind still reeling from the revelations Clint had shared. He almost wished he didn't know the truth. He had enough problems of his own without taking on something this volatile. In the end, though, he knew he would do what he could. It was the right thing to do.

"I'm in," he said to Clint.

"I already knew that," the detective said. "But be ready, because we're upping this game."

"How's that?"

"You'll see." He finished off his beer and rose from the booth. When he reached for his wallet, Zielinski waved him off.

"I got this," he said.

Clint nodded. Then he peered a little closer at Zielinski's face, and pointed toward his lip. "You should have kept it. You look older without the mustache."

"Screw you, Ward."

Clint didn't seem offended. He walked away from the bar, leaving Zielinski alone with his envelope.

When Margie returned, he ordered another pair of shots. She eyed him for a moment, but seemed to see something in his expression that satisfied her. She walked away to fill his order. He waited patiently until the shot glasses were in front of him, then picked up the first and sipped it. He knew there was a lot of work in front of him, and probably some danger, too. But he didn't have to face it today.

Today, he drank.

Chapter 79

After he left the Maxwell House Tavern, it took Wardell Clint only fifteen minutes to locate Earl Ellis. He was at the Vietnamese restaurant he seemed to be fond of. Clint waited another five minutes before Ellis left the restaurant. He drove north. Clint followed, waiting until the two of them passed into a light industrial district before he activated his emergency lights. He didn't touch his radio to advise dispatch of the stop.

Ellis pulled to the side of the road. Clint got on his public address system and ordered him to pull around the corner, off the main arterial. Ellis complied.

Clint exited his car and approached Ellis's on the passenger side. When he reached the window, he rapped sharply on it. Ellis dropped the window several inches and stopped.

"Is there a problem, Officer?"

"Step out of the car."

"What did I do?"

"Out of the car," Clint ordered, his tone sharper this time.

Without waiting for Ellis to comply, he turned and walked to the rear of the man's car.

Ellis hesitated, but after a few seconds, he shut off the engine and got out. He met Clint at the rear of the car. Clint stood with his arms crossed loosely, appraising the tall man in front of him. Ellis returned the look, evaluating him in turn.

"Was I speeding, Officer?"

"I'm a detective."

Ellis smiled easily. "My apologies. Why did you stop me, Detective?"

"How long have you known Leonard Strayer?"

"Who?"

"Leonard Strayer," Clint repeated.

"I don't know the name."

"White male, long black hair." Clint traced a line from the corner of his mouth halfway up his left cheek. "Ugly fishhook scar on his face."

Ellis shook his head. "I think I'd remember someone like that."

"He's memorable," Clint agreed. "Had a substantial criminal record, too. Which is why we have his fingerprints on file."

"He sounds like someone I don't want to know." Ellis's tone was easy, almost cultured.

"No chance of that, anymore," Clint said. "He's dead."

Ellis shrugged.

"Shot and killed, actually, after murdering a police officer," Clint continued. "We took his prints off his dead body and ran them through the system. That's how I found out his name, if you want the truth. I didn't know it before that."

Ellis reached into his pocket.

Dropping his hand to his gun, Clint growled, "Keep your hands out of your pockets."

Ellis used his thumb and forefinger to pinch the edge of his phone and pull it out. He looked at the screen. "Officer, I'm late for a business appointment, so—"

"Not with Strayer, though."

"I told you, I don't know this man you're talking about."

Clint reached into his own pocket and dropped a photograph onto the trunk of Ellis's car. The man didn't immediately look at it, only stared back at Clint. Curiosity got the best of him, eventually, and he tore his gaze away to look. His eyes flared slightly, but he otherwise concealed his surprise.

"Didn't know him, huh?"

Ellis brushed some dust from his sleeve. "He must have used a different name. What's your point?"

"I dug into Strayer's record. I found a report from four

years ago in which he was arrested. In that same report, you're also listed as a suspect."

"So?"

"So, you knew him. I've got the report, and I've got that." He pointed to the photograph.

Ellis leaned forward toward Clint and sniffed. "Is that whisky on your breath, Detective?"

Clint ignored the question. "Let me ask you something else. Do you know Tyler Garrett?"

"The police officer in the news? No, not personally."

"You're lying."

Ellis looked at him coolly. "Why do you say that? Was I mentioned in some obscure police report that he was also in? Or do you have another photograph to show me?"

Clint forced a crooked smile onto his face. "I've shown you enough of what I have."

"I think I'd like to talk to your supervisor, Detective."

"Well, I'd prepare yourself for disappointment, then." Clint reached into his pocket and pulled out a business card. "But do me a favor and give this to Garrett next time you see him." He held out the card to Ellis.

Ellis stared at him, not reaching for the card.

Clint waited a few moments, then set it on the trunk, facedown and exposing the handwritten note he'd scrawled on the back. He turned and walked back to his car.

Ellis's curiosity got the best of him, which Clint knew it would. He called after Clint, "'I've got you.' What the hell is that supposed to mean?"

Clint opened his car door. "It means if you hang out with shit birds long enough, you'll get shit on yourself."

"I'm not a shit bird," Ellis said.

"I wasn't talking about you," Clint replied.

He got into his car and drove away, leaving Ellis to stare after him.

Chapter 80

Farrell was staring at his academy picture on the wall behind his desk when the knock came at his door. He spun in his chair to see Sergeant Kelly Ragland's round face leaning in his doorway.

"Yes?"

"You said you wanted to see Yang before she out-processed?"

Farrell stood up. "That's right."

"I'm done with her." Ragland disappeared from the doorway.

For a moment, Farrell wondered if that was it. Then a woman's hand extended through the threshold and knocked lightly on the open door.

"Come in," he said.

Officer Jun Yang stepped into his office with a duffel bag slung over her shoulder. She wore a loose green sweatshirt and jeans that were tucked into her black combat boots.

Farrell mimed for her to close the door behind her. She hesitated, but reluctantly did so.

"Please," Farrell said, "have a seat."

Yang slid the bag from her shoulder and leaned it against the chair furthest from Farrell. Then she sat down, her body remaining erect in the position of attention. "What can I do for you, sir?"

Farrell cleared his throat. "Sergeant Ragland said you were out-processing?"

"Yes, sir."

"Have you turned in all of your equipment?"

She nodded.

"Including your gun and badge?" In his experience, those two most emblematic of items were always the last to go.

Yang frowned slightly. "Especially those."

Farrell gave her a long look. With her military background and the way she handled the testing scandal at the academy, he thought he had a firm grasp on who Jun Yang was. But her decision to quit had surprised him. Hadn't she seen death in the military?

"Why?" he asked her. "Why are you quitting?"

Yang didn't answer right away. In that moment of silence, Farrell realized he'd had a very similar conversation with Gary Stone after he was removed from city hall. He'd stopped Stone from quitting and put him on ACT. He wondered for a second if he was doing right by trying to stop her now.

"I realized this is not what I want for my life," Yang finally answered. "Seeing Gary lying there that day, I...I couldn't wait any longer."

"But you're good at this job," Farrell said. "You were an MP. You excelled in the academy."

Yang shrugged. "I'm good at something else, too."

Farrell took a deep breath and let out a sigh. He contemplated how much he could tell her. How much was enough to get her to stay but not so much that it put her in danger? Or him, for that matter.

"I need your help," he said. "Just a little longer."

"I'm done."

"Look, I know I probably rushed you by putting you in ACT so early on in your career, and I'm sorry for that. But I needed someone with a clean background and clear-cut ethics."

"Why?"

Farrell stared at her, silent, wondering again how much he should say.

"That right here. That silence. It's the problem," Yang said. "There are too many secrets. Everyone on this department has secrets and they want you to believe they're acting in your best interests, but they're not."

Farrell listened to her words. She was right. He considered telling her about Garrett, but he couldn't bring himself to do it. Regardless of the truth she spoke about secrets, it was just too dangerous. He'd started to share these terrible secrets with Stone and the man ended up dead. He couldn't risk another officer knowing too much. He and Clint would have to bear the burden themselves.

But he didn't want to lose a quality officer like Yang. He took another stab at keeping her on the job.

"You're a good cop, Jun. Don't quit."

"I already have."

"Don't stay to help me," Farrell said. "Stay because it's the right thing to do. You're already off ACT. You'll go back to patrol."

She shook her head.

"Please," he said, almost pleading. "Pick your shift. I'll make sure you get it."

"I can't."

"Why can't you?"

"Because I don't want to end up like the other three," Yang said.

Farrell gave her a confused look. "Other three? What do you mean?"

Yang raised her fingers and counted off each one. "I don't want to be a burnout like Zielinski. I don't want to end up dead like… dead like Gary. And I sure as hell don't want to end up as whatever the hell Garrett is."

Farrell stared back at her in silence. He didn't have an answer for that.

Whatever the hell Garrett is.

After a while, Yang must have realized he had nothing more to say. She stood and hefted her bag onto her shoulder. Then she left the office without looking back.

Farrell let her go. He stared at the empty doorway after she'd gone, and he thought about her words for a long while.

Slowly, Captain Tom Farrell turned his chair back around to see his framed academy class photo again. In the glass, he caught a faint, dark reflection of his own visage, tired and worn. In the photograph itself, all the bright and shining faces of yesteryear gazed hopefully out at him, but right now he couldn't recognize a single one of them.

Chapter 81

As the sun settled, he returned to the gravesite, the dirt still fresh over the casket.

Tyler Garrett wondered what the headstone might look like. Perhaps it would be a modest granite slab. Or maybe the parents would make a big show of how their son died a hero's death. He imagined the former, but who knew how people would react to the loss of their child?

Before he spoke, he glanced around to make sure no one could hear him. Only Tiana waited for him at his car, half a football field away.

"Hey, Stoney," Garrett said, "I'm sorry, man."

He stood there for a moment, considering his words.

"That's not true. I'm not sorry. You forced me to do it. You didn't have to lie. You could have told me the truth from the jump, and we would have figured everything out. We could have gotten it straight. Instead, you put me into a situation where this was the only answer."

Garrett nudged a clump of dirt with his toe.

"You would never have stood up if they pushed on you. You realize that, too, don't you? I should have seen that before we became friends. I was naïve for thinking a leopard could change his spots. When we first met, I thought you were a politician with a gun. That's like an armed chameleon. I was hoping that meant you might be opportunistic, like me, someone who could blend in. Besides being a good hider, Gary, do you know what a chameleon is? It's a liar. Don't get me wrong. I don't mind lying, especially if we did it together, but when you did it to hide ratting me out, that's something I couldn't abide."

Garrett shoved his hands in his pockets.

"But I gotta thank you for showing me the truth in the situation. I've played everything too reckless. So it's time to get out. I can do one of two things. Either I leave now which sort of feels like I'm sneaking out the back door with my tail between my legs. I don't like the thought of that. Not my style at all." Garrett's mouth was a thin, hard line. "Or I can go back to work, take care of some loose ends, then walk out of that department on my terms, with my head held high. That's how I want it to go."

He kicked at a rock and sent it skittering across the fresh dirt. He looked up into the clear blue sky and felt the sun on his face. It was going to be a hot day. Maybe he could take Tiana to the lake. He'd have to convince her not to bring Fia, though. She'd be a downer today. Gary's death had hit her surprisingly hard and he didn't want to listen to her cry about it anymore.

He glanced at the dirt pile a final time. "Take care, Stoney."

Tyler Garrett left his friend behind as he walked slowly toward his car.

Authors' Note and Acknowledgements

While this police procedural is based in a real city and mirrors reality in many ways, it is a work of fiction. The authors have taken a great many creative liberties in the interests in the telling of this series. For instance, no characters are directly based on anyone, with the exception of some positive homages done with permission. No actual incidents are rendered here, either. Some police codes or procedures are slightly different than in reality. Additionally, the political structure and history of both city government and the police department has been modified for dramatic purposes. While we're certain that astute readers will notice those differences, we're equally confident they'll forgive the discrepancies.

The authors would like to thank:

Chris Rhatigan, for some excellent editing.

Zach McCain, for another killer cover.

Carla Warren, Judy Orchard, Bonnie Conway, Cheryl Counts, Dave Mather, Melanie Donaldson, Brad Hallock, John Emery, and Kristi Scalise, for reading this book early and giving invaluable feedback to make it better.

Marty Hill, for inspiring his namesake character.

Good cops across this nation who stand in stark counterpoint to those few who do evil deeds.

Journalists and civilians who keep watch for those same few and stand against those actions when they occur.

It is said that the best disinfectant is sunlight. If you're a faithful reader that has come this far, know that while the world of Charlie-316 will always be a gray world to match our own, the sun will shine in the final installment of this arc, *Code Four*.

About the Authors

COLIN CONWAY is the author of the 509 Crime Stories, a series of novels set in Eastern Washington with revolving lead characters. They are standalone tales and can be read in any order. He served in the US Army and later was an officer of the Spokane Police Department. He's a commercial real estate broker/investor, owned a laundromat, invested in a bar, and ran a karate school. Colin lives with his beautiful life partner, their three wonderful children, and a crazy, codependent Vizsla that rules their world. Find out more about him at his official website: **ColinConway.com**.

FRANK ZAFIRO was a police officer in Spokane, Washington, from 1993 to 2013. He retired as a captain. He is the author of numerous crime novels, including the River City novels and the Stefan Kopriva series. He lives in Redmond, Oregon, with his wife Kristi, dogs Richie and Wiley, and a very self-assured cat named Pasta. He is an avid hockey fan and a tortured guitarist. You can keep up with Frank at **FrankZafiro.com**.

Are You Ready for the Next Book in
the Charlie-316 Series?

CODE FOUR

The last two years have been tumultuous ones for the Spokane Police Department. On the surface, the agency has suffered from scandal and police officer deaths. Underneath, a secret and deadly game of cat and mouse has played out.

Now the Department of Justice has sent investigators to determine if federal intervention is needed. Their presence disrupts everyone's agenda and threatens to expose dark secrets. Goals shift from winning situations to simply surviving.

Not everyone will.

In this tense and explosive final installment of the Tyler Garrett saga, everyone's true nature is laid bare. Garrett scrambles to maintain what he has built. Chief Baumgartner tries to protect his department. Captain Farrell's plans crumble around him, and Officer Ray Zielinski's career is at risk. Meanwhile, DOJ supervisor Édelie Durand diligently follows the facts where they lead. And through it all, the unflappable Detective Clint keeps his eyes firmly on the prize—Officer Tyler Garrett.